Symphony
OF HER
eart

SYMPHONY OF HER Heart

SHERI ROSEDALE

EMPOWERING WOMEN EVERYWHERE

Symphony of Her Heart
Sheri Rosedale

ISBN: 978-1-948018-02-9
Library of Congress Control Number: 2017956609

First Printing, 2019

Published by EWE ~ Empowering Women Everywhere

EMPOWERING WOMEN EVERYWHERE

DEDICATED TO:

Sura, my mother

Marum, my sister

TO ALL WHO READ THIS STORY

I never wrote the story with the intention of anyone ever reading it. Its purpose was to permit me to disclose and reveal, in a safe environment, emotions and issues I kept tightly sealed and tucked away. The issues of the past were constantly haunting me and the pressure and exhaustion of living with the lies, secrets, and fears took their toll physically, mentally, and emotionally.

When I decided to record the emotions and events, the task of writing became a physical release, much like the eruption of steam from a pressure cooker. Without forethought, I was compelled to regurgitate the words swirling around in my head. Crying, exercising, solitary walks, and screaming into my pillow didn't help. It was only the continual flow of words onto the page that became my only relief. I couldn't stop... I would write when I became most vulnerable. I would write when some passing thought actually became an insight or revelation. I would write when I cried feeling alone and frightened wondering how my life could ever be or would ever be different.

I kept a legal pad in the car because invariably as I drove my mind would wander and become fixated on something and the words and thoughts demanded to be put on paper. I would have to pull off the road in order to get them out of my head having relief only when I did so. This continued for a long time until I realized something was happening. It was scary but I chose to take the first 10 pages with me on an appointment to a new doctor. I don't know why.

During the appointment, after all the routine questions, answers, and general information was acknowledged and disposed of I meekly made a confession of sorts about the story and how it came to be written. The doctor was kind and supportive and asked to read what I brought. When I returned for a follow up visit she shared some personal information of her own and acknowledged how important it would be for other women to share in the main character's story. It was this response and others like it that led me to eventually consider making the story public. The story had value as I began to believe the same about myself.

The main character and story resonates with many women. They know her because she is a part of who they are. The story provides an opportunity for the reader to participate in sharing the insights, knowledge, pain, and struggles that hopefully they recognize in themselves that Lyla, the main character, could not throughout most of her life. This enables the reader to grasp the tools they need to reshape their lives and affect others in the same way.

I believe there is a bond that exists between women that transcends familial ties. We share a unique ability to communicate in ways unknown to others. We are able to recognize one another's essence and in doing so we become sisters of the heart each with our own unique symphony.

The story was written not only for those who, by whatever means, find themselves in compromising and/or abusive relationships. It also has value for those who remain untouched by toxic relationships and/or know of someone whose life has become compromised. Hopefully, the story will help those women understand the women who have become victims in order to become a supportive member of our community of women.

It is my belief we are all making a journey with many paths to follow. These pathways are formed by our decisions, choices, behaviors, perceptions, and outside influences. If the choices we make cause us to falter, we need to be able to create a new path with the assistance from others to alter and ultimately continue the journey creating a way for us to blossom. When our voice has become silenced and our lives compromised remember we are not alone.

Our voice, our flame, our essence may be smothered as a fire is to become burning embers. But those embers never die they merely await the time when they are fed with life-giving breath to enable us to say and believe, "I will never again permit anyone to extinguish the flame within me."

Share with others and share your symphony with me. I can be reached at symphonyofherheart@gmail.com.

Your sister of the heart,

Sheri

Symphony
OF HER
Heart

THE CATALYST...THE ADMISSION

With hesitation she began, "I'm a bit of a mess, you see. I don't think I want my husband, Juliano, to return. It's been almost two years now since he abandoned the children and me and returned to Miami to work at his previous job. He quickly reestablished residence with a friend there, forgot about his family, ignored that he had been diagnosed with a motor neuron disease, and then decided to reappear."

Hours earlier Lyla had greeted a morning sky filled with large white clouds. The air was cool with soft winter sunshine reflective of a typical day in Houston, Texas in November, 2009. Lyla arrived at the doctor's office just minutes before her scheduled appointment. This was the first time she was to see the doctor's nurse practitioner. Her anxiety was increasing daily, accompanied by fears and uncertainties, and she needed to see someone, anyone. She admonished herself out loud in the car on the way over. "How bad can this woman be? All I have to do is tell her what I need and that's, that. Stop crabbing. I can do this."

But minutes later in the waiting room, the nurse's assistant opened the door to the inner examination rooms, called Lyla's name, and looked around to see if anyone responded. "Lyla Rose Masselli?" she repeated.

Lyla looked up, then acknowledged the call by raising her hand as though she was still in school, got up from her seat, and walked to the open door.

"How are you this morning, Miss Lyla?" the assistant asked.

Lyla responded with an automatic reply, "OK."

Lyla was directed down the hallway where she stepped onto the scale. After her weight was recorded, she followed the assistant into an exam room. Her vitals were taken, an update on her medications was checked, and she was asked why she was there.

"I'm here to have my thyroid meds checked," Lyla said without emotion.

"All right," said the assistant. "Dr. Horne's nurse practitioner, Charlie, will be with you shortly."

Lyla knew the drill and was ready for the wait. She took out her Nintendo DS and continued a Sudoku puzzle she had started earlier. Her attention was drawn to a faint knock on the exam room door. A woman walked in who looked to be in her late thirties, dressed casually in a pair of trendy, multi-colored trousers and sweater.

Great looking earrings, thought Lyla. *I like her style.* The woman looked at Lyla, smiled, and spoke.

"Hi, my name is Charlie. I'm Dr. Horne's nurse practitioner. How about we talk about why you're here today. How can I help you?"

What a loaded question, Lyla thought. *I could never divulge what was really wrong and why I was feeling fearful and anxious.*

Lyla dutifully recited the litany of illnesses, surgeries, and medications. Charlie's questions were asked and answered as they moved from issue to issue with ease. Lyla's rapid speech and body language exposed her fragile emotional state that had been intensifying daily. She never trusted anyone but for one brief moment she let her guard down. It only took an instant, but Lyla, on an instinctive level, knew she could trust this woman, she barely knew, who was about to hear Lyla's innermost feelings. Lyla was going to allow the mask to fall and for the first time disclose the truth.

After telling Charlie she didn't think she wanted her husband to return Lyla looked up at Charlie and felt something she hadn't felt in a very long time...safe.

She went on. "I presumed from my husband's barrage of phone calls and complaints he was no longer able to perform his job. He constantly complained how difficult it was for him to do simple tasks without assistance. Juliano, my husband, didn't discuss his plans or reasons for what appeared to be his sudden decision to depart his job and return to our Texas home.

"But, I know my husband well. He rarely told the truth, and I suspected he was trying to elicit my sympathy. He was manipulating me; he wanted something. All I knew was that he was coming back, and I was not emotionally equipped to deal with him." Lyla paused, then said to Charlie, "I feared I could never reveal the kind of life I lived with him and my lack of compassion for him, given his diagnosis. You would think I would be looking forward to his return, but I'm not; at least I don't think I am. In fact, I know I'm dreading it, and I feel so guilty for saying this."

Lyla couldn't believe the words had actually come out of her mouth. She began to feel this uncomfortably large lump of emotion rising from her gut to the pit of her stomach to her throat. Tears began to well up in her eyes and she knew if she didn't practice some sort of self-control she would begin to weep unrestrained.

With eyes lowered, steeling herself against an onslaught of tears, she continued in a whisper, "I shouldn't have spoken. I'm not quite sure how to explain how I feel except to give you a visual image." She swallowed hard to get rid of the lump then gathered her strength and described the following:

"You see," she said, "I feel like I'm wearing a necklace of rocks. The rocks aren't the beautiful polished kind, they are ugly jagged rocks of all shapes and sizes, most with razor-sharp edges. They are gray, black, dark multi-hued rocks hanging unevenly spaced from a string of leather. And every time a significant event occurs causing me to feel pain or become upset, another rock is added to this necklace that has become so heavy that I can scarcely hold up my head. I am afraid, at some point, I will not be able to lift my head at all.

"These rocks represent the emotional effects of what has already occurred in my marriage and what I believe will happen when my husband returns to our home in Texas. They symbolize a tidal wave of feelings. I'm drowning. I am in a constant, heightened state of anxiety, never knowing what demands he will make and what might happen to me.

"When I was cleaning and making preparations for his return to Texas, I discovered he had hidden a bottle of Viagra pills and a set of handcuffs, real handcuffs, in one of his dresser drawers. I became terrified, wondering, "My God what had he planned to do with me and what might he do once he returned?"

"The triggers, even insignificant things like hearing Latin music, smelling his brand of cologne, or cleaning the glass stand for his huge television, cause fear in me. Every time I have to wipe that glass, it feels like I'm caressing his skin and I want to vomit. Innumerable items and circumstances trigger extreme anxiety and distress I'm unable to manage. And when I get so anxious, my gut starts grumbling and churning, my heart races, and I can't catch my breath.

"I have a terrible aversion to touching him but especially being touched by him. I resent, even before he arrives here, having to attend to his personal needs of being dressed or undressed. I don't think he's as helpless as he appears. I just wonder why he continues to put me through his barrage of requests that feel more like orders and demands.

"I can't stand his incessant teasing. It causes me to become upset, and when I complain about it, he accuses me of being too sensitive. I feel he picks at me like a vulture picks at a carcass. Will I have to use all my strength to take care of him and have nothing left for me? Does he do this because he knows I hate him and it's emotionally painful for me to do it? Does he get pleasure or feelings of superiority and power knowing and doing this?"

Lyla lowered her head and with her eyes downcast tears began to flow freely. She could barely catch her breath when she revealed, "And the children. I'm not quite sure how to explain this but when he asked for and demanded sex, I kept seeing visions of the young woman I know he violated against her will many years ago, and somehow, she became me. I was pregnant seven times in seven years and had non-consensual pregnancies, several that ended in miscarriage. And...I was unable to shake the feeling I was being raped every time he wanted to have sex, over and over and over again. I was always too afraid to say no or too weak or too sick to fight back."

Lyla was emotionally spent and embarrassed by her admissions. She closed her eyes, took a deep breath and could not look at Charlie let alone speak any more. Charlie was quiet, listening intently as Lyla described her necklace and divulged her feelings. Charlie chose her words carefully, not wanting to minimize the significance of Lyla's pain and obvious terror. When she finally spoke, she made several recommendations.

"I believe it is imperative that you be given the opportunity to talk about theses feelings and issues. If you are uncomfortable talking to a stranger in a therapeutic setting, perhaps you can begin a journal. Writing about the feelings and issues you must deal with is one way to get those things outside of you. Even if you never read what you write, it is better to get it out than allow it to stay inside and devour you from the inside."

Of course, Charlie was unaware that Lyla's secrets, fears, and anxieties about her life with her husband and what she endured, had consumed, transformed her into someone else. Lyla had become someone she no longer recognized or liked. The real Lyla was neatly tucked away in a corner of herself, safely covered up with layers upon layers of protection by withdrawing emotionally from her immediate and extended family and anyone who attempted to reach out to her. Lyla politely agreed with the suggestion of keeping the journal and walked out with her prescription and unknowingly, the seed of what was to become an idea that would help her heal and allow her to be free.

According to the plans that Juliano formulated without Lyla's input, she was to fly to Sarasota, where they would meet, and she would accompany him as he drove them back to their Texas home. As Lyla began the final preparations for her trip to Florida, she entered the master bedroom closet to look through documents related to the trip. While searching, she discovered old files that caused once distant memories to move to the forefront of her consciousness.

Strange, she thought, *that I happened upon that particular set of papers, ushering back many disturbing feelings. I thought I had tightly wrapped up everything associated with that event in my life and hidden it safely away, along with the pain.*

But seeing those papers caused a rush of painful feelings as ugly and disturbing as though the incident had just occurred. Lyla was surprised at her reaction and felt the need to escape to the openness of her backyard. She called to her little pack of furry friends to take a stroll around the grounds, compelled to retreat to the nurturing atmosphere of the garden. She instinctively knew that being outside and feeling the warmth of the sun and wind brush against her face, would help put things back into perspective for her.

Lyla walked over to her little blue bench nestled underneath the flowering crabapple tree. She sat on the bench in a spot of dappled sunlight and was joined by several of her cavaliers who made themselves comfortable on her lap and on the bench. They cuddled together in the warmth of the sun and the hush of the afternoon, serenaded only by the sound of the wind through the trees.

During these moments of reflection, Lyla allowed her mind to meander and become fixed on what Charlie had suggested. The beauty of the gardens and the well-kept verdant lawn was nearly obscured by the memories that came creeping back. It was at that moment that she entertained the idea of writing. Suddenly she knew exactly how and what she would do; it was as though a magician had snapped his fingers and made it appear out of nowhere. She spoke to her cavaliers.

"I know what I'll do. I'll write a story, my story. Only I'll make it a fictionalized account, use a young woman's life as a vehicle to finally tell the truth and talk about those things that have been haunting me. Perhaps this way I can share the heartache and the mistakes of not realizing I was viewing life through a veil and was unable or unwilling to recognize how I became involved in toxic relationships, and their effect on my life."

Lyla slowly walked back to the house to get her laptop, feeling relieved and energized, by her decision. She sat on the small family room couch near the freshly lit fire and propped up her laptop on a small throw pillow on her knees. Her companions snuggled close to her on the couch beside her and on the floor by her feet. She clicked the desktop icon to stream one of her favorite radio stations, listened to the music, and allowed her mind to go back to the beginning, to when she was young, uncompromised, and free.

She began her story.

THE WORLD AT HER FEET

The day was bright, sunny, and warm, a flawless May morning, 1972, in Miami Shores, Florida. Lyla felt proud and satisfied, knowing she had successfully completed her college education. Her parents never believed she would complete her degree when she interrupted her college experience after her first two years to work. But she surprised everyone, even herself, by returning to finish her undergraduate program and was certified to teach Kindergarten through Grade 6. Lyla joined other students as they filled the intimate auditorium of the small women's college, with her cap on her head, her hands white gloved, and her gown pressed.

The ceremony was planned for every graduate to carry a lighted white candle down the aisle to their seat. The president of the college spoke, along with the valedictorian and others. Diplomas were distributed, the dutiful handshake and congratulations were spoken, and the women migrated out to the lawns to visit with friends and family. Lyla ran into a friend and fellow classmate.

"Well Maxie, we did it, we finished in spite of ourselves and we're not any worse for wear," said Lyla. "There were a few classes when I thought I wouldn't make it like the philosophy class with Sister Agnes. Do you remember that one? Ha! I knew I was in trouble on the first day when she asked for a show of hands of those students who believed in angels. I didn't know much when I began that class, but she turned out to be one of the best teachers I had. I'll never forget her.

"I don't mean to cut you off but, I need to find my mother before she thinks I'm trying to avoid her. Oh, before I forget Maxie, Mother is having a gathering of some friends later to celebrate; will you be able to come?"

"Sure, said Maxie "wouldn't miss one of your mother's soirees for anything. It will give me a perfect excuse to go shopping."

Lyla's mother's condo glistened in the reflection of the evening sunset. It was bathed in sherbet colors of a Technicolor sky. Sunsets in Miami

Beach, but especially at her mother's location on Bay Harbor Island, were spectacular, just like the people who spilled out onto the terrace and the music that streamed from the windows. Lyla's mother, Sura, was well-known for her gatherings of beautiful people. The surroundings were meticulous, the service impeccable, and the food was glorious; it was a veritable smorgasbord feast for the senses.

Sura greeted her guests with a regal air as though she were holding court, dignified, and always self-assured. She was dressed in a pale-yellow chiffon summer dress that glittered from the colored sequins scattered over the bodice and skirt. Her exquisite jewelry sparkled in the twilight and reflected the beauty of her dewy, iridescent skin, and bright violet blue eyes.

Lyla promised to be on her best behavior that evening and not upstage her mother. Sura never liked too much competition, especially from Lyla. It was not competition for men as much as it was for attention. Sura demanded it, Lyla shied away from it, and lived in the shadows of her glamorous mother. It was important for Lyla to look good but not too good. Lyla had no difficulty giving her mother the spotlight and the space she required. While she rarely attempted to garner the attention, it was something that just happened. Men were attracted to her and women were fascinated by her simple, natural beauty and carriage.

Lyla arrived fashionably late to her mother's building on the south side of Bay Harbor Island, an island between Miami Beach and Miami. She chose to wear an off-the-shoulder, pale lavender fine spun cotton dress. The neckline of the dress accentuated her neck where she wore a strand of tiny diamonds that nestled gently in the curve of her throat. The necklace was a graduation gift from her parents. The dress, casual but elegant, draped her sensuous form, flaring out in soft folds around her long shapely legs. She looked like a luscious marzipan-like confection with a hint of sparkle around her hazel tinted brown eyes and on her lips. She was fresh, alluring, irresistible.

Well, here goes, Lyla thought, as she ascended in the small elevator to the third-floor condo. With two apartments per floor it was obvious where the party was. Her guts were churning, doing somersaults, and her anxiety climbed as she went from floor to floor. When Lyla stepped out of the elevator, she was greeted by Lucille, her mother's housekeeper, confidant, and friend. Lyla sighed with relief that Lucille was the first person she encountered. Lyla embraced Lucille and felt surrounded by genuine warmth and love.

"Congratulations," Lucille whispered in Lyla's ear. "I knew you could do it. I'm so very proud of you." Lyla whispered in return, "Thank you. Your loving arms give me the strength and support I need to enter the crowded room and find mother."

Lucille was the only stabilizing force in Lyla's family. Sura depended on Lucille for emotional support throughout her marriage. And Lyla depended on Lucille for the love, attention, and support she was unable to get from her mother. Lucille's stature in the family was hidden only because Lucille wanted it that way. It was no longer necessary for her to work, but she believed she could not abandon Sura and her children; they needed her.

Lucille arrived in the Rose household as a young woman when Lyla was about ten. She was 5'6" tall with a delicate frame. Her smooth nutmeg colored skin was flawless, and her long hair now sprinkled salt-and-pepper was tightly pulled back, neatly tucked close to the nape of her neck. She was soft-spoken, genteel, and rarely provoked to anger or bitter words. She possessed omniscient wisdom coupled with a gentle manner and used soaps and lotions that had the scents of fresh roses and lavender. She became the buffer and chief consoler when emotions and conflicts rose.

Her introduction into the Rose family dynamics occurred one fateful afternoon several months after she arrived in the home. Apparently, Lyla had made some seemingly minor transgression in her father's private rooms that resulted in him verbally and physically assaulting Lyla. She accidentally left the roll of toilet paper slightly unrolled and resting on the tile floor. When her father asked who had committed the act she admitted without hesitation not realizing the seriousness of the crime she had committed. Harry stood over Lyla yelling and berating her. When she stood silent he became more enraged and he began to hit her in the face, on her arms, and about her body. The red hand marks and the marks from his large ruby ring were imprinted on her skin. She ran screaming and crying to her wing of the house and threw herself on her bed sobbing, repeating over and over that she hated her father. Lyla's mother never interceded on Lyla's behalf during the confrontation and assault. Afterward, Sura stood at Lyla's bedside and attempted to soothe her and calm her down, by trying to convince Lyla she would recover and be OK, and that she didn't hate her father.

Lucille was downstairs in the kitchen area when she heard Lyla scream and quickly ran up the back staircase to Lyla's bedroom. Lucille instinctively sat on Lyla's bed and cradled and rocked Lyla in her arms softly consoling her wiping away her tears. Lucille was the calming maternal influence, took her job as caretaker of the family seriously, and was an integral member of the Rose family.

Lyla walked through the kitchen to the Florida room past the throng of people and pulsating music to find her mother who was surrounded by her usual entourage.

"Mother," she said, leaning in to dutifully brush each cheek with the breath of a kiss.

"Everything is beautiful; thank you so much for doing this for me."

"Oh, please," Sura responded. "It's the least I could do for my little Rosebud." As the words trailed off into the room, she followed with, "I've been waiting for this for a long time. I was so worried you wouldn't finish."

Lyla turned away from her mother and searched frantically for a friendly face or a safe place to retreat to, thoroughly embarrassed and humiliated by her mother's words.

"Where ever are you going?" Sura quipped, sounding somewhat annoyed. "There's someone I want you to meet."

Lyla felt the color drain from her face. The churning in her gut that had begun earlier had returned and was reaching its peak. *Oh, no*, Lyla thought. *Here it comes, another one of mother's introductions.* Her mother was forever trying to find a suitable husband for Lyla and tonight would be no exception. Lyla had to behave, she had already been forewarned. *I wonder who it could be this time*, she thought.

Lyla watched as her mother searched the room and then felt her mother grab her arm and they swirled through the sea of people and onto the terrace. She wondered *how her mother was able to see that far and through all those people? Incredibly, the woman must have had some sort of laser vision.* Once her mother locked on target, Lyla knew there was no getting away from her.

Sunset had just descended when her mother tapped a rather tall, neatly dressed man on the shoulder. He appeared to be in his early thirties with dark hair and soft hazel eyes. Sura began her introduction.

"Hello Herbie, so glad you could make it. I'd like you to meet my daughter, Lyla," she said as she swung Lyla around to face him. Sura bent close to Lyla as though to give her a kiss on the cheek. It was a movement that gave Sura the opportunity to whisper in Lyla's ear. "I thought you might want to know Herbie is indeed single, a CPA in a large firm, available, and by the way, drives a snazzy Porsche convertible.

"Please," Sura begged, "give this one a chance," and she re-entered the condo through the sea of undulating people.

Dutifully polite, Lyla stood still under Herbie's intense gaze and pretended to be interested in the small talk being made. Lyla continued the banter by asking, "Mother mentioned you are a member of a large, successful firm in the Miami area. How long have you been with them and do you ever do any traveling?"

Well, that was all she had to say. Herbie then embarked on a ten-minute dissertation about the work he did, how he was in line to become partner soon, no less than the youngest partner-to-be in the firm, and how he enjoyed the traveling he did for the Latin American clients.

Lyla spied her friend Maxie coming towards them as she began to fall into a somnambulistic coma of boredom and quickly held out her hand, eagerly introducing Herbie to Maxie.

"Herbie," Lyla said sweetly, "I'd like you to meet a friend of mine from school, Maxie, short for Maxine. Maxie, this is Herbie. I am so sorry but if you two would please excuse me for a moment, I see someone I must acknowledge."

Lyla left Maxie and Herbie to get acquainted and began to maneuver around people through the room in the direction of the bar. She noticed a tall, attractive man standing at the bar, waiting to be served, swaying to the sensual rhythm of the rhumba being played. The man at the bar caught a glimpse of someone in pale lavender and intriguing coming toward him, a raven-haired classic beauty with a mane of thick, begged-to-be-touched locks that framed her oval face. She gazed from behind hazel tinted, velvety brown eyes adorned by a forest of lashes and well-formed brows. Her long shapely legs carried the feminine torso of a woman who was modestly endowed, yet lean and muscular from years of dance and movement. She learned to carry herself well, not with pride, but with the stance of a dancer.

Men were struck by Lyla's unsuspecting knowledge of her natural beauty, and easy-going manner. She never spent hours primping and cooing to herself in the mirror. A toss of her hair, some shine on her lips and lashes, a comfortable outfit, and she was on her way. Her sense of style and color were characteristics she unknowingly learned from her mother.

What a beautiful diversion. I wonder who she is, the man mused as Lyla came within striking distance. As she approached the bar, she heard the song "Temptation," sung by Diana Krall and thought to herself, *what a beautiful temptation, I wonder who he is?*

She greeted the gentleman as she approached the bar. "Hello," Lyla said with a voice bright and sensual, a quality so natural to her. "My name is Lyla Rose, what's yours?"

"Beautiful name for a very beautiful young woman," he said smoothly, causing Lyla to blush. "My name is Mark Weiman. I'm a friend of a friend here from New York City for a week or so for some sun, fun, and feminine diversion."

"Working on your tan, I see," she said with a chuckle.

"Yes," he laughed, eager to draw her in. "I've been spending some time on the beach and rented a sailboat the other day. The sun's amazing down here."

They spent the next 20 minutes sharing information and small talk, unknowing seductress and experienced seducer. Lyla was eager to move this forward and asked Mark if he would enjoy listening to some live jazz. He accepted her invitation to go to a local jazz club with the interest of pursing her further.

"Excuse me for a moment, Mark, while I say goodbye to some friends. I'll return in a few moments and will be ready to go." She searched for her mother to say thank you again for the party and whoever that friend was who brought Mark. As she was about to leave, Maxie caught up to her.

"Hey, Lyla, the guy you introduced me to, Herbie. I need to ask you something. Are you interested in him? If you are I'll back off, but if you're not, I'd like to get to know him better. What do you say?"

As Lyla turned to go, she said to Maxie, "Take him, he's yours. I think I've found something more to my liking," as she disappeared out the door on Mark's arm.

Lyla and Mark left Sura's condo building en route to Miami in Lyla's little sport sedan. Her intended destination was an intimate jazz club near the airport. It was one of those places inhabited by the locals where good drinks and masterful sounds of live jazz filled the dark, smoke-filled air. They stayed there for the remainder of the evening and late into the night.

Lyla didn't realize that the handsome man she encountered embodied the characteristics of a brightly colored serpent in the way he patiently, cautiously, and quietly waited for his unsuspecting prey to appear in order to wreak devastating emotional damage. What a foolish girl, like a moth to a flame, she was about to get burned.

That initial encounter was the beginning of a relationship Lyla would never forget and the catalyst that sent her on a reckless path of regret. She was unaware that what she had experienced emotionally with her father and witnessed between her parents was not the way relationships were supposed to be. This attitude and perception of men was her only frame of reference and experience.

Lyla was drawn to men who were demanding, emotionally distant, and almost aloof with flash and flair. They appeared to be strong men who were in control and did not treat women with respect nor apparent consideration. They were beautifully colored reptiles slithering their way in and out of women's lives, leaving behind a path of pain.

No wonder she spurned all the advances of boys, and later men, who were tenderhearted and treated her with kindness and romance. She was disinterested and quickly disposed of the men who were most unlike her father. They made her uncomfortable, perceived them as ineffectual, and had no idea how to communicate with them. She misunderstood their interest and tenderness as weakness. Instead, she was drawn to the ones who made her cry.

MEMORABLE ADVENTURE

Lyla became convinced that Mark, her current lover, this perceived suitor, was the one she wanted to make permanent. Mark made the trip to Miami Beach several times a month. When he was in town, Lyla was his constant companion. Mark's condo was one of many overlooking the ocean on Collins Avenue. Lyla prepared Mark's condo for his arrival stocking it with his favorite food and beverages. Lyla was available at all times, no questions asked, and no demands made.

The couple kept busy playing in the sun on the beach, on the boat, and traveling to the Keys and the Bahamas for more diversion. The relationship with Mark lasted until September of that year. It culminated in an invitation from Mark for Lyla to visit him in New York City. The plan was for her to stay with Mark over the weekend at his Fire Island beach house and then spend a couple of days in the city with him to celebrate the Labor Day Weekend.

This is it, thought Lyla. Although he never ever mentioned anything about marriage, Lyla, for whatever reason, was certain he was planning to ask her. The scheduled weekend on Fire Island with the accompanying days in the city was evidence to her he was serious. She became excited to think this was going to happen and decided to tell her mother of his invitation and her presumptions. Sura was skeptical at first but chose to ignore any possible warning signs regarding the legitimacy of a marriage proposal, his business, or standing in the community. If this was as serious as Lyla led her to believe, Sura decided perhaps it was time to prepare her Rosebud for an exciting weekend and possible future with this man.

Sura took Lyla to an exclusive women's shop in Bal Harbour and purchased the perfect wardrobe for the trip to New York City. It was a kind of preemptive trousseau. While they shopped, Sura asked Lyla if she was happy and if she loved him.

"Mother, what do you mean? I like him, he's good looking, has money, and he's Jewish. I thought you said love was not the most important part of the marriage equation, and you could always learn to love your husband as long as he took care of you?"

"I didn't mean love wasn't important; only that if you chose someone who had all the other 'right' qualities, you could learn to love him in time."

Every outfit Lyla tried on looked like it was custom made for Lyla and Sura was indeed thrilled thinking this would be a perfect opportunity to start making wedding plans. After Lyla left for New York, Sura began making lists and phone calls in preparation of wonderful news from Lyla upon her return and impending proposal.

When Lyla arrived at the airport's baggage claim in New York City, there was a gentleman holding a sign with her name on it. She immediately thought it was strange that Mark hadn't come to meet her.

"Good Afternoon. Are you Miss Lyla Rose?" Lyla acknowledged with a nod of her head. "I'm sorry Miss," he said. "Mr. Weiman was unable to leave an important meeting and asked me to pick you up and take you directly to his apartment in the city where he will meet you later."

The gentleman collected her luggage and directed her to a large dark-colored sedan. Lyla was so eager to see Mark that her earlier sense of anything amiss quickly dissipated.

Perhaps she should have paid more attention to those earlier feelings.

She was taken to a handsome sophisticated apartment with floors covered in fine marble and oriental rugs and was greeted by the housekeeper.

"Good afternoon, Miss Lyla," said Carmen, the housekeeper. "Mr. Weiman asked me to get you settled and offer you a small snack before he arrives, in case you're a little hungry. Allow me to show you to your room so you can freshen up after your journey."

Although his absence from the apartment at her arrival should have been another red flag, Lyla chose to ignore it and made preparations to leave for their trip. Mark finally arrived, greeting Lyla with a warm embrace and quick kiss.

"So sorry for not meeting you at the airport and not being here when you arrived. There were loose ends to tie up so we could spend more time together," he said.

That's all Lyla had to hear. She was now more eager than ever to begin their weekend together, thinking she was about to become Mrs. Weiman. To Lyla's delight, Mark chose to drive and they were alone in the car. *This was another sign*, she thought, he was going to ask her as they made small talk during the drive. He pointed out local places of interest and showed Lyla other places unique to the area.

Their journey ended when they arrived at his beach house. It was a large frame structure with gables, a dark steep roof, with a wide porch that wrapped around both front and rear. Mark parked the car and they walked up the front steps where they were met by three women and two men. Lyla was surprised and couldn't understand why there were other people there. She ultimately concluded this was an impromptu surprise party he had planned and was eager to meet everyone.

Mark introduced the other people as his roommates as they met on the porch. The roommates ushered Mark and Lyla into the house, laughing and talking about things only Mark's friends were familiar with. Once inside the house, Lyla was directed to the room she was to share with Mark.

"*Strange*, she thought, *roommates. Why in the world would he share his home with other people?*" Her thought immediately faded when she heard someone telling her to change into her bathing suit and meet them on the back porch to go to the beach. Mark's room was simple and sparsely furnished but quaint. Lyla wasted no time and changed into one of her little suits, walked to the back porch where she met the rest of the roommates, and walked with them toward the beach, expecting sun and surf. The beach was not inviting; it was rough with substantial wind, chilly air, and few people in the water. Chairs were set up with groups of people crowded around fires to keep warm. She was freezing and didn't dare go near the water; the beach was covered with course sand mixed with rocks and pebbles with scattered tufts of grasses, and the water looked dark, foreboding and cold. It was not exactly the kind of place she was used to.

Lyla was withdrawn feeling out of her element not knowing anyone. Mark was not particularly attentive, so she was left on her own to get to know the others. They all appeared much older than she; she almost felt like a child. What she failed to realize was that they were Mark's friends, his age group, and Mark was more than ten years older than she.

The roommates organized and prepped food to cook over the open fire. The menu consisted of lobster, fresh fish, fresh asparagus, and corn in the husk and a large bowl of creamed slaw. One of the women brought out pitchers of what looked and tasted like some white wine fruit drink which was interesting but not to Lyla's liking. The group members shared prior Labor Day exploits peppered with current political thoughts as they huddled around the large bonfire. Mark eventually joined Lyla and began to be attentive. She relaxed and soon felt the effects of the wine.

The women were curious to know more about Lyla. One of the women asked again, "Well, who are you and where do you come from? Are you Mark's latest?"

"Excuse me?" Lyla responded and repeated with emphasis. "I'm not quite sure I understand you. Exactly what do you mean by Mark's latest? Like I said before, my name is Lyla. I live in North Miami. I'm here for a short visit, and I'm a friend of Mark's, not that that's any business of yours."

Lyla quickly changed the subject to something other than herself as she began to feel like a minnow in a school of barracuda. The women looked at one another with a look of poor thing, she doesn't know.

The sun began to set with the light waning across the sky. There was no Miami Beach sunset here. The air had become colder, and everyone decided it was time to retreat to the warmth of the fireplace in the house and enjoy a hot toddy and good music. When they reached the house, and gathered in the large living room, someone took out a cigarette of marijuana. It was offered from one person to the next.

Lyla did not indulge in recreational drugs but took the joint when it was passed to her, not wanting to appear innocent and out of place. She had observed the others' behavior and mimicked them by puffing deeply and holding her breath before exhaling the heavy, burning smoke. First one breath and then another and she began to lose her sense of balance and her touch with reality. Mark, feeling the effects of the marijuana, took Lyla's hand and led her to the bedroom. Lyla felt strangely uncomfortable and was unaccustomed to losing control of her senses. Instead of their romantic interlude being a heightened sensual experience, Lyla unwillingly conjured up dark and foreboding images.

When Mark was satisfied, Lyla asked if he would bring her to completion. But Mark was finished and ready to sleep; he mumbled, "Finish yourself, I'm tired," as he rolled over and fell into a deep sleep. Lyla knew the others could hear everything that was said. She crawled to the other side of the bed mortally wounded and embarrassed. She curled up and wept softly as she fell into an exhaustive and dizzying sleep.

Lyla was uncomfortable the next morning, knowing everyone had heard what happened the night before and chose to avoid breakfast by walking on the chilly beach until Mark was ready to make the drive back to the City. He took no notice of her distress and obvious absence at breakfast. She didn't speak during the ride back, staring out the passenger window, wondering what in the world had happened. Eventually, he noticed her silence, turned, and spoke to her.

"Hey there, Sunshine. Why so quiet? Want to go into town and do a bit of shopping? There are some nice shops in the area. You might want to find something to take back to remember the weekend."

Remembering the weekend was definitely not on her agenda and was more likely to become a haunting nightmare.

"I don't understand," she said quietly. "Why did you ask me here? Why did you treat me so badly?"

"Badly, what do you mean, badly? Oh, you mean last night? Don't worry about that. Sometimes that happens when I smoke. It's just... I was so satisfied and the weed was so incredible, eh, don't give it another thought. It doesn't have anything to do with you."

"I thought," she spoke barely above a whisper, "I thought perhaps you invited me here for something special, something special like getting serious, special, as in asking me to...

She couldn't finish her sentence. The car became deathly silent as Mark attempted to extricate himself from a messy situation and salvage what was left of her visit for his own selfish reasons.

"It must have been a terrible misunderstanding," he said with a sincere and apologetic voice. "Why don't we sort of start over when we get back into the City? I have to go to work for several hours tomorrow, but I will be home for dinner. We can go out, have dinner, and go to the theatre. Would you like that?"

Should she believe him? She looked over at him and wanted to trust him. He looked at her with a huge smile and a twinkle in his eye. After a long pause, she said.

"Sure, that sounds like a nice thing to do."

That night, Mark was attentive and loving. He took Lyla to a small Italian restaurant in the City called Grotta Azzura. They walked down a flight of steps from the sidewalk into a room filled with wonderful aromas, small tables covered in white tablecloths, and candlelight. A waiter greeted Mark with familiarity and escorted them to a small table sandwiched between others. It wasn't really intimate, but it was very romantic. Mark never took his eyes from her, making Lyla feel they were instantly transported to some cozy restaurant in Italy.

Lyla eventually shook her feelings of anger and rejection with his constant attention. She let her guard down and she became vulnerable to his every desire. Mark gave her no reason that night to think anything was wrong or have misgivings about their relationship. He held her emotionally captive throughout dinner gazing lovingly and intently into her eyes, holding her hand, and reaching over to kiss her periodically during the short ride back to his apartment. He kept her physically captive throughout the night, pleasuring her in ways he had not done before, never giving her doubt about his unselfish interest in her.

He left for the office mid-morning the next day and mentioned it would be several hours before he would return. Suggestions were offered that she explore the City and shop while he was away. He left her on her own, hoping he had smoothed things over. She was hesitant to attempt to explore the City on her own and chose to make a romantic dinner at the apartment. The local fresh market was a short walk giving her immediate access to everything she needed. Armed with a credit card Mark had given her, she collected her courage, went to the store, and purchased food, wine, and flowers for their evening.

She began feeling more confident about Mark and their relationship and successfully buried her memories of what had occurred on the

Island. Her dinner preparation was interrupted to look around the apartment for a vase for the fresh flowers she purchased. Her plan was to place the flowers in a vase on the table between the candles and have the wine on the table chilled and ready for consumption at the perfect moment. *This is a great way to show him I have the skills to entertain with confidence and sophistication*, she thought.

An intricately cut crystal vase was sitting on one of the end tables in the living room. It appeared to be the perfect vessel for the flowers, and she took it to the kitchen sink. Before adding the water and powder to keep the flowers fresh, she noticed a folded piece of paper inside. She removed the paper to keep it from becoming wet, partially unfolded it, and placed it on the kitchen counter by the phone.

Dinner was almost done and the table was set. As she was leaving the room to take her shower and change, she remembered the piece of paper she left on the counter. *Whoops*, she thought, *I forgot to make sure I put this someplace where it won't get lost and make a point of telling Mark.*

As she lifted the paper from the counter, she saw someone had made notation of flight times and dates written on the paper. *Hm*, she thought, *he did care; this must be my flight information.*

She studied the paper and it was indeed flight times, but it was for a flight out of Paris in several days and there was someone else's name and phone number written by the flight times. Her name was Monique. She was scheduled to arrive on Friday at 4 p.m. on flight...on flight. The words began to blur as her eyes filled with tears. From the scribbled notes, Lyla surmised Monique was a flight attendant and Lyla presumed she was coming in to be with Mark for the weekend. No wonder he scheduled Lyla to leave when he did. He needed to make room for the next one and didn't want either one of them to meet accidentally.

Lyla was in shock, could barely take a breath, and stood motionless with the paper until the sound of the door brought her back to reality. She walked into the foyer with the paper as though it was stuck in her hand. Mark greeted her with an attempted kiss from which she withdrew.

"What's the matter, honey?" he asked, looking at her face and then to the paper in her hand.

She began to speak with a slight stammer.

"I thought, that is, I was trying to do something nice and decided to make dinner for you tonight instead of going out, and I ...and I ...you see, I bought flowers for the table," she went on in a whisper with her head bent down and her eyes glued to the paper looking guilty. "I found this when I went to put the flowers in the vase."

He looked at the paper, snatched it out of her hand, and suddenly realized what she had found. He immediately raised his voice and accused her of snooping. He was treating her like she had done something wrong and she felt she needed to run. Their time together was nothing but a lie. It must have been some sort of game he was playing with her. He was juggling her and who knew who else. It was meaningless, nothing. He used her, and when he was ready he would let her go, in pieces. She was merely another one of his toys, and when he was tired of her he would throw her away like he had the others.

Driven by a force she neither understood nor acknowledged, she continued to make incongruous choices in the men she encountered. Why would someone with her abilities and potential make so many bad choices? Her decisions led to relationships and brief encounters that ultimately ended badly for her. She was left behind, left out, used, and hurt, never understanding why it didn't work. The obvious always eluded her; perhaps it was the decision to embark on the encounter in the first place that led her to failure and heartache.

BROKEN PIECES

Lyla listened to the plaintive but soothing sounds of blues and jazz chanteuses who sing of love both lost and found. Ella Fitzgerald, who sang George and Ira Gershwin's rhapsodic "Good Morning Heartache," sweet and sultry, was Lyla's recurring emotional theme regarding the men she chose to become involved with.

Lyla was unaware that her father and her relationship with him, her parent's relationship, and the dysfunction within her own family formed her perceptions of herself and the kind of relationships she entered into. The role she inhabited within her family unit became the same role she played in all her relationships.

Harry Rose, Lyla's father, was a perfectionist who strove to be the best and without blemish. His exacting measure and intolerance of error in himself was translated to his family and others who worked for him. Lyla was never really comfortable in her father's presence. She was fearful and hesitant to speak up. Asking for anything created physical symptoms impossible for her to control. Her hands would sweat and shake, her heart would beat faster, and when she spoke her voice would become a whisper. Walking into his room to ask for something was like the scene from the "Wizard of Oz," when Dorothy and her companions walked into the great hall and were confronted by the image and voice of the Wizard for the first time.

The ever-present fear of her father drove Lyla to achieve perfection, always hoping for his acceptance. She avoided, at all costs, confrontations or questioning his authority and longed for her father to show her any measure of love and recognition but received neither.

Harry influenced Lyla by instilling in her a strong work ethic and teaching her the importance of living up to her responsibility. As a result, she never shied away from hard work and rarely took short cuts to accomplish tasks set before her. Harry had a chip on his shoulder he often dared others to knock off. He held his emotions in check and was not demonstrative with his feelings toward his family yet in public was charming, theatrical, and a risk taker. He enjoyed being in the spotlight and adored being adored. Women flaunted themselves at him, and he rarely resisted their advances only to leave one for another feeling no remorse for his actions.

Although Harry was married to Lyla's mother all his life, they didn't live a happy life together. Lyla's mother felt ignored, cheated on, and abandoned, and comforted herself with material things and a life outside her marriage.

Lyla didn't pursue a teaching job the summer she graduated. Preparing for Mark's visits was more important than trying to get a job for the fall. When she came back from her fateful weekend in New York, teaching positions were already filled and contracts signed.

She was bored, depressed, and feeling generally out of sorts. She drifted from one insignificant job to another as a secretary or receptionist, anything to keep her busy. She made bad choices for jobs and equally bad choices in men that left her feeling alone and used. She began to harden herself, burying her feelings deeper and deeper.

What was it that caused her to continue to repeat the same self-destructive decisions causing her to roam aimlessly through life without structure or plan for what was beyond the end of the day? Would she ever recognize her behavior, and if she did, would it be too late?

It had been six months or more since her trip to Fire Island when Lyla got a surprise phone call from Mark. He was in town to relax and wanted to know if she would have dinner with him. At first, she hesitated but accepted his invitation to show him what it was like to be treated with disdain and disrespect. He was waiting outside, under the portico, when she arrived. *Too bad*, she thought, *he still looks good.*

They went to a casual restaurant on Treasure Island not far from Mark's condo and engaged mostly in small talk. Throughout dinner Mark watched Lyla intently as though he was looking for a clue to how she felt. She began to feel uncomfortable under his probing stare. Mark couldn't put his finger on it, but there was something different about Lyla. The more he stared the more uncomfortable she became. She looked at him and pretending not to care, asked, "What is it, what is the problem, you keep staring?"

"You see," he said, "I've been wondering all evening what is so very different about you. I wanted to see you because I've had time to think about what happened that weekend when you came to visit, and I wanted to say how very sorry I was about how I treated you. I don't see Monique anymore."

"It's none of my business who you see," said Lyla.

He thought, *she's still very angry and hurt.* He said nothing more; he deserved it. And then he finally recognized what had changed about her. She had lost the beautiful carefree-like innocence that was so alluring.

They parted cordially when Lyla deposited him at his condo. She watched him as he walked slowly into the lobby through the glass doors without once turning back to say a final good-bye. *I showed him,* she thought, *and I don't care if I never hear from him again.*

While Lyla was drifting aimlessly from one insignificant job to the next, her friends were becoming established in their career fields, finishing graduate degrees, getting married, and having babies. Somehow, Lyla was not aware that she was moving in a far different direction than the people around her. Securing a teaching job that year was unrealistic and she discarded the field completely. She discovered that she was either overqualified or under-skilled for every job she attempted, became frustrated at her failures, and grew tired of straying from job to job. The thought of a possible career change led her to attend a technical school to obtain the skills she needed to become a paralegal. *I can do this,* she thought.

She never told anyone of her early desires to become an attorney. How did she get so far off course? If her desire was to become an attorney, why become a paralegal? Her secret fear was her lack of self confidence in passing the LSAT entrance exam and successfully completing law school.

Lyla's choice to participate in a program that was established for women who did not have a college degree was ironic. She spent her days taking typing classes, speed writing, and basic grammar. The most challenging and interesting classes were the ones taught by guest attorneys who came to teach the basics of each area of the law. Every case fascinated her, particularly when she was required to research case law in the courthouse law library and write briefs.

She successfully completed the course and was prepared to be a working paralegal. Finding a job as a legal secretary was easy but finding one as a paralegal was more challenging as those jobs were traditionally filled by men at the time. Undaunted by the rejection, Lyla answered an ad published by two young attorneys just starting out on their own. They needed a secretary and couldn't pay much. Lyla needed a job, a place to get experience, and took what was offered.

Another, more experienced, secretary was hired and she and Lyla were responsible for working for both men when necessary; Lyla didn't mind. She enjoyed being busy, was a quick learner, and had a sincere interest in everything completing tasks with accuracy. The job gave her confidence and a strong sense of accomplishment. It appeared she had finally found her place.

THE REPTILE SLITHERS IN

The office had been particularly busy and Lyla didn't notice when a client was ushered into one of the attorney's offices. The case was criminal and currently being handled by the other secretary. The client was in and out of the office often during the next several weeks. Lyla met him on one of those occasions when she delivered documents to the attorney preparing the client's case. She knocked on the closed door and the voice from inside responded.

"Who is it?"

"It's Lyla, sir. I have those docs you're waiting for," Lyla said as she entered the attorney's office.

"Thank you, Lyla," the attorney said. "By the way, this is our client, Mr. Juliano Masselli. We're handling a case for him."

"Hello, Mr. Masselli," she said. "Very nice to meet you."

"Nice to meet you as well," he said, looking at her. Then he turned to his attorney and said with a smile, "With secretaries like Lyla, I'll have to think about breaking the law more often just so I can find reasons to come see you."

The two men laughed at the client's humor; Lyla blushed and asked if there was anything else she could do before she left for the day.

"No, thank you," the attorney answered. "I don't think I will need anything further for this case now."

Lyla couldn't get the client out of her mind. He was well-dressed, good looking, and had a great smile. There was something about him that attracted her and she couldn't wait to bump into him again.

Several weeks passed when Lyla caught glimpses of Mr. Masselli during his appointments. On occasion, she was able to have short conversations with him as he passed her on his way in or out the door. Judy, the other secretary, noticed Lyla's interest and subtly tried to warn her to stay away from him; he was a client. But Lyla was drawn to him and didn't stay away.

Her eyes followed him each time he appeared, and she did everything she could to be in his way or find a way to speak to him. It was becoming obvious to everyone in the office that Lyla was interested in him and he was interested in her. One last time, Judy tried to warn her.

"Lyla," she pleaded, "stay away from him. You're taking a big risk stay away."

Lyla looked at her incredulously. "What do you know about him? Is there something I should know?"

"I can't tell you," Judy said softly. "Just trust me."

Juliano Masselli was not forgotten, just neatly tucked away in the back of Lyla's mind. Several months had passed since her last encounter with Mr. Masselli. As usual, the office was busy and Lyla had little time to do anything other than type pleadings, take information for interrogatories, and balance the checkbook, a task she never liked. On one particular evening, Lyla arrived home worn out from a long, stressful day, grateful to be home. She changed from her work clothes into something comfortable to lounge in, a loose-fitting cotton dress that looked more like a huge T-shirt. It wasn't great fashion but it was comfortable. Lyla piled her hair on top of her head, fastened it in place with a plastic hair clip, and went to the kitchen. She opened several cabinets and the refrigerator and spoke, "Hmm, what can I put together for something tasty tonight?"

Lyla's favorite radio station, WBUS, was playing soulful jazz as she poured herself a large glass of sweet vermouth and seltzer over ice with a wedge of fresh lemon when a knock on her apartment door interrupted her. When she opened the door, she was face to face with Juliano Masselli, who was holding a large bouquet of fresh flowers. Lyla stood at the open door unable to move or speak. There was a lengthy silence which Juliano broke by introducing himself.

"Excuse me, I am Juliano Masselli and you are Lyla Rose?"

Silence, long uncomfortable silence continued as Lyla stared from the flowers to Juliano's face and back to the flowers again.

"Excuse me," Juliano said. "You are Lyla Rose, are you not? The Lyla who works for..." and then suddenly the sound of Lyla's voice brought her back from her shocked silence.

"Uh, yes ... yes, well, yes, I am." Lyla instinctively closed the door slightly and took two steps back into the safety of her apartment.

Juliano reached up with his free hand to open the door wider. He gestured towards Lyla with the bouquet of flowers and said, "I was just in the area and thought you might like these."

Lyla's eyebrows arched in surprise and her velvety brown eyes grew wider and wider. The silence became uncomfortable for them both, and Lyla finally cleared her throat and spoke.

"Ahem, well, yes, no, that is. Sorry, I'm mumbling and rambling. Yes, I'm Lyla Rose. How ever did you find me?"

"It wasn't difficult. I have my resources, but that's not important. The important part is I found you and ...would you mind if I came in? It's a little uncomfortable for me to talk to you standing outside your door."

Lyla hesitated for a moment wondering if she should let him into her apartment and then with a wave of her hand smiled and let him in.

"Yes, forgive me, please, do come in."

And another brightly colored serpent slid his way into Lyla's life.

Juliano stepped through the open doorway into Lyla's apartment. He looked at her and promptly surveyed her small, neat, fashionably decorated living room. Her walls were covered with hanging art work and objects d'art were scattered about on shelves and tables.

Lyla felt uneasy in his presence and tried to bring calm by explaining how she started collecting art and art objects.

"When I was a teenager, the grocery store rewarded purchases with green stamps. As an incentive, a promotion was initiated where customers could collect stamps when they purchased groceries and were encouraged to redeem them for houseware items only available in the store.

"My first art purchase was with green stamps. It was a 6"x 6" ceramic tile that Robert Fabe, a local artist, had drawn on and fired, an ordinary bathroom wall tile transformed into art. This was just the beginning of my love affair with art and all things artistic. My pieces reflect different aspects and events in my life."

Juliano was impressed at the number and diversity of objects and commented, "I can see you're an avid art enthusiast; you have a very interesting collection."

"Yes," Lyla responded, "thank you. I think that was a compliment. Can I get you something to drink?"

Juliano turned to face her, "Sure, that would great, whatever you're having."

"Well, I've got some M&R sweet vermouth over ice with some fresh lemon."

"Perfect."

Juliano followed Lyla into the small kitchen and asked about her day at the law office. She continued to feel uncomfortable and responded without turning to look at him, struggling to concentrate on pouring and mixing his drink.

Busy, we were very busy, very busy, today ... with lots of pleadings and other court documents requiring completion in time for several different cases. It was a relief to come home and only have to think about what I was going to make for dinner."

Lyla spoke rapidly and appeared to be seriously preoccupied with the drink preparation. Juliano's constant staring at her caused her to become even more nervous while she was making his drink, working as quickly as possible without spilling and making a mess. She turned and handed Juliano his drink.

"Here you are; I hope it is to your liking."

"Yes, it's just fine."

Juliano noticed Lyla's hand shaking slightly as she handed him his glass. To put her at ease he raised his glass with a smile and mischief in his eyes and said, "Well, it's a good thing I wasn't up to my old tricks, otherwise you would have had my court documents to deal with as well. Let me ask you something." As he motioned with a wave of his hand he asked, "Do you always dress like this when you're making dinner and entertaining?"

Lyla's cheeks became flushed. She took a long sip of her drink and responded, "Actually, no, not always; sometimes I dress somewhat more casual."

There was a brief moment of silence, and then they broke into laughter. The humor and accompanying laughter broke the tension and the wine helped Lyla to let go.

"Listen," Juliano spoke, "how about we finish our drinks and I take you out for a nice meal? You've worked a long hard day. You deserve to be waited on. How about it? Nothing fancy, just a good meal and quiet conversation."

The wine on Lyla's empty stomach was already affecting her. She let her guard down and said, "Why not? That sounds like a good idea. Thanks, just give me a moment to change."

Lyla crossed in front of Juliano, dangerously close enough to smell the warmth of his cologne. When she did, she felt a tingling sensation and an almost unrestrainable urge to be even closer to him. The sensation and her reaction to him caught her off guard. She did not give in to the urge but went directly to her bedroom and closed the door, leaving Juliano alone wondering what had just happened.

She looked in her closet and decided to wear a pair of wide-legged trousers in pale beige linen. Then she chose a dark beige sleeveless tank top of fine spun cotton edged with darker-colored lace embroidery. The clip in her hair was pulled out, she gave her hair a fast brush through, refreshed her makeup, and grabbed one of her pashmina shawls to keep her warm in the air-conditioned restaurant. A little bit of spray from her favorite bottle of perfume completed her preparation as she stepped into her low-heeled sandals. She refreshed her lipstick, took one last look in the mirror for confirmation, and off she went through the bedroom door.

From the bedroom door Lyla could see Juliano sitting comfortably on her couch drinking his vermouth with his eyes closed, listening to the soft melodies of the music. The alluring aroma of Lyla's perfume announced her presence, whereupon Juliano interrupted his reverie and fixed his watchful eye upon her.

"Stunning." he whispered.

"Why, thank you," she responded with a slight blush. "I'm ready if you think you can tear yourself away from your drink and the music."

Juliano rose from the couch with his drink in his hand and motioned to Lyla's glass. "Why don't you finish your drink and then we'll go."

"Oh no, no more for me, I've had my limit; I'm not much of a drinker. I like to keep my head about me, you know."

Juliano drank what was left in his glass and handed it to Lyla. She placed it on the counter and Juliano ushered her out the door of the apartment. As they walked down the outside hallway, Juliano described the destination he had chosen, which was a perfect little Italian restaurant close to her neighborhood.

The subtle and beautifully colored serpent charmed his prey.

The evening was warm and already filled with the familiar sounds and aromas of a south Florida evening. The night birds were chirping, frogs were calling to one another, and the breeze from the ocean smelled of the sea. The restaurant Juliano chose was an unobtrusive-looking little place hidden in a small strip plaza off a side street in a residential area. When they walked in, they were immediately greeted and seated at a table in a darkened corner of the small dining area. The décor was refined but simple with semi-formal service and candlelit tables that were covered with white tablecloths and matching cloth napkins, crystal, and silverware. A small vase of fresh flowers was placed at the center of the table and a bottle of chilled wine was waiting.

And Lyla thought she was only going to dinner.

The dance had begun.

The menu was limited but pleasing. Lyla looked across the table at Juliano and told him what she wanted to order. His lips parted in a soft smile, and he nodded to Lyla and motioned for the waiter who had been watchfully waiting for a signal. The wine was poured, Juliano made a toast to Lyla's loveliness in the candlelight, and conversation began. Juliano spoke very little about himself personally, revealing nothing, but instead focused the conversation on Lyla and her family. After a serving of the restaurant's special lemon ricotta cheese cake was consumed, Juliano and Lyla left the restaurant for the short ride back to her apartment in silence. Lyla was tired from a long day, satiated with a wonderful meal, and had too much wine with dinner and dessert.

Juliano patiently waited.

Juliano walked Lyla back to her apartment, unlocked her door, and walked her inside. He closed the door behind him, turned to her and said, "Thank you for a lovely evening. I'm glad I stopped by."

He made no movement toward her to reach out his hand or kiss her. She stood in the apartment almost bewildered by his manner, and she responded, "It was lovely, thank you. I enjoyed dinner. Perhaps we can do this again some time."

He looked into her eyes, handed her keys to her and said, "Perhaps we can. Good night, Lyla."

He closed the door softly and left Lyla standing there in stunned silence.

She was his.

Lyla stood still for several moments, feeling the soft pounding of her heart. Small beads of perspiration trickled down her arm, and she became aware of the tingling sensation she felt earlier. She held onto that for another moment, then took a deep breath, ran her fingers through her hair, and walked to her bedroom, wondering what had just happened.

Lyla left for work the next morning feeling different, pondering her encounter with Juliano. Her work kept her busy without time to think about her dinner date until lunch time when her co-worker, Judy, came into her office.

"Hi there, Lyla. Are you too busy for lunch today?"

"No, I'm just finishing up reconciling the personal account and could use some diversion and sustenance. Be there in a moment. I'll meet you at the elevator."

As Lyla and her co-worker, Judy, rode down in the elevator, her friend noticed something different about Lyla.

"Hey Lyla, there's something different about you today. Did something happen? Did you have an encounter of an extraordinary kind last night?"

"Oh, do you mean the stupid bank reconciliation on the trust account I finished last night? You know how I hate numbers and hate doing that chore. It's always such a relief when I balance with the bank."

"Yeah, I know what you mean. But I didn't mean that. You look different today, just different. What happened last night? Did something happen after work? I thought you were going right home."

"I did go right home after work but the strangest thing happened. While I was planning my dinner menu, there was a knock on my door, and you'll never guess who it was."

"Do you really want me to guess? Or do you want to get the suspense over with and just tell me?"

"No, I mean, sorry, I didn't mean to keep you in suspense. It was Juliano Masselli, you know that client of Mr. ...."

Before Lyla could finish her sentence, Judy closed her eyes, tilted her head back with her hand to her face to cover her eyes. She shook her head and groaned.

"Lyla, what did I tell you? What did I tell you about him?"

"Don't get nuts, Judy; I didn't call him. He just showed up at my door with this huge bouquet of flowers and sort of invited himself into my apartment. I didn't do anything wrong."

"What do you mean he sort of invited himself into your apartment?"

"Well, I sort of invited him in."

Judy's voice raised about three octaves.

"I can't believe you let him in after all the warnings I gave you about that man."

As the girls traveled from the 17th floor down to the main floor of the building, Judy recited her litany of reasons why Lyla had no business being in that man's company. All were perfectly good reasons, not the least of which, she reminded Lyla, was that it placed her in jeopardy of losing her job. Secretaries were not to socialize with clients, ever—office rule.

The elevator door opened to the crowded lobby packed with lunchtime employees. Lyla and Judy walked a short distance to one of the local lunch places away from the ears of people who worked in the building. When they reached their table and ordered lunch, Judy began again, "What were you thinking?"

"I didn't think it would be a problem. All we did was grab a bite to eat. He was a perfect gentleman. He didn't even try to kiss me when he left me at my door. I can handle him. There's nothing to be concerned about. After all, it was only dinner; it wasn't a marriage proposal."

By the time the girls were on their way back upstairs to the office, the subject had been dropped but not forgotten by either one. Lyla spoke to Judy before they reached their respective offices, "Don't worry Judy, the whole thing was one innocent meal and won't happen again."

First lie.

First secret.

One of Lyla's admirable qualities was a strong sense of fair play and the importance of the truth. It was indeed curious she would feel so strongly about truth yet work so hard at living a life of falsehoods and lies about who she was and the secrets that haunted her. Looking at her, one was reminded of a piece of exquisite Scalamandre' fabric with two very distinct sides. There was an exposed side showing the beauty of color and design and an underside with the complicated, intricate patterns of threads, which once woven together, produced the finished product. One side of the fabric was simply beautiful, the other a detailed complicated picture of interlocking and overlapping stitches.

Lyla's announcement was an assertion to Judy and a warning to Lyla. Her relationship, if there was to be one with Juliano, was going to have to be kept secret from Judy and everyone else at the office.

Secrets.

Isolation.

THE SEDUCTION

The relationship Lyla had established with Juliano was easy, almost refreshing to her. There were no expectations she had to live up to or questions to establish some kind of religious community connection. The object of their time together was playful, pleasurable, and open-ended. There was no thought of a future with this man and nothing was ever discussed. His time and life away from Lyla was not known to her, she didn't ask and he never included his friends or other couples in the relationship. It was always just the two of them. He completely filled her time, her space, her life when she was with him. Juliano seemed to be a gentleman lover who was patient, almost feminine, in his understanding of a woman's sexual desires.

In the initial stage of their relationship, Juliano would appear at Lyla's door with no phone call to forewarn her of his presence. On occasion, when Lyla was not home from work or was out with friends, Juliano would leave a short note taped to her door. He never appeared on the same day or at the same time. Initially, she found his impromptu inconsistencies exciting and challenging. In the beginning, it was the anticipation of his presence and the wonderment of what he had planned that made their relationship so electric. Lyla swiftly became accustomed to this impromptu kind of life with Juliano.

It was not long before Lyla changed her routine after work in order to anticipate Juliano's presence. She began to decline invitations to the local gathering place after work or shopping sprees with friends. Stops on the way home to the grocery became infrequent as the need to keep her refrigerator stocked with food for potential menus was becoming unnecessary.

She withdrew from her friends at work so she would not be tempted to reveal what she was doing and with whom. The unannounced visits from Juliano increased, and he became a constant companion on the weekends when he was available. Lyla would race home after work, refresh her makeup and clothes, and sit and wait, sometimes with success, other times to spend a lonely evening disappointed. But she didn't deviate from her new routine of rush home and wait.

Juliano kept Lyla busy and engaged whenever they were together. Each outing was as exciting and wonderful as the one before. Their time together would begin the same. He would appear without notice on her doorstep with a bouquet of flowers with no promise or commitment of a next time. They flew, by private plane, to the Bahamas for a weekend of sun, fun, gambling, and shopping. They ventured to the west coast of Florida to Marco Island, Captiva Island, cruises on the Gulf to Key West and the Dry Tortugas.

When they weren't traveling, they frequented the clubs and restaurants from south Miami Beach to Ft. Lauderdale. They often visited the club in the Mutiny Hotel at Sailboat Bay in Coconut Grove where Juliano was one of the undisputed champions of backgammon. There were live jazz performances close to the airport, stone crabs at Joe's, Mediterranean food on Miami Beach, and more drinks and dancing at Numero Uno, one of the local popular Latin establishments.

Juliano was always impeccably dressed. His clothing was beautifully coordinated and tailored with exacting attention to detail. Lyla's appearance was exotically intoxicating and sensuous, with a dignified sense of style and grace: simply, classically beautiful.

Numero Uno became their favorite place to end an evening. The pounding, throbbing rhythms of the congas and brass instruments of Latin music greeted them as they entered the smoke-filled club jammed to capacity with beautiful people. The live band hovered above the tiny dance floor on a seemingly invisible platform. At the edge of the dance floor, small tables were set up as sentinels to keep the floor clear for the throngs of people who crowded there. There were tiers of tables mounted on ever-ascending-risers that reached into the darkness filled with people and the muffled sounds of voices that could barely be heard over the music.

The hostess escorted Juliano and Lyla to a table just above the first row of tables on the first riser. This was a perfect spot for them to watch the dance floor and listen to the brash, wild, and romantic sounds of the live band. The waitress appeared and took their drink order. Juliano ordered drinks for them both as Lyla became more entranced by the pounding of the drums, the percussion instruments, and the brass. The club was hot, the music was hot, and the people were on fire. Although Lyla sat silent, Juliano could tell she was yearning to move to the dance floor.

Their drinks came quickly. Juliano emptied his glass and stood with his hand outstretched to Lyla. She rose gracefully and placed her hand in his as he led her onto the dance floor as though she was royalty. He moved Lyla around the dance floor with ease and grace, and Lyla loved every moment. She was drawn to the music, the dance, and the fire it created within her. Her graceful movements made her appear as though she and the music were one. When she danced, those around her couldn't help but stare and become mesmerized by her.

The couple melted into the crowd and disappeared for several moments, when suddenly people began to leave the dance floor. The onlookers respectfully walked to their tables or stood back on the sides of the club to watch the two who dominated the floor.

The music changed from a wild mambo to "Besame Mucho," played in a sensual rhythmic rhumba. Everyone was immediately caught by the beauty and grace of the two as Juliano moved Lyla around the floor. They moved in complete unison, almost entwined in each other's arms and at other times mirroring each other's moves as though they had always done this together. He spun her around and turned her out away from him, while their hips moved undulating and rolling with the rhythm of the music.

They parted briefly, an arm's length away, and glided to the side in time with the beat. As he retreated, he drew her back to him closer and closer with each sensual movement. He then took her in his arms pressing her body close to his as they moved in unison with the music, almost close enough for their lips to touch. When the music finally ended, they remained still, capturing the moment, the heat between their bodies, and the flame ignited within them.

Lyla never thought about this relationship as serious. The time with Juliano was fun and in the moment, and she never asked for anything more. Everything was exciting and satisfying, from the food, music, and dance to the passionate sex that left them both wanting more ... of everything.

Lyla was so busy she barely had time to catch her breath. She found herself in a whirlwind of activities with Juliano as her director, allowing little free time for Lyla, her family, or friends. The red flags so disturbing to others eluded her. She was having a good time. Although Lyla was totally unaware of what was happening, the initial isolation continued and was nearly complete.

Sura's concerns and suspicions were brought on by the infrequent phone conversations and lack of encounters with Lyla from the time Lyla began her relationship with Juliano. Lyla seemed to be constantly engaged between her job and her newfound companion. Sura knew something was wrong, she could feel it. This was not a healthy relationship but one destined to destroy Lyla.

Sura knew only what Lyla chose to reveal about Juliano but was able to discern enough to surmise that Juliano had nothing in common with Lyla. She was Jewish and came from a reputable family. He was Catholic. Who were his parents and/or his family? Where did he come from? What was his background? Sura thought, *he doesn't even seem to have any kind of job. Where in the world does he get the means by which he lives? Something is very wrong.* Sura could see it, feel it, but couldn't figure out how to extricate Lyla from that man's grasp.

Lyla eventually accepted an invitation from Sura to join her for lunch at one of the trendy restaurants in the Bal Harbour Shops on Miami Beach. They were to meet for lunch and spend time shopping, an exercise they both enjoyed. Sura tried to find a way to warn Lyla about the kind of man Juliano was and hoped to change Lyla's mind about continuing the relationship.

They met at the outdoor restaurant in the Bal Harbour shopping plaza located half way between Nieman Marcus and Saks Fifth Avenue. Small tables were set amid lush foliage, providing some tables a modicum of privacy. When they were seated among the foliage and were served their drinks, Sura tried to convince Lyla to look elsewhere for companionship. Sura began, "Please forgive my intrusion into your private life. I did not ask you here to interrogate you but to help you."

Lyla cautiously responded, "I didn't know I was in need of help."

"I'm worried about you. I know you were devastated about what happened with Mark; I understand that. But you have moved into a relationship with someone who I fear will have a much worse impact upon you and your life."

Lyla began to feel defensive. "Mother. How in the world would you know who Juliano is and what kind of person he is? Besides, it's not a serious relationship."

"I was young and vulnerable once and have met men like Juliano. I recognize the demeanor, the charm, and the enticement, and am concerned about you. I do not want to suggest restricting who you see but need to caution you about continuing this relationship. Please don't shut me out. I'm here to help and to let you know I love you and want to protect you."

"Mother, I'll be sure to let you know when I need protecting. Thanks for your concern; but this relationship is not serious. I told you that. Let's drop the subject and enjoy our afternoon together."

Lyla was uncomfortable knowing how her mother felt. She resented her mother's intrusion and was unable to talk about where she went and what she did. They drifted farther and farther apart. Lyla rarely made an appearance at any of her mother's events. It was more seldom that Lyla came to visit and Sura's invitations to lunch and shopping went unanswered as Lyla continued to drift farther from her family.

One evening after work, Lyla received a phone call from Mark Weiman. She was surprised. He was back in town and wanted to see her. He asked her to go out to dinner with him, and she decided meeting him at his condo was all she would do. Although she did not consciously know why she responded, she made sure she looked irresistible.

Her mother's condo was on the way to Mark's condo. She decided to stop by and tell her mother Mark called and she agreed to meet him. Sura was astounded that Lyla would consider seeing him again after what happened in New York. Sura was not one to forgive easily, if at all. Lyla wanted her mother to know she was willing to see other people hoping to get some relief from the pressure of her relationship with Juliano. After doing her due diligence at her mother's, Lyla drove the short distance to Mark's condo.

The night was beautiful with the warm balmy breezes common in south Florida. Lyla parked her sedan and walked up to the guarded front doors leading to the entrance of the opulent lobby. She gave her name to the doorman who had been made aware of her impending arrival, was ushered inside, and called Mark on one of the house phones in the lobby. Mark asked her to come upstairs to his condo.

Lyla responded without hesitation, "I think it would be best if we met somewhere in the lobby downstairs."

"Not a problem," Mark responded. "I'll be right down."

Lyla waited patiently and looked around for a private place for them to meet. Mark came out of the elevator and approached Lyla with a warm smile and open arms. His embrace was not well received but she allowed an acceptable brush of a kiss on her cheek. He looked at her intently and noticed she had changed, again. She had grown into her womanliness and had become mature in her looks; she was breathtaking.

Her snug fitting little red T-shirt was neatly tucked into her close-fitting jeans and her beautiful legs looked a mile long in the high-stacked shoes she wore. Her skin was tan and smooth, and her hair had been cut short to frame her face and hug her neck. Lyla had grown up, and he was impressed. He couldn't help but stare, and she soon became uneasy as he drank in her image.

"I'm back in town," he said.

"I know, I see that," she responded.

They both chuckled and were a bit uncomfortable. He looked around the lobby and found several chairs almost out of sight and out of the way of people entering and leaving. He motioned for Lyla to follow him, and he asked her to sit in one of the empty chairs. He sat next to her but gave her personal space.

"I'm back in town," he repeated, "and wanted to see you. I've been thinking about the last time we met."

"Hmm," she said with her eyes fixed on his face. "And, exactly what was it you were thinking about?"

For the first time she noticed he appeared tense. He was not the cool Mark she had known before.

"I wanted to tell you something I had not told you before and hoped it would help to explain why I'm here now. You see, technically, I was married when we saw each other."

Lyla was silent wondering what kind of bombshell he was planning to drop.

"Technically?" she said, "Exactly what does technically mean? Is that anything like being a little pregnant?"

He laughed softly and went on.

"Well, you see, I was married but not living with my wife. My wife became ill, and when she was too ill to live at home she was placed in a private hospital. I never intended to leave her, but after several years she became worse. She had some type of mental issue and eventually no longer recognized me and became someone I didn't know. I stayed married to her as long as I thought there was a chance she might recover. But once the doctors gave me no hope, I initiated divorce proceedings. I'm now single and want to know if you would consider going out with me, start over, so to speak. I would like to spend time with you and see if we could find a way to have a serious relationship, and a possible future."

Lyla couldn't believe what she just heard. These were words she would have given anything to hear when she was in New York for that fateful weekend. But now? And the story about his wife? She could barely digest everything before she spoke.

"I don't know what to say. I mean, I'm sorry to hear about what happened to your wife." Lyla was sincere in her condolences to him but was unequivocally resolute about not attempting to have another relationship with him.

"I'm sorry, Mark. You see, I have been seeing someone on a regular basis, and I'm not interested in seeing anyone else right now."

"Yes, I know," he said. "I've heard you're seeing Juliano Masselli."

"How on earth did you know that, and how do you know him?"

"I don't know him personally, but I have heard about him. Lyla, you should stay away from him. He's not the kind of man you should be with."

He stopped short of saying Juliano was dangerous with an equally dangerous personality.

"Did you talk to my mother by any chance?" she asked. "Did she put you up to this? She must be getting desperate to ask you to intercede for her."

"No," said Mark, "she didn't ask me to intercede, but if she had I would have gladly tried to change your mind about him."

Lyla was done with this conversation. She rose to her feet and held out her hand to Mark.

"Thank you, Mark, it was lovely to see you. I must go now. I appreciate and am flattered by your offer but you see, I've made my choice, and I'm going to continue to see Juliano, for now."

"Are you sure you won't reconsider and give me another chance?" he asked.

"No, Mark. I won't reconsider. I really must go now."

Mark walked Lyla to her car and once again made an offer.

"Please Lyla, listen to me; if you ever need anything, anything at all, please don't hesitate to call me. You know where to find me."

"Thank you," she said, "but I don't think it will be necessary. It was good to see you, Mark. Take care."

She drove off into the night and Mark felt a chill come over him at the thought of her being with Juliano. *She has no idea what she's getting herself into*, he thought.

RETURN

Lyla continued her relationship with Juliano, ignoring pleas from her family and friends. She no longer answered phone calls or invitations to anything, anywhere, for any reason. Juliano, to her surprise and delight, suggested they move in together. He chose a location unfamiliar to Lyla, far from her family and friends. She left her legal job and planned to fill her time slowly unpacking boxes and becoming familiar with the area. She decided to wait until they were settled to once again look for a job at her new location. She purchased a puppy for companionship to fill her lonely hours and tried to meet other young couples in the neighborhood.

They had been in the house almost a month when their pseudo idyllic life together became a nightmare of epic proportions. Juliano didn't appear to have a job and was gone for hours, sometimes days. Lyla had no idea where he was, what he did, or who he was with. He never confided in her and became angry when she asked. It did not take her long to learn not to ask and to wait dutifully for him to return. On those nights when he would return late at night, obviously drunk, she would lie awake waiting for him to come home and when he arrived, was afraid to confront him.

Often, she would wait to hear him fumble for his keys, trying to unlock the front door, and then stumble through the front door. The sounds she heard were of him bumping into things, tripping, and catching himself as he nearly fell, finally reaching the bedroom. She would lie there, pretending to be asleep, as she listened to him undress and fall into bed. Then, after he began to breathe in deep even breaths, she would cry softly and fall to sleep.

On the night before Valentine's Day, Juliano came home in the late hours of the night and his behavior led her to believe he was very drunk. He was supposed to have been visiting with an old friend although Lyla had no idea where he was or who he was with. She was up early the next morning, anxious to piece together some kind of relationship, hoping to resurrect the light-hearted fun-loving excitement of their past. Lyla's inability to see the reality of the situation influenced her decisions. Unfortunately, she thought what better way to celebrate the Valentine's Day holiday in a way they would not soon forget but to have a romantic dinner?

Didn't she see what was happening? How could she ignore all the red flags?

When she returned from grocery shopping, although Juliano's car was there, Juliano was gone. Nothing had changed from the time she left, not a glass in the sink, not a fork, nothing. Lyla did not give this much thought. Lyla didn't deviate from her mission. Even though she had not seen Juliano all day, she was certain they had talked about having dinner together that night.

Lyla was at the sink, washing stem glassware when the phone rang.

"Hello," a man's voice on the other end said. "Is this Lyla Rose? Do you know a Juliano Masselli?"

Lyla was hesitant to speak. She was bewildered and uncertain she should answer yes to any of his questions.

"Excuse me, but who are you and what is it you want?"

"I am Detective Sergeant Oliver and I'm with the police."

She was confused and quickly thought, *why would the police be calling me and what did it have to do with Juliano? He was very drunk the night before, maybe he was involved in a traffic accident. This must certainly be some kind of a mistake.*

"I don't understand," she said. "Why are you asking about Juliano? And no, I don't know exactly where he is at this moment. I do expect him to be home later today. Is there some message I can give him or a number I can take for him to return the call?"

"No. There's no message. I'll check back some other time."

Lyla hung up the phone and froze with her heart pounding. What in the world was going on? What did the police want with Juliano? Was he dead? She knew Juliano did things she didn't want to know about but this sounded ominous. After a few minutes, the phone rang again and the same voice as before identified himself as Detective Sergeant Oliver.

"Miss Rose," he began, "I apologize for probably upsetting you with the prior phone call. I wanted to advise you we have arrested Juliano Masselli and have him here at the County Jail. He has asked to talk to you, and we think it might be helpful, for all involved, if you were to come see him."

The confusion became shock and Lyla couldn't speak. She began to perspire profusely; her heart began to beat faster. A strange feeling of heat overcame her body, she became dizzy and nauseated, and the room began to appear as though it was spinning.

"Why does he want to talk to me? I'm, I'm, uh ...what happened? What is all this about? What does this have to do with me?"

The Detective continued, "I think it would be best if Mr. Masselli were to tell you when you get here. I'd like to give you some directions to the county courthouse. Do you have something to write on?"

"Yes, yes, just a moment," Lyla said, as she fumbled for a pen and something to write on. Her hand shook as she took down the information.

"We would like you to come down as soon as possible. Can you do that?"

"Uh, um, I have to ... yes, I can do that. I'll be there in about a half hour."

"Thank you. I'll meet you in front of the courthouse and take you to see him."

Lyla began to have waves of nausea and felt as though she were in the middle of a waking nightmare. Without thinking she began to function automatically: she found her purse and keys, put the puppy in her crate, and drove to her destination. She had no idea what to expect and had never known anyone who had been arrested and in police custody. Her familiarity with criminal law was limited to the clients requiring help for speeding tickets and other minor criminal offenses. This was different; this frightened her.

Traffic was congested around the courthouse. The parking lot was within walking distance. It was a busy place with a diversity of people coming and going, attorneys with clients, and police everywhere. A man dressed in an inconspicuous dark suit, white shirt, and scuffed shoes came up to her in front of the courthouse. She instinctively placed her handbag on her shoulder and clutched it close to her body. A slight tremor swept through her slight frame and her eyes became fixed on the approaching figure. The man introduced himself as Detective Sergeant Oliver.

"Are you Lyla Rose?"

"Yes," she answered softly.

Detective Oliver motioned with his hand for her to follow him up the steps of the building.

"Thank you for coming, I'll take you to him. Please follow me."

They entered the building through heavy glass and metal doors, walked to the elevators and waited for the doors to open. They exited the elevator on the third floor and walked down a hallway to a room where the door was locked. Detective Oliver knocked faintly and the door opened. Lyla walked into a small room that was bathed with natural light from a large rectangular window on the outside wall that was criss crossed with an iron decorative pattern. The room was uncluttered with a long, unpolished wood table that was surrounded by six brown wooden chairs. The walls were bare painted in a light coffee color that made everything appear yellowish brown. There was a large overhead light above the middle of the table. The room was cool but the air smelled stale. Juliano was sitting at the table facing the window. He had handcuffs on and was staring down at the table top, transfixed, as though the table held guarded secrets.

When Lyla entered the room, he looked up and met her confused and frightened expression with worn, sad eyes. Juliano looked terrible. His clothes were crumpled, as though he had slept in them, and his face was covered with a growth of dark stubble. He looked forlorn and frail, characteristics she had never seen before.

The detective motioned for her to sit next to Juliano and said he would give them some privacy. Lyla followed the instructions. She sat in the chair next to Juliano but not close to him and made no motion to move closer or touch him. She sat erect on the edge of the chair, her back stiff and straight with her feet tightly crossed at the ankles. Her hands gripped her keys and her handbag that she rested on her lap. When she looked at Juliano, she did not recognize him. She thought, *who was this person and why was he here like this*? He avoided her eyes and her questioning look. It was then, she spoke barely above a whisper,

"Can you tell me what's happening here?"

Lyla clutched her handbag and keys as if some awful stranger was about to wrench them out of her hands sitting even taller and stiffer in her chair in grave anticipation of hearing that Juliano was involved in someone's demise from drugs. Then she pushed her chair back slightly and waited for Juliano to speak. Something happened; something she was unprepared to hear.

Juliano lifted his chin from his chest, his face drawn, his expression serious. He had a difficult time looking at her. Instead, he stared at an invisible spot across the table. Then, shaking his head from side to side he said in a barely audible voice, "I have done something. I have done something. I have done something terrible. I have told the police every-thing, and now I'm going to try and explain it to you." He continued in the slow gravelly voice of a man who look emotionally beaten, broken, and guilty.

"I met my friend, Lenny, after his shift at the restaurant. It was late, but we were both hungry so we stopped at a local bar for something to eat and we started drinking. I don't remember how long we were there, but by the time we left it was late. We both had had too much to drink. The party that started at the bar had moved to Lenny's house in Coconut Grove. Within moments, Lenny's house was filled with people, most of them I didn't know. Lenny and I went out to the back of the house to his workshop to avoid the crowd. You know Lenny, the ever-present addict, always has some stash around."

Thoughts rushed to Lyla's mind. *Lenny? Lenny who? I don't know any of his friends. Drugs...alcohol...arrested.*

She sat up straighter in her chair with her shoulders pulled back and her chin pulled even higher. Her breathing was shallow and rapid, nerv-ous perspiration was dripping down her arms, and her fingers began to tremble. Juliano spoke in a monotone, still staring at the spot across the table.

"Then Lenny took out some stuff he had recently purchased and asked if I wanted some. He said it was really great, and I couldn't resist. I don't know how much I did but I remember walking away from the house and into one of the bars close by."

Juliano became a predator, a lone wolf, searching for vulnerable prey.

He knew the bar would afford him easy access to female patrons. He used his charm and found a woman who was initially receptive to his advances and vulnerable from a night of drinking. Juliano lured the woman to a dark and deserted garden in the back of the bar. His initial preamble of intimacy became aggressive and violent. He took his prey, against her protestations and her struggle to free herself.

"I confessed, he added.

"It was ... against her will."

It was nonconsensual.

It was...rape.

An act of violence, power and control.

Juliano's voice was devoid of any emotion as he recounted what had occurred. His words bounced off Lyla's psyche and she was unable to process what he was saying. The words, "against her will" echoed in her head. She listened in shock retreating mentally and emotionally to a place of safety, and several times felt like she wanted to scream, run, and throw up. She was unaware she was pushing her chair farther and farther away from Juliano, looking for a way out of the room. The door was behind her, he was handcuffed, and the detectives were outside the door. Lyla was still. She waited until he had finished speaking, but thought only of leaving, getting away from him, and the awful things he had done. She relaxed her fingers from around her purse and keys, pushed back her chair, and slowly rose to her feet. She was finally able to gather her thoughts and move her lips. She chose her words carefully to make sure Juliano understood.

"There's something very wrong with you and you need help, help I can't give you. If what you told me is the truth, and I believe it is, then there is nothing I can do for you." It became a monumental task to keep her composure as she turned her body to the door.

"Lyla," he called out to her. "Lyla, please, listen to me for a moment."

"I've heard enough, Juliano; there's nothing more to say. I must leave."

"Lyla, before you go, please listen. The detective told me there's a program for people who have problems like me and there's a possibility I can be placed in it and get help. Are you going to leave me? Will you help me? I have no one else to turn to."

So, this was his reason for the face-to-face meeting. There was no apology from him, no request for forgiveness; he needed her.

There was a long heavy silence that filled the room's stale air. Lyla felt as though she were about to choke, but turned to Juliano, and said, "No, not right away. I'll make sure you get an attorney and into the program you need. I can't, I won't, do any more than that."

"That's understandable. I'm just grateful you're willing to do that; I have no one else to turn to."

She was still his victim.

Lyla needed to wake up from the shock and move. At first it was impossible because her feet were rooted to the floor. She managed to push the chair out of her way and stepped back toward the door. Looking at him was difficult. The pathetic, rumpled figure seated at the table was a stranger whom she found difficult to acknowledge. She said good bye, not knowing when or if she would see him again. He was now in a system that took complete charge of his life.

Lyla drove back to the little house in shock struggling to believe what had just occurred was real. She took the puppy out of the crate and walked her in the backyard, focusing on this simple reality because she wasn't ready to accept the other was true. The kitchen and its contents remained untouched and she had no sense of hunger or pain. She fed and walked her new puppy and then changed into her nightgown. Lyla cuddled with the small ball of fur, feeling the warmth of her little body, and fell into a deep sleep until morning.

A night of rest helped Lyla see that she needed to go back home. She wasn't sure how or what would transpire between her and her mother, but she needed to tie up loose ends with the little rental house and go home. There was a contract, and she was obligated as one of the signers on the lease. Her first priority was to see the leasing agent that morning, knowing she had to leave the house as soon as possible.

Lyla was direct and unequivocal, telling the rental agent it was necessary for her to break the lease. Her hope was to leave without financial obligations and was willing to forfeit her deposit if he would let her go. The agent asked why. Her answer was a condensed version of the truth. She acknowledged the circumstances were unusual, but she was resolute about leaving and asked for his cooperation. He was surprised by her forthrightness and courage and agreed to her request. He destroyed the contract and gave her until the end of the week to pack up and move out.

Her success in accomplishing the unpleasant task without further penalty gave Lyla the impetus to do what was next on her agenda, call her mother. If she hesitated she would lose her courage.

"Hello Mother," she said, "it's Lyla. I have something to tell you. It's very bad."

Lyla's mother was silent as Lyla related the entire incident from the detective's phone call to her conversation with the leasing agent. Lyla waited, fearing the worst but her mother spoke in a calm voice.

"I will take care of everything. Pack your things immediately and I'll come down to help. I will make arrangements to get a moving truck and I will find an appropriate place for you to live close to the condo, by family. Just do as I ask you to do."

There were no recriminations, no accusations or "I told you so." Lyla cried in relief and sorrow. She sobbed uncontrollably, feeling the pain of deep wounds.

"Lyla," Sura said with conviction. "Lyla, listen to me. Cry until you can't cry anymore, dry your eyes and don't cry for him again. You're going to survive. I am here for you."

Lyla did as she promised. With Juliano's written permission, she sold his car and through her contacts obtained an attorney for him. Months passed as the legal system moved slowly. Juliano's case finally came before the Judge. She attended the court proceeding to witness his final disposition. He was sentenced and remanded to a locked facility in a program where he would get the help he needed. Finally, it was over. The promise had been fulfilled and she could move on with her life. Or could she? Would she?

Lyla tried to move on with her life by preparing and decorating her new apartment. Her mother decided they could all use a little R&R. She invited Lyla, Lyla's cousin and her mother on an excursion to the Bahamas for an extended weekend of shopping. When Lyla returned she received a short note of apology from Juliano. She obtained permission to visit him where he was incarcerated in the facility. This meeting convinced her she had to try to understand why and if he could be helped. During this time, she attended a therapy group formed especially for the friends and family of the offenders, who had been ordered by the Court to the program.

The group met at the facility and was attended by those who needed to understand the men they supported. They were given an opportunity to learn about themselves and why they had embarked on such a journey. Lyla learned how to function in a group and to give valuable feedback but did not come away with the knowledge of how to let go. She was unable to recognize in herself what she saw in many of the other women.

What made her stay? What caused her to think she could fix someone who was broken? Lyla became a rescuer, unconsciously trying to fill her overwhelming void. She had an extreme sense of personal obligation to fix him, to make his life better, and to give him what she believed he never had. It felt better to find someone to rescue than be rescued or become aware that she was in need of being rescued.

THE CONSEQUENCES

Sura believed she needed to keep Lyla close to her and help Lyla heal. She opened a floral boutique/gift shop in a fashionable shopping area across the bridge from Bay Harbor Island that catered to an upscale clientele. She offered Lyla a potential partnership as an apprentice. As preparation for the floral design aspects of the job, Lyla and her mother took a course in floral design from a local florist. It was Lyla's responsibility to design the fresh and dried flower arrangements. In addition, she spent one day a week combing the wholesale nurseries for beautiful and unusual plants that were sold in the store. Customers looked forward to what Lyla discovered on her once-a-week journeys, and the store became a gathering place for the beautiful people to shop for equally beautiful and unique items.

Lyla rarely went on dates, but when she did they were to appease her mother's fears that Lyla would somehow renew her relationship with Juliano. During the day, she was the young, hardworking apprentice entrepreneur, while her mother watched her every move. Once she left the store, she became someone else. One evening a week would be spent with Juliano, getting to know him, talking about his progress and his setbacks, and what would happen in the future, to him, to them.

How could she possibly think there could be some kind of, any kind of future with this man, especially after what he had done?

Lyla embarked on the ultimate rescue journey. Her flawed reasoning led her to believe that only she could give Juliano everything he needed and in doing so would cleanse him of his anger and unhappiness. She mistakenly believed that with her constancy and help he would change and his demons would be gone.

Lyla was unable to understand how it couldn't work. It seemed so obvious, so simple to her. Lyla did not consider the consequences or ramifications of her decision, and how it might affect her life. She dove into the deep end, thinking she could swim ... forever.

According to the doctors in the therapeutic program, Juliano made significant progress. It was determined by the doctors and other staff members he was ready to be released from the program. One criteria to be considered for release required that a family member sign him out of the facility for weekend passes for a specified period of time. It became a record of how well he continued to improve and an indicator to the court if he was going to be able to succeed once released.

Lyla and Juliano discussed all the possible options. He had no family to take him out and to be responsible for him during the time he spent away from the facility. In the end, Lyla offered to marry him in order for him to be able to go through the court ordered therapeutic process. She saw no other way for him to complete this necessary step. It was simple; she would do this for him, give him the chance to have a life, and help him move on successfully. Once he established himself, if necessary, they would separate and move on with their lives. She saw nothing wrong with this plan and thought, "I can do this."

Once she made this fateful decision, she needed to leave her mother's shop to make sure her secret marriage and life was kept from her family. Legal secretarial jobs were plentiful and she chose to take a job in a law office where no one knew her past.

What was she thinking?

Lyla was the ultimate rescuer. She found a person who needed the comfort and care of someone who was willing to give everything. She agreed to share the burden of his secret; a burden that would ultimately destroy what she believed was her initial love for him. Her choice, unknowingly, significantly shaped the greater part of her life.

The plan was for Lyla and Juliano to be married in secret in her apartment by a notary, away from the wise, knowing, and loving eyes of her family. Arrangements were made for Juliano to be signed out of the program for his first pass by someone who was approved by the authorities, the doctor, and by someone who Lyla trusted not to divulge her secrets. During the initial pass, Juliano and Lyla would be married in order for Lyla to continue to take him out. It was not the kind of wedding Lyla pictured herself having. There were no joyful celebrations or bridal shower, and no beautiful dress. She would not become a princess for a day and be whisked away for a romantic honeymoon. Instead, she was alone and unable to tell anyone what she was about to do. A friend who worked in a floral shop agreed to make a glamelia bouquet for her in muted shades of pale pink, in place of a traditional bouquet.

Lyla wore a white cotton, off-the-shoulder, eyelet peasant blouse cinched at the waist over long flowing wide-legged cotton trousers that had intricate floral satin embroidery along the hem. A wreathe of entwined fresh baby's breath was made for her headpiece. She wore delicate, pastel single pearl earrings, that were given to her years before by her aunt, and a single strand of pearls her mother had worn when she was married. Lyla was breathtakingly beautiful, and alone. There were no family or friends to share in what should have been one of the happiest days of her life, no one to walk her down the aisle, and no hoopa canopy.

The ceremony was conducted in the small living room of Lyla's apartment. It was brief and the promises limited to the essential words that ended with, "Do you take this man" and "I do." The notary had them sign the appropriate document, and it was over. That was it, nothing significant, just "I now pronounce you man and wife." You may kiss the bride." They were legally married. She did what she promised and made it possible for Juliano to leave on passes in preparation for his eventual release from the program.

Moments after the ceremony was complete, Lyla excused herself and retreated to the sanctity of her bedroom and left the notary to chat with her new husband in the living room. Where were the feelings of joy and the anticipation of a long life together built on trust and love? She walked through the bedroom towards the bathroom and looked at herself in the mirror in wide-eyed disbelief at what had just taken place. In a matter of moments, words were spoken, promises were made, and she was legally Mrs. Juliano Masselli.

So many things were running through her mind. She covered her face with her hands and began to weep. *This feels so wrong,* she thought. *This is all so wrong. I've gotten myself into a mess and don't know how to untangle everything.*

Lyla's thoughts were interrupted by Juliano's voice filled with excitement.

"Hey, Lyla, where are you? What's taking you so long? How long does it take you to freshen up your face?"

The slight irritation in his voice forced Lyla back to reality. There she was stuck in shock in front of the mirror, and he was waiting in the living room, ready to celebrate with a cold bottle of champagne. She couldn't stay in there forever; she had to come out some time.

Lyla ran her fingers through her hair, shook her head slightly to re-set her hair, and adjusted the small white crown of baby's breath that encircled the top of her head. She held her head up, pulled her shoulders down, and told the mirror image, "I can do this." With foolish courage and determination, she walked across the bedroom and crossed the threshold into the living room, into a life she was totally unprepared for.

As a result of her decision to support and marry Juliano, who Lyla was, what she wanted, and her growth as a person came to a crashing halt. She left all of herself behind in order to function and survive in a world she had to create, with only rare moments of reality.

REALITY

When Juliano returned to court, he was granted probation, and they began a life together in Lyla's apartment. Lyla decided, after six months of marriage, it was time to stop pretending and tell her parents what she had done. Prior to this, she was careful not to wear her wedding ring or mention anything about Juliano or her secret ceremony. No one had a clue. Her parents were together at the condo on Bay Harbor Island, which was a rare event, and Lyla believed this was her opportunity to tell them.

There she was again, riding up the elevator to the third floor, having a hard time with her churning guts, wondering if they would ever calm down. Her parents had just finished dinner and were relaxing in the lounge. Lyla wore her wide, gold wedding band as proof of what she had done.

After entering the condo, Lyla walked over to the lounge and greeted them. Her father made a sweeping gesture with his hand for her to sit with them. Instead, she declined the request and stood stiffly before them, with her hands folded in front of her. She had to get it over with and speak fast before she changed her mind and continued to keep the secret. Her voice was soft and trembling.

"There's something I came here to tell you both, and I know you're going to be very upset with me. I wanted to tell you myself before someone else found out and told you. I wanted to explain hoping you would understand, although I don't think you will."

Sura's eyes opened wide and she began to breathe heavily. Before Lyla could tell them and explain, her father asked in an angry accusatory tone. "What is that ring on your finger and where did it come from?"

Harry's demeanor changed. His face became beet red, his eyes began to bulge, and his entire body began to quiver. Her plan was spoiled. She had to defend herself and couldn't think fast enough on her feet except to say.

"I...uh...it's a wedding ring, Dad, I got married.

Harry spoke with clenched teeth and lips pursed into a snarl. "To whom, may I ask?"

"I married Juliano, Juliano Masselli. We were married in private by a notary."

Sura began weeping bitterly and asked Lyla, "How could you do this to yourself, to us? Do you realize what you have done? You have to undo this immediately ... immediately. Do you understand me? Do you hear me? What in the world have you done? My God, what is the family going to say? What will our friends say? What have you done to yourself?"

Sura continued to sob hysterically and looked to her husband to say something, anything. Through her tears she said, "Harry, do something, please, do something, there must be something you can do."

After pleading with her husband, Sura spoke, in a much calmer voice, almost devoid of emotion, "Perhaps we should have her committed."

Lyla had never seen her father so angry before. He let out a horrible guttural sound like a cornered wild animal and Lyla was frightened.

"Where is he, where is he? I'm gonna kill him. What has he done to you, to my daughter? He's mesmerized you with some kind of horrible spell, and I won't let it happen. I will not stand for this. Are you pregnant? Did you believe you had to get married?"

Once her father stopped screaming, she was able to compose herself enough to say to him, "Listen, Dad, everything is going to be all right, really. We're doing OK, really, I'm working, Juliano is looking for work, and we're OK. Really, we're fine. I know you are both very angry, and I didn't do this to hurt you. At the time, I thought it was the best thing I could do. I was trying to help him, help Juliano. I'm sorry you are so upset. I'm sorry, I'm so sorry."

The room became deathly silent. Lyla's parents were in shock. Sura was sobbing and Harry was sitting next to her with a grimace of pain and anger on his face, shaking his head. Lyla saw Lucille enter the family room from the kitchen. She was outside the room listening and came in to see what she could do to calm things down.

Lucille whispered to Lyla, "Baby you need to go. I'll take care of your mother and father; they need some time, they need time. This is a whole lot to take in. I will light a candle in church for you. You need to go."

Lyla was visibly shaken by their response and heeded Lucille's advice. She walked hastily to the elevator, trembling and shaking, with large tears streaming down her face, and then ran to her car.

There was little Lucille could do to console Harry and Sura. For the first time, in a very long time, they held each other and cried. It would be a long time before Lyla would see her parents or any other family member. News spread quickly about her marriage, the circumstances surrounding it, and the man she married. Now, Lyla was really alone.

Lyla never married Juliano in an attempt to elicit a reaction from her parents. Their attitude and response were most unexpected and she was completely unnerved by this show of parental protection and affection.

The intense roller-coaster journey of her life began after Lyla and Juliano were married. There were ups and downs with short-lived plateaus falling to swoops and swerves that led to an eventual drop. Lyla spent her life navigating this cyclical journey, giving up more and more of her life as time went on. Her ability to overcome the spirals of her relationship and her she-bear protection of her children left her worn and exhausted. Climbing back became a monumental, if not impossible, task.

ROLLER COASTER

Although Lyla's decisions created isolation from her family, she liked the idea of being married, and wearing the gold wedding band. She believed she belonged to someone who would take care of her, she was wanted, and valued. Unfortunately, the wedded bliss was short-lived. Juliano was still adjusting to being free and on his own, although he was obligated to report every week to group therapy and a probation officer.

The short honeymoon period lulled Lyla into a false sense of normalcy. This quasi-euphoric feeling obscured her ability to see the reality of what she had done and who her husband was. The periods of calm and seeming contentment would invariably precede a storm. During the quiet periods, Lyla tried to believe the difficulties of the past had disappeared in a brief respite from the pain and memories and she happily rode along with the waves of calm, not realizing they would end.

Juliano's inability to sustain a good marriage could only be hidden for brief periods. Something would trigger an outburst that Lyla was always unprepared for.

Juliano had too much idle time without a job which allowed his anger to simmer and build. He was absent from the apartment most of the day and would eventually return late, often drunk. He would rarely confide to Lyla where he was going, who he was with, and what he did. Although her days were spent at work, she spent her evenings alone and isolated.

Juliano was mandated to attend court ordered group therapy sessions as one of the conditions of probation with others who were on probation. He would return home after therapy with group conversations buzzing in his head. The sessions created insurmountable obstacles, or perhaps, it was Juliano who caused the problems. One evening during the session, the men of the group decided that Lyla was too high maintenance and Juliano needed to take control and become the reigning head of the household. As a result, Juliano returned to the apartment after the meeting with an attitude and began accusing Lyla of being difficult.

He became verbally abusive and insulting. His speech brutally berated Lyla and she could no longer bear the onslaught of offensive language. Juliano hated Lyla's family, especially her parents. He believed they exerted undue influence on Lyla, and he could not allow that. The conflict instantly escalated into harsh words spoken by both. Juliano began to chide her about her family. It was as though he needed to reinforce the continued distance between Lyla and her family to keep her in control.

"You need to understand you are married to me now. Your family has no say in our marriage, especially your parents. I'm the boss, here. Your parents are overbearing, controlling, and interfering. Your meddling mother needs to stay out of our marriage. Dot. Period. None of them are welcome to visit and, someday I'll make sure they are never around.

"I don't care how much money your family has," Juliano would say, "or who your father knows, it means nothing to me. He's just some old man who likes to dominate and manipulate everyone he deals with just like he does in business, and he's not going to do that to me. You belong to me now."

Lyla couldn't understand what precipitated his barrage of insults and condemnations or what the catalyst was. Her marriage had already isolated her from her family and she had no friends. What was he talking about? After his outburst and bombardment of verbal assaults, Lyla retreated from the living room and collapsed in tears on the bathroom floor. Her sobs and moans reflected her intense pain and suffering. She clung to the side of the bathtub, resting her head on the cool porcelain, not knowing if she was going to faint or throw up. Juliano finally followed her to the bathroom, silent and angry.

"Please," she pleaded, "please, leave me alone. You need to go, you're killing me ...you're killing me," she cried in a hoarse whisper, "This must end."

Lyla was emotionally and physically exhausted from the confrontations. The walls of the apartment were thin. She knew this because she would often hear the young couple next door arguing and she no longer cared if anyone heard her or not. She needed to get away from Juliano because he was sucking the life out of her.

Through the sobs she begged and then demanded, "Just go, don't come back. Please don't come back."

He frightened her with his explosive anger and potential for violence and she never forgot his past and the stories he recounted to her. He thought his stories were a measure of his power and subjugation over others, but in reality, they were frightening examples of someone she didn't know. She was so afraid. He spoke to her in a venomous voice.

"You are demanding, he said. You nag me to death and are high maintenance; you're never satisfied. Money, money, money and bills, bills, bills, that's all you talk about. You should have married that stupid dentist, Barry, what's his name, you used to talk about."

He left her in the bathroom, sobbing, clinging to the tub.

"You have no business knowing my business. If I want you to know I'll tell you."

He looked at her collapsed, shaking form in the darkness of the little bathroom, turned, and walked out of the apartment. She did not see or hear from him for days. His absence eliminated the tension and Lyla's anxiety slowly began to disappear with each passing day. Her normal routine working in the law office continued, never allowing anyone to know what happened to her. An important part of the deception was to carry on living a life that was not real. To everyone else, Lyla appeared to have a normal life; but in reality, it was a lonely, anxiety-filled existence of uncertainty and pain. Her only companion was the little dog she purchased prior to their marriage.

Juliano returned to their apartment nearly a week after his initial disappearance and waited for Lyla to come home from work. When she entered the apartment and was surprised by his presence, she immediately began to feel the uncomfortable churning in her gut. It was an experience occurring too often from the tension and anxiety in their marriage. Juliano walked toward her and could see the distressed look on her face. He stopped just before reaching her, giving them personal space, as he wasn't sure what her response would be.

"Hello Lyla. I was hoping we could talk."

Lyla didn't know how she was supposed to respond to this surprising truce, if that's what it was. Her eyes grew wide with astonishment and bewilderment, and she found it difficult to speak. She could feel herself getting stiff and was unable to move from the spot. It took extraordinary effort for her to remain calm and she drew in a deep breath for courage and strength.

"What are you doing here? I asked you not to return. I thought I made myself quite clear," she said. Her voice was steadier than she was actually feeling, and she surprised herself at her ability to get the words out without shaking. She felt like she was walking a tightrope between remaining steadfast in her words and inciting him to anger. This was a delicate balancing act she would learn to do very well to keep his anger and rage from reaching the surface and spilling onto her. He attempted to inject some humor to lighten the uncomfortable tension between them.

"I thought I'd come by to get some of my things. After all, I walked out without anything and would like to have a change of clothes and a toothbrush," he said with a soft chuckle. He was a master manipulator and knew exactly what to do. Things were moving as he anticipated. It was only a matter of time before he would have her back.

"By all means, Juliano, take your stuff. I would not want to deprive you of brushing your teeth."

Lyla's sarcasm exaggerated her discomfort at his appearance and her unwillingness to bend, at that moment.

"Listen," he said, "I'd appreciate it if you would come over to the couch and take a seat so we could talk. I promise you, I'll remain at a safe distance."

Lyla hesitated for several moments and finally walked to the couch, remaining a safe distance from Juliano, choosing a spot at the far end. He followed her and sat as far as he could from her at the other end squarely on the seat, but slightly forward, and looked at her. She noticed his body language and felt herself backing up to the arm of the couch as far as she could go. Juliano observed her movement and began to speak in a slow hushed voice.

"I've come to apologize. I've come to tell you how sorry I am. I behaved so badly. The men in the group have been trying to influence me in a very bad way. After all, they're just like I am, and I never noticed I fell into the same pattern each week when I attended the meetings. I don't want to upset you, make you cry, or make you miserable. I have no business being with those men and have asked to be in a different group.

"You are so right about all this, the group, the men in the group, and my treatment of you. You were right; I'm the problem, not you. You have been so wonderful to me; I owe my life to you. Without you, I would have been rotting in some prison or dead, and I'm so grateful for everything you have done for me. You are so special."

Juliano sat back, watched, and waited for her response. He observed as she digested his words and was waiting for a sign, a sign indicating he had her where he wanted her, so he could reel her back in. Her eyes began to soften. That was it, the sign he was waiting for. As her eyes softened, she spoke barely above a whisper.

"I can't do this anymore. I can't have these fights and emotional roller coaster confrontations. I appreciate your apology, but this has to stop."

That was the other sign he was waiting for. As soon as she spoke those words, he knew it was time.

"You're right," he said, apologetically and with great remorse, or so it seemed. "All this has to stop. I never intended to hurt you, and I'm so very sorry this happened. I don't want to be without you. I need you, and I'll never do this again, I promise."

As soon as the words crossed his lips he broke into an alluring smile knowing that would cause her to relent and come to him, or all was lost. She softened even more and allowed him to move closer to her. He bent towards her, took her hand clasped tightly in her lap, looked into her eyes, and spoke lovingly.

"You're the best thing that ever happened to me, and I don't want to do anything to lose you. You're so special."

With a moment of hesitation, he then moved ever closer to her and right before he reached her lips he stopped. Lyla moved toward him ever so slightly and they kissed gently.

Manipulation.

Reconciliation.

Completion.

The beautifully colored snake had charmed his prey.

He knew this would be enough for now and did not dare fully embrace her, knowing it would cause her to retreat. Instead, he proposed they celebrate by going out to dinner, and afterward stop by to see Tito Puente and his band in person at a small club near the airport. Because of his non-aggressive approach, he was successful in convincing Lyla it was a good idea to go out for an evening of good food and music.

"That sounds like a good idea," she said with a more lighthearted tone in her voice. "If you'll give me some time, I'll shower, change, and be ready to go."

"Take all the time you need," he called back to her. "There's no need to rush."

The thought never crossed her mind of how he got the tickets to get into the club on such short notice and how he knew she would be willing to go? She was so relieved the entire mess had ended that she became completely involved in choosing her outfit in anticipation of the evening. As she walked back to the little bathroom to shower, she called over her shoulder to him, "What a great idea; this is going to be a nice evening, and I'm so glad you thought of it."

Lyla never realized this entire scene was not some impromptu event. Juliano was masterful at getting what he wanted. He rarely left things to chance; he made sure to be in control, always.

Juliano took her to a popular Spanish restaurant on SW Eighth Street in Miami for paella and sangria. The meal was filling and delicious, and they left with Lyla feeling a bit light headed and vulnerable from the wine and food. It was a short drive to a club near the airport. Juliano left the car with the valet and walked Lyla into the darkened room already pulsing with the music of Tito Puente.

The club was small, exploding and reverberating with the crushing sound of the rich, brassy Latin music, always so well received by the crowd. Couples were on the dance floor swaying and moving to the rich magical music. Juliano ordered drinks and they left the table to join the others on the dance floor.

Lyla did not have a habit or tolerance for consuming much alcohol. When she had more than she should, she usually became amorous, a trait Juliano was well aware of. The young, good-looking couple moved to the music through several pieces. They retreated back to the table to listen attentively to enjoy the "in person" experience, the mood, the people, and the night.

One more time, Juliano took Lyla's hand and led her to the dance floor where the sultry, sensual music overtook them. They became intoxicated while in each other's arms, moving to the heart rhythm of the music. It magically transported them to another place, and when the music began to fade to a faster tempo, Juliano whisked Lyla off the dance floor, out the door, and home.

Lyla was still enraptured by the events of the evening, feeling the effects of the food, wine, and the subsequent drink at the club, along with the music that filled her with desire. She felt as though she were floating and danced into the apartment into the living room. Juliano followed closely, not wanting to lose the moment and took the opportunity to make a move. He quietly moved behind her, taking her waist in his hands, and began to move with Lyla as she swayed to the tune she hummed.

Softly, easily, he began to kiss the back of her neck, making certain he did not move too fast. They moved this way to the bedroom where Juliano turned Lyla to face him. She closed her eyes, mesmerized in the moment, moving sensually to the music that lingered in her head and on her lips. He gently touched her face and began to softly kiss her lips. The softness gave way to passion, as they responded to the rhythm they both seemed to feel. He caressed every inch of her beautiful skin, maneuvering easily into place to bring them to passionate completion. Lyla, exhausted from the evening and alcohol, fell into a deep sleep in the arms of the man who charmed and seduced her without her realizing it.

Why did she let Juliano back into her life? Why did Lyla continue to stay? She believed she saw some very deeply hidden but good aspect of him that surfaced briefly only to recede back into the depths of his being. It was these brief moments of gallantry, seeming gentleness, even loving-like actions that significantly influenced Lyla to hang on, waiting...waiting for these to resurface. Had she convinced herself there was something good in him that only she could perceive? Is this the false picture of him that drove her to save him and keep trying? Unbeknownst to Lyla, the few redeeming qualities she thought she saw and hoped to nourish and nurture were not enough for Juliano to be able to overcome the greater part of himself.

Waiting for this to occur was like waiting for Godot.

STABILITY

Over time their married life, although tentative, became more stable. Juliano appeared to be serious about finding a job but had no immediate success and blamed everyone and every circumstance. He soon discovered he was not qualified for any specific type of job and had few marketable skills, at least none he could identify. He could no longer associate with most of the people he knew prior to his arrest. His network of friends, those who were left, were of no assistance, as they didn't work either.

He applied for and was hired in the marina/boating industry where jobs were plentiful. He started working at a local marina driving a forklift, loading boats off racks from storage and back in again. He soon had other responsibilities such as cleaning boats and running them when owners were too busy to take them out. It was demeaning and didn't pay a lot, but it was a bona fide job and he was outside and felt free.

Juliano had no vehicle and didn't make enough money to qualify for a loan to get a motorcycle, something he desperately wanted in his life. Lyla was eager to do whatever she could to make things easy for him. This spawned an idea for her to go to her mother's banker and take out a non-collateralized loan with her excellent credit.

When Lyla picked him up from work the day she received the check, she made conversation about the day and then pretended to be perturbed over having to pick him up. With a little smile she suggested they look at motorcycles and window-shop. Juliano, at first put off by her suggestion, gave in. He thought she was trying to give him a hard time and was not in the mood. He had been up since 5 a.m. that morning and had been out in the hot sun all day.

When they arrived at the dealership, they walked around and Juliano's mood lifted. He explained exactly what motorcycle he would get and what he would do to customize it. He was like a little kid in a toy store. When his mood began to darken again, Lyla took his hand and asked what he wanted most. He shrugged and longingly stared at a motorcycle standing near them.

He said, almost lovingly, "That one; I want that one … in black with a different exhaust, different handle bars, accessories, and one of those Bell helmets."

As he came out of his reverie, he became angry thinking he was being teased. He threw off her hand, turned, and walked out of the showroom to the car. Lyla followed him and when they got to the car, Lyla got in her seat and reached into her purse.

"You know the bike you want, the black one you pointed out?"

"Yeah," he said with some disgust, "so?"

"Well," she said, smiling sweetly, "I think you should go back in and get it."

His eyes grew angry and the tone of his voice began to change.

"Now look, I don't want to talk about it anymore." He took out a cigarette, took a long deep draw and blew a stream of smoke in Lyla's direction. When his anger subsided, he spoke softly to her. "I just don't like it when you tease me. It's so demeaning having my wife pick me up from work and begging rides from the other guys."

Lyla waited until he finished speaking, hoping his anger would remain subdued, and pulled the check from her purse.

"Well, I guess it's time you get your own transportation."

She held the check for Juliano to see. At first, he didn't realize what she was doing. It was a cashier's check in an amount providing more than the cost of the bike and everything he wanted to do to it, plus more. He took a better look and was speechless when he discovered what she had done.

"Where did you get this?" he said. "I know better than to think it came from one of your parents. Lyla, where did you get this money?" His tone began to have that annoyed sound to it. Before his anger rose any more, Lyla spoke weakly, almost afraid.

"It came from me. I went to my mother's banker. I was able to get a signature loan because of my mother's relationship with the bank and my good credit. All I had to do was ask. Was this enough? Was the amount enough to get what you wanted? I just wanted to do something nice for you. Are you angry with me? I don't understand."

This was not the reaction she had anticipated and she began to feel she had done something wrong. Simultaneously, the horrible grumbling rose from her guts to her stomach. She was afraid, and she tried to find a comfortable position in her seat and unconsciously held onto the door handle.

"Hey, listen, I'm sorry, I'm so sorry I jumped the gun here. That was a really great thing you did, I'm so lucky to have you, you're so very special. Thanks, thanks for the money, that was, that was really, something else. Hey, wait here, I want to run in the dealership and talk to the sales guy for a minute, make some arrangements to come back and stuff."

Before Juliano left the car, he gave Lyla a quick kiss on the cheek. He had a huge smile on his face and a bounce to his step and practically flew into the dealership. *Things were finally going his way* he thought to himself. *Finally, on his own again, what a relief; it had been too long.*

Their relationship improved when Juliano began producing more income on a regular basis. When the tension subsided and the fighting ended, Lyla decided to stop working in the law office. The legal environment continued to reinforce painful and discomforting memories and she applied for a teaching position at a small, private parochial school. This school and parish didn't pay as well as the public school, but it was close to their apartment, and it gave Lyla the opportunity to make a change.

Lyla liked the close-knit family environment and was looking forward to working with the children. She hoped to develop a close relationship with the other teachers, the children, and parents. Perhaps this was a way for her to feel like she was part of a family. It had been several years since she graduated and completed her internship. It was scary and exciting, but she knew she could do it. She was filled with innovative ideas and believed she belonged in the academic environment. Although Lyla never discussed her plans with Juliano, she chose to pursue a graduate degree as a reading specialist. This would make her schedule very hectic, teaching all day and going to class at night, but she knew this was right for her.

Their life was relatively simple and busy with both of them working, only Lyla had a future in mind. Juliano never discussed a future for himself outside of his current employment. Lyla loved her teaching job and was recognized by the other faculty members and the principal as a hard worker, dependable, and caring. The students genuinely loved her.

Many of the little girls followed her everywhere outside of the classroom and talked about her beautiful clothes. When she discovered that the school didn't have enough funds to provide extra items such as small tin paint sets and brushes, markers, colored chalk and children's paperback books she bought these for every one of her students. She brought a portable record player into the classroom and introduced the children to classical music by Debussy and other masters. She purchased rolls of unprinted newsprint and kept it in the room for special projects and rewards when children finished their work early or were well behaved. The school was not air conditioned and when the weather was exceptionally warm it was difficult for the children to sit for long periods of time without becoming fatigued and crabby. So, she instituted one of the most favorite activities of all, the seventh inning stretch.

It was a bright, sunny day in early April when Lyla took her class out to the volleyball court for PE. She chose to stay outside for a short time to watch the class and as she leaned against the fence, felt a nagging annoying backache and other symptoms she tried to ignore. She became tired easily and got violently nauseated from the cigarette smoke in the teacher's lounge which was the only air-conditioned room in the school. She was arriving home after school with an insatiable craving for ice cream, sour dill pickles, and peanut butter and jelly on toast. She developed a routine in the late afternoon fixing her snacks and falling to sleep on the couch watching the Merv Griffin show.

During a regular exam, a small lump in her breast was discovered and she became horrified it might be cancer. That same afternoon, the doctor ordered an x-ray. The only appointment Lyla could get on short notice was during the afternoon on the next school day. She was reluctant to take it but had no choice.

The principal and other female faculty members were understanding. Lyla had never missed a day at school and was concerned about her students. The principal of the school told her not to worry, her class would be taken care of, and to let them know the outcome. Lyla waited impatiently for the images to be taken and nervously waited for the phone call from the physician for the results.

"Hello, Mrs. Masselli, this is Dr. Block's office. We have the results of your breast image study and need to let you know it was an enlarged milk duct gland. It's nothing to be concerned about, except we would strongly urge you to get to your obstetrician to have a pregnancy test."

Lyla hung up the phone in stunned silence. Milk duct gland? Pregnant? She had no idea. It was not possible, not possible.

She never thought of becoming pregnant. Surely this could not be possible. The thought was dismissed and she refused to consider the possibility until she skipped a second month. How ridiculous. It was impossible; she used protection. It couldn't be possible. A home pregnancy test confirmed what she didn't expect; a positive result.

Their marriage was based on some convoluted belief that if things didn't work out they could simply get divorced and go their separate ways. They never discussed the possibility of having children. It was an unspoken understanding between them. Lyla became uneasy and the anxiety she felt was growing. She wondered, *how do I tell him? What is he going to do?*

Juliano, like some spoiled child, began nagging Lyla incessantly about getting a dog of his own in the midst of Lyla's anxiety and emotional turmoil. She couldn't deal with the impending pregnancy and his childish behavior and believed it was easier to give in to him than fight. He chose a beautiful black and tan female Doberman puppy and registered her for obedience classes.

Lyla decided to tell Juliano of the pregnancy about four weeks after she got the test results. She planned for them to go out for dinner after one of the puppy's obedience classes and tell Juliano then when he was in a good mood. Juliano was proud of his puppy, Gretel's, performances and agreed to the celebration. Lyla was quiet throughout the meal. Her speech had been rehearsed all day, but when they were actually together, none of her ideas seemed to make any sense.

Lyla looked at Juliano and said, "Juliano, I've been thinking. I wanted to let you know that, uh, have you ever heard the expression, the rabbit died?"

Juliano was engrossed in his ice cream sundae and looked up at her with a puzzled expression.

"Wasn't Gretel great tonight? She's so damn smart, the smartest one in the bunch and the best looking, too. Not like that Ralph. Did you see him? He spent more time rolling around on the ground with all four legs in the air than he did standing on them."

Juliano was now laughing out loud. "That's the happiest dog I've ever seen."

Lyla was quiet, staring at him, waiting for him to respond to her question.

"A rabbit died?" he said shaking his head confused. "What rabbit, where, how come?"

"No, no silly, I mean do you know what the expression means?" she said softly.

"NO," he said, clearly annoyed. "Tell me," he said, his voice growing more agitated.

Lyla hesitated and then spoke. "It means I am pregnant." As she spoke, she lowered her eyes, afraid to see the expression on his face. He looked at her in shock and disbelief.

He finally said. "You're pregnant? How did that happen? Don't you take precautions? Didn't you use something? Anything?"

"I ... I did take precautions, but it just happened," she said faintly.

Juliano sat mute for a few moments, and finally responded with little emotion. "Well, I guess this means you're going to have a baby."

He wasn't proud, he wasn't happy, he merely commented she was pregnant. He didn't take credit for assisting in something remarkable and never showed interest in pursuing the subject. He was more excited when he got his motorcycle. Lyla couldn't understand his response and didn't know which was greater, her relief that he wasn't angry or her hurt that he appeared not to care. This was not the way it should have been. There was no shared, loving moment in response to her announcement. She was alone even in this. They didn't mention the pregnancy again that evening, but the next day after work Lyla with some apprehension brought it up again.

"Do you think we really ought to go through with this, with the pregnancy? After all, it's 1980 and we do have the option of my having an abortion. This was not something we planned or expected."

Juliano ignored her, said nothing.

Lyla was sitting on the edge of the bed and he had his back to her looking for something on the dresser and was not focused on her. Again, Lyla tried to talk to him. "We never talked about children; we never discussed anything that alluded to a future or anything long term, and this is a responsibility we never addressed."

Continued silence from him, when all of a sudden, he turned to face her and spoke with a harsh tone of voice that frightened her.

"You are not getting an abortion; you are having this baby, and it will be taken care of, end of discussion. This baby was not an accident. Although, I think the entire evening, especially Tito Puente, surely must have had something to do with it. If we had not gone to the club and had such a good time seeing him perform, this baby might not have been conceived. That was such a great night, wasn't it? Hmm, the music, the drinks, you looked so great and ... anyway, this baby is here and that's that."

His reaction caught her off guard. There was no more discussion. She was confused. What she didn't know at the time was that he had fathered other children in other relationships and had never taken responsibility for them. Perhaps this time was different for him.

To him this event was nothing special just the end result of a night of drinking and dancing, just another fact with no emotional attachment.

The more she considered her situation and condition, the more she thought, *Can I do this? Should I do this? The marriage had already been difficult, and I am so uncertain about staying. If I should have the baby, it would change everything for me. Did I misinterpret his detached matter-of-fact response? Did he want this baby?*

Lyla made it through her first trimester of queasiness and finished the school year. During the summer, she felt physically wonderful, shopping and eating, eating and shopping, but alone. There was no one to share her pregnancy with, no baby shower, and no real friends. She casually ambled through baby stores and baby accessory departments alone. Juliano had no interest in shopping. Some of the treasures she discovered were a beautiful bentwood rocker, an Italian perambulator, and matching stroller, spending money they really couldn't afford to spend. She loved everything she saw and spent hours rocking in her chair imagining how it would be.

How was she going to tell her family? She couldn't stand the stress of hiding something else and she was hoping this might change the way they felt about her and her husband. The stress drove her to confide in her mother. Sura could barely hide her dissatisfaction but wouldn't deny support if Lyla needed her, or so she said. Lyla decided not to renew her contract with the school for the coming year. Her due date was early December and she had no desire to spend the day on her feet in a hot classroom.

There was little enough room in their small apartment for the two of them, much less a baby. Lyla was feeling frightened, vulnerable and alone, and believed she needed help. She called her mother.

Sura proposed a plan that Lyla couldn't resist. Sura decided it would be best for Lyla and her husband, what's his name, to come to Cincinnati, Ohio, Lyla's birthplace. It was the family's place of residence during the summer months, and the base of operations for Harry's business. The plan was for Juliano to work for Lyla's father in one of his establishments. He would have a job and Lyla could again be with her family. In time, Lyla hoped her father would find a job for her as well.

Lyla instantly accepted the idea and looked forward to being with her extended family and back in her home town. Juliano was not so thrilled but had little choice. He hated the cold weather, hated the Cincinnati Reds, especially Pete Rose, and hated Lyla's family. Sura found a house for them, arranged a mortgage in their names, co-signed the loan, and the rest was up to Lyla to pack and move up there. Lyla was in the seventh month of her pregnancy when she arrived at the Greater Cincinnati airport. It was mid-October and the weather reminded her of an Indian summer.

HOME

The trees were dressed in their late summer wardrobe and the front lawn was covered with a blanket of tall green grass dotted with dark red geraniums that matched the brick of Lyla's new home. The home, built in 1937, was a modest yet sturdy northern home in a quiet residential neighborhood. The house was a two-story red brick with a large bay window covered with a weathered copper roof flanking the left side and a small front porch on the right enclosed by a black iron railing. The back of the house had a wooden deck that opened onto a generously sized back yard under a canopy of mature trees perfect for children and pets.

The large master bedroom, off the living room, was bathed in bright light by the front bay window with a covered window seat underneath and another window near the bathroom that let in an abundance of natural light. The pass-through bathroom led to a second bedroom designated as the baby's room. It too was bright and sunny. The dining room and kitchen were in the central part of the house and the staircase leading to the second floor seemed to secretly appear in the wall near the dining room. The second floor had ample closet and storage space and another large bedroom and bath.

Sura was an animated tour guide. The banter between Sura and Lyla echoed throughout the empty house with exclamations of oos and ahs over the old-fashioned architectural details of the home's features. The crown molding, the wood window sills and frames, and the tile kitchen counter tops had been restored and/or renovated to their original beauty.

Lyla was silent lost in thought as she climbed the steps from the basement to the kitchen. She walked into the kitchen first stopping to gaze out the side kitchen door window at the house next door, walked into the kitchen, and brushed her hand across the cool square tiles of the counter top. Sura became concerned hoping that the steps and excitement hadn't become too overwhelming for Lyla and was causing her or the baby distress.

Lyla walked into the dining room, out to the wooden deck, and held tightly to the wooden rail. Sura followed her and stood beside her as they looked into the yard and listened to the birds and the wind through the trees. Sura, without speaking placed her hand on Lyla's and held it tightly. Lyla turned to her mother with tears in her eyes overcome with emotion.

"Mother, I don't know what to say. Thank you. The house is beautiful and I'm so happy to be home."

They embraced holding each other for several moments then Sura stepped back and suggested they celebrate with some Graeters ice cream. The invitation was irresistible and they left the house laughing and talking about how Sura would decorate the house, with Lyla's help, of course.

Juliano and his dog arrived with the moving truck several days later and the move in began in earnest. Lyla unpacked the kitchen first and then moved on to other non-essential boxes. Juliano started working right away and Lyla was left on her own.

Each time Lyla invited Sura to shop there was a different excuse. "Sorry Lyla, I have other plans. You know your sister is having her baby at the end of the month, she needs me, I have to go help her. Sorry, Lyla, I have this horrible sinus headache." No one else in the family responded to her inquiries for company either. It seemed as though Sura and the rest of the family had disappeared once Juliano arrived. His presence made everyone uncomfortable and the isolation continued.

One afternoon, Sura arrived at Lyla's house unexpectedly. She had returned from helping Lyla's sister with her sister's children and her sister's new baby. Sura walked in dragging a large dark brown garbage bag. Lyla took a few steps toward her mother when Sura threw the garbage bag toward Lyla that landed at Lyla's feet.

"Here," Sura said. I went baby shopping with your sister at one of the outlet malls and I got you some things."

"Uh, thanks mom, I...uh, thanks for the stuff."

"Sorry I can't stay, it's late, your father and I are having company for dinner this evening."

"Oh, OK," answered Lyla. OK then see you some time later, I guess."

Lyla, saddened by her mother's angry display, threw the garbage bag of baby items down the basement steps. She thought, *perhaps it was a mistake to come here, they hate my husband and they must hate me.*

Lyla was left on her own to figure out where to go to furnish the baby's room with furniture and accessories and fill in the gaps of necessary baby items. The days grew cooler and shorter and Lyla's belly grew even bigger. She couldn't remember the last time she saw her toes and the one dress and pair of maternity trousers she had were no longer stretching big enough to cover her. Her coat no longer fit because she couldn't close it and her shoes were getting uncomfortably tight.

Lyla's father kept Juliano busy working long shifts, he left early in the day and didn't return until late in the evening. Lyla and Juliano rarely had any time together. Tension began to build. Lyla was spending too much time alone, and there was barely enough money to cover their expenses. Harry, Lyla's father, wasn't going to give Juliano any more hand outs than he already had with the house and the job. Lyla couldn't figure out if her father was punishing her for marrying Juliano, getting pregnant, and becoming dependent on him to provide Juliano an income.

Juliano arranged to have a free evening to take Lyla out to dinner for their anniversary thinking it would appease Lyla for his lack of attention to her. He made reservations at a popular upscale restaurant in downtown Cincinnati. Neither of them had the appropriate formal attire and looked like street urchins when they arrived in the dining room. The room was tastefully decorated with hanging crystal chandeliers, the tables were covered with white tablecloths each adorned with long white candles and gleaming silver cutlery.

The restaurant slowly revolved as it revealed a 360-degree view of the city and across the river into Covington, KY. Lyla and Juliano were shown to their table and sat without speaking hiding behind their menus when Juliano began to complain, "It's cold and dark here, what happened to the sun? I can't ride my motorcycle anymore, the customers at the store are a pain in the ass, my boss is lazy and stupid, and don't they ever fix the roads around here?" After a long pause, "Just so you know, I'm naming the baby after me and he's going to be called Junior."

Lyla looked up from her menu at Juliano trying to figure out what had prompted his pronouncement. He had led her to believe he was indifferent about the baby, had something...had he changed? Was this his way of getting back at her and thumbing his nose at her family? Suddenly she felt a wave of heat move through her body that began in her toes and climbed rapidly to her head making her nauseated and dizzy. She excused herself from the table without saying anything and exited the dining area and went to the ladies' room.

The bathroom was softly lit decorated in muted tones of smoky taupe on the walls and the accessories. The attendant approached her with a damp hand towel and asked if she needed any assistance.

"Thank you, Lyla answered. I just need a few moments I felt a bit queasy." The attendant smiled and asked how far along Lyla was in her pregnancy. "Oh, I have maybe four weeks to go but it sure doesn't feel like that right now."

The attendant answered, "You just stay here as long as you need to. If you want I can let someone know you're OK. Who are you with, honey?"

"Oh, no that's not necessary, I'll be fine, thank you, I just need a little time."

Lyla needed time to think how she could leave the restaurant and get back home without involving Juliano. She had no money to pay for a taxi and was afraid to call her mother. She was stuck. She saw the same sad eyes in the mirror that she saw the day she was married.

When the queasy dizzy feeling subsided, she got up and saw her full reflection in the mirror. She hardly recognized herself. The only dress she had was an unbecoming grey corduroy jumper that pulled taught trying to cover her belly with an equally unbecoming bright yellow long sleeve heavy cotton shirt underneath. Her face was puffy, her hair had outgrown it's cut and was unshapely. She wore heavy maternity tights in dark grey that sagged and had become bunched around her fat ankles, and her swollen feet were stuffed inside her scuffed worn loafers. She was a mess.

Lyla returned to the table and Juliano was noticeably angry. He had a scowl on his face and began to interrogate her.

"Why did you get up? Is there something wrong? I thought you liked this place and wanted to go out? You left suddenly without saying anything. What's the matter with you?"

"I'm upset. You decided to name my child, my Jewish child, after yourself."

"What? There is no discussion here. I'm Latin; it's tradition. The first-born son is named after the father dot period, no discussion."

Lyla hesitated to speak but charged ahead no matter the consequences. "Well, it's not done like that in my family. This child is going to have a Jewish name. If you wanted a 'junior' you should have married a girl who wasn't Jewish. End of discussion."

Juliano sat across from her leaning back in his chair wide eyed his mouth dropped open, dismayed at her reaction. Where did she get this bravado all of a sudden? It must have been influence from her family. He had a million reasons to hate them, and now he had one more. He thought, *the sooner he got out of Cincinnati the better.*

Less than a month later, in the hush of the night, Lyla's son was born. He had pale creamy skin and a shock of ebony colored hair that stood straight on top of his head. Lyla was breathlessly in love with her child. Whatever hurt angry feelings she had for her parents and Juliano were set aside. Her priority now was to protect and preserve this new life.

Her skills in caring for her newborn were lacking but she quickly learned with the aid of her mother and her cousin. Her mother came over to help Lyla bathe the baby. Her mother filled his little plastic bath-tub with warm water and placed a washcloth in the bottom to keep him from slipping down into the water. Then Sura took another small cloth with baby soap and gently rubbed his skin from head to toe. She ended with shampooing his hair and rinsing it with fresh warm water from a separate container. Lyla's cousin showed her how to burp the baby after being nursed. Burping him on her lap or over her shoulder was easy. Getting him to sleep was her biggest challenge but she soon learned from her cousin that the rocking chair was an invaluable tool to accomplish that.

When weather permitted she took the baby out for walks in the per-ambulator. It was the perfect vehicle that kept him safe and warm bun-dled in his fleece bunting. Although Juliano was rarely around he did manage to have some free time one Sunday to accompany Lyla and the baby on one of her walks around the neighborhood. The air was crisp and cold but the sun was shining. They met another young couple walking with their daughter and the two little families spent the afternoon together. The new mothers shared their birth experiences and the fathers talked about sports. Lyla and Juliano were finally a family.

Lyla needed to feel like her old self and got her hair cut and permed and began exercising to return to her pre-pregnancy weight. She thought her life was moving in a positive direction until one Sunday morning in February when Harry came to the house, ostensibly to visit.

Harry walked into the living room and sat on a chair opposite the couch facing Juliano. Lyla greeted her father and then left the room to take care of the baby. When she returned to the room she heard her father talking in whispered tones with a serious expression on his face. He was sitting on the edge of his chair leaning aggressively toward Juliano; he never took his coat off. Juliano sat quietly listening with a blank look on his face. She heard the words "fired" and "I won't contact the authorities."

"Dad, what's going on here? Did you just fire Juliano?"

"I have to leave now, Lyla, you need to talk to your husband."

"But, Dad, what do you mean he's fired? How will we live, where will we get money?"

"I'm sorry Lyla, that's no longer my concern."

Lyla's father rose from his chair and walked out the front door saying nothing more. Lyla was in shock and Juliano was relieved.

Lyla began to question Juliano. "What just happened here Juliano? What's going on? Are you really fired? Did you know this was going to happen?"

"It's over, there's nothing more to say. I'm going out for a while, I'll be back later."

"What do you mean you're going out and you'll be back later? What are we going to do, how will you get a job?"

"I don't know."

Juliano disappeared and Lyla was left alone in shock.

Juliano never confided in Lyla why her father fired him. She never knew if Juliano had purposely sabotaged his job or if this had become part of the enmity that existed between Juliano and her father.

Lyla learned years later that Juliano drank alcohol on the job, was often drunk, and had been accused of stealing money from the bank deposits. Juliano's behavior was a violation of his probation and rather than report him to the police which would have sent Juliano to prison, Harry fired him.

FIGHT OR FLIGHT

Juliano failed miserably in Cincinnati. It was a strange city with obstacles he could not overcome. He had to report to a probation officer weekly and was required to have a job. When he began applying for miscellaneous jobs he had to report he was a convicted felon, his crime, and that he was on probation. No one wanted to have anything to do with him, especially when he had to explain the crime he committed. Lyla turned to her brother for help, he wouldn't. Then she turned to her cousin, he couldn't. Juliano stopped trying and Lyla didn't know who else to turn to.

They were running out of money, fighting, and Lyla became more estranged from her family than before. Her humiliation and embarrassment overwhelmed her good judgment. In her moments of desperation, she decided they had two choices, fight to stay and overcome obstacles or leave. Juliano's only desire was to get as far away from Lyla's family and Cincinnati as possible but had no idea how.

Spring training announcements on the television were the catalyst that sent the little orphan family on their journey. Lyla refused to consider returning to the Miami area. She was afraid Juliano might be tempted to repeat drinking and drugs and ultimately rape again or return to his previous criminal friends and equally criminal habits.

She thought mid-Florida would provide some familiarity, yet distance. The house was listed for sale and Lyla began to pack. Juliano contacted someone from his past who lived in Tampa, promised to immediately find a job, and a place for them to live. Juliano never told Lyla who he knew and how and Lyla was too afraid to ask. How was she supposed to pay for the mortgage? How was she supposed to buy food, diapers, and pay utilities? How was she supposed to get around without a car? With little fanfare and empty promises, he packed their only car with his clothes, took his dog, left Lyla and the baby, and never looked back. She wondered, *would he ever return for her?*

Was this a move of desperation? Did Lyla really think this through? Could she really trust Juliano to do what he said he would? This would have been the op-portune time for her to leave him and finally confide in her parents. What kept her from doing that?

What happened to the 'she-bear'? Why was she trying so hard to preserve a rela-tionship she knew was wrong and wasn't going to work? Was the fear of the un-known and of not being able to count on her family a stronger motivating force than the fear of her husband and fragile marriage? Did she consider this, and if so did she take the lesser of what she thought was two evils?

She was too naïve to understand that distance from Miami did not determine Ju-liano's behavior. She was too naïve to understand that she could never, would never be able to influence or control his behavior. Part of the game he played was to allow her to think she did.

Juliano called Lyla when he arrived in Tampa, Florida but never told her where and who he was staying with. She began to panic, he was gone, she didn't know where he was, and she couldn't manage him to make sure he didn't misbehave.

Days turned into weeks. Spring and warmer weather arrived and Ju-liano did not call or return. Lyla was forced to beg her father for money. Harry gave her $25.00 a week for food and gave her one of his old deliv-ery cars for her to use. It was dirty inside and out, leaked oil, and the interior smelled of gasoline. The driver window didn't roll up or down and the tires were bald. She was being punished because she married him, got pregnant, and didn't leave him when Juliano left her.

Lyla was forced to face the reality of being abandoned and was afraid to ask her parents to help her divorce Juliano and help her find a job. She timidly read through the classifieds but had no self-confidence to believe she could take care of herself and the baby. She couldn't ask her father for a job, she presumed he'd say no, he had had enough.

Juliano's calls were infrequent. The last time they spoke he was at a party. She could hear the background noise, music, and loud voices and he was noticeably drunk. She hated it when he was drunk it always caused her anxiety and when she became anxious and fearful her guts would grumble and she would be in and out of the bathroom in pain. She finally convinced herself she needed to find a way to begin a life in Cincinnati without Juliano. Her plan would be to sell the house, take the profit and put it towards a small rental apartment and find a job as a secretary. Before she could follow through, Juliano called and told Lyla he had a job opportunity, a place for them to live, and he wanted his family with him. He sounded strong and self-assured. She gave his news some thought and in reality, was relieved. Her fear gave up her plan to start her own life, and she chose to follow him to Florida.

Why?

Lyla made arrangements for movers to pack, load, and deliver the contents of the house and then told her parents she was leaving for Tampa with the baby. There was no feedback from them, no questions were asked. She felt as though they were relieved she was leaving. Sura offered to take Lyla to the airport. The ride to the airport was deathly silent and uncomfortable. Lyla's guts churned, and her mind raced to find the words she really wanted to say. "Mom, please help me, don't let me go." But the words were never spoken.

When they arrived at the airport the silence continued between them. Sura carried the baby for the last time and walked Lyla onto the plane. When Lyla turned to say her final goodbye to her mother, she felt a huge lump rise in her throat, her chin began to quiver, and her eyes welled up with tears.

Lyla was in conflict, afraid to leave and afraid to stay worrying that what she was about to do was going to end badly. She was afraid to trust a man whom she had learned not to trust, not only with her life but now with the life of her child or face the uncertainty of trusting her family who she believed held such enmity for her. Sura handed the baby to Lyla and kissed Lyla and the baby goodbye. Sura was unable to hold back her tears. Lyla cried as the plane pulled away from the gate.

Lyla sat holding the baby during the flight and covered herself with a receiving blanket when he needed to be fed. She had plenty of room in her bulkhead seat when he had to be changed but he slept most of the flight. When Lyla deplaned, she followed the signs to the baggage claim area. Lyla expected Juliano to be there to meet her but he was nowhere to be seen. She waited by the designated conveyor belt for her luggage to arrive. When it did she struggled to lift the luggage from the conveyor while holding the baby. She unfolded the stroller and strapped the baby safely inside. She stacked the rest of the pieces by her side and waited for Juliano to appear.

SYMPHONY OF HER HEART

She became anxious fearing that she might have misunderstood Juliano's instructions and perhaps was supposed to meet him outside. Her heart beat faster, she began to perspire, and she grabbed the luggage and dragged it to the doors to the passenger pickup area.

No Juliano.

She waited.

It was too hot and muggy to remain outside. She pushed the stroller and dragged the luggage back inside the waiting area and began to walk up and down baggage claim pushing the stroller and dragging the luggage watching the exit doors. The longer she walked and waited, the angrier she became. Every time another group of passengers arrived in baggage claim and then departed, she grew angrier.

The minutes became hours. She could not ignore the cries of a tired, hungry baby and became overwhelmed with worry and anxiety. She was exhausted, her hands were bruised and swollen, her legs ached, and she had to find a place to feed the baby. She couldn't walk and drag anything anymore. She saw a bank of elevators that transported passengers to other floors including the airport hotel.

Lyla decided to get a hotel room, call her mother, and ask if she could return to Cincinnati on the next available flight. Lyla thought. *The worst thing that could happen is that Sura would say no. But, if she agreed to help Lyla, then Lyla would find a way to begin her life without her husband.*

Lyla stood staring at the elevator doors, waiting for them to open when she heard someone calling her name. Juliano came running down the aisle, frantically waving his arms trying to get her attention. She turned to look in the direction of the sound and saw a figure running towards her. She froze momentarily, but when the doors opened she stepped forward to walk inside. Juliano caught her by the arm and dragged her back out of the elevator dragging the stroller with her. She wrenched her arm free from his grasp, and Juliano began apologizing for being late. A security guard witnessed the scene and walked over to offer his assistance. Juliano babbled about being out late the night before and oversleeping. It was that simple.

The guard spoke calmly and placed his hand on his revolver. "Do you know this man, Miss? Is he bothering you?"

The guard stepped closer to Lyla and the baby. Lyla's face was stone and her eyes were like steel. She answered, "I'm all right sir, I know this man."

"Are you certain you're OK?" the guard repeated.

"Yes," she replied, "I'm fine."

The guard moved a short distance away from her but watched the scene in case he needed to return to her aid. Lyla moved away from the elevator doorway and stood directly in front of Juliano. She spoke slowly with as much strength and determination as she could muster.

"I've been waiting for over three hours, and I'm not going anywhere with you. I have been traveling since early this morning. It is now 4 p.m. I'm tired and so is the baby. You have abandoned us. I don't care about any of your stupid explanations. Get out of my way. I'm leaving; I have nothing more to say to you."

When Juliano tried to bar her way, the guard moved closer and Lyla motioned that she didn't need his help. Again, Juliano gave his litany of excuses until he was breathless. When he realized she meant what she said, he changed tactics. If nothing else, he would try to buy some time.

"You're right," he said. "It's late, and you are both exhausted. The movers came yesterday and the house is ready. Why don't I take you there? You can stay the night, and if you still want to leave in the morning after you've had a good night's rest, I'll take you to the airport. I won't try to stop you."

He intended to do whatever he could to manipulate her into staying. He hoped when she saw her furniture and other personal items and heard his plans, she would acquiesce. She hesitated, wondering if this was more lies and games, but she was also feeling tired and suddenly frightened. The weight of the luggage, the length of the day, and her overwhelming responsibilities for her child caused Lyla to relent and accept his offer.

"All right," she said. "I'll go with you, but only for the night. I'm leaving in the morning on the next flight back to Cincinnati. I mean it."

Juliano breathed a sigh of relief. He couldn't do enough now. He carried the luggage and loaded the car for the short drive to the house.

Lyla remained silent with her eyes transfixed on the unfamiliar people, buildings, and streets that she saw through her passenger window. When they arrived at the house, Lyla began to cry. The tiny, unassuming house was in a depressed neighborhood Lyla would never have visited, let alone lived in. The houses were faded painted concrete block in need of repair. Yards were unkempt many with abandoned cars on cement blocks in the front yards. She gasped in horror at what she saw. What kind of place had he brought her and her child to?

Juliano was gracious and helpful unloading the luggage and taking it into the baby's room and their room with Lyla in a cocoon of silence. Lyla fed and bathed the baby and rocked him to sleep in her rocker. She searched through boxes to find her bed linens and made the bed. Juliano offered to get fast food but she declined. She used her last ounces of strength to shower and crawled into bed, curled up, listening for the baby, and fell deeply to sleep.

The baby's sweet cries of hunger and discomfort being in a wet diaper awakened her. She felt as though she had just fallen to sleep, but it was morning, and she was being summoned. The morning sun was bright, and Juliano was by her side, snoring. She got out of bed without waking Juliano, changed the baby, rocked and breast-fed him wondering how and why, she relented the night before? This is what she left Cincinnati for? She admonished herself for not having the strength to find a way back to Cincinnati. What was wrong with her that she couldn't follow through?

When the baby was satisfied, she held him tightly feeling she needed to protect him from being snatched from her. She wandered through the house into the living room and kitchen. *Funny,* she thought, *it looks just as bad in the daylight as it did the evening before.*

The rooms appeared to be miniature in size with barely enough room to turn around. The walls looked like they had been recently painted an off white and the carpet was dark brown and looked new. Perhaps it was cleaner than she thought. The worn vinyl floor in the kitchen was an ugly gold color in a marble like pattern that had begun to curl in the corners. The stove was old but clean and there was a dishwasher.

Then she walked from the kitchen to the garage. Most of her furniture didn't fit in the house and the single car garage was filled from floor to ceiling with furniture and boxes. Juliano was waiting for her in the kitchen when she re-entered the house from the garage.

"Well, what do you think? I know it's not as big as our house in Cincinnati, but it's the best I could find on such short notice." He continued without waiting for a response, "And guess what? I know I said I would take you back to the airport this morning, but I've got this job interview this morning. Once I'm done, I promise, I'll take you wherever you want to go. How does that sound? Do you want to know anything about the job?" he continued again, not giving her a chance to respond. "It should be great. I get a car and everything. It's not far from here, real convenient. What do you say? How about it? I need the car."

She stood there expressionless and was somehow not surprised he had lied to her.

"Do what you want Juliano, I don't care about your job. You can pick me up when you're done, I'll be ready to leave. I guess I can wait."

Juliano showered, dressed, and left. She bathed the baby and put him in the stroller to take a walk. She was right, it was just as bad in the daytime. Lyla was afraid to walk alone and took Juliano's dog for protection.

The sun was shining and the air was warm. The other houses in the neighborhood looked like the house Juliano brought her to. They were small concrete block homes with faded paint on the outside. Trash was scattered throughout, yards looked like modified junk yards, and old dirty children's toys littered the bare dirt lawns.

She saw no one as she walked and was afraid to go too far. By the time she returned to the house it was time to feed the baby and put him down for his nap. There was no phone in the house, making return reservations would have to wait, she was trapped. While the baby slept she walked into the kitchen and stared out the back glass sliding door. The yard was enclosed on one side with a six-foot wooden plank fence, on the other three sides with a chain link fence, and the grass was filled with huge bald spots and weeds. Everything was old, everything was dirty, everything was horrible.

The afternoon dragged on and the baby awoke from his nap hungry and needing to be changed. Once again, she fed the baby, walked the neighborhood with the dog for protection, and waited. At 5 p.m., Juliano finally walked into the house with a handful of flowers and a big smile on his face.

"I'm sorry it took me so long. I didn't realize the interview would take the whole day. I know I told you I'd take you to the airport. But guess what?" He ignored her lack of response and continued. "Guess what? I got the job. Isn't that great? Wait till you hear all about it, it's going to be great. I start tomorrow morning. By the way, they want to meet my wife. They think it's really important the wife be involved. Sounds great, don't you think? How about we go out and celebrate? What do you think? Honey...did you hear me?"

"Yes, I heard you. I want to go home; this is not going to work."

"Oh, you mean yesterday." He took her hand, still holding onto the flowers, and she pulled away from him. He motioned for her to sit down and she reluctantly walked to the couch and sat down still holding the baby.

"Listen, I am sorry about yesterday; that was a horrible thing I did to you and the baby. I was a louse and believe me, I'm so sorry the whole thing happened. It was never my intention to hurt you. I'm sorry. How about we kind of start over? I have a job now and can support my family. How about it? Will you forgive me and give me another chance?"

He held the flowers for her and gently took her into his arms. At first, she was stiff and unresponsive, but she began to soften and allowed herself to be held. He whispered in her ear, "I'm so sorry; I promise, I will never hurt you or the baby again. I promise.

I'm so sorry.

I never intended to hurt you.

I promise, it will never happen again.

ON THE MOVE AGAIN

Lyla spent months trying to adjust to the city, find a friend, and feel comfortable. Feelings of depression and desperation caused her to pack the car with essentials and drive north, aimlessly for hours; roaming, crying, and thinking. She tried to summon the courage to leave and head home to Cincinnati but she always returned, feeling worse than when she began. Her attempts to leave were always thwarted by her fears. Could she find a suitable job to make enough money to support her child? If she did, could she trust anyone with her baby? Where would she live? Her parents sold the home they purchased for her. Would her family accept her and her baby? She was ashamed of her marriage and felt like a failure. Her agonizing conflict was whether to stay with Juliano in a situation she knew and was miserable in, or return to Cincinnati, uncertain if her family would accept her even if he wasn't with her.

Her feelings of entrapment and melancholia propelled her to go somewhere familiar and safe. She escaped several times to Miami Beach staying with her cousin at her cousin's home. She didn't tell Juliano her plans until she reached her destination. Her cousin never made her feel unwanted but Lyla realized she was not prepared mentally or financially and could not stay with her cousin indefinitely. More fears overwhelmed her. Did Lyla have the courage to tell her cousin she wanted to leave her marriage? What would her family think of her? Would they help her? Were they still angry and upset with her for marrying Juliano in the first place?

Did she really want to escape or was she testing herself to see if she could successfully leave for good or testing him to see if he cared?

Irrational fear.

Inability to trust the only people she could trust.

Another lost opportunity.

Juliano knew he was the consummate manipulator and soon became successful at his job in sales in the automobile industry. Old debts were paid off and Lyla saved money. Juliano's ego was fed by his success, making money, and being recognized by his peers making him easier to live with. He worked long hours and played hard, drinking and socializing after work with friends and co-workers. He soon began to complain about his immediate superiors and others in management. Lyla was unable to deal with his late-night wanderings and being drunk upon his return home. The stench of alcohol on his breath and the cigarette smoke on him and his clothing disgusted her. She was unhappy and alone; he was socializing with someone else.

The melancholy increased and was ever present. Juliano's probation officer, who openly showed her disgust for Juliano, the crime he committed, and his gift of probation, was making unannounced visits to the house and harassing Lyla when Juliano was not home. Why harass Lyla? Juliano was the one on probation. The landlord was finding excuses to show up unannounced and coming on to her. The house was infested with roaches. And the big dog next door jumped the fence and ate Lyla's favorite bamboo storage container that was airing on the back patio concrete slab. That was it, she had to do something.

Once again, she tried to gather the courage to make a plan to leave. While the baby took his afternoon nap, she cleaned the house and did laundry, she even washed the walls. She started making a list. How much money would she need to drive back to Cincinnati for gas, food, hotel? Was returning to Cincinnati a reasonable, practical option? Where would she stay once she arrived? What were her job skills? Could she call her mother for help? Did her mother think she could get her father to give her a job? Get moving quotes only for necessary pieces of furniture if anything at all. What would she pack for herself and the baby? Would it all fit in the car? Did it matter what she brought back?

Juliano walked into the house as she completed her list. She barely acknowledged his presence as he passed her on his way to the bedroom to change out of his work clothes. She took the opportunity to hurriedly fold up her list and tuck it under the chair cushion to retrieve later when he wasn't around. Juliano returned to the living room, saw Lyla's face, knew there was something troubling her, and thought he was probably the cause.

Lyla said nothing then slowly turned to him. "I can't live like this anymore, I feel like I'm living a nightmare.

She recounted her encounters with the probation officer, the landlord, and her fears, rational or not, living in the neighborhood across
the street from the biker gang members. "I am 34 years old and don't
want to be, can't be in this position ten years from now; I need this to
be over. I'm afraid it will never end."

Juliano reached for her hand and she withdrew it. She was feeling
empty, tired, worn. Juliano, the slithering serpent, began his dance of
lies and manipulation, falsely reassuring her, luring her, manipulating
her to believe things would change. He was going to surprise her with
news that very evening. He heard about a job opening for a better position in another city to the south, in Sarasota. It would be better hours,
more money, and the change would do them both good. He begged
her, pleaded with her, promised her things would change.

*It was fear that kept her there and the delusion of hope that Juliano would
change, that their circumstances would change. One more chance he would beg.*

I'll change, I'll be different.

It was never my intention to hurt you.

Please don't leave me, I need you.

INFIDELITY

Sarasota was a quaint city with soft white sand beaches and an active arts community with downtown streets dotted with antique shops and galleries. It had an interesting combination of laid back culture with banks and brokerage houses bordered by luscious botanical gardens surrounded by the beauty of the large bays and waterways.

The change in location appeared to be what they needed to revive their relationship, or so it seemed. They rented a small, newly constructed house in a clean, middle class neighborhood of young professionals with families. Lyla walked with the baby on the clean wide sidewalks with the baby in the stroller and felt safe.

Lyla easily transitioned into their new home and community. The beaches were beautiful, fresh bakeries abounded, and she shopped the sales for adorable clothes for her son. Juliano was able to provide financially to cover bills. All of this deluded Lyla into believing her life had improved and was not distressed at learning she was pregnant again. She had no idea her life was about to change abruptly. Reality stepped in without warning one afternoon while she was separating laundry and her little boy was napping. Juliano had convinced her that only she could wash and iron his dress shirts for work by telling her about all the compliments he got from co-workers about how terrific his shirts looked. She believed him. As she was taking Juliano's shirts out of the dirty laundry basket, she noticed lipstick on the collar and a strange perfume smell. The lipstick color and the perfume scent were not hers.

She flew into a rage and began throwing Juliano's dirty shirts everywhere in the laundry room and didn't know if she wanted to throw up or scream or both. He always came home late, and she knew he socialized with his friends from work but did not suspect he was seeing another woman. She wasn't thinking. She called him at work and confronted him.

"Hello Juliano? Yes, it's me, yes, fine? Fine? You can dispense with the pleasantries. Would you like to tell me how someone else's lipstick and perfume got on your shirt collars?

"Listen, I can't talk to you right now; I'll have to call you back."

"Don't bother, she sneered, "don't bother to call me, and don't bother to come home. You can stay with whomever it is you're seeing and sleeping with. I don't want you here, ever."

She gently hung up the phone. She was enraged; she didn't know what to do. Her first thought was how would she take care of her little boy and the child she carried? She had no money of her own, only the money Juliano gave her to pay the bills and get groceries. While her son napped, she took her anger out on all of Juliano's precious clothes, the things he loved most. She pulled his clothing off the hangers in the closet, put everything in leftover empty moving boxes, and threw the boxes onto the front lawn. Then she went for the dresser drawers and jammed his underwear and socks in garbage bags that joined the pile on the lawn. She used another smaller kitchen garbage bag and wiped the bathroom counter clean of his toiletries, soaps, shampoo from the shower, brushes, razors, everything and pitched that onto the front lawn as well. The last things to go were his shoes. He loved his shoes. They joined all the rest of his stuff on the lawn. *Damn him*, she thought.

Juliano finally called back, but Lyla gave him little opportunity to give her excuses.

"Honey," he said, "honey, listen to me. You have to listen to me. You're wrong; you've got it all wrong. I haven't been seeing anyone."

"And I suppose the lipstick and perfume on your shirts is all my imagination? You must think I'm so stupid."

Bang, she slammed down the phone. The phone rang again; Lyla picked it up and listened saying nothing.

"Listen honey, I can explain, you have totally misunderstood. I know what it looks like to you but I promise you I..."

Bang, she slammed the phone again. One more time the phone rang, and Lyla picked it up.

"Don't come back, don't show up here. I've locked you out and will not let you in. I've thrown all your clothes, shoes, and other stuff on the front lawn; you can pick them up there. Do not. I repeat, do not call me back."

She calmly hung up the phone. The phone rang again, but Lyla didn't answer. Lyla waited for her heartbeat to slow down and the feeling like she couldn't breathe to subside. It seemed like the walls of the room were closing in on her and she panicked to get out of the house. Her little boy woke from his nap and she took a long stroll around the neighborhood. By the time she returned to the house, she had calmed down enough to feed her son, bathe him and put him in his pajamas. She was emotionally and physically exhausted and retired to her bedroom. It was after midnight when the phone rang and awakened her.

"Hello, is this Lyla? You don't know me. I work with Juliano. In fact, both my husband and I work with Juliano. I wanted you to know he's very upset about what's happened, and I wanted to try to explain for him since you won't talk to him."

Lyla was confused hearing a strange woman's voice. She sat up in bed, trying to overcome her drowsy state. She could feel the rage and pain of Juliano's deception come over her. She finally spoke.

"I have no intention of speaking to you or to Juliano."

The woman interrupted. "Juliano's here, by the phone, and he wants to talk to you. Will you talk to him? Please? I'd like to put him on the line. He needs to explain what happened."

"No, I have nothing to say to Juliano or to you. Who are you anyway?"

"I told you," the other woman said. "My husband and I work with Juliano. I feel badly about what happened and wanted you to know he has not been seeing anyone else. This has been a terrible misunderstanding. He loves you, Lyla, and wants to come home."

Lyla could barely contain her emotional wrath. She spoke through clenched teeth, struggling to remain calm.

"I have already told him, and I'm going to tell you. I have nothing to say to him or you. He can stay wherever he is tonight because I'm not going to let him in the house, and I don't care if he never comes back. If he wants his stuff he can pick it up on the front lawn. I don't care what he has to say and I don't care what you have to say. Don't ever ... don't ever call me again and don't ever tell me anything about what my husband has done or not done ... it is none of your business."

Lyla put the phone down and cried herself to sleep.

The next several days were tense as Lyla waited for Juliano to collect his clothing and other personal items from the front lawn. She went over everything in her head a million times: the shirt, the lipstick, the perfume that wasn't hers, and his insistence he had not been unfaithful to her. She didn't know where to go or who to turn to for help. She wasn't sure how her parents would react to the situation. She didn't call them until she could no longer stand the stress of not knowing. At least she would find out where she stood.

She called her mother's house in Cincinnati and was surprised when her father answered the phone.

"Hello, Dad, it's me, Lyla."

"Yes, Lyla," her father responded. "How are things in Florida with you, your son, and your pregnancy?"

"Not so good Dad, that's what I wanted to talk to Mom about. Is she there?"

"Mom, no, she's off on one of her trips and should be somewhere in Europe or Israel, I think. I don't remember and don't know her itinerary. She won't be back for several weeks. Is there anything you want to talk to me about?"

Lyla hesitated for several moments.

"Lyla, Lyla, are you there?" She could hear the impatience in her father's voice. "Did you want to talk to me or not? I don't have time to stand here and listen to silence."

"Uh, yes Dad, uh, well, you see."

"Get it out Lyla, what is it?"

"Well, Dad, you see, I'm having some difficulties."

"What do you mean difficulties? Difficulties with your son, the pregnancy? Is everything OK over there? Did he do something to you?"

"No, well, Dad listen to me, please. I'm having problems with Juliano. You see, there's this other woman and things are a bit messy."

Before Lyla could go into any detail, none of which her father wanted to hear, her father interrupted her.

"All right Lyla, what do you want to do? Do you want to come home? If you do, and you don't want to wait for your mother to return, I'll send a moving truck, have you packed up, and get you and your little boy back here. Is that what you want? Well, talk to me Lyla, tell me, is that what you want? I haven't got all day here. If this is what you want, consider it done."

Although Lyla wasn't sure what she expected or wanted, she heard her father's exasperated voice, the "get it done" business-like tone of getting another uncomfortable situation taken care of and out of the way.

And even though she knew she was better off leaving and desperately wanted to return home and have someone take care of her, she heard herself saying, "No, that's OK, Dad, not right now; I'll take care of it. I will handle it. There's no need to tell Mom I called. Thanks anyway, I'll be OK."

"All right, Lyla," her father responded, sounding somewhat frustrated and confused. "You take care. Let me know if you need me."

"OK, Dad, I need to go now."

It was just before dark that same evening when Juliano arrived at their home. He knocked on the front door after picking up the boxes of his clothing that were strewn on the front lawn. Lyla looked through the peep hole in the door and hesitated to open it. She waited a long moment, stepped back several steps, then stepped forward again, and opened the door just enough to speak.

"Hello Lyla, I just wanted to know if I could come in to explain things to you and see our son."

Lyla looked at him and wondered if she should let him in. She said nothing and made no move to allow him to enter for several minutes, and then spoke in a soft voice devoid of emotion.

"I suppose you can come in for a moment to see our son; he's in the family room watching television."

Juliano walked into the house and went directly to the family room to see their son. The little boy jumped up immediately when he saw

Juliano and gave him a big hug.

"Hello, Daddy," he said with his curls flopping everywhere. "Mommy and me had a good day today. We played with the hose and got my toys all wet. Do you want to come see what I did outside?"

"No ... not right now. Daddy will see you another time; you go back and watch your television program. I'll see you later and kiss you nighty night."

"OK Daddy."

Lyla watched as this exchange took place. She wondered how her son would feel without his father. She took a deep breath and sighed heavily, not wanting to think of what was to come.

Lyla motioned with her hand for Juliano to sit in the living room. He purposely took a seat on a chair close to the front door. Lyla walked over to the couch that was a reasonable distance from his chair.

"Don't worry," he said. "I'll sit way over here so I can duck easily if you decide to throw something at me. I know you don't believe me. I realize I have little credibility, but I want you to try to understand what happened."

How could she believe anything he said? The room was eerily quiet except for the sounds that drifted in from the television in the other room. The tension between them filled the air, and Juliano's discomfort showed in the beads of perspiration that dripped from his brow and under his arms. She saw he was being forced to reveal something and knew it was going to upset her.

Lyla could feel her guts rumble and heat rise throughout her body. Nausea was overwhelming her and her head started pounding. Her anxiety caused small drops of perspiration to trickle down her neck, her complexion turned a dull shade of grey, and she felt dizzy and faint. Juliano noticed her distress.

"Can I get you something, a glass of water or something, are you OK?"

"I'm fine. What is it you want to tell me? All this has been a very stressful and uncomfortable ordeal, and I'm tired. Can we just get this over with?"

He was careful not to lean forward too far in the chair, hoping to keep her from becoming more anxious, but he wanted to be closer to her. He moved to the far end of the couch she was sitting on, she responded by moving as far back as she could without leaving the couch. He began.

"Well, you see, there was a party after work. I know I didn't tell you about the party, and I'm sorry. Anyway, there was a party after work because we were celebrating what a good month we had, record numbers ... anyway ... everyone decided to go to a local club where we were drinking and dancing. I was just having a good time dancing with some of the girls there; you know how I love that Latin music.

"Anyway ... I was just drinking and dancing and one of the girls who I danced with got a little too close, I guess, and got her lipstick on my shirt collar. That was all. I didn't do anything else. I never kissed her. I just danced with her and some of the others. Please believe me, that's all there was. I never even noticed what happened with the lipstick. If I had, I would have taken the shirt to the cleaners and not given it to you to wash and iron. Well, you know what I mean, if I had been fooling around and wanted to cover it up, I would have done things differently."

His voice trailed off when he realized he was making the situation worse the longer he spoke. Lyla said nothing. Lyla never moved and never took her eyes from him. Juliano became uncomfortable under her intense stare. He cleared his throat and continued.

"So, anyway ... because you were so very upset with me, I didn't know what to do. I had no place to go, and Gary and his wife offered to let me stay with them at their house. Do you remember my friend Gary at work? Besides, you were so mad at me I was thinking maybe it was a better idea to stay away to give you time to calm down. It wasn't my idea for Gary's wife to call you. She saw I was upset when you got so angry, and she tried to help, that's all, that's all. Please believe me.

"There is something else I need to tell you, and I want you to hear it from me and not find out any other way. The other issue has to do with another woman, someone I knew many years ago when I was in college. You see, I was seeing this girl. I wasn't serious about her but we dated and you see, we were just dating, nothing serious. She got pregnant and said the baby was mine. I wasn't serious with her or with anyone, and when she told me she was pregnant, I told her I didn't want to marry her and was not interested in the baby. She chose to keep the baby, and I never had anything to do with her or the baby all these years.

"It was a very long time ago, almost 15 years ago. She contacted my friend Lenny, and Lenny told her how to find me. Well, the girl I got pregnant contacted me. She lives here in Sarasota, and I've been seeing her. I mean, I've been going to see my daughter. I have a daughter, and I have been trying to establish a relationship with her, you know, trying to be a father because she doesn't have one. I guess I understand how important having a father is now that I have my son. I know I didn't do what was right in the beginning with this girl, but I would like to do it now. I'm sorry I didn't tell you any of this; I should have, I mean, about my daughter. I never intended to hurt you. Please believe me."

Lyla sat there catatonic, trying to digest Juliano's confession. When she finally spoke, it was barely above a whisper as she fixed her gaze on a spot beyond him.

"I'm pregnant," she spoke softly. "I'm pregnant with your second child. This has been a difficult pregnancy with a substantial risk of losing this baby. The doctor told me not to get upset and to take it easy. Not... get... upset ...and here you sit telling me you have another child you have been secretly seeing along with her mother."

"Well, I remember you said the doctor told you not to get upset and that's why I didn't tell you."

"When did you plan on telling me about this other child?"

"I don't know, certainly not until after our baby was born. I didn't want to do anything to endanger you or the baby."

"How convenient of you to, all of a sudden, be so concerned about me, our son, and the baby I'm carrying. I find it all so difficult to believe."

"All right Lyla, all right, don't get crazy."

"Listen to me," Juliano said, "it's late and I would like to ask if I can stay on the couch, at least for tonight. You're right, it's a lot to take in, and we have a lot to talk about. We won't resolve this tonight. It's going to take time. How about we give each other some space tonight and take the next few days to try to sort things out? I promise to stay out of your way and sleep out here on the couch. That way, we can see if it's possible to work all this out or not. Then we can decide how best to deal with it all. What do you think?"

She looked at him surprised at the reasonable and mature suggestion and at the calm he was exhibiting. She was too tired and too worried about the child she carried to fight with him.

"I have a good idea," he said. "Why don't you let me give our son a bath, read him his bedtime story, and put him nighty-night. How about it?"

She said nothing else as she contemplated the reasonableness of his suggestion.

"Yes, she finally said, "I suppose so. I guess you can't do any more damage than you have already done by doing that. Yes, go ahead. I don't think I can do this anymore," she said in a very emotionally weary voice as she got up from the couch. "I can't do this now, I am finished."

She thanked him, turned, and went into the bedroom for the night. She barely had the strength to prepare for bed. Physical and emotional exhaustion overcame her. Her greatest concern was for her unborn child, what might happen to her baby as a result of the stress, shock, and near hysteria she was feeling. The numbness she experienced reacting to Juliano's revelation hopefully protected her. She stepped out of her caftan, lowered her nightgown over her protruding belly with barely enough strength to wash her face, and crawled into bed. She fell to sleep hearing the laughter of her son playing with his father.

For the remainder of that week and several weeks after, Juliano left work early to be home for dinner and did whatever he could to help Lyla with their little boy. He bought a small inflatable pool and put it in the sunny part of the small yard. Their little boy played with Juliano while Lyla relaxed and watched them. Their son went to bed early, exhausted from the sun and water, and Lyla and Juliano had time to talk. It also gave them time to be a family which was an essential component that had been missing from their life.

One evening after their son was put to bed, they sat in the living room and talked visiting old and current issues long unaddressed. Lyla began.

"I don't know what you want Juliano. You say you want a family but you're always someplace else working or socializing with someone else. You need to decide what's important to you. Do you want this family, your daughter and her family, or do you want to be on your own?"

After a long silence, Juliano answered. "I want to have my wife and children and I want to be able to provide for them financially. I want to do what's right with my daughter whatever that is and I want you to be OK with that. I want to live with you without this constant fighting and tension and I'm not sure how to do that. Do you?"

"Honestly Juliano, no, I don't know how to do that. I just know what has happened is not working. It's difficult to trust you and I doubt that you're happy with me constantly complaining and finding fault with you."

"All right, Lyla, how about we start by being honest with each other. I need to pay more attention to my family and include you in my decision making. I will have to curb my socializing with other people and spend time with you. I will try to help you at home especially when the baby's born. I don't know what will happen with my daughter but I won't keep you in the dark about her. If nothing else, I would like to stay together for the children. I think we should try. After all, we've been through a lot. What about you?"

Lyla took time to contemplate his words and then answered. "Ok Juliano, it sounds like you're asking me to trust that you'll change. I have tried to do that in the past and it didn't happen. I would hate to keep you from the children but..."

Juliano interrupted her. "Please Lyla, I'm asking you to trust me this time. I think staying together and working on our issues is better than going our separate ways. I'll try to do whatever it takes to be a good husband and father. I promise. I know I've messed up in the past but I realize I can't keep doing that."

How was Lyla supposed to trust him? He sounded so sincere. Was he really going to follow through? Although weary of Juliano's broken promises and endless requests for forgiveness, Lyla wanted to trust him but didn't know why. She was hopeful, for the sake of the children, Juliano would follow through and their married life would improve.

Juliano stopped drinking and came home after work. They went to the shark tooth festival, gathered shells on the beach, and enjoyed creamy ice cream cones on St. Armand's Circle. Lyla never brought up the infidelity again and tried to be accepting of Juliano's daughter. She suggested they invite his daughter for dinner one late afternoon to give them all an opportunity to meet. They both appeared to be trying.

Lyla prepared for the birth of her second child. She interviewed and hired someone from an agency, set up the crib in her bedroom, and waited for labor. As her due date got closer she became more anxious. Labor began three weeks early; Lyla's water broke in the middle of the night. The woman from the agency came to the house and Juliano took Lyla to the hospital. This labor and delivery was very different from her first. She was given a drug to induce labor and she progressed rapidly. Her baby boy was born early the next morning.

Reality descended upon her while she was in the hospital with the after baby blues. She was alone in the hospital, in the dark, and cried for herself, her children, and for a marriage she feared was unstable. Juliano only appeared at the hospital when Lyla and the baby were due to be discharged. He waited to explain to Lyla why he didn't visit her and the baby until he and their other son arrived in her room.

"Hey there, we're here to take you and the baby home. What a great big brother this little one is going to have. We wanted to surprise you with the good news. I arranged for some vacation time from work so I could stay at home to help you with the kids. Isn't that great?

"I...I'm... yes, that's great," Lyla said with surprise.

Lyla's days were filled with her children, getting back to her pre-pregnancy weight, and establishing a relationship with her husband. The marriage and the little family, although fragile, remained intact. It appeared they were both trying and had made the right decision to stay together.

And then the inevitable happened. Juliano's income deteriorated and they descended into the familiar wormhole. "Juliano there's not enough money to pay the bills. What's happening at your job?"

"Business has slowed and the store is having financial difficulties. My boss is stupid and I think I should look for another job someplace else."

"Someplace else? Where else? Doing what?"

"I heard about a job in the Tampa area that should be lucrative. I've already had the interview and accepted the job. I begin in two weeks, just enough time for us to move in someplace else. Don't worry I'll find us a place that's clean and affordable."

"But," Lyla began. Juliano interrupted her.

"Lyla, this is a good move, a good opportunity for me. You'll see. I'm doing this for us, for our family. It will work out, I promise."

Lyla had no choice. At least she believed she had no other choice. Again, she was not included in the decision and resented being left out.

Lyla did not recognize his consistent behavior of failure and his inability to sustain a job. Each time circumstances became challenging he was either fired or quit and moved on without explanation.

Juliano did as he promised. He found a small, newly built rental home on a street with other young families. His income increased and was consistent, they lived close to the dealership, and his hours were better. He requested his attorney pursue early release from probation and it was granted by the court. For the first time, they believed they were free of the past.

Lyla enrolled her eldest in a neighborhood pre-school and adjusted to the new town. Although the house was larger than the home they occupied in Sarasota, their current home wasn't large enough for her to empty all the moving boxes that were stored in the garage. Lyla was successful in paying old and new debt and began to save money. Juliano's job gave a reward for jobs well done and the little family embarked on its first vacation, Disneyworld in Orlando.

THERE'S NO PLACE LIKE HOME

Lyla heard no complaints from Juliano, only glowing reports of how the owner of the dealership liked him and what a good job he did in his finance department. Lyla went on adventures exploring the area with her little boys and made new friends with other pre-school mothers. She was careful not to reveal their past and focused her attention on her children. One evening Juliano approached Lyla for sex. "Hey there Lyla, I had a great day at work, made lots of nice money, how about we celebrate?"

"I don't know Juliano, I'm tired, I've had a busy day with the kids and it's late."

"Aw, come on Lyla, you know how much you turn me on, let's have a glass of wine and mess around especially now that the kids are asleep."

While Lyla was in the bathroom washing her face, Juliano snuck up behind her, grabbed her, and began to grope her body. He was rough and demanding in his touch, looking for selfish pleasure.

"Juliano, stop that I can't rinse my face." He continued his foreplay and began to manipulate her to move to the bed. "Aw, come on Lyla, you know you want this as much as I do. I need this," said Juliano.

"Juliano, this is not a good time, I don't want to be pregnant again, not now. I don't want another baby." But she eventually gave in knowing he would nag her, bully her, and become insistent and demanding. She didn't have the strength to fight him off or change his mind.

"All right Juliano, all right. Stop, give me a few minutes to finish and I'll be right back."

Lyla slowly finished her night time routine, made sure her contraceptive was in place filled with extra anti-sperm, and slowly walked back into the bedroom. Several months after their family vacation Lyla was surprised to learn she was pregnant, again.

This was not a good time. Her youngest was still in his crib and needed her. She was miserable emotionally and physically. The depression of being pregnant so soon after her second child smothered her and her belly blossomed quickly into the pregnancy making her uncomfortable.

The children were asleep for the night and Lyla was in bed by the time Juliano came home from work. She had been crying. Juliano entered the bedroom.

"What's wrong Lyla, is everything OK with the kids?"

What a stupid question, she thought.

"OK? You ask if everything is OK? No, it's not. Both of the kids are miserable and covered with chicken pox. I'm bathing them in oatmeal baths every three to four hours and slathering them from head to toe with calamine lotion. I'm exhausted, my body is swollen everywhere and I'm tired, just plain tired. I don't want another child, I don't want to be pregnant, I can't take much more of this."

Juliano sat on the edge of the bed and tried to calm her down.

"Lyla, I know this feels like it's never going to end but it will. The kids will get better and soon things will get back to normal. Trust me. Maybe you could go next door and ask our neighbor for some help with the kids especially when you go into labor. Someone will have to be here with the kids when I take you to the hospital. Just try to get some rest."

All Lyla could think about was his selfish, bullying behavior. She thought, *what does he think normal is? I feel like I'm always pregnant, will it ever end?*

Labor and delivery were the last things Lyla wanted to talk about and rest remained elusive. Lyla began labor at her weekly appointment with her ob/gyn. She didn't have time to give in to labor or anything else. She had sick children and needed to get them to their pediatrician. During her visit to the pediatrician she continued to experience early labor and rushed home to plan for someone to take care of the children. It was apparent she was going to have a baby that evening.

She continued to labor the rest of the day. Her water broke around nine that evening and Juliano was still not home. Lyla went to her neighbor for help and when Juliano finally arrived they left for the hospital. The baby was born by cesarean section several hours after she arrived at the hospital. Another little boy, a beautiful cherub with pale pink skin, a shock of strawberry blonde hair, and what she hoped would be bright blue eyes, like her mother's.

Lyla was lulled into a false sense of security. Juliano had yet to complain about his job and she had saved enough money for them to consider purchasing a home of their own. One evening Juliano approached Lyla with a plan.

"Lyla, I want to talk to you after the kids are in bed."

"All right, I'll meet you in the living room in a moment," said Lyla.

"OK I've taken a look at the savings and believe we should have enough for some kind of down payment for a mortgage, if the lender will accept my terms. We need to find a local builder, draw up some plans, and get a house of our own. I'll handle the financing. What do you think?"

Lyla was intrigued and delighted at the prospect of having their own home. "Do you really think we can pull this off?"

"Sure," Juliano reassured her. "We're doing just fine. Let's draw up some plans to show a builder and move forward."

They found a neighborhood in the initial stages of development by a local builder where lots and homes were affordable. The lot had ample room for a home Juliano and Lyla thoughtfully planned with a fenced yard for the dogs and children and a flower garden for Lyla.

Juliano and Lyla were busy with their respective roles. Lyla was responsible for the house and children and Juliano provided the money they needed to live. He was proud of his accomplishment in building and owning his own home. Business was good and Juliano continued to have a good income and was promoted to head finance manager in the dealership. Being recognized and successful in his job became the foundation upon which Juliano's anger would rest.

Even though there was little time for Lyla and her husband, she never complained. She filled her time with her children and found creative outlets that kept her from feeling the lack of a partner. One Saturday afternoon Lyla packed up the boys and headed east toward Orlando towards the strawberry fields. She found a 'u pick' field and gave each little boy a plastic pail to fill with fresh strawberries. This adventure was repeated at the citrus orchard when they picked oranges and made fresh squeezed juice.

Their most successful adventure took them to Tarpon Springs visiting the sponge docks, eating Greek sweet treats, and bringing home sponges for their shell collections. Lyla never let the number of children, the distance, or the sheer logistics of planning adventures keep her from taking her little band of boys everywhere she could.

During the warm summer days, Lyla kept them busy with a large inflatable pool. By the time the day was over, the children were exhausted, bathed, and easily put to bed. When Juliano had a day off, he would join the boys outside in the pool. Lyla planned and executed outdoor projects like the shaving cream party and fence painting that delighted and kept the children busy. Juliano's job appeared to be going well for him, Lyla was taking care of her responsibilities at home, and the family appeared to be stable. The school year was ushered in buying new clothes and supplies. Everyone was eager to get back to school and their friends.

Lyla discovered in the spring of the next year that she was pregnant. This was another unplanned pregnancy. She knew she had to do something to end this cycle. Giving in to Juliano's desires was easier than finding excuses or fighting with him, fearing the consequences. She knew exactly when it happened. Juliano had had a few drinks and was feeling amorous, as usual. He approached her for sex.

"I don't know Juliano, this is not a good time. I don't want another baby, I don't want to be pregnant. It's only been a couple of months since the miscarriage and it's not a good idea. I'm too old and worn out to be having another baby."

"When will it be a good time? He asked as he tried not to let his anger and frustration show. Things are going great for me, I'm thinking of leaving the dealership for a job that will make me rich and you have nothing to complain about."

Lyla had no idea he had become restless and was looking for another job.

"What? Another job? It's just...it's just that I don't want to get pregnant. I don't want to get pregnant anymore. What job? Where? Doing what?"

"Don't worry," he said with a twinkle in his eye. "You're so regular. When was the last time you had your period?"

Lyla hesitated and began counting on her fingers. "Seven, this is the seventh day," she said quietly.

"Ha," he laughed, we've got plenty of time, trust me."

Lyla became pregnant, her seventh pregnancy in seven years, this had to be the last for her with him. One evening she approached Juliano after the children were asleep.

"Juliano I need to talk to you. Do you think you can stop what you're doing and listen?"

"Yeah, sure, sports scores won't be on for a while yet. What is it?"

"I don't want to have any more children, I don't want to be pregnant any more. My body is sending signals with the last miscarriage and I'm asking you to have a vasectomy. Will you?"

Juliano looked at her in shock. His eyes looked like they were going to bulge out of his head and his face turned beet red. "What, what did you say? A vasectomy? Are you kidding? No one is going to touch my equipment. Ever."

When he finished speaking he gave a shudder at the thought and left the room.

The fourth little boy was born in December of that year. Lyla decided, after consideration and consultation with her doctor, to have a tubal ligation after the birth and didn't hesitate when the doctor questioned her more than once to confirm her agreement to the procedure.

Juliano arrived at the hospital with the three older children to introduce them to their baby brother. Without forewarning he decided he was naming the baby. "OK, Lyla, just so you know, I'm choosing the name for this last kid. He's going to have a name that reflects my heritage. You got your way and named all the other kids."

Lyla quietly listened to the name Juliano considered. "I don't think so Juliano. That name sounds like this child is a member of the mafia." She secretly wished she could write whatever name she wanted on the birth certificate but was afraid. She relented but put a Jewish name for his middle name.

Lyla needed to gather her family around her, hoping to have them accept her children, her little family. She handwrote invitations to her immediate family asking them to gather together to share in the birth of her final child and give Hebrew names to her children. To her delight and surprise, everyone she wrote to responded. The date was set, plans were made and Lyla was relieved all were able to attend.

Lyla did not anticipate that Juliano would use this occasion to exercise his control over Lyla and ultimately show her family, he was boss. Her Jewish family was arriving to gather for a Jewish ceremony for her newborn son and her other children. It seemed incongruous this would occur in the shadow of an 8-foot live Christmas tree. But Juliano would not be dissuaded.

Lyla worked hard cleaning, dusting, and vacuuming the entire house. The bathrooms were spotless and the play room was clean with all the toys, books, and games organized on shelves. The dining room table's leaf was added, the table was dressed in a clean white cloth, and set with napkins, cutlery and glassware.

Lyla ordered fresh deli platters from the local grocery filled with meats and cheeses, local fresh rolls and bread, and accompanying sides of salads. Lyla made her mother's recipe of noodle kugel and blintzes, and she purchased some smoked fish for her father.

Everyone assembled in the living room. Lyla's brother stood next to Harry, who held the baby, and Sura stood next to Harry. The room was bright with light that came streaming in from the bank of windows and French doors on the opposite side of the room. Lyla's brother spoke prayers in Hebrew, gave each child a Hebrew name and blessed each one. Lyla stood behind the group watching, took a deep breath, and sighed feeling she had been accepted. The time, distance, and cir-cumstances of her marriage appeared to have melted away.

For the past seven years, Lyla had been anxious, lonely, isolated from her family, and dying of emotional thirst. She was hugged, kissed, and held by everyone there and felt she was being filled with the nour-ishment of love she so desperately missed and needed. When the last person left and the house was once again quiet, Lyla believed she had reestablished a connection to her family. She didn't realize at the time this was the bridge that had to be built, giving Lyla access to her family when she was in need.

Sura decided to stay after everyone had departed to spend time with Lyla and the grandchildren. Lyla went to the bedroom to put the baby down for his nap and Sura was in the kitchen feeding the other children. The baby had just fallen asleep when the phone began to ring. Lyla answered the phone in her bedroom. As she listened to the voice on the other end, her face turned a pale shade of grey and she felt like she couldn't breathe. "I understand," she said quietly not wanting to wake the baby. "You do what you feel you need to do." She hung up the phone as though in slow motion. She was in shock.

Sura and the children were having a hilarious time having lunch at the kitchen table. Sura had made her 'old fashioned spaghetti' recipe that Sura's mother used to make. The children were laughing and giggling slurping up long strands of pasta with sauce all over their faces and pointing to the brother who was sitting in the highchair. He was hanging strands of spaghetti from the bars of the highchair for the dogs to eat.

When Lyla walked into the kitchen Sura saw Lyla's ashen face and became concerned. Lyla reassured her mother with basic Yiddish and sign language that Harry and other family members were fine.

"Then what is it? Sura asked?

"How about we get all these terrific spaghetti eaters cleaned up and into the playroom to watch some cartoons so mommy can take care of the kitchen?"

The boys hopped down from their chairs and had their faces wiped. The extra spaghetti on the highchair tray was quickly consumed by the dogs and the children settled into their little chairs in front of the television.

Sura took Lyla's hand. "Lyla, I can see by the look on your face that the phone call was serious. What happened? Who was that and what was the call about? Come sit down, the dishes can wait, come over here, I'll make us a cup of tea, tell me, tell me what happened."

As Sura filled the tea pot and put it on to boil, Lyla took their favorite china cups from the cabinet and sat at the kitchen table. Sura joined her and waited for Lyla to begin. Lyla sat at the table with her eyes downcast while she played with the edge of her tea cup. There was a long uncomfortable silence.

"Well, mother, you see, the phone call was from Juliano. He called to tell me he would probably not be home tonight and if he did make it, it would be late."

She took a deep breath, let it out slowly, and began to tell her mother the story of Juliano's daughter in Sarasota and the child's mother.

"What has this got to do with the phone call, Lyla?

"I'm getting to that mother. Juliano called to tell me his daughter was out with friends riding motorcycles and was involved in a terrible automobile accident. She and the others were badly injured and have been taken to a local hospital near Sarasota and it's uncertain if she will survive."

"Lyla, is there anything I can do or will my presence here make things more difficult?"

"Well, to be honest with you mother, I have no idea what you could do, but thank you for asking. I think it would be best if you go. Juliano has a difficult time dealing with adversity and this now puts more responsibility and pressure on him. He will have little patience and will want his privacy. I'm sorry."

"It's understandable Lyla, I'll make arrangements to go home. But if you need me for any reason please call me right away."

Sura returned to Cincinnati on the next available flight and Lyla was left to deal with Juliano. For the next several months, Juliano spent many hours at the hospital and rehab providing support to his daughter and her mother. His daughter did survive but was paralyzed and would likely not walk again, her life forever changed. Lyla tried to ask about his daughter and her circumstances. Each time Lyla asked, Juliano ignored her or said he would handle everything and the topic was never to be discussed again.

COMPLICATIONS

Lyla went to her standard, after-baby, follow-up appointments with the doctor. Routine blood work indicated there were abnormalities. From this point forward, Lyla would begin a long journey into doctor's offices and hospitals for diagnostic procedures and surgeries. They were challenging, cascading, life-changing events that dramatically shaped the remainder of her life. She would be tried beyond measure and would need the support and strength from her family. The emotional damage she endured showed in physical symptoms. Several months passed with endless doctor appointments, pain and discomfort, diagnostic tests, and no definitive answers. She was given medication to lower her blood pressure that was causing headaches and nervousness, changes in dosage of her thyroid medication that either made her more nervous and anxious or caused her to feel exhausted. She began to have sharp squeezing pain in her upper right quadrant that moved to her back that made her feel faint, she was spending more time in the bathroom than normal, and she was losing weight.

It was late morning when Lyla finished tasks of morning laundry, feeding the baby lunch, and putting him down to nap. She had been in and out of the bathroom numerous times during that morning and had begun to feel weak. Twice she had to rush back to the bathroom and her toddler ran after her with his bottle hanging from his teeth asking, "Mommy, mommy, where are you? You got a boo boo?"

"Mommy is OK, sweet boy, I'm right here."

When Lyla got her son down for a nap, she was close to collapsing. She left his room and started walking to her bedroom to lie down. She never made it to the bed. The cramping and pain became intolerable and she collapsed on the floor and began to weep.

"Please God, please. Just give me enough strength to take care of my children. I have to get up off the floor. Please, God, get me off the floor."

She stayed on the floor until the pain subsided and crawled into bed to rest until nap time ended. She had to function, the other older children would be coming home from school on the bus at the front of the neighborhood and she needed to be there to greet them.

Lyla never complained or asked for help with the children knowing Juliano would refuse. She went to all her medical appointments alone that were scheduled when the older children were in school. She never left the baby unless it was absolutely necessary. Her frustration grew into worry about what might be wrong with her. Doctors were talking about her gall bladder, her liver, her intestines, she was frightened. What was wrong with her?

She was exhausted. She was afraid. She had no support from Juliano, he always seemed to be lost in his own reality retreating into silence and secrecy. Juliano became increasingly restless and Lyla grew frustrated and fearful never knowing the real reason for his behavior. She was consumed with her health issues and couldn't deal with Juliano's problems. Whenever Juliano was angry, she learned to keep peace at home at any cost. If there was a problem with the kids, she took care of it. She wasn't willing to take a chance that he might harm her or the children.

In the midst of all this, Juliano impulsively changed to the new job he alluded to when the last baby was conceived. He told her he was the financial officer of a company that assembled desk top personal computers. He explained he was getting in on the ground floor of something profitable. But he couldn't give her any details.

"Juliano, where's the company? Do you have an office, an employment contract, a salary?"

"I don't know why you worry so much Lyla, don't you trust me? I know the owner, he was a customer at the dealership, I can trust him. I'm telling you for the last time, everything's just fine. You need to concentrate on taking care of the kids and the house and leave the rest to me. Besides I know what I'm doing and you don't have a clue about business."

During this same time, Lyla's favorite aunt and uncle, who lived in Miami Beach, were celebrating their 50th wedding anniversary with a formal black-tie event. Lyla yearned to return to Miami Beach, to the places that were familiar, and be close to her family. She was encouraged by her cousin, who's husband was a physician, to get another opinion by a physician her cousins knew and trusted. Lyla and Juliano were invited as a couple and Juliano agreed to attend the event. Special arrangements were made for someone trustworthy to stay at the house and care for the children during Lyla's absence. They didn't anticipate being gone any longer than the weekend. Juliano decided a romantic weekend was in order and booked a fancy room overlooking the ocean at the Fontainbleau Hotel.

Although Lyla was thin and pale, she looked stunning in a full-length, black and white tuxedo gown she purchased for the occasion. Her shoes were mid-heel black silk with a rhinestone bow on the toe, and she carried a small black satin bag adorned with a white satin rose. She looked like a model who stepped from the front pages of Vogue.

On the night of the party, the evening sky was clear with warm tropical breezes that wafted perfumes of the ocean and tropical flowers through the air and displayed, as the sun set, sherbet colors splattered and steaked across the sky. When Lyla and Juliano arrived at the event, a large crowd of guests had gathered in the reception area socializing and enjoying drinks and hors d' oeuvres. At the flickering of lights, the guests retreated from the front reception room to the main ballroom for dinner and entertainment by a full formal orchestra seated above the dance floor on a stage. It reminded Lyla of the Paul Whiteman, Benny Goodman, and Glen Miller orchestras famous from the 1920's to the 1950's. During the summer when she was young, her parents frequented a park above the Ohio River where one of the big bands played all evening under the stars. When she was lucky enough to be brought along, she dreamed of one day dancing with her partner just like her parents.

Lyla's parents were the first ones on the dance floor, much to the delight of everyone. They were a beautiful pair, Harry with his dark hair sprinkled with grey and athletic body in his formal attire, looking like Tyrone Power, and Sura, a platinum blonde, Marilyn Monroe look alike with her curvaceous body, radiant skin, and eyes. They were graceful and glided across the floor effortlessly as though they were inseparable, magical.

Although Lyla was hungry and the food smelled delicious, she was careful about what she ate. Almost everything she ate, of late, caused her gastric and abdominal distress and she didn't want to spoil the evening. By the time the desert was served, Lyla was uncomfortable with pain radiating from the top of her right shoulder down her right arm. That was followed by nausea and a stabbing, squeezing pain in her upper right abdomen, causing her to feel faint. Beads of perspiration formed on her upper lip and she had trouble taking a breath. She turned to Juliano who was sitting next to her finishing his desert.

"Juliano," she whispered. "Juliano, I need to leave, I need to go back to the hotel, I'm not feeling well. Please take me back to the hotel now."

She approached her mother who was seated at a nearby table. "Mother," Lyla whispered in Sura's ear. "Mother I'm having some difficulty and don't feel well. I need to go back to the hotel now. I'll see you tomorrow at the house for brunch."

"All right, Lyla, is there anything I can do for you? Do you need to contact a doctor now?"

"No, mother, I think if I just get some rest I'll be OK. I'll see you tomorrow."

The ride back to the hotel was quiet with the exception of the Latin music playing on the car radio. Juliano was back in his element; south Florida was his favorite place to be. He felt at home and sorely missed the streets and surroundings, the music, and the salty air. They arrived at the hotel and walked across the glittering lobby past guests in evening clothes and casual wear.

While they waited for the elevator to arrive, Juliano watched as everyone stared at his wife. He was acutely aware she attracted attention and liked that everyone noticed her. Lyla's demeanor and silence hid her distress feeling anything but beautiful. Her discomfort was from the excruciating stabbing abdominal pain, waves of nausea, and weakness that began at dinner. She couldn't wait to get into the room and undress.

As they rode, alone, in the elevator, Juliano moved close to her. She knew exactly what his intentions were. He didn't care she was in pain. He didn't care about her; he was only thinking about his desires. After all, with every man looking at his wife and wishing they were riding in that elevator with her, he was, and he was going to get what all those other men were wishing they could have.

He ushered Lyla into the room with fanfare, and she slowly walked in, wondering what she could do to stall until she found a way to distract him and avoid what she feared would be the inevitable.

She said. "Why don't you pull the curtain and open the balcony doors to let in the ocean breeze? It's so beautiful tonight. I know how much you love to hear the sound of the ocean."

She was desperate to alter his plans for the evening and hoped he would focus his attention on the view and the ocean long enough for her to think of something else to distract him.

"Hey, Lyla. Why don't you come over here and look at this; it's really beautiful. Nice room, huh? Nothing is too good for my honey."

She hesitated for a moment, afraid to go to him fearing if she didn't it would lead him to coerce her in some violent way if she didn't comply. Lyla slowly walked to the balcony and stopped at the dresser to begin taking off her jewelry.

"Don't bother with that stuff now. Come on over and take a look at this," he said, showing some impatience. He was happy to take in the salty air and feel the wind in his face.

Lyla reluctantly joined him on the balcony and knew how rejection affected him. It caused him to become angry, sullen, vengeful, and cruel. She allowed him to take her in his arms. He began to kiss her softly until his passion grew nearly unbridled. He took her hand, eager to take his prize, and nearly dragged her to the bed. Lyla knew she would have to give in to him, pain and nausea or not. They were her issues; he had totally forgotten about that.

"Juliano, wait just a moment while I slip out of my dress and freshen up; I'll be right back."

He watched Lyla intensely as she moved away from him and into the bathroom. Juliano undressed in eager anticipation of what was to occur. He folded his trousers, hung up his jacket, and let the rest of his clothing drop to the floor. He slithered under the cool, clean sheets, comfortable in his nakedness, and waited for her. He found a local radio station that played soft, mellow, Latin jazz he knew would be conducive to encourage passionate sex and turned the volume low enough to be heard but not distracting. "Ah, perfect," he sighed.

Lyla stepped into the beautifully appointed bathroom and closed the door. The towels were neatly folded, hanging from the ornate, golden towel bar. The pain she had earlier had begun to subside. She searched in her toiletries bag for something to calm the discomfort, and took several pills, hoping they would quickly take effect.

She unzipped her dress as she stared in the mirror with a profound sadness in her eyes and allowed the gown to drop from her shoulders to the floor while she stood still, transfixed. Her eyes reflected her truth. Her furrowed brow accentuated the lines between her eyes. The skillfully applied makeup artistically camouflaged the dark circles under and around her eyes and her long thick black lashes hid her emptiness and agony. Her eyes no longer had the bright enchanting luster, vibrant color, and wide-eyed wonder of her youth. She was alone and afraid of the consequences of rejecting him, and unsure how she would deal with her husband's insatiable desires.

Lyla began to question when the sexual encounters they had in the beginning of their relationship stopped and the coercion began. Although she had been reluctant to accept Juliano's sexual advances since the birth of her second child, she continued to acquiesce until her last child was born. From that time on, she spurned Juliano's advances and requests making excuses of not feeling well. She couldn't stand for him to touch her body, to violate her, as if her body didn't belong to her anymore. She knew he didn't love her, she knew he wasn't being romantic and passionate, he was an animal who used her without compassion.

Against her will, that's what it was, and it was more and more difficult to conceal her true feelings. He succeeding in killing whatever feelings she originally believed she had for him. The act with him was not love making or romantic, it became a duty, an obligation she had to perform to make sure he did not find some way to punish her if she were to say no. Her fear was real. She was so convinced of this that he didn't have to do much to cause her to believe in her fears. Her body was beginning to break down. Things were happening she didn't understand. She was sick, something was very wrong; she had never been weak and physically disabled with pain before.

Lyla's mirror image was not compassionate and did not offer a way for her to escape. The image's voice in her head said, *I understand. I know how you feel and how difficult this is. You will get through this.*

This was not the voice she needed to hear. This was the voice of the child who had been abused by her father and convinced that submission was the only way to survive.

Lyla rinsed her face and prepared herself as she had done so many times in the past. She splashed some perfume on her shoulders and powdered her breasts and body with her perfumed powder. Her trembling fingers picked up her dress and draped it over the towel bar and she covered her body with a robe. She lingered for a moment, took one more look at her reflection, stepped from the bathroom, and turned off the light.

It was obvious he was ready. Juliano's eyes were closed concentrating on the music, as she slowly walked to the other side of the bed. He opened his eyes, pulled aside the sheet to usher her into bed, and she slid in next to him. He took her in his arms and kissed her passionately, running his hands over her smooth skin. He was easily aroused and eager to take his prize concentrating only on bringing the act to a climax. He didn't recognize her as a person, her desire, if she actually had any. She had become an object, a vessel, for him to use to accomplish his physical needs. Once the act was complete and he was gratified, he held her momentarily and then rolled over in satisfied exhaustion. He muttered goodnight and fell into a deep sleep.

Once he was asleep, Lyla crept back to the bathroom. She turned on the shower feeling the warm water and steam fill the air. Her lungs filled with the warmth of the mist, and she breathed deeply, taking long, slow breaths. Her disgust of him and compulsion to wash off his smell and his touch over came her. The water trickled down her face and over her body as small pearl-like tears fell from her eyes.

She didn't scream this time, she never screamed. She didn't fight, she never fought. From the time she suffered the abuse from her father she learned screaming and fighting back accomplished nothing. She learned to remain stoic and withdraw to survive, that whatever happened to her would eventually end, and she would have to go on without support from anyone. So, all her rage, disgust, and horror were pushed into the shadows of her being.

Juliano awoke early the next morning, anticipating another one of his lovemaking sessions and was surprised to see Lyla in the other bed.

Juliano moved into Lyla's bed to wake her with his passion, eager to have more. Again, he took her to him, and she acquiesced to his demands knowing he would end quickly and would leave her alone.

"I can't help it," he whispered to her. "I just can't help I'm so attracted to you; I can't keep my hands off you. You're so great in bed, and you feel so good."

Lyla remained silent and still although what she wanted to do was scream and run out of the room far away from him. Juliano leapt out of bed feeling re-energized and invited Lyla to go for a morning swim. The day was sunny and beautiful, and he couldn't resist. Lyla didn't move. It took all her strength not to reveal her real feelings of disgust and despair.

"No thanks, Juliano. I think I'll just lounge up here in the room and take a nice long bath while I have the chance. I'll order up some things to nibble on and have them here by the time you come back."

"Great idea, I won't be long. You think of everything," he said. He put on his bathing suit, bathrobe, and beach shoes, and was out the door.

Once Juliano was out of the room, Lyla immediately got out of bed, washed, showered, and got dressed. She hurriedly packed her clothing and accessories and was ready to go. Room service knocked on the door and delivered a luscious breakfast of fresh fruit, croissants, strong coffee and juice. Juliano returned from his swim and joined Lyla on the terrace for breakfast. Lyla reminded him they needed to be at her aunt's house for brunch.

"You go to your aunt's house. I'll stay here. Better yet, why don't you stay here with me? I'm really not in the mood for more of your family, particularly your mother."

Lyla knew Juliano was not comfortable around any of her family, her mother in particular. She worked hard to keep peace between Juliano and her parents. Being in the middle of people who detested one another was a constant strain. Juliano never wanted to hear anything about Lyla's parents. He resented anything they gave to Lyla and was always trying to prove he was worthy and able to provide.

Whenever Sura came to visit Lyla and the children, which was not often, Juliano was civil and Sura was polite. She stayed at a hotel not far from their house and Lyla had to wait until Juliano left for the day before she could pick her up. He often chose not to come home for dinner and when he did the tension in the house was palpable. Sura would try to converse at dinner if Juliano was there.

"Well, Juliano," Sura would begin, "How were things at work today? I guess this is probably a busy time of the year. Lyla tells me you work with many of the famous sports figures. What's that like?"

"Sura," Juliano answered. "I didn't know you had an interest in athletes or followed any kind of sporting event. Yes, I do have an occasion to work with some famous and not so famous people, that's the nature of the business."

"Okay," Lyla would interject. "Is anybody ready for desert and then a stroll around the neighborhood to walk off dinner?"

Lyla tried to ignore his remarks and reminded Juliano he needed to shower. He grudgingly went into the bathroom, turned on the shower, and stepped in.

Rejection, would there be consequences?

Lyla saw her opportunity to escape and poked her head far enough through the bathroom door for him to hear her. "I'll see you downstairs near the valet as soon as you're ready. In the meantime, I'll do a bit of window shopping. Don't be long." She closed the bathroom door, picked up her bags and walked as fast as she could to the elevator.

It was a short automobile ride to her aunt and uncle's home. It was just down the street over the canal, past the hospital and down Alton to N Bay Road. She'd driven these roads so many times when she lived there, and it was comforting to return to a place that was like home. The house was packed with guests from the night before. Everyone had gathered at her aunt and uncle's house to enjoy each other's company, eat, and visit until they couldn't eat or visit any more.

Upon their arrival to the house, Juliano parked the car in the last available space of the driveway. Lyla got out and walked into the house carrying her luggage past several guests and went directly into her cousin's old bedroom. The room hadn't changed. The oversized twin beds with the pale lilac fabric tufted headboards were neatly made with the large rolled bolster pillows standing against the headboards. The chaise with matching fabric sat under the bank of tall windows reminding her of the times she and her cousin talked through the night. The same TV was perched on the rod iron stand between the lounge and the French styled dresser topped with oversized frame mirrors gilded in gold. The drapes were pulled back to the side wall and the wooden window shutters were open showering the room with bright daylight.

Lyla looked wistfully at the room that was filled with memories and felt safe and comfortable. Lyla and her cousin shared secrets and caring times together especially when her cousin's parents were away on an extended Asian tour one summer. Lyla and her cousin became inseparable that summer. They spent long summer days swimming in the pool, sun bathing on the dock, and fishing for fresh fish for dinner. Lyla made beer battered fish and her cousin made her famous key lime pie. Lyla unpacked, feeling a rush of nostalgic memories of their happy, carefree youth, wanting somehow to go back to those times.

Lyla walked from the bedroom wing to the main foyer. She crossed through the formal living room into the crowded Florida room. Along the way, she was greeted by family members and others she had known since she was a little girl. Glass sliding doors from ceiling to floor extended for 40 feet across the rear of the Florida room, framing the view of the bay and the Julia Tuttle Causeway Bridge. The water on the bay was still, like glass. The sky was clear and blue with puffy white clouds so distinctive of a south Florida sky.

Juliano was being held hostage by one of her aunt's friends in front of the buffet that displayed the salads and smoked fish. The black and red caviar was piled high on top of two different mounds of finely chopped egg salad surrounded by gourmet crackers. The smoked salmon and white fish were plated to one side accompanied by enough creamed herring and sour cream for one to swim in.

Juliano motioned to Lyla to come over, wanting to be rescued from the old woman's clutches. Lyla dutifully joined him and gave him an excuse to move on. Juliano went to the bar for a drink and Lyla made her apologies and looked for her mother. Sura was on the other side of the room near a mountain of fresh fruit that was cascading from multiple containers. Lyla observed how beautiful her mother looked that day. She was dressed in an aqua and white Lilly Pulitzer floral print sundress that complimented her bright blue eyes and fully feminine form. The off-the shoulder dress flared out from the cinched waist to a full skirt that swung gracefully when she walked.

Lyla was apprehensive about an in-hospital procedure scheduled for the next morning that was necessary to determine a diagnosis. The test had been scheduled in Miami Beach as a second opinion so Lyla could be close to her family during her time of uncertainty and anxiety regarding her health. Lyla sought out her mother to make sure they had coordinated efforts about details for the next day. She surveyed the Florida room from her buffet vantage point and saw her mother chatting with a tall dark-haired man and a woman; they appeared to be a couple. Lyla walked toward her mother and tried to get her attention.

"Lyla," Sura beckoned with her jeweled hand. "Come, I want you to meet someone; I've been talking about you. You looked so lovely last night; it was unfortunate you had to leave so early. How are you feeling today?"

Sura's eagerness to tell Lyla all she had discovered about her new acquaintances contrasted Lyla's obvious impatience and discomfort. Sura spoke to Lyla.

"We share so many things in common I'm surprised we've not somehow bumped into each other sooner. It turns out we've been playing a bit of Jewish geography and have discovered Alex's mother, Ethel, has a home in Palm Beach, and we're both members of the Hibel Society." She continued. "Lyla, I'd like you to meet a lovely couple, Alex and Annie Blum. They're both teachers, lovely people."

Alex stood almost six feet tall and was lanky with a shock of jet black hair and warm brown eyes. His smile was boyish and full of mischief. Lyla reached out her hand to Alex and felt a spark as they shook hands. Lyla withdrew her hand quickly not understanding what happened. She then clasped his wife, Annie's, hand and felt great warmth and comfort as though Annie was an old friend.

Lyla spoke hoping she didn't show her extreme anxiety. "How lovely it is to meet you both. Do you live here?"

Annie responded with a warm smile. "No, we're just here for a visit, and we're having a wonderful time. Miami Beach is such a beautiful place. We've enjoyed the weekend immensely." Her face was bright and her hazel eyes were soft and gentle.

"Yes," echoed Alex. "We're so glad we could make it for the party. We're both teachers and so lucky to get the time to attend."

Lyla could no longer contain herself, she interrupted Alex. "Excuse me, I don't mean to interrupt," Lyla said, "but Mother I need to speak to you for a moment … now."

Just as Lyla and Sura were walking away, Juliano walked up to them and announced he was leaving Miami Beach and returning home. Lyla, with wide-eyed terror, was barely able to speak as tears began to roll down her cheek.

"What do you mean you're leaving? I thought, well, I thought you were going to be with me, take me…You're leaving? Why are you leaving now? You know I have that horrible test at the hospital tomorrow; how can you leave now?"

"Excuse us Sura," Juliano said as he took Lyla's arm and walked her hurriedly out to the car. Lyla did her best to keep up with his long strides but felt she was being dragged like a child.

"What's the matter with you Juliano? Why are you in such a rush? And why aren't you staying tomorrow? You know I'm having that horrible…"

"The test," he mumbled; he had forgotten. "I have to get back. I'm very busy and can't stay away any longer. Besides, I would think you would want me to get back to check on the children."

"You know the children are well cared for. It's me who needs you now, Juliano."

Juliano hesitated as though he were giving it thought and then replied, "I'm leaving, and you've got your family." Lyla reached for his hand. He pulled away from her.

"Let me go. I've got to go check out so I'm not charged another day for the room. I'll see you when you get back home."

Juliano gave her a quick kiss on the cheek, hopped into the car, and hastily exited the driveway. Lyla stood there in disbelief. "He left," she said to herself. "He left me when I needed him. He left me … where is he when I need him?"

Lyla slowly walked from the street, back up the driveway through the oversized double front doors, and into the house. Sura saw Lyla's facial expression and body language and knew immediately that Lyla was in distress. As Lyla came closer, Sura was hesitant to make an inquiry concerned she might be making matters worse. "Lyla, did you want to talk to me earlier?"

"No ... yes ... no, maybe ... well, Juliano's not staying. He's going back now."

Sura took Lyla's hand and led her back to the bedroom where they could have privacy.

"It's all right, Lyla," Sura said in a reassuring voice. "It's all right, Lyla. I'm here for you, and so is the rest of the family. I'll take care of you. I'll be there for you."

Lyla remained unaware that her family had always been her sole source of support. She never understood or recognized this fact before. Did she, could she, now?

Lyla and Sura were up early the next morning for the test, the ERCP. The sun was shining and the air was warm when they arrived at the hospital by 8 am to meet with several of Lyla's cousins who were there for support. When the time came for Lyla to be prepped for the ERCP, Sura reassured Lyla she would be there waiting for her to wake up from the anesthesia and not to worry.

Lyla was prepped and the IV drip was started to put her to sleep. The procedure revealed a significantly distended gall bladder filled with sludge. Unanticipated complications arose. Lyla was not given enough drugs to keep her asleep during the entire test. She suddenly awoke, on a cold stainless table being flopped onto her belly like a flipped pancake. She tried to scream but couldn't, she had been intubated. She began to flail about with her hands and arms, was drugged again, and the test continued to its conclusion. Lyla couldn't wake up on her own after the extra dose of drugs and was administered another drug to help her become conscious.

When Lyla woke up, she could barely stand or walk, she was experiencing excruciating pain in her abdomen, and couldn't stop throwing up. When Lyla and Sura went to the doctor's office to discuss the results Lyla slumped over in the chair and the doctor called to have Lyla immediately admitted to the hospital. The doctor tried to reassure Sura that his patients did not usually have this type of reaction to the procedure. Sura didn't accept the explanation and ordered the doctor to call her nephew immediately and apprise him of the situation. "Tell my nephew to find me when Lyla is taken to her room."

Sura took Lyla to admitting in the wheelchair and then to her room. Her cousin's husband, a surgeon, explained to Sura that Lyla would be sedated for pain and surgery would be scheduled for early the next morning to remove Lyla's gall bladder.

Lyla remained in Mount Sinai Hospital, on the 8th floor for several days, recovering from the surgery. She was in a VIP room attended by the nursing staff. Lyla's cousin's husband came to check on her every morning during his morning rounds and Sura was there every afternoon for tea time.

Lyla completed her recovery and recuperation at her cousin's house. It was a long and painful recovery with drainage tubes still in place. After the final tubing was removed and Lyla was feeling stronger Sura announced the time had come to SHOP. Sura, Lyla, Lyla's aunt and cousins met at the Bal Harbour Shoppes. Sura always said nothing made a woman feel better than a day of lunch and shopping. Everyone decided that Lyla needed a "make over" and Sura made an appointment at Saks' cosmetic counter for Lyla to have a guest make-up artist give her "the works."

Not once during Lyla's recovery did she ask about Juliano and not once did Juliano make any inquiries about her, her condition, or when she anticipated returning home. Several days after the shopping spree Lyla was so disappointed that Juliano never called to find out about her. She decided to call his office and was told by the operator that Juliano no longer worked there and no one knew how to reach him. Lyla called the sitter and asked if she knew where he was and the sitter didn't know. Lyla was scared and confused and tried to hide her concerns. How was she going to tell her mother? What should she tell her? What was happening to her life?

When Lyla was able to travel, Sura accompanied Lyla home. Lyla left messages with the sitter with the arrival day and time. The plan was for Sura to stay with Lyla until Lyla was strong enough to take care of herself and the children. Juliano dutifully showed up at the airport and the ride back home was quiet. Sura could feel the unspoken tension between Lyla and Juliano but did not interfere. He barely acknowledged Lyla, was distant, and dutifully polite to Sura. He was not acting like a husband whose wife had been through the trauma of surgery and was gone for almost four weeks.

The children were ecstatic to see Lyla with the exception of the baby. He was a year and a half and screamed every time he saw Lyla. He was traumatized by her absence and refused to allow Lyla to touch him. Lyla was heartbroken by his pain and confusion and didn't know how to re-assure him and reestablish a connection with him. Sura took over and began to cuddle the baby and cradle him. Sura cooed to him and stroked him until he finally calmed down and Lyla was able to re-establish the bond between mother and child once again.

Sura bathed and prepared all the children for bed while Lyla rested. When they were ready for bed they all cuddled around Lyla in her bed for her to read them a story. Lyla and Sura were equally exhausted after the trip and soon after retired to bed. Lyla had no chance to ask Juliano what had happened with his job.

Although Lyla was relieved to be home in her own bed with her children around her, it was several weeks before Lyla recovered enough to care of herself and her children. Sura's farewell was tearful and anxious. Neither Sura or Lyla was able to share the fears and anxieties plaguing them. They had fears about Lyla's health, the care of the children, and the marriage on the precipice of collapse.

Lyla approached Juliano one evening anxious about the status of his job. Juliano spoke to her with an offhanded attitude. "Look, there were problems at work, the guy who owned the company took a lot of money and left the country."

"What has that got to do with you getting fired? And if he did leave the country with all the money why was someone answering the phone telling me you were fired?"

"I told you," he said in an irritated voice, the owner stole a whole bunch of money I got from the bank as a line of credit and split the country and now no one knows where he is or the money. That's it dot period. I don't need an inquisition here."

"Does that mean you are responsible for the money you got and he stole?"

Juliano didn't respond.

"OK, Lyla said, if you aren't working there will you be working some-where else?"

"I don't know," he said. "I haven't made any definite plans yet. I'm working on something I'll let you know. There's a game on I want to watch. Is there anything else you want to know?"

The tone of his voice was enough to keep Lyla quiet.

MORE COMPLICATIONS, WHAT ELSE COULD GO WRONG?

Lyla said nothing to Juliano or anyone else about residual issues she continued to have after the gall bladder surgery. She felt weak, dehydrated, lost weight, and was spending hours in the bathroom. When Lyla called her cousin in Miami Beach about her symptoms, Lyla was advised to go to a gastroenterologist immediately. Lyla chose someone at random who was a provider in their insurance network. Lyla was diagnosed with ulcerative colitis and was scheduled to undergo a sigmoidoscopy in the doctor's office. When Lyla was prepped and asked to lie down on the cold, metal examining table, the nurse explained to Lyla what would happen. Lyla's heart began to beat wildly and her anxiety skyrocketed.

"Wait a minute, now," Lyla said to the nurse. This can't be right. You said the doctor's going to stick a tube where? And it's going there without any anesthetic of any kind? I'm going to be awake for that?"

The doctor entered the room with a big smile on his face. Lyla thought to herself, *I don't see anything here for anyone to be smiling about.*

"Hello, Lyla," said the doctor with his big friendly smile. "How are you?"

"Well, doctor, I'm not so sure I'm OK. I understand this is going to be done without any kind of numbing or calming medication and I'm concerned because I'm so inflamed and I'm already in a lot of pain."

The doctor patted her on her hip as he stood over her and reassured her this was a procedure that would not be painful, he'd done lots of these before.

"Now, then let's get started. Nurse, would you please assist me?"

The nurse instructed Lyla to roll onto her left side and the procedure began. The flexible tube was inserted into her and snaked through her colon. The excruciating pain felt like she was on fire. She grabbed the edge of the table with her right hand and tried to bury her head in the crook of her arm. She closed her eyes and tried to focus on something other than the burning pain inside of her and could not.

"Stop, please stop," she begged the doctor. I can't stand this anymore. I don't care what else you have to do."

He ignored her pleas and sobs.

"Just a little bit farther, just a little more and it will all be over," he said.

"No, No, No, you have to stop now, I can't take it anymore." She began to scream and tried to pull herself off the table with her right hand. "Stop, stop, I'm begging you to stop."

Lyla was beginning to hyperventilate and felt faint. That's when the doctor began to withdraw the tubing. It was just as painful being withdrawn as it was going in.

Stupid doctor, she thought.

"OK," said the doctor, it's all over now. You can get up and get dressed. The nurse will come in to help you."

The doctor exited the room and left Lyla slumped over the edge of the cold table weeping.

"Are you all right?" asked the nurse. "Mrs. Masselli, I'm asking you, are you all right? Open your eyes please and answer me."

Lyla slowly opened her teary eyes and looked at the nurse.

"OK, that's good." In a cheery voice the nurse gave Lyla instructions. "Now, let me help you sit up for a moment. You need to swing your legs over the side of the table. There we go, that's great. Now, just sit here for a moment and I'll help you get down."

Lyla began to make soft moaning sounds. "There's something wrong with me. I'm cramping, I'm bloated, and feel like I'm going to explode."

"Oh, that's normal," said the nurse. That will pass and it will feel like gas. Let's get you to the next room where you can dress and go to the bathroom."

Lyla was given her clothes and insisted on dressing herself and being given privacy. When the nurse left the room, Lyla fell onto the waiting chair. Her hands were shaking so badly she could barely get dressed. She was bleeding, cramping with a swollen belly and was nauseated.

She needed to get home.

Lyla dragged herself from the room to the reception area toward the office door. A young receptionist asked, "Well, I hope your procedure went well. Would you like to make a follow up appointment?"

"No, not now."

"All right then," the receptionist said in her stupid cheery voice. "The doctor wants you to have this prescription filled. And remember to call back and make a follow up appointment. Have a good day."

Lyla never looked back and walked out of the office door to the elevator. No matter how she felt, she had to act like she was ok. Falling apart would prolong the time it took her to get to her car. She stepped into the elevator and leaned on the wall to keep from falling down. The elevator went down to the first floor and Lyla slowly walked out the front door of the building to her car parked nearby. The bright sun filled her face with warmth and bathed her shivering body. She reached her car, got in, and sat there in the warmth of the car's interior. Tears were streaming down her face while she tried to calm down and will the pain to subside.

The doctor prescribed Prednisone, a steroid medication her cousin had warned her about. Lyla followed the label instructions and began to feel like she was losing her mind. She was easily upset, nervous, moody, and couldn't sleep. She told her cousin the doctor's diagnosis, ulcerative colitis, and the medication he prescribed. Her cousin sent Lyla books and pamphlets from the Crohn's Colitis Foundation to learn and understand how to live with the disease.

Lyla made a follow-up appointment and was determined to confront the doctor and request he prescribe something else. The doctor entered the exam room with a cheery smile on his face and extended an outstretched hand. Lyla dutifully shook his hand and when the doctor asked how she was doing she responded with the truth.

"To tell you the truth, doctor, I'm not doing very well. I feel like I'm going crazy. I nearly had an accident on the way here, I'm screaming at the kids and the dogs and I can't get my hands to stop shaking. I am requesting that you take me off the prednisone and give me something else. I have read these books here and have spoken to my cousin who also has ulcerative colitis and is married to a physician that..."

"You did what?" the doctor interrupted.

"I read these books," Lyla said looking at him like it was a stupid question. "I read these books and pamphlets about ulcerative colitis and…"

The doctor interrupted again. "Why are you questioning me and what I prescribed for you? Exactly, who do you think you are to question me?"

Lyla began, "but doctor, it says here and I've talked…" he interrupted again.

"I don't care who you talked to and what you read; you shouldn't be reading that anyway. You have to do what I tell you to do."

"I would," Lyla said standing up to face the doctor. "I would if I felt that it was the right thing to do and if I wasn't so miserable taking the drug. But this doesn't feel right."

The doctor's face got red and he began to yell at Lyla. "If you don't want to do what I tell you to do you can go see someone else."

Lyla was afraid to finish the confrontation and be dismissed by him as her doctor. Lyla backed down, apologized for her outburst, and sat down submissively.

"Lyla," he said condescendingly, all you have to do is trust me and do what I tell you and everything will be fine.

Lyla walked out of the office no better than when she walked in. She didn't have any new medication and had already decided that she was not going to continue taking the poison. It caused more problems than it helped. She also decided that she would not return to this doctor.

Visits to doctor's offices, painful procedures, hospital admissions, and surgeries dominated Lyla's life. She had inconsistent or no support from Juliano emotionally or physically. He was either too busy, wasn't interested, or just didn't want to know. The burden of her bad health and the responsibility of the children were carried by Lyla alone.

Lyla's health deteriorated without proper care from a physician. She was having difficulty taking care of the children. She got progressively weaker from dehydration and pain. She bathed and put to bed the two youngest but was unable to take care of the other two who were five and seven. She prepared the bath for them and then sat on the floor next to the tub and watched as they bathed themselves and played in the tub. The boys were tucked into bed with their books. There would be no story from Lyla that night.

Lyla had no strength left to take care of herself and collapsed into bed. She was unable to take care of the boys the next morning, the seven-year-old was in charge. Lyla called her cousin in Miami Beach and Sura. Her cousin arranged an appointment for Lyla with the doctor who was head of the Crohn's and Colitis Foundation in Tampa. Lyla explained to Sura what happened and that she could no longer take care of the children. Lyla was afraid she was going to die.

"Please mother," Lyla cried. "Please, take care of my children; take my children, please. Don't leave them here with Juliano. Something's very wrong with me and I'm afraid."

Sura answered. "I'm on my way Lyla, don't worry about the children. I'll be there as soon as I can catch the next flight out."

"Mother, listen to me, listen to me. I'm not going anywhere until I know my children are safe with you. Do you hear me, mother?"

"You're not going anywhere Lyla, I'm coming to you, I will be there."

Sura arrived in Tampa later that afternoon at the house to find the children unsupervised and Lyla barely conscious in bed. Sura took over, took care of the children, and then Lyla. The doctor's appointment was scheduled for early the next morning.

Where was Juliano?

When Sura and Lyla arrived at the doctor's office, Lyla could barely walk from the car to the office. Sura helped Lyla onto the exam table in the exam room and was so weak she couldn't sit up. When the doctor arrived Sura introduced herself and brought the doctor up to date on Lyla's medical history.

The doctor was an older gentleman with a soft, gentle voice and kind eyes. When the exam was complete the doctor asked Sura to step outside the room so they could talk.

"Sura," the doctor began. "I want you to understand that Lyla must be admitted to the hospital immediately. The dehydration alone is serious let alone the other issues that are occurring. I want you to take her to the hospital now and get her settled. I will schedule some tests for tomorrow and make suggestions how best to proceed."

Sura returned to the room, Lyla was very still and pale. Sura stroked her hair and whispered. "Don't worry Lyla. I'll take care of you and get you the help you need. We'll be going directly to the hospital. Don't worry about the children, I will take care of them as well."

Once again, Sura went through the admission process with Lyla. When they reached the room, Sura helped Lyla change into a hospital gown. The nurse assured Sura the doctor had already called in orders for Lyla.

Lyla reached for Sura's hand. "Mother," Lyla whispered in a weakened voice. "Mother, please, my children."

"Everything will be fine, Lyla, I'm here now, I will take care of the children, I promise."

Sura then left and the nurses began to prep Lyla for the IV and ordered medications.

Lyla was hospitalized for three weeks. Sura remained in Florida until Lyla returned home and was able to care for herself and the children. Lyla slowly recovered under the care of her physician and began to wonder about Juliano, a job, income, and bills.

One evening when the children were safely tucked into bed Lyla entered the master bedroom to find Juliano engrossed in a televised sporting event. She hesitated to interrupt him during one of his programs.

"So, Juliano, what's happening? Anything new, interesting, whatever?"

Juliano gave her a story about having another job but the new company he was working for either fell to pieces or was swallowed up by another company. The bottom line was that he was jobless and broke and responsible for IRS debts incurred by the company that supposedly no longer existed.

"Where have you been all this time if you weren't working? Have you been paying the bills? How did my mother pay for all the food for the children?"

Juliano barely acknowledged her and stayed focused on the television screen. "Listen, Lyla, I'm taking care of things. I've got an interview at a dealership this week and will have a job by the end of the week. Stop worrying."

End of conversation. Juliano neglected to tell her everything.

Lyla was having one of "those days" when nothing seemed to go right. Her guts were working overtime and she was having cramping and backpain. She barely slept the night before and she couldn't shake the uneasy feeling of impending disaster. It was 9:00 am and she was still wearing her nightgown and ragged bathrobe. She couldn't even re- member if she brushed her teeth and she knew for sure she hadn't brushed her hair. The robe was old and comfortable but was threadbare. One of the loops for the cloth belt had torn off, she couldn't remember how, and the other loop was only attached on one end and was hanging on by a thread, much like how she felt. Her slippers were terry scuffs that made that slap slap sound as she walked or actually slid across the floor and needed to be washed. They too had seen better days.

She didn't have the luxury of giving in to anxiety or pain. Laundry had to be done, the house cleaned, and the children cared for. She as- sembled snacks of dry cheerios, hard-boiled egg mixed with cottage cheese and crackers to munch on for her youngest as he sat in his high- chair in the kitchen. She then slapped her way into the laundry room to put her third load in the washing machine, took dry clothes out of the dryer, and dumped them into a large basket to fold. She sat the basket on one of the chairs at the table to monitor her youngest as he tossed cheerios off the tray to feed the dogs. Another routine day in her household.

As Lyla quietly folded the little pieces of clothing, her thoughts turned to the reality of her life and she became more upset. She thought, *here I am still in my bathrobe, not showered, taking care of everyone else. I feel like some pack of dogs has been dragging me around a junkyard and I'm falling to pieces.*

Her thoughts and her task were interrupted by the front door bell. She took her little boy out of the highchair, slung him onto her left hip, and went to answer the front door. A plain looking woman in a dark frayed suit stood in front of her. She held up a small card as she intro- duced herself to Lyla.

"Hello, I am agent Gardner from the IRS, here's my card," as she flashed a small paper card in front of Lyla's face. "I need to gain entrance to your home. May I come in?"

"Entrance to my home?" Lyla answered. "What do you mean?"

"I said, I need to come into your home and take inventory of all your property."

"Uh, what for?" Lyla wasn't going to let some strange person into the house she didn't care who this person said she was.

"Well, you see, Mrs. Masselli, if you don't cooperate and let me in to make this inventory, I'll go back to my office and have your husband arrested. I have no qualms about doing that."

Lyla stared at the agent in disbelief with her child slowly sagging on her hip. The agent waited for a response and when she didn't get one from Lyla, turned around and walked to her car that was parked in Lyla's driveway.

Lyla ran after her with the baby bouncing up and down on her hip dragging the broken belt from her bathrobe. "Wait, wait, please wait Miss...Miss... I'm so sorry if I have offended you but I just can't allow some stranger to come into the house without warning. I think you have been quick to judgment and would appreciate some understanding or at least an opportunity to resolve this in another way. What has to be done here to work things out? I don't even know why you're here."

The agent looked at Lyla and began to realize that it might be possible that Lyla was not complicit in her husband's actions.

"All right, Mrs. Masselli. I'll give you a chance to work things out. Be at the IRS office downtown on this date with your husband. An agent will meet with you regarding your debts and how this debt to the IRS will be repaid. If you miss the scheduled meeting, I will issue an arrest warrant for your husband. Is that understood?"

"Yes, quite," said Lyla. "Thank you for giving me this chance, I appreciate it."

The agent left and Lyla went into the house shaking. She put the baby down in the playroom with the other children and picked up the folded clothes and put them in the children's rooms. The phone rang as she left the baby's room. *What now*, she thought. She picked up the call in her bedroom. The man's voice on the other end identified himself as a representative from the mortgage company. Her heart began to race and she began to shake.

"I'm calling to advise you that you are three months in arrears in your mortgage payments. When are you going to make the next payment?"

Lyla was unable to speak.

"Mrs. Masselli, did you hear me? When are you going to make your mortgage payment?"

"Uh, yes sir, yes. You see, I know we can make a payment, my husband is trying to get the money. Can we have a little more time?"

"Look. You need to put that house on the market or make payments right away. If you don't make a payment and it's not on the market, I'm going to issue a notice to the sheriff and you will be evicted."

As Lyla listened to the man, she stared out the bedroom window at the sycamore tree in the yard wondering what was going to happen to her and her children. She whispered into the phone. "Please sir," Lyla begged again, "please don't take the house, please just give us a little more time; I'm certain things will be better."

"You have one month and that's it. If you're not caught up in payments and/or the house is not on the market, you'll have to leave. I will follow through, believe me, I'll send out the sheriff and lock you and your possessions out."

Lyla was stunned into silence; she was going to be homeless. The phone call was more than a warning to Lyla and she wondered if she was the only one in the marriage who was concerned about what was about to happen.

Juliano refused to talk to the mortgage company, put the house on the market, or consider a way to find his family a home. He was determined to stay in the house he had designed and built. The memories of the home and the life they had planned and built were lost and rapidly faded along with many of Lyla's personal items left behind when the sheriff locked them out.

For the next six months they lived like gypsies moving from one temporary rental home to another until finally Lyla found a little grey house in a development near citrus groves where she could safely settle her tribe. It was Lyla's determination and resilience that kept the family from totally disintegrating.

Again, a rented moving truck packed up and then unloaded their boxes and furniture to the citrus grove house. This one was small so many of the boxes remained in the garage unopened. Lyla unpacked things important to the children and necessary for daily life. She jammed as much as she could inside cabinets and closets and nestled her boys, the youngest in pre-school, into their rooms with all their precious objects.

Juliano decided it was best to declare bankruptcy, wipe out whatever debts could not be paid from his salary, and start over. Lyla was mortified by Juliano's use of legal maneuvers to avoid the responsibility of debt. The shame and embarrassment drove her farther away from her family.

Lyla's health became a mirror of her marriage reflecting the issues that caused her to remain stressed and anxious. The colitis became unmanageable and the doctor threatened to put her back in the hospital for an extended stay. It was in December of their first year in the little grey house near the groves when Lyla was at her worst with the disease. She refused to go back to the hospital and convinced the doctor she could be cared for at home with home health care. He ordered IV medication and Lyla was followed by nursing personnel who came to the house on a regular basis. The steroids had an ameliorative effect on her symptoms but never got her into a place of sustained remission. Eventually the IV medication was stopped and Lyla was given one last chance to improve with oral medication. It didn't work.

Lyla was called into the doctor's office to discuss her options. She was alone. The doctor walked into the exam room. He picked up Lyla's hand and cupped it in both of his hands to give Lyla some reassurance.

"Hello Lyla, how are you doing? We need to talk about your progress and discuss your options for treatment of the disease."

It doesn't sound like this visit is off to a good start, Lyla thought. She smiled a weak smile and the doctor continued.

"It would seem," he said, that you're unable to be weaned from the steroid and without it your symptoms are unmanageable. To date, we've tried every medication on the market and in trials and you have been unresponsive. The only other option we have is surgery. The procedure I'm referencing is radical but by removing the diseased portion of your intestines you can be free of the disease and medication. There's only one surgeon here doing this procedure and I've made a referral for you. Please make an appointment, you must bring your husband. Lyla left the doctor's office numb and frightened. How would she convince Juliano to go with her?

After a doctor's visit, the only place Lyla felt comfortable was sitting in the warmth of the car's interior that had been baked by the sun. The seat comforted Lyla's thin body and helped her recover from the chills from the doctor's cold office. The doctor's words continued to echo in her mind: intractable, medically unresponsive, radical surgery. *My God,* she thought, *I'm going to be butchered.*

It was nearly time to pick up her youngest at preschool. She slowly drove down the street, turned into the grass lot, and entered the carpool line. She opened the car windows to feel the warm breeze, turned off her engine, and watched her son playing with the other children. The sound of the children's voices and laughter lifted her mood. *Ah, thank God,* she thought, *he's been behaving, he's not on the naughty bench having time out today.*

Lyla said nothing to Juliano that night about her doctor visit. She was tired and he was not in the mood to hear anything. He was tired and grumpy and immediately began to complain about some customer and his boss. Lyla knew she would have to wait to tell him. After several days, Juliano took a morning off and Lyla tried to tell him about her doctor visit.

"I know you would prefer not to go with me but my doctor insisted. Would you mind?"

"Just make the appointment when I don't have to take too much time off work."

"Well, when would that be?"

"I don't know, just tell me the day and time and I'll meet you there. Are we done with this?"

"Yes, yes, we're done with this. I'll let you know as soon as I..."

He left the room and turned on the television, blaring sports scores.

Lyla called the doctor's office to make the appointment. "Yes, thank you, not a problem, I think that'll be fine. Do you know about how long the appointment will take? You see, my husband is coming with me and will have to leave work and..."

"Don't worry Mrs. Masselli, the doctor won't make you wait too long. I really don't know exactly what will be involved."

"OK, yes, I understand. I was just wondering."

Lyla's voice trailed off knowing she would not have the answer she needed and hoped Juliano wouldn't give her a hard time and become inpatient at being kept waiting.

The surgeon's office was like all the other doctor offices she had been to. The room was cold, uninviting, and sparsely furnished with uncomfortable chairs. Small tables were scattered around the room littered with old magazines that Lyla had no interest in reading. Juliano immediately picked up a copy of Sports Illustrated.

After a short wait Lyla and Juliano were called into the exam room. Her vitals were taken by the nurse and they waited for the doctor. Lyla was familiar with exam rooms, she knew them all. They were all the same filled with instruments, cotton balls, a sink, exam gloves, lubricant, and the walls were covered with pictures of internal and external body parts.

She and Juliano did not speak. Her mind was occupied by the room's interior and her fears of what the doctor had to say and Juliano's mind was, well, she had no idea what he was thinking. The doctor knocked on the door, entered the room, and introduced himself to Juliano. He read Lyla's chart and the reports.

"Hm, very interesting," he said. "Unresponsive, unable to be weaned, and an issue here in the pathology report, dysplasia. Do you understand what that means?"

Juliano and Lyla looked at the doctor with surprise.

"It is a general term that means there has been abnormal growth and development of cells or tissue. This often occurs with chronic inflammation and you certainly have that environment in your gut. The grade of dysplasia is very concerning with a good possibility of cancer."

The doctor handed Juliano and Lyla pamphlets explaining the surgery he was about to recommend. He continued, "I'll give you a few minutes to read these pamphlets and then return so we can discuss this further."

Lyla began reading the pamphlet trying to understand. Juliano took charge and immediately decided that surgery was her best option.

"Lyla, listen to me."

"I'm reading," she said, "I'm trying to understand all this, just a minute. You haven't read the pamphlet, Juliano. You don't know what it has to say and what the surgery involves. Do you know what that doctor is going to do to me?"

"No, I haven't read the pamphlet, but I'm trying to tell you this is something that has to be done. The doctor says you have cancer in your gut and it has to be removed. It makes sense."

"But, Juliano, the surgery is a big deal, he's going to take..."

"Let's not talk about that now. We need to focus on what will make you better."

Lyla sank back into her chair and said nothing else. The doctor walked in and Juliano told him they both agreed to the surgery. The doctor took them to the office manager who booked the surgery date and time according to Juliano's and the doctor's schedules. No one asked Lyla. She sat there without contributing, listening to them schedule her butchery at their convenience. Once they concluded their business, Juliano and the doctor chatted about football and cars, the doctor loved cars and Juliano was obsessed with sports.

Lyla sat her little band of boys down at the kitchen table and explained she was sick and needed to have an operation to make her better. Fear showed in their faces, they were speechless. Their mother was sick and leaving them again, and they had no idea when or if she would return.

Juliano was at the hospital on the day of surgery. He made no inquiries, no attempt to visit, send flowers or cards during Lyla's hospital recovery. His office was five minutes from the hospital but he never returned until the day of her discharge. Instead, he scheduled time off work to take the children on vacation.

Recovery from surgery was long and painful but Lyla was determined to regain her strength. Juliano's presence and support was nonexistent and their relationship became distant. He occasionally made inquiries about how she was feeling but Lyla believed these were either polite inquiries or interest in determining if she was able to have sex. The better she got, the more often he asked until one night he asked her.

"Hey Lyla, looks like you're feeling much better, how about we mess around?"

She looked at him and curled her upper lip in disgust. Her body was ugly, swollen with a large red scar from under her breasts to her bikini line. She had an ostomy bag hanging on her side with a piece of her intestine sticking out, and sex was the very last thing on her mind.

Juliano must have been able to read her mind or was excellent at reading her facial language. "Don't worry, honey," he said. That bag doesn't bother me. It's been so long, I really want you."

"Please Juliano, not now, not like this. Please. After the next surgery is done and the bag is gone, then..."

"I understand," he said. "Sure, not a problem. I'll wait."

He rolled over and went to sleep. Lyla curled up on her side of the bed, thankful she was able to convince him, this time. Although Lyla suffered complications, had to drive herself to the hospital emergency room for an obstruction, and additional surgery, she finally began to gain strength. The boys became dedicated helpers. They dragged their laundry baskets into the laundry room, separated their darks and lights and threw everything into the washing machine. They ended up with a lot of grey socks and underwear but at least clothes were clean.

For months Lyla was unable to move beyond depression and reasoned she couldn't continue to live without support. Juliano's only interest was in having sex. She knew she couldn't take care of the boys and herself the way she was but she couldn't live with a man who had no empathy or compassion for her either. One evening when she was particularly melancholy, she summoned the courage to tell Juliano how she felt. Her desperation for change and a release from the emotional pain drove her to speak. The children were asleep and Juliano had not retired for the night.

"Juliano, I need to talk to you. I need support in my recovery and in my life."

He was standing half way in the bedroom doorway when Lyla began to speak. He turned around to face her and walked toward the bed standing over her with a confused expression on his face.

Where was she going with all of this? he wondered. *It must be all the medication.*

Lyla sat up and plumped her pillows behind her so she could get some distance between them and not feel like he was intimidating her.

"Juliano, listen to me, please. I have not had your support. I need a partner. If you're not able or willing, I will deal with that. And if that's the case, I need for you to let me go. Just think about it. When you've decided or want to talk, we can go from there."

This was something Juliano did not expect. He took a couple of steps back away from the bed and looked at Lyla's face long and hard as if he were making an indelible imprint of her face on his mind and turned to leave the room. When he got to the door he turned to face her and said, "I'll think seriously about what you've said."

The more Lyla thought about her talk with Juliano the more she realized she had faced death without her husband's support. Lyla may not have understood her rationale but her speech to Juliano marked the process of Lyla mentally severing her relationship with Juliano.

Several days later, before retiring to bed, Juliano informed Lyla he didn't want to leave her now or ever and wanted to do whatever it took to give her the support she believed she needed. For him, leaving her was not an option. And so, it began again—the marital relationship that wasn't a marriage, a partner that wasn't a partner, and a life that was devoid of real love and affection.

The family stayed together in the little grey house and passed the next seven years paying off debts and saving money. The owners of the house advised Lyla they were determined to sell and made the initial offering to Lyla and Juliano. Instead of purchasing the rental house, Lyla and Juliano chose to purchase a new home that was more spacious in a new neighborhood. Juliano's enthusiasm for the new house was infectious. Lyla began to believe that perhaps their life would change.

The cycle of push back, acquiesce, pull away continued without any real change.

ANOTHER MOVE UP

Lyla lovingly placed her worldly possessions in the new house and set up the study as her special room. At last, after almost 8 years she unpacked all her precious books, pictures, and meaningful objects. There were so many things she had forgotten about. The house fit Lyla's maturing family. The eldest would begin his last year of high school, the two middle boys were in high school, and the youngest would be in his last year of elementary school.

The boys were busy, productive, and content with their friends, schools, and activities. The upstairs loft was her eldest's bedroom. It became a popular place for her boys and their friends from the neighborhood. Lyla's sister and parents moved into the area and were within short driving distance. She had missed them terribly and was grateful her children now had grandparents and cousins to be with.

Lyla deluded herself again into believing she made the right decision to stay with Juliano. She became so preoccupied with furnishing the house and re-establishing a relationship with her family she thought nothing of Juliano's silence or brooding. She might have known this wouldn't last.

Lyla and the children spent the summer swimming in their pool, getting to know their neighbors, and then the school year began with a flurry of activity. One evening after the children were asleep or busy in their rooms, Juliano told Lyla he thought it was time for him to move on. He recently read a book called, *"Who Moved My Cheese?"* that convinced him he needed to change to a different, better job. He didn't tell Lyla that reading the book had prompted him to decide to move back to Miami without her input. He asked her to read the book that evening hoping his decision would then make sense to her and she would not object to his absence and their eventual move.

"Why do you want me to read this book?"

"Well, you see," he began, "I think it's important you understand what's happening at my current job, and what it all means."

Lyla said nothing.

He became irritated with her silence and obvious resistance. "Why don't you just read the darn book tonight and then we can talk. It's a short read. Let me know when you've read it and we'll talk."

"I don't understand why you're in such a hurry for me to read this. I'm tired. I have so much to do for tomorrow and must get up early for the kids."

"Lyla, why can't you do this one little thing I ask? Is that so difficult? I'm out there working hard to take care of my family, and you give me a hard time about one small request."

"Fine, fine, Juliano, I'll read the book if it'll make you happy."

Lyla read the book before going to bed that night. The next morning was business as usual, getting the children off to three different schools. The book and its implications or meaning were forgotten until Juliano brought them up that evening.

"Hey, honey, did you have a chance to read the book?"

"Yes, Juliano, I did."

"Well, what do you think?"

"I understand what the book has to say, but what does it have to do with you?"

"Well," he hesitated, "Well, you see, I think this book is telling me I shouldn't wait around to see what's going to happen with my job. I need to move on now. You know, move on to something better."

Lyla didn't like what she was hearing. Her guts began to grumble and groan. "You mean you want to look for another job somewhere else? Where exactly?"

"Well, yes, I believe I need to go someplace else."

"Does that mean you have found something else already?"

"Well, you see. I'm leaving for Miami tomorrow."

"Miami? Tomorrow?" she interrupted.

"Just a minute, just a minute, take it easy. I'm leaving tomorrow but will come back the same day." Juliano began to speak rapidly and gave Lyla no chance to speak. "You see, my old boss is in Miami now and he's paying for me to fly down to talk to him about a position. Can you believe it? He's paying for me to fly down and back on the same day. This is great, isn't it? It's a good opportunity for me and I want to go. I'm going, I've made up my mind."

Deja vu?

Lyla was dumbfounded and could barely think. Finally, she spoke softly, "I don't understand. I don't understand why you have to leave. You already have a perfectly good job here. We have such a nice house, finally, and the children are happy; everything has been working out so well. I don't understand. We haven't been here that long."

Did he stop to think about the children, Lyla, their friends, her doctors and the life they had established for over a decade? What kind of impact would it have on the children to leave their schools? Apparently, his only interest was himself.

The discussion was over, he was finished. "I have to go, Lyla, I have to go. I'll come back and tell you all about it."

The 'talk' ended with Lyla spending the night trying to figure out what went wrong and why Juliano was so unhappy. What was it she didn't do? She gave him everything and it was still not enough.

Lyla didn't realize Juliano's satisfaction with his life, his job, everything, had nothing to do with her or the children. When would she?

Juliano flew to Miami the next morning and returned home the same evening. He took Lyla into the bedroom and explained to her he was offered, the job of a lifetime, and he agreed to take it. This would mean the 'big time' for him, and he wasn't going to let this opportunity go. This was his chance. He told her he would be gone by the end of the week and had already made arrangements for a place to stay on a temporary basis.

Although she tried to convince him to stay, there was little Lyla could do to dissuade him. He was driven, his mind was set, and his plans were made, without his wife and children.

Before Juliano left for Miami, he made the announcement to the boys. They were assembled in the family room and had no idea what was coming. The shocked expression on their faces was heartbreaking. They didn't understand why their father was abandoning them. What did they do wrong? They'll do better in school; take out the garbage without being told. What was happening they wondered?

Juliano packed his clothing and other personal items. A dealership vehicle was delivered to the house for him to drive back to Miami. The children said goodbye, in shock, not knowing if he would ever return, but somehow clung to the hope he would.

"Don't worry," he said, "don't look so glum. I'll come back to visit maybe once a month. You'll never know I was gone."

He walked out of the house, got in his vehicle, drove off, and never looked back. Lyla and the children's feelings of anger and abandonment were palpable. Lyla gathered them around her and assured them they would survive, together. She made appointments for the boys to get counseling and promised, with conviction, she would take care of them. The next several weeks were difficult. The children descended into despair and depression.

Although it took time, Lyla and the boys established a life routine without a husband and father. Lyla did her best to conceal her fears and the problems with her gut but the added emotional stress exacerbated her ongoing medical issues. She refused to allow it to destroy her; she suffered in secret.

Not long after Juliano left, Lyla met an acquaintance who had recently acquired a small companion dog breed known as the Cavalier King Charles Spaniel. One of the predominant characteristics of the breed was its loving and loyal personality. It was known to be the consummate companion, eager to please, and affectionate. Although Lyla never consciously sought to replace her absent husband, she fell in love with the dogs she met, purchased one who became her constant companion, and soon joined a local cavalier breed club. She volunteered to develop and run cavalier rescue for the club. As her children grew older and more independent, this companion and the others to follow filled her emptiness.

Once a month, Juliano did return home for an overnight visit. He became a stranger but attempted to exercise authority over the boys causing confusion and resentment. His presence caused discord and Lyla begged him to reconsider, but he would not return home permanently. He promised to look for a job in the area to placate her, but he never followed through.

He called home every so often but never spoke to the children. His conversations with Lyla were short and he always had an excuse. "Listen, Lyla, I have to go I have someone waiting to come in my office." This was his standard get off the phone speech Lyla had heard for years. Lyla got tired of the excuses and tired of not having a husband and marriage. She no longer waited for the phone calls and the visits. The physical separation created a divide she no longer desired to bridge. She was angry.

Before Juliano left for Miami, Lyla was too afraid of his threats and too sick to attempt a legal separation. But, the longer they were physically separated and the more uncomfortable the infrequent visits became, Lyla's secret thoughts and desires began to move her closer to take legal action.

Decisions made during emotional desperation can lead to severe, unintended, sometimes dangerous consequences.

Juliano and Lyla had been separated for nearly eight months. One evening during Juliano's infrequent visits, Lyla's frustration and anger over her empty marriage and absent partner prompted her to explode over something insignificant. She lashed out at Juliano without forethought or planning and told him she wanted a divorce.

"A divorce?" he quipped. "A divorce? Ha. Just where do you think you're going to go? What do you think you're going to do? How are you going to take care of these kids? You're sick and you haven't got skills. Besides, if you leave me, I'll make sure you get nothing," he said in a threatening voice. "I'll sell this house and you'll be out on the street with nowhere to go. Don't push me, Lyla."

That was enough to frighten her into submission. After all, he had made her and the children homeless in the past.

Multiple attempts at leaving an abuser is very common, especially when there are children. Without forethought and planning, it is difficult for a woman to be successful unless she is escaping imminent danger to her and/or her children.

"How to Stay Away for Good" by Sydney Martin. https://www.breakthesilencedv.org/beat-that-seven-times-statistic/

On average, a woman will leave an abusive relationship seven times before she leaves for good, according to The National Domestic Violence Hotline. And although society might question this statistic, and how it is possible for survivors to return to their abusers, there are many factors that play into leaving an abusive relationship permanently.

Divorce was not an option for Lyla. Juliano's threats were real enough to frighten her into submission. She questioned herself, could she provide for herself and her children financially? Did she have any marketable skills? She was convinced she could not, did not. She was trapped.

Lyla's life was strange. She was a married woman yet she was alone without a partner and had little social contact outside of people she met through the children's schools. She never looked outside of her marriage for companionship, believing doing so was wrong. Her Victorian attitude kept her faithful and Juliano never considered she would move beyond the confines of their relationship to find anyone else.

It was no longer possible for Lyla to turn to her parents for help. Harry had Alzheimer's that was rapidly progressing and her mother had her hands full with him. "Her Harry wasn't Harry anymore, only sometimes," Sura would say. Lyla knew her problems with Juliano and her marriage would have to remain a secret.

Lyla saw Juliano out of the corner of her eye when his car pulled into the driveway but refused to make eye contact or acknowledge him when he exited the car. He had to walk up to her before she took notice of him. He was grinning, happy about something, but his presence did not elicit any joy from her.

"Hey there, looks like you're doing some serious weed pulling. Kind of a hot day for that isn't it?"

Lyla didn't respond.

"Yea, well, I'm home, I'm home for the weekend, the whole weekend What do you think about that?

Lyla didn't move from the spot and continued to concentrate on her weeding. After a long pause she finally said, "Well, I see that. I need to finish this weeding so I can start dinner at a decent hour. Why don't you let the boys know you're here?"

She had nothing to say and was not interested in him. She continued to focus on the ground, hoping Juliano would leave her alone. He got the message and entered the house, calling for the boys.

Dinner was strained that evening. The conversation excluded Juliano. The topics the boys and Lyla talked about were out of his realm of familiarity and he sat there without participating. He was like an observer, a stranger. All through dinner she thought, *he's going to be in the bed, he's going to want to have sex, and that is going to be a problem.* Little did Lyla realize that was not going to be the only problem she would have to deal with that night.

After dinner, the boys helped Lyla clean up the kitchen while Juliano sat in the family room watching sports on the television. When the boys were done, they migrated upstairs to play video games and use the computer. It gave Juliano an opportunity to talk to Lyla about his news, the reason for his visit. Lyla wiped the last counter, the kitchen table, and the dogs were taken out. When Lyla returned, Juliano approached and asked her to join him in the bedroom. She followed him into the bedroom and stood at the foot of the bed with grave anticipation. Juliano stood near the window by his side of the bed.

"Hey, dinner was great. Do you know how long it's been since I've had a home-cooked meal, one of your meals? It was great, real great. Well, uh ... there's a reason why I'm here and why I took the weekend off, which you know is something I rarely get to do."

Lyla remained silent, unsure of where this was going. Juliano continued, "Well, I've been thinking and have decided it's time you and the boys come to Miami. My job is going great, and I have no intention of leaving Miami. We need to sell this house and buy one down there. I'll find us a nice place to live in a great neighborhood, and we'll all be together."

Juliano waited for a response, there was none. So many things were going through Lyla's mind. Did she have the courage to say them or was she going to stand there and let him bully her again? After a protracted silence, she spoke slowly with reservation.

"Nice for whom? I don't know, Juliano. The children and I are doing well here. We love living in this house and being with my family. They have their schools and their friends. I don't want to move to Miami. I don't know why you suddenly want us."

His obvious anger showed in his tone and words. "I've always wanted my family, and I've been working hard to get you down there; you seem to have forgotten that. Who do you think sends you money to pay the bills around here?"

Juliano's voice hardened, his anger rising. He was becoming agitated and frustrated at Lyla's defiance. "What do you mean you're not going to Miami? I'm telling you, you are."

"No, Juliano, I can't do this. I can't do this anymore. You left us Juliano. You left us. You abandoned us and we've learned to live without you." Lyla was surprised she was able to tell him what she and the children had been through. "You went down there and have been having a great time. I know. I know." Her voice began to rise in volume and pitch. "My uncle agreed to let you stay at his beautiful home on Miami Beach for nothing. I heard from my uncle how you go out on the town and don't get back to the house until late at night. I know. Don't bother to lie."

He said nothing in his defense. He didn't seem to care. As Lyla poured out her feelings, she began to sob. Juliano tried to calm her, regain control, and make sure the children did not hear them. Controlling her into submission was of paramount importance to him.

Juliano began with a whisper. "Listen, Lyla, I did what I had to do. I had to find another job and that was the best job out there."

"No, you didn't," she responded. "No, you didn't. You could have taken a job locally but you didn't want to. You said you didn't want to be put out to pasture. So, you left us. I can't take my children away from their home and the only life they've known. They are all so vulnerable."

Juliano believed he had to regain his domination over her and became hostile. The old threats began and in a sinister voice he continued, "All right, you want to stay here? Then perhaps you should. But, I'm warning you, if you stay you won't be staying in THIS house. I will sell it and you will have to find someplace else to live. The house is in my name, and I hold the mortgage. I can do what I want. How are you going to take care of all of these kids? Huh? Tell me, how? I'll make sure you get nothing ... nothing. You'll be out on the street, homeless with a bunch of kids. Then what?"

When he finished his threatening tirade, he left Lyla sitting on the floor next to the bed sobbing and shaking, and walked toward the door of the room. As he approached it, he turned back to Lyla and spoke to her with malice and disgust in his voice.

"Just think about that Lyla, just think about it, and then tell me you're not going to Miami."

Her victimization was so complete she never considered the veracity of his threats. Her isolation and lack of someone to confide in and a voice who saw her situation clearly kept her from realizing and understanding the truth about her rights to property and support.

Lyla buried her face in her hands and sobbed uncontrollably. She had nowhere to go, no way to take care of the boys, and she was not well. She was stuck, and he knew it. Juliano's behavior convinced her that her attempt to stand up to him had failed. Without the needed emotional and legal support, she was weak in her attempt to establish herself as an independent person, and she failed miserably. When Juliano returned to the room, Lyla was still sitting on the floor weeping softly.

Juliano bent down close to her face, invading her space, knowing it would intimidate and frighten her. He reassured her he would find someplace nice for them to live. He whispered to her leaving no room for her to defy him.

"This is best for all of us Lyla, believe me. I'm thinking of all of us. We'll be happy down there; we'll be together; you'll see."

He tightly grabbed her arms, helped her off the floor, and put his arms around her in an attempt at a hug. She was unresponsive but Juliano didn't care. He got what he wanted. With some effort, she broke away from his arms, making the excuse she needed to wash her face.

"Good, I want to get the boys together and give them the good news." As he spoke he chuckled, "I don't want you out there looking like I've been beating you up."

Juliano gathered the boys in the family room and was warming up the audience with tales of customers from his job and sports trivia. Lyla came out and joined them while Juliano made the announcement.

"Now listen boys," he began. "I know things have been difficult since I've been gone, and I'm sorry about that. You see, I had to leave town

to find another job and make sure this new job was going to be permanent. Well, it's taken awhile but I'll be staying at this job and I've decided
it's time for you and Mom to move to Miami."

The boys were frozen in their seats, their faces ashen. They were
stunned into silence. Juliano continued, "The house here will have to
be sold, and I'll buy something for us down there. It'll probably take a
year or so to get all this accomplished, but I think it's best for everyone.
Anybody have any questions?"

They all began to talk at once. "What about our friends, our schools?
What's going to happen to our activities? This is our town; our home.
How can we leave? Why can't you work here? There are plenty of jobs
here; why can't we stay?"

Juliano's voice was harsh and commanding. "We can't stay because I
have a job someplace else and this is the way it's going to be. Everything
will be fine boys, trust me. It's going to happen and you are all going,
like it or not."

The boys were unresponsive. He dismissed them and Lyla retreated
to the bedroom. She showered and got ready for bed and for the first
time refused Juliano's advances. "Not tonight, Juliano, I'm very upset;
it's been a very difficult evening. Not tonight."

"Yes, I guess it has. We have plenty of nights to come."

*Lyla carried the stigma of her husband's behavior that contributed to her isolation.
This complicated her life and influenced her decisions to remain with him. Each
time she gathered the courage to leave, the fear, the disgrace, and the threats
would draw her back. She had no self-confidence and believed all the lies he used
to control her.*

One year later, the house in the Fort Lauderdale area was built and
the house Lyla and her boys loved and called home was sold. Juliano
was proud of what he had accomplished. He was a player in the big
time, no longer a little fish in a little pond, and he liked it. Juliano's decisions were all about him with little thought given to the carnage he
inflicted on the family he was supposed to love.

Lyla and the children packed their precious lives, and the moving
van arrived to load the boxes and furniture. Just before they were finished loading, Lyla made two phone calls and made her final farewells
to her family. She went to the patio for privacy and spoke to her parents.

She spoke to her father first. "Daddy, I have to go, do you understand? I will miss you. I don't know when I'll see you again. I love you."

She dissolved into a pool of tears at the end of her conversation, it was so final. She and her mother had a very short, emotional goodbye. Lyla promised to stay in touch and to finalize plans for her parents to come and visit. With extraordinary sadness, Lyla knew this would never happen.

One of the reasons Juliano chose their community was the privacy; it was guarded and gated. No one entered the neighborhood through the guarded gates without permission, and he wasn't about to give Lyla's mother access. Juliano had often threatened not to let Lyla's parents, her mother in particular, come to the new house, and this time he would keep his promise. Lyla's greatest fears would come to pass. That was the last time she would talk to her father as she knew him. This felt wrong, the same way she felt after her brief marriage ceremony. Lyla was living a waking nightmare, and couldn't stop it. She knew this was not the beginning of another new life for them it was the beginning of the end.

Juliano planned, and intended to execute, a short family vacation on the beach in Sarasota, Florida for several days. He rented a beach cottage a short distance from the ocean and beach that was along the route to Miami. He never consulted Lyla and waited to advise her of his plans until the day they finished packing. He told her he believed it was best for them to spend some quality time together, to have an opportunity to once again become a family.

The little caravan of husband, wife, children, and dogs began their journey down the west coast of Florida. The family arrived in Sarasota at the rental cottage on the beach at dusk. Lyla was weak from emotional and physical exhaustion and could barely drag her bags up the steps to the cottage bedroom. Juliano ignored her. The boys helped Lyla with the dogs, crates, and baggage. Juliano was eager to get out, have dinner, and stroll around St. Armand's Circle, the Sarasota mecca of shopping and restaurants.

Lyla showered and threw on comfortable clothes but couldn't shake the weakness. She was exhausted, dizzy, lightheaded and nauseated but thought if she got a little food, she would feel better. Juliano found a small Italian restaurant on the Circle who could accommodate a party of six for a late dinner and he ordered a bottle of wine to celebrate. The boys and Lyla ate quietly while Juliano rambled on loudly. "Trust me, guys, everything's gonna be great, now that we're together. Wait 'till you see the house and the neighborhood, you're really going to like it." No one spoke; they were tired, worn out, and no one else shared his optimism.

After dinner, Lyla wanted to immediately return to the cottage, but Juliano ignored her feeble request. Lyla dutifully waited on a bench outside the ice cream parlor while Juliano and the boys devoured their treats and meandered around the circle of shops. An hour later, Juliano and the boys returned to her. Lyla needed every bit of strength and determination to get from the car to the cottage, up the steps, undressed, and into bed where she collapsed and stayed for the next three days.

Juliano and the boys brought in groceries to make simple meals while Lyla languished in bed either reading or sleeping. The boys helped her by walking and feeding the dogs and Juliano spent his days on the beach baking in the sun, playing volley ball with the boys, and his evenings on the Circle. It didn't seem to concern him that Lyla could not get out of bed and didn't care enough to ask. He did nothing for her.

On the day of their departure, Juliano announced he was leaving early that morning for Miami. He told Lyla that he made reservations for one night at a local hotel near Ft. Lauderdale beach because the closing was delayed by a day. His plan was to meet them at the hotel in Ft Lauderdale. Lyla didn't ask and didn't care about the reason for his abrupt departure and welcomed his absence. She dragged herself out of bed, bathed and dressed, and marshaled the boys to gather everything and load the remaining cars for the drive. They drove down the west coast of the state across Alligator Alley, into Ft Lauderdale to the ocean, and checked into the hotel for the night.

Juliano eventually arrived at the hotel in the evening without explanation of where he had been or why. Lyla didn't bother to ask. The closing on the house was scheduled for the next morning. Lyla was not included and was instructed to go directly to the house by noon the next day and wait for the moving truck to arrive.

Juliano's attitude and behavior set the tone for the remainder of their relationship and marriage. Juliano reminded Lyla his working hours were long and he had events and job obligations to attend after work. When he was in the mood, he would share stories of his evening rhapsodies while rubbing elbows with the rich and famous or the lavish events he was obligated to attend, without her. He would often return home only to complain about the rich food and wines and how he had overeaten. There were times when he would be out until the middle of the night, returning home drunk, reminding Lyla of the early days. At those times, fights would begin and end without resolution, or there would be deadly silence. Juliano was the only one who loved being in Miami with his friends and coworkers who were more of a family to him than his wife and children.

Lyla spent her time finding ways to stay busy by participating in a local cavalier owners' group, cavalier rescue, and creating sewing projects that gave her limited opportunities to meet people. These activities did little to fill the void of not having a partner. The boys had difficulty transitioning, felt isolated, couldn't make friends, and hated not having their old friends and schools. Miami never felt like home.

Juliano attempted to revive his marital relationship with Lyla by taking her to Captiva Island, Florida for a romantic getaway. His idea of romance was to have sex immediately upon arrival in the hotel room, bake in the sun on the beach or by the pool, have sex, eat and drink lots of alcoholic beverages, and have more sex. During the trip, he took Lyla window shopping at one of the many quaint, upscale shops that dotted the island and nagged her to buy something. She knew this activity fed his ego and provided the justification he needed for his treatment of her.

Occasionally, Juliano would take Lyla out to dinner to a local restaurant and find something to complain about whether it was the service, the food, anything. Other times he would make time for an anniversary dinner or the annual obligatory take mom out for Mother's Day brunch. Otherwise, Lyla's days were spent cooking, cleaning, doing laundry, and fostering dogs. She rarely had an opportunity to enjoy the restaurants, art events, concerts and entertainment, or social events of the area.

Nothing had changed. Juliano would make fun of Lyla in front of the boys, and belittle her especially after a difficult day at work. Most of the anger, frustration, and rage associated with his life, particularly his job, was taken out on Lyla and she became his punching bag.

"Did you pay that bill? What was the exact date and how much was the bill? I know you keep a list of monthly obligations, where is the list? Did you pay my credit card charges and if you didn't why not? I told you I want those paid the day you get the bill. What did you do with the money I gave you this month?"

In response, her guts would rumble and churn. She would perspire and her hands would shake. It was difficult to conceal her anxiety. Juliano would catch her off guard and fire questions at her that she was unable to answer fast enough. On one occasion, to maintain control, he frightened her with accusations of financial subterfuge.

"You know a lot of my friends have told me when their wives go to the grocery they steal from their husbands by taking extra money from the checking account that is used to pay for groceries. They would write a check for $20.00 over the amount of the groceries and get the cash back and stash it for themselves. Stealing...downright stealing. You would never do that, would you? I trust you so much."

"Of course not, Juliano. I would never think of doing that."

These were times Lyla learned to lie convincingly in order to protect herself.

There were rare occasions when Juliano would come home in time for dinner. Although Juliano would join everyone at the table he never ate as though he enjoyed the food or had an appetite. He would pick at the small portions or shove the food around his plate without finishing his meal. On the nights when Juliano arrived home after nine he often acted drunk. Lyla listened as he slipped and slid his way down the hallway to their bedroom banging and bumping into the walls dropping anything he had in his hands. When he was like that, he would perform his nightly ritual of taking off and hanging up his clothes and shower in silence unless he was interested in sex. If not, he would meander to the family room to finish the evening watching television. It wasn't until many years later he revealed he routinely consumed an entire bottle of wine every evening as he drove home after work.

As they drifted farther apart, Lyla, again, turned to thoughts of leaving. She was dependent upon him financially, and her health was precarious. She was receiving special IV treatments in the hospital for the ulcerative colitis every six weeks. These two factors alone kept her attached to him unable to break away, or so she believed. Her thoughts were the only hope she had to cling to.

Lyla spoke to her mother often but was forced to make excuses each time Sura asked to see her, the children, and the house. Juliano made it clear Lyla's parents would not enter his home and Lyla was afraid to defy him. Every three months or so, when Lyla believed there would be no repercussions from Juliano, she would make the four-hour drive to see her parents who were declining in health. Her father was in advanced stages of Alzheimer's and Lyla's voice was the only stimulus he responded to. She would enter his room in the cottage on her sister's property and sing the song, "Dark Town Strutter's Ball," as he mouthed the words along with her. Sura was moved to an assisted living facility. Every time Lyla left her parents, she worried it would be the last time she saw them.

Sadly, Sura was diagnosed with lymphoma and the last time Lyla saw her was in the hospital when Lyla and her siblings gathered around her to discuss treatment options. Sura never survived the initial treatment and died three weeks from the initial diagnosis before Lyla was able to return. Three weeks later, Harry died and Lyla was overcome with grief. She was inconsolable, angry at herself, and angry at Juliano.

THE FALL FROM GRACE

Lyla's persona was altered and concealed by Juliano's threatening and bullying behavior, his disinterest and disdain for her. She lost her vivacious and carefree attitude and lost or buried her rich sense of style. Her wardrobe consisted of plain baggy trousers and loose-fitting shirts or dresses, things she believed would keep her from appearing provocative or sensuous around Juliano. She rarely wore makeup and chose a short, plain, almost unbecoming hairstyle. While Lyla misunderstood the dynamics of Juliano's need to dominate and control, she did not want to do anything to arouse Juliano's desires for sex and instinctively shied away from appearing inviting to his eye. Even more so from the time they moved to Ft Lauderdale, Juliano saw Lyla as an object to dominate when he was drinking and when he was not drinking Lyla was careful never to be naked or without a robe.

Juliano seemed oblivious to Lyla's health issues unless he was interested in sex. He would make polite inquiries only to ascertain if she would comply. When she didn't consent, he would nag her until she acquiesced. If the nagging didn't work, he tried cajoling her or using emotional blackmail to get her to submit. None of his behavior changed.

"How are you feeling, are you feeling all right? How about we mess around? I'm really in the mood. It's OK if you're not feeling well. I know you would if you could. I know how much you like it. Remember the new car I was looking at for you? What color did you want? What kind of accessories do you want?"

Juliano would take out his arsenal of arguments based on his interpretations of Christian biblical verse and try to convince her she was subject to him, as he was head of the household. His religious views regarding marriage were tyrannical and never subject to discussion. When he engaged in this abusive, bullying manner, Lyla remained quiet, knowing she could not prevail, and kept her anger and resentment hidden.

Six years had passed from the time they moved to Ft. Lauderdale and Juliano was working in Miami. By this time, Lyla dreaded him coming home. She would function with little fear or anxiety throughout the day but her anxiety would rise and become almost uncontrollable when the hour grew near for him to be home. The closer his arrival got the more her guts churned. Often times, she would focus on any kind of craft activity she believed would keep her from being vulnerable as a way to survive.

On many occasions, she pretended to be asleep, too exhausted, or too weak to engage in conversation or anything else when he appeared late in the evening. On those nights when she was awake, she piled all five of the dogs on the bed and acted as though she was thoroughly engrossed in some movie or television program. Those tactics worked sometimes but not often enough to discourage him completely. She knew she would have to give in at some time and only gave in when she believed she was in peril. If she had no other option than to perform, she would acquiesce and let him do what he needed to do. After the act was complete and he rolled over to sleep, she would escape to the bathroom to shower his smell and touch from her body. Although she may have been able to wash him from her body, she couldn't wash away the mental and emotional damage and pain he inflicted.

In early January, 2007, their pseudo idyllic life ended abruptly. Lyla suspected, intuitively, that Juliano's job was coming to an end. She begged him to find a job in the Tampa area so they could move back to the place she and the children considered home. Her attempts to talk to him about those feelings and her desire to return to Tampa were ignored.

As usual, Juliano went to work one morning and Lyla conducted her routine errands that included picking up groceries. When she arrived home late morning, Juliano's car was in the garage. As she walked up the driveway, Juliano came out of the garage dressed in a pair of old shorts and a T-shirt. He walked toward her and announced he had been summarily fired. Lyla said nothing as she continued to walk through the garage into the house, her arms laden with packages. He never offered to help.

"Hey there ... Lyla. Hey there. Aren't you going to say something?" he called after her, obviously irritated at her indifference.

Juliano gave Lyla a brief synopsis of the morning's events and waited for a response. He was in shock and stopped functioning at the idea that he was a dispensable commodity. Lyla, without input or assistance from Juliano, started thinking for them both. Her fears of being home-less again after so many years caused her to make desperate, foolish decisions.

Juliano's insatiable need to live well, beyond his means, kept them in financial jeopardy. "All right Juliano, Lyla said, "if we can't pay the mort-gage and other expenses without your income, we have to sell the house. We have some options. You can look for a job here, we can move back to Tampa and you can look for work there, or we can look elsewhere."

At the time, she could not foresee that Juliano's past would influence and alter their options. Lyla contacted an old friend who was a real estate agent to list and sell the house. Arrangements were made for the home to be updated and ready for market.

Why would she continue to stay, given their current financial situation and her desire to leave the marriage? It seems like this would have been a good opportunity for her, except there was no income to take care of her and the children, and she remained in a fragile state of health. Did her old rescue mindset return or emotional hysteria?

Another potential problem reared its ugly head and was about to complicate their already complicated lives. Juliano failed to disclose to Lyla that he had been having some physical issues. His gait changed, he had difficulty running, and he complained of a loss of balance. His morning bike rides grew shorter in length, and he was falling off his motorcycle. Lyla never knew if this was caused by depression, drinking, or if there was something dramatically wrong with him. Lyla made ap-pointments with local neurologists and accompanied Juliano on every visit, exam, and diagnostic procedure. There was no definitive diagnosis or consensus of opinion except for 'wait and see' advice. She would not abandon him if his symptoms were real.

After several weeks, Juliano emerged from his emotionally comatose state and decided starting over someplace else might be the answer. Without explanation, he refused to return to Tampa. Lyla suspected his past arrest, conviction, and possible inability to pass a background check, could become an obstacle if he were to remain in Florida. Texas was discussed as a possible alternative. Cost of living was less, jobs ap-peared to be prevalent, two of the children wanted to go to Texas uni-versities, and their eldest was already working there.

Before Lyla would agree or even think of making such a major move, she insisted Juliano make a short reconnaissance trip there. She warned him she wasn't going anywhere, especially that far away, unless he was certain he wanted to be there and could get a job. After searching through the local Texas papers, they agreed on the Houston area. Juliano went to Houston to job search and look for housing. The market there was healthy and homes were much less expensive than in south Florida. Juliano interviewed for a job, successfully passed the background check, and was scheduled to begin in October of the same year. It had already been a little over 9 months from the time he was fired, or so he said, and money was running low.

The relief was brief.

Juliano met Lyla's conditions and she agreed to the move. The house remained unsold and Juliano's Texas boss was applying pressure for Juliano to begin his job. Lyla found temporary accommodations for Juliano at a hotel specializing in temporary lodging for executives in the Houston area until the family could be reunited.

Suddenly, Juliano announced he wouldn't go to Houston without his family, and he let the job go. He convinced Lyla that finding another job, an even better one, would be easy. She should have known better. The Florida house sold on Thanksgiving Day and Juliano immediately insisted on returning to Texas to find a home.

Why was Juliano suddenly so insistent on having his family with him?

Why was Juliano so anxious to get his family to Texas?

They found a beautiful home in an affluent neighborhood on an acre in an area covered with forestation. It was beautiful country and reminded Lyla of her home in Ohio. Juliano arranged the financing with the proceeds from the sale of the Florida home. The Texas house was a handsome Tudor style traditional brick. She thought perhaps they finally made the right decision. What she didn't realize was that it might have been the right decision for her, but not for Juliano.

ON THE ROAD AGAIN AND ABANDONED

The loading date and move was just before Christmas, 2007. The boys were responsible for packing their own rooms; Lyla had to do everything else. When that was accomplished, the boys flew to Texas to stay with their eldest brother until the movers arrived at the new house. The load onto the van was uneventful and took approximately five hours. Upon its completion, the moving van began its journey west. Lyla was relieved to leave south Florida. She mistakenly thought the road trip to Texas was an opportunity for them to work on their estrangement and re-establish whatever was left of their relationship.

When is she going to wake up?

They drove out of the neighborhood, onto the highway across Alligator Alley, up the west coast of Florida, and began the journey to Houston. The car was loaded with all the dogs and enough supplies for several days.

Lyla didn't recognize Juliano's silence as anything but contemplative and didn't notice the red flags until it was too late. The road trip Lyla anticipated turned into a nightmarish marathon of endless driving, horrible hotels and take-out joints, causing Lyla's guts to go crazy. Juliano insisted on doing the driving and refused to participate in any other way. He complained viciously about his leg, his inability to keep his balance, and to walk.

Every time they stopped for more fuel, Lyla had to fill the tank, clean the windshield, pay for the gas, and walk the dogs. When they finally stopped for the night, Juliano would remain in the car while Lyla checked them into the room. After that, she got the luggage carrier from inside the motel and dragged the luggage from the car to the room. She removed each dog from the car in their respective crate to the luggage cart and wheeled the cart piled with the crates to the room. Lyla walked the dogs when they reached their destination for the night, before retiring to sleep, and again before they got back on the road the next morning. This activity was a horrific ordeal Lyla would barely re-cover from. Juliano had no interest in helping Lyla with that activity and never offered. Juliano thought, *why should I help? They aren't my dogs.*

By the time they reached the Houston area, Lyla was overcome with exhaustion and Juliano was anxious to attend the closing the following morning. One last time, she performed the horrific motel ritual with her gentle and patient companions and the luggage, hoping she would have the strength to survive. This time Lyla was included in the closing and her name appeared on all the documents. Juliano insisted they spend the night in the house even if they had to sleep on the floor. He dragged Lyla to Wal-Mart to purchase an air mattress and other supplies, and they waited for the movers to arrive the next morning.

Why was he so anxious to sign closing documents and get Lyla and the boys into the house?

The moving van arrived at the Texas house the day after closing and all the boys arrived at the house soon after the movers. It was a long and hectic day. The house buzzed with activity and excitement as boxes were unpacked, the boys set up their computer equipment, and beds were made. Lyla focused on the kitchen, directing movers where to leave boxes. It took most of the day to unload, and boxes were everywhere. Although Lyla was worn out, she was relieved to have her belongings with her even if most were still in boxes.

Juliano did nothing to assist anyone with unpacking. His priority was for his precious, large screen television to be connected and working. Lyla ignored him and knew not to ask for his help. When Lyla walked into the master bedroom Juliano was quietly emptying his boxes diligently organizing those items that were important to him. He ignored everyone unless he needed help with electronics for the television.

Lyla spent the following days and weeks unpacking and checking contents of high priority boxes for damage. Juliano spent his time watching television and disappearing for long periods of time in the only car they had at the time.

Before Juliano left Miami he had purchased a vehicle for himself. Lyla had no idea what their financial status was, he shared nothing with her, and she initially wondered why he got himself a car when dealerships usually provided a car to managers. Juliano's new car and the children's cars were transported and delivered to the new house a week after the furniture arrived. Lyla hoped this would improve Juliano's attitude.

Why did she keep hoping he would change?

Why did she think anything would help?

Lyla, Juliano, and the children started the New Year together as a family, dysfunctional as it was. Juliano made a speech at dinner on New Year's Eve. He lifted his glass of wine and spoke. "Well, it looks like this is going to be a great year, especially with the family back together again. We have a chance to start a good life here in Texas, here's to success for us all." Juliano and the boys tapped their glasses and drank their wine, Lyla sat at the other end of the table as a quiet observer of the scene.

But he soon began to complain. When the temperature dropped to below freezing for several days and enough snow fell to put a light covering on the ground, Juliano was beside himself. Soon after the snow shower, he complained about the weather, the traffic, the bugs, anything and everything. He wasn't in Miami anymore.

During the month of January, Lyla and Juliano traveled from their home in a northern suburb to the medical complex in Houston. Appointments were made with a team of doctors from the neurology clinic who conducted diagnostic tests to get a definitive diagnosis. Lyla never left his side. In the end, the diagnosis and prognosis remained uncertain, it was a degenerative, incurable motor neuron disease. The doctors strongly suggested Juliano function as nearly normal as possible including getting a job. They advised that working was a good way to keep his attitude positive for his self-esteem, not to mention their finances. Juliano's attitude did not improve and he grew even more depressed. Lyla never knew if the cause of the depression was disease related or if he was unhappy with the move, her, the house, and no job. He was uncommunicative about it all.

Every week Lyla looked through the classified section of the newspaper for jobs she thought Juliano would be able to apply for. "Hey, Juliano, I found a couple of jobs that sound like they're right up your alley. How about you take a look and see if you'd like to apply?"

Juliano would accept the information and Lyla would not hear from him for days. Finally, she had to ask. "Did anything work out?"

"No, I didn't get through to my contact; no, I didn't get an answer back. I couldn't get through to the GM; the rep didn't get back to me."

It sounded like the same old excuses she heard in Florida and she began to worry and get anxious about how they were going to pay bills. As the weeks passed, she began to make subtle inquiries again about employment. Juliano made an unenthusiastic attempt at scheduling an interview with someone and upon his return from the appointment, appeared angry and sullen.

Lyla was busy emptying more boxes in the master bedroom when Juliano walked in presumably from his job interview and threw his briefcase on the chair. Lyla saw the scowl on his face and asked, "How was the interview?"

Juliano answered with clenched teeth and a deep raspy voice. "That... stupid...bastard."

Lyla did not look at him or respond. He continued, "The guy I had an appointment with had the gall not to show up for the interview. Then on the way out of the showroom I lost my balance and fell when I stepped off the curb. There are no jobs anywhere and people in 'this town' don't move around like they did in Florida. Openings are scarce and nobody here knows who I was, what a big deal I was in Miami. They think I'm just an old cripple."

His vain attempts at job hunting were short and unproductive and tension began to build. He would pretend to contact different dealerships or reps for dealerships looking for possible job openings. In a city as large as Houston, there wasn't one dealership that was looking for someone with Juliano's skills and talents. Lyla found that hard to believe. Juliano kept a tight rein on the money and refused to be responsible for paying the bills. Lyla was forced to beg him for money and had to wait until the finances were almost completely depleted before he would part with enough for bills and food.

No job, no income, and the tension grew worse. Lyla continued to be busy with household chores and observed that Juliano spent his days lounging in the living room all day watching sporting events or absent all day returning late afternoon around dinner time with a strong buzz. By this time, they were picking at each other with Lyla confronting Juliano about his responsibilities. The more she pushed, the more he retreated, leaving the house for longer periods, returning and smelling of alcohol. He did nothing.

Juliano was constantly on his cell phone with his friends and cronies in Miami without explanation to Lyla. His conversations were whispered or he would retreat outside to speak freely. Towards the end of March, Juliano and Lyla were openly hostile when the last confrontation occurred.

"I hate it here. I can't get a job, and nobody wants to hire an old man. I hate the weather, I hate the driving, and I hate everyone because they don't appreciate who I was, who I am. I am a Somebody, and they don't know it."

Juliano's family, his wife, and children, who he couldn't live without became irrelevant. He hated it and didn't want to be there. It was that simple.

Lyla was unloading the dishwasher in the kitchen listening to Juliano rant. She had become numb and couldn't find words to respond right away and then she spoke.

"I am tired of your excuses, of your feeling sorry for yourself, and just tired in general. You have done nothing to act like you're a member of this family. This move to Texas was supposed to be a positive move for the two of us as a couple and the family as a whole. It has become nothing more than what it was in Florida."

And then the inevitable: the final conflict.

"It's your fault, Lyla. Yes, that's right, it's your fault. You brought us out here and now that we're here you don't have sex with me often enough like a real wife should. You don't do anything for me, you're always busy doing something else."

Lyla, unable to control her feelings any longer, began to express her frustration and outrage at Juliano's inability to function, his lack of responsibility for their family, and his failure to follow through on his promises.

"Look, Juliano," she began. "Now is not the time to start on me about the lack of sex in our life. The real problem here is that we're running out of money and something needs to happen with you and a job. You're not functioning. You're not looking for a job. You sit in front of that stupid television all day starting with good morning earth or sunrise or whatever the hell it is and you don't end until late at night with sports. We're not much better off than we were in Miami."

More angry words and accusations flew back and forth and ended up with Juliano walking out of the house. Lyla was left crying, frightened, and confused. Juliano drove off, and Lyla had no idea when or if he would return and almost didn't care. She went outside in the backyard to her little blue bench under the crabapple tree followed by her faithful companions and sat in what remained of the afternoon sun and cried from exhaustion and frustration, knowing something happened that had not happened before. It was different this time. The confrontation had a finality to it she never experienced before.

She had been abandoned; one of her worst fears was realized. Lyla flashed back to when Juliano made his fateful announcement years earlier when he decided to leave his job in Tampa and move to Miami without consulting her. He was going to do it again only this time she was in a strange city without friends, family, or anything that was familiar.

Lyla was in a tangle of emotions that were difficult to sort through and the old fears descended upon her. How would she take care of herself and the boys? What would she do? She was convinced she had no skills and was in a fragile state of health. The more her fears preyed on her the angrier she became. She tried to calm the disquieting thoughts and decided if this was the end of her marriage there were things she would have to address, like get a job. The luxury of time no longer existed and she couldn't give in to her medical issues, whatever they were.

Juliano walked into the house that same evening and walked into the kitchen to find Lyla. At that same moment Lyla was bringing the dogs in through the kitchen back door after their mid evening walk. Juliano was calm as was Lyla. He smelled of alcohol and cigarette smoke. Juliano approached Lyla with caution.

"Listen, I've been thinking about what happened today and I've decided this is not going to work for me." Lyla listened. She was waiting for his exit speech. "I've spent a lot of time thinking about all the things we said to each other, and you're right about some of those things. I do need to be working, and we do need the money. It just so happens I talked with my old boss in Miami, and he said I could have a job if I wanted to return to Miami. I told him I would take the job.

"I leave in two days to make the drive back. I've contacted an old friend who said I could live with him in his condo near the office, so I've pretty much got everything already arranged. I don't know when I'll come back, if ever. That's something we'll have to wait and talk about. At least I'll be working again, and we'll have some income and medical insurance coverage."

Lyla was unemotional, "Juliano, I won't try to stop you."

There wasn't much left to say. He had already made the decision to go, and it was now only a matter of physically packing the car, and getting on the road. She recognized the pattern. When things got too difficult for him, or he was overwhelmed with responsibility, he packed all his things into his car and drove off to someplace else, alone. She thought, this is the last time he's going to do this to us, the very last time."

Was abandonment of his family his plan all along?

When he first left, she was relieved to be alone without the constant fighting and tension that existed between them. She often fell asleep emotionally exhausted, too tired to even realize her aloneness. When the fatigue wore off, the awareness of her singularity troubled her at night, alone, in the dark. Feeling afraid at night in her bed became a familiar feeling. She struggled to convince herself she had nothing to be afraid of, at least nothing physically.

The weeks since his departure had passed and Lyla developed a routine that helped to ease her discomfort. She was no longer filled with anxiety and fear of him demanding sex and the uncertainty of his moods. She took care of her canine companions every night maintaining vigilance especially when the coyote pack was heard howling and hunting in the area. Each little girl was rewarded with a cookie after a successful time outside. Lyla put her water on to boil and steeped her herbal teas and added a biscotti for herself as a sweet comfort before brushing her teeth. She sat in her bed, her pillows propped behind her back, with her bedside lamp on sipping her tea, munching on her biscotti watching something engaging on television. When she finished her biscuit and tea she took her time finishing her night time routine and crawled back into bed under the sweet-smelling sheets. The last thoughts on her mind were, the doors were locked, the dogs were in the house ready to give warning, and the alarm system was armed. *I'm safe, I'm okay,* she would repeat in her head. Most nights she watched television until her eyelids grew heavy and she drifted off to sleep hearing the voices gradually recede from her consciousness never understanding why those voices helped to make her feel safe.

HER WORST FEARS REALIZED

The circumstances under which Lyla functioned colored and significantly influenced the way Lyla thought of herself, the decisions she made, the consequences of those decisions, and how it all affected her choices and the person she became. When this awareness became evident to Lyla, she began to wonder who she was as a woman. Her contemplation forced her to look back on how the prior events with Juliano had shaped her attitudes, her personality, and how she interacted with her children and others around her. She had become so embroiled in the life she made up to protect herself and her children that she began to wonder who the real Lyla was and who the Lyla was that she became. Her days were filled with constant anxieties and fears.

Who was Lyla Rose Masselli? Was she the woman Lyla Rose could have become?

Lyla mourned her broken marriage, the loss of a husband, the feeling of being unwanted, abandoned, and left alone. She was thrust into a situation where she was out of her comfort zone of tending to the house and children and was not prepared to meet and engage new people and situations. By sheer will, she tried to regain self esteem and composure and decided to venture outside the house into the community. She thought. *There must be something I can do, I can't be that inept, stupid, or afraid.*

The community newspaper advertised summer adult classes at the local community college. She scanned the available classes and programs and found a program where people with bachelor's degrees were being invited to apply for a one semester program in the fall to become certified to teach. The state was short of teachers and was trying to fill vacancies for the fall. All she had to do was convince herself she was not too old, too stupid, or too scared to sign up and take the class.

She could feel her guts beginning to grumble and groan from anxiety as she drove to the community college campus. She got lost twice, probably from nerves, but eventually arrived on the campus and found visitor parking. The registration building was alphabetized and numbered and she followed the signs pointing to the registrar's office. She took a deep breath, opened the heavy door and walked up to the counter. The young woman behind the counter was welcoming and polite and helped Lyla to complete the right forms and sent her to the next office to choose her class schedule. Lyla didn't dare stop and think otherwise she might lose her nerve and not follow through. Once she completed the process, she felt better about herself and crept out of her aloneness into the world.

Class was tedious, the reading was often boring and put her to sleep. The homework was at times frustrating and surprising. One assignment was to explain her philosophy of education. "What?" she moaned. She spoke to herself again as she waited for some kind of epiphany to occur. "What does she, her professor, mean philosophy of education?" If Lyla ever had one she had no idea what it was. What initially looked to be an easy assignment was turning into something annoying. She sat at her computer staring at the question on the blank page wondering where to start. She immersed herself in the different philosophies of education she found in her text books and in different articles on the internet. Interestingly enough, she discovered she did indeed have a philosophy of education. She made an outline of the salient points she wanted to cover and began to write. The words poured out one paragraph after another tumbling onto the page. After an initial edit, she produced a final product that surprised even her. *Wow,* she thought, *I didn't know I had a philosophy, let alone all of that.*

When the practice test for certification was administered in class she achieved a passing score and thought teaching could be something to fall back on. It was evident her marriage was falling apart and the words, "...if I come back..." from his final speech haunted her. After their last uncomfortable verbal phone confrontation, Lyla made a concerted effort to keep topics neutral. The verbal abuse was painful. It left her weepy and feeling like a failure; it was a feeling she had experienced too often before and didn't want to revisit.

Lyla finished her class with a sense of accomplishment. The regular interaction with others opened a door more important and significant than she realized. Throughout the semester, Lyla battled a new medical problem, an abdominal hernia, that required surgery to resolve. Although she was uncomfortable and suffered, she did not schedule surgery until after she completed the class. Surgery was scheduled for early December, 2008, and once again she prepared the boys for the news. They were strong and supportive and reassured her they would take care of her. Initially, she had no intention of telling Juliano, but decided to mention it about a month prior to the scheduled date. He never asked or inquired after that, which was so typical of him. She forgot, December was his busiest time of year. Nothing else was more important to him. Why would he change now?

Two of the boys, who were still living at home, accompanied their mother to the hospital on December 8th the day of surgery and her eldest arrived to meet them. Even though she was apprehensive about the surgery, the boys were a remarkable comfort to her. This was the first time she was in the hospital without having to face an ordeal alone. Surgery went as planned, or so the surgeon thought, and her eldest did as he promised. He was there to pick her up the next morning, take her home, and put her to bed. He made chicken soup with matzoh balls for her, lasagna for his brothers, and stayed with her until he believed she was stable.

But later the same evening things went wrong. She became weak and dehydrated and knew it was time to call the doctor who advised her to get to the hospital if she had no improvement. By the next morning, Lyla could barely lift her head. The boys took her to the emergency room where they waited for hours for her name to be called. Pain medications and IV fluids were administered. Tests were done and she was admitted. The boys never left her side until she was moved to a temporary unit, awaiting transfer to her room. She kissed them goodbye and thanked them for staying with her releasing them from their vigil reassuring them she would be all right.

Lyla began what would become a living nightmare. The pain was excruciating that emanated from the squeezing feeling in her abdomen, her veins had collapsed and a central line was introduced into her upper right chest. Her heart continued to race from anxiety and her body began to shiver and shake when she was told she had to have an NG tube. She was exhausted and in pain, they could do whatever they wanted to her, she was too exhausted to fight back. The drugs entered her body through the central line and she began to drift into a mindless sleep for a week. At some point, Lyla awoke long enough to understand that her body was not responding to the therapy for the ileus and other related issues. Surgery was not an option to resolve the issue and she began to fear she would not recover. And the best plan the doctors had was to watch and wait.

She called one of her sons and asked that he contact Lyla's brother for appropriate documents related to Jewish law and burial should she not survive. She once again drifted in and out of consciousness for another week until her body suddenly began to recover and her guts began to function. The NG tube was removed, she began to take fluids and nourishment, and although pale and weak she began to gain strength.

The doctors ascertained she was making such good progress that she could be discharged the day before Christmas. The boys told her Juliano, to her surprise, was flying into town to rescue her from her ordeal at the hospital and something strange happened to her. She was so grateful Juliano was taking the time to rescue her that she thought of nothing else. Her excitement grew throughout the day he was to arrive. She gathered the strength and with the help of hospital personnel bathed her body, washed her hair, and tried to look as good as possible. She instantly forgave Juliano of his foibles and faults, he was coming to take her home, to rescue her.

He arrived in her hospital room, around nine in the evening, the night before her discharge, accompanied by all the boys. The moment she saw them all she reverted to someone she used to be. The new Lyla was gone, lost somewhere. She was appreciative, submissive, and thankful for the small crumbs of affection Juliano offered. He was a bit cool and distant, but she ignored his behavior. She reached out to him when he came by her bedside and tried to wrap her arms around him and hug him. He withdrew. He was there, that's what counted. She was blind to any other red flags of reality.

The next morning Juliano arrived in her hospital room to take her home. The progression of Juliano's affliction, had become obvious. He walked slowly, with a cane, and a profound limp. Lyla and Juliano waited for the next two hours for her to be discharged and Lyla became anxious. She knew Juliano had no patience and was fearful he would either make a scene or leave without her if the doctors and the nursing personnel didn't complete the paperwork and get her out of there.

Her anxiety climbed to an intolerable level.

And this was her rescuer, her white knight.

Lyla's arrival home was celebrated with a delicious meal cooked by the boys. The aromas emanating from the kitchen made her mouth water. Everyone gathered at the table in the kitchen and behaved as though she had never been away laughing and talking about their lives. The dogs were especially happy to see her jumping up and down, barking, and wagging their tails. They refused to leave her side. She had missed them all and had been so fearful she would never see her children again. Although weak and frail, she insisted on staying in the kitchen until she was no longer able to sit up and then retreated to her bedroom thankful to be back in her own bed. Juliano dutifully stayed with her until she fell asleep.

The next morning, she awoke after a good night's rest, thankful to be with her family. Her next day was spent becoming acclimated to her home and being on her own without the assistance of the hospital staff. She was too weak to take care of herself and relied on the boys to make her morning tea and toast and then crawled back into bed to rest. Juliano did nothing for her.

She was eventually joined by Juliano late in the afternoon. He turned on the television and she attempted to cuddle next to him. He seemed distant, almost cold, but Lyla ignored it. During a moment of weakness, Lyla looked up at him as he sat there comfortably engrossed in some sporting event.

"Juliano," Lyla whispered. "Juliano, did you hear me?"

"Uh, yes, what is it?"

"I've been thinking and…" she noticed he never turned the volume down on the television, "I think I've been a very foolish old woman." His face was expressionless and his eyes were fixated on the television screen. He made no move to acknowledge her in any way and her words hung in the empty air.

When he spoke, his voice was without emotion. "Lyla, I'm leaving tomorrow morning. I'm returning to Miami; I can't stay."

She interrupted, "But, I thought since you came to get me…"

Before she could finish her thought, Juliano continued as though she had not spoken, "I never said I would stay, Lyla. I have to go back; they need me. You know how it is, end of the month, and end of the year. It's very busy, and they need me, I have to be there. They need me."

Lyla had some wild fantasy about being rescued when Juliano appeared but that fantasy could never be fulfilled. His plan was to stay for Christmas Day because the dealership was closed and return on a very early flight the next day.

This reality check was harsh, but it forced her to face the situation and the man who she mistakenly thought came to rescue her. She was a foolish old woman, foolish enough to think this man would ever take care of her. It was a painful lesson she would not forget. When Juliano left her again so helpless, frail, and weak, the emotional residue for Lyla was suffocating. But instead of falling to pieces and into depression, she chose to concentrate on recovery and become strong enough to function. Now her path was much clearer than it had been before. She needed to take care of her.

Initially, Lyla was unable to take care of herself. She hired a woman to come in daily to help her out of bed, shower, and put on a clean nightgown. The woman made Lyla a simple breakfast of warm rice cereal, slivers of dry toast, and tea with honey. At first Lyla was only able to eat several tablespoons of cereal but she began to regain her strength and appetite. After several weeks, Lyla was able to walk and shower without assistance.

Her diet improved and she began to gain weight. Her thoughts turned to what she could do to take care of herself and how she would survive. Juliano made no commitment to return to Texas, and he didn't want her in Miami. His infrequent phone calls were newsy, short, and polite. She knew it was over and the reality of this produced a fear-based anxiety that she had to overcome; she was determined.

ANOTHER NEW BEGINNING

The overwhelming, all-consuming, paralytic fear she used to have at the thought of him leaving her was reduced to a dull, aching, gnawing feeling. She reasoned, *Well, it appears I faced death again, without him again, and if I can do that and survive, I can face the world and survive, at least I hope I can.*

Lyla ached for someone to be with who would fill the void. She listened to the plaintive, haunting song, "Someone to Watch Over Me," sung by Ella Fitzgerald. The melody and words sung by the queen of jazz and blues washed over Lyla, engulfing her and bringing her to tears. She listened alone in the dark, with only the glow of the light from the fireplace, as she played the track over and over again and sang softly with Ella.

How well it described her pain and musings. Each time she listened to the CD, she wondered if she would ever find 'the man I love' who would watch over her. She thought her life would be fulfilled if only she would meet the man who would make her happy and make her life complete. Her life was unsettled, unstable, and without purpose. Her mistaken belief was that all she had to do was find the right man. Surely there was someone out there waiting around the next corner. The music took her on flights of fancy that wrapped her in a soothing blanket of comfort, easing and filling the aching emotional void.

Regrettably, Lyla had yet to discover it wasn't the 'right man' who was going to make her life whole. She was the only one who could that. And perhaps by chance, if a man did come along would she recognize him? If not, would she ever feel complete unto herself?

Lyla was filled with unproductive anger and needed to figure out how to redirect and channel the anger in some fulfilling, creative way. In the beginning, baking bread was a way for her to remove herself from her reality and become absorbed in the process itself and not focus on the unpleasant and painful feelings.

She was spoiled coming from south Florida where good fresh bread was plentiful. Bread-making was a challenge and Lyla couldn't resist. All obsessed people would agree immersing oneself completely helps to focus on an activity that can shield you from everything else. Ultimately this activity gave Lyla an opportunity to be momentarily removed from herself and her circumstances.

Lyla consulted the Internet for recipes and bread baking techniques. She was tenacious once she decided to tackle a task and became engrossed in everything she could find about it: books, people, the Internet; nothing was overlooked. Without realizing it she had created a productive purpose. It didn't matter to her that she had no prior knowledge or experience. Nothing would be impossible as long as she took the time and effort to learn.

She casually dabbled in baking bread but became drawn to the complexities and challenges of baking good specialty breads and turned to making bread the 'right' old fashioned way. Lyla's first goal was to make a good challah, the egg bread baked on Friday afternoon for the Shabbos (Sabbath) dinner table. A friend provided an uncomplicated recipe from a Jewish cookbook, and Lyla thought, *I can do this.*

All of her first loaves were colossal failures and came out of the oven flat or blobby. They were under baked, over baked, dough was too dry or too wet, or the braids swelled all over the pan. Lyla was over-anxious, impatient, and not carefully following the recipe. She eventually discovered that reading the instructions for using the proofing ovens was an important step in succeeding. Lyla was learning critical lessons.

As she surfed the internet, she found bread blogs, bread sites, bread forums and bread books, and became immersed in everything bread. She had more questions than answers even with the information on the blogs she read, and she could not figure out what went wrong and why she was failing.

She thought, *my recipe is simple. What am I not doing? Am I doing anything right? It must be something so obvious I just can't see it.* The boys were not so critical. They ate all her failures, every crumb, without complaint. But she didn't stop.

Over and over again she repeated the steps of the recipe, carefully making sure not to leave anything out. Eventually, she began to see the dough as a living, changing organism with unique properties she needed to interact with, not fight. Although each batch of dough was unique, she began to understand it was necessary for her to partner with and become intimate with her dough.

It was then she realized the necessity of just the right touch and how the dough needed to feel and look when the kneading process was complete. Once she understood this vital relationship, she used her mixer to do the initial kneading, but then turned her dough onto the counter and hand kneaded the dough until it was ready. She was using her senses, her intuition, her newfound knowledge, and her relationship with the ingredients to make the determinations when the dough was ready to move to the next phase.

"I can do this. I can do this." She kept repeating. And then it happened. The loaf looked like a loaf of bread. It came out of the pan golden brown and smelled delicious, filling the house with the aroma of fresh baked challah. The enticing sweet aromas of egg and butter from the freshly baked bread brought her sons to the kitchen eager to taste her creations. She did it, and then she did it again.

Baking specialty breads became her life-giving passion. Her success with the challah in the loaf pan led to success of the braided challah and more. She gathered recipes from the Internet and selected several to try. The loaves were puffy, shiny from the egg wash, with dark caramel colored crust and smelled like the fresh ingredients of oats, cheese, butter, and herbs. The boys were delighted and couldn't wait to grab the fresh warm loaves as they came out of the oven. Soon, there was so much bread they couldn't eat it all. One of the boys commented that the bread was so good, she should sell it.

And that's how it began. Lyla posted a message on the neighborhood Internet group announcing she was making homemade fresh bread. She began with one loaf of challah (egg bread), and before long she was making nine varieties of specialty bread. At first, she baked every Friday, but due to the overwhelming response, she had to bake daily except Saturday and Sunday. Her days began early in the morning taking care of her pack and the house, and by 9 a.m. she would be busy in the kitchen, covered with flour, mixing, kneading, proofing and baking loaves of bread.

The house was filled with intoxicating aromas. Lyla had become productive at something she was proud of. A little business had been created without her even realizing it, and she was soon filling up her kitchen drawer with money. She opened a bank account just for the bakery and decided the bakery needed to pay for itself. If the bakery couldn't sustain itself paying for supplies, she wouldn't continue, but it did. In fact, by the time the holidays arrived she added other goodies like her famous pumpkin bread and cinnamon rolls.

Neighbors were buying for themselves, other neighbors, and friends. The front door of the house resembled a revolving door. People came in and out visiting, purchasing, and tasting bread. They couldn't get enough and Lyla couldn't work fast enough or long enough hours to make what was ordered. The interaction with other people and the euphoric feeling of accomplishment was exhilarating. They liked the bread, and they liked her.

Lyla's cottage industry bakery had been in existence for about six months and her business was outgrowing her small kitchen. Her thoughts turned to how and where she would go to increase her production, and how she would get her bread to more people. One of the residents admired Lyla, her baking talents, and her bread. She approached Lyla with an offer for them to become partners in a small bakery establishment in one of the upscale areas of town. Lyla was flattered by the offer but believed her talents at bread-making were not professional enough yet, and she was not ready to take on the responsibility of a partner. But it was tempting and provided the emotional support Lyla needed.

During those months she spent baking and making friends, she had few thoughts of Juliano. One of her goals was to learn from someone who was an expert in making bread. A customer alerted her to classes offered at the flagship supermarket store in Houston. Lyla found the web page and clicked on the link for the class, thought about the time, cost, and the fear of the unknown, and signed up. The decision was made: she was going to attend the bread-making class at the cooking school taught by a well-known baker and chef. She was anxious to learn new skills and improve upon what she currently produced.

On the appointed day, she awoke early, took care of her pack of cavaliers, and drove into the city. The huge Central Market store was already bustling with people shopping and browsing. Lyla climbed the steps to the second story and found the classroom empty, except for the staff who were dressed in white chef coats making last-minute preparations.

Soon other members of the class arrived and took their seats at their respective tables. The walls of the room were lined with shelves packed with all sizes of pots and bakeware. Large rectangular ovens lined the back wall with a huge, double, stainless steel sink on one side. Kitchen Aide mixers were lined up along the front counter, waiting patiently, like sentries, for the students to begin their lesson. On the other end of the front counter were two very large braided loaves of challah (egg bread), one more beautiful than the other. They had multiple braids that were completely uniform and the crust was a dark golden color that shined brightly in the overhead lights.

Moments before the class began two women walked over to where Lyla was sitting and chose seats at her table. The other women Arlene and Lorraine and Lyla introduced themselves to one another as the chef put on her microphone and started the class. Lyla could tell from the banter back and forth between the two ladies that they were old friends and colleagues and were enjoying the time out together. Lyla immediately became aware of her aloneness but brushed the feeling aside. Lyla was there to learn and was intrigued by the bread and the process of making it.

The class began with some basic definitions about the different kinds of yeast and other baking materials the class would be using during the class. The chef walked to the front of the group with a large book and asked for volunteers to talk about challah and its significance to the Jewish community, it was the first bread they would be making. One of the women at Lyla's table was Jewish and offered some general information, Lyla remained silent. The chef finished her explanation about challah, read an interesting passage from the book, and asked everyone to take a taste of both breads. They tasted the rich egg flavor, the spongy texture, and the soft crunch of the crust and Lyla was determined for her bread to be as good or better.

The participants at each table were instructed, as a group, to come up to the work area to their respective mixers. The table where Lyla sat had only three participants. That meant they would have more hands-on opportunities individually. They followed the directions given to them and listened as the chef explained and demonstrated each technique and step.

When the dough was mixed, Lyla noticed it was much wetter than her dough, almost to the point of being sticky. She made a mental note. After the dough was finished being kneaded by the mixer, they turned it onto the floured surface and kneaded by hand for a moment or two just to get the feel of the dough and notice its smoothness and shine. When the dough was ready, they proceeded to make braids. That day, they were making four braided challah, something Lyla had anxiously wanted to learn. She picked up the braiding technique as though she had been doing it for years. When the other ladies at her table had difficulties, Lyla offered to help, and they all began to share and laugh together.

After their loaves were braided and sent to proof, they returned to their table to begin the next recipe. It was a calzone filled with chopped peppers, roma tomatoes, mushrooms, and mozzarella cheese. It was a special treat because they were going to eat the calzones fresh from the oven. The challahs were in the ovens and the calzones were ready to be brushed with an egg wash and put into the ovens as well. While they waited for the bread and calzones to bake, they attempted their next recipe: breadsticks. These were long, skinny, twisted breadsticks with orange zest and fennel seeds. The dough was soft, smooth, and had a different texture from the other dough. Lyla enjoyed the company of the other women who were now engaging freely and including her in their conversation.

Lyla lost all track of time and didn't realize how late it was. She could smell the freshly baked bread coming from the oven, challahs were put on racks to cool, and calzones were brought to the tables for everyone to enjoy. When Lyla broke open her calzone, the steam escaped like a puff of smoke and it smelled of cheese and peppers. Her seat mates did the same as they broke open their calzones and began to enjoy the fruits of their labors, all except for Arlene. Lyla watched as Arlene ate nearly half of hers, and then said to her table companions, "This is delicious and I'm so tempted to eat the rest, but I'm going to save it. I want to take it home to my husband. He was so excited when I told him I was coming to the class. This way he can share in what I've done, and we can enjoy the experience together."

Lyla said nothing and cast her eyes down at her plate as she finished her calzone. She didn't know how that felt, to have someone who wanted to share her experiences. Arlene's words hung in the air like a small dark rain cloud over Lyla's head, and her mood began to darken.

The finished challah and breadsticks were distributed to the students. Compliments and a round of applause were given to the chef and her staff. The class participants departed talking and laughing. Lyla was the last to leave. There was no one to leave with, no one to go home to, and no one to share anything with. She walked down the steps beyond the cash registers and the front doors into the depths of the store with the darkness of the little cloud above her head.

She explored the busy store in wide-eyed wonderment, jostled and bumped by the crowds of people shopping. That store was as much a social experience as it was a place to purchase food and accessories. As she strolled through every department, she stopped for a long time in the bakery. She stood watching the bakers work with the dough and smelling the just-finished bread as it emerged from the ovens. It was an adventure just walking the aisles with delectable surprises waiting around each corner and down every aisle.

Lyla completed her tour of the entire store but was not tempted to make any purchase. With a heavy heart, she exited the store feeling the pain of her solitude and walked to her car in the parking lot hoping that window shopping would lift her spirits. It was a Saturday, and every Saturday, weather permitting, a different band played outside on the veranda to entertain customers as they watched and devoured the goodies they purchased inside. Couples had gathered on the veranda at tables for customers who stopped to listen to the music and some were even daring enough to dance. The longer she watched, the darker and lonelier she became.

Lyla drove across the street to a strip of enticing upscale stores. She donned her hat and sunglasses and walked briskly, at first, entering and exiting new and interesting shops. The shoe store was her first stop and when she walked in she remembered it had been such a long time since she bought a nice pair of shoes. Dress shops were next and then on to other stores that normally would have been enticing places. As her feelings intensified, she began to walk slowly, aimlessly past the stores, only occasionally stopping to peer inside windows. The melancholy had become intensified and she could no longer contain feeling overcome by her singularity and the absence of a significant partner to share her life.

The slower she walked the heavier she felt, and what had begun as an exciting adventure turned into a sorrowful moment. When she reached her car, small tears filled her eyes, and she took a deep breath to dampen the feelings of emptiness that had descended upon her. She listened to soft classical music as she drove down the monotonous highway home on a long, sorrowful ride and thought.

I am struck by my aloneness, my awful singularity, and the painful oneness that engulfs me.

THE BREAD LADY AND THEN

Lyla returned from her baking class with new skills and the confidence to continue baking. She modified her recipes, honed her techniques, and had more orders to fill than equipment to produce the quantities needed. More loaf pans and a larger, better mixer were purchased. Now she was really in the business of baking bread. Regular customers from her neighborhood had stopped buying bread from the local grocery. Kids were boycotting school sandwiches made with store-bought bread and their mothers complained that their thighs had fallen in love with Lyla's bread.

Lyla was becoming a successful businesswoman, making deliveries in and out of the neighborhood and named her bakery, Sweet Aromas. Her kitchen drawer was filled with money, evidence of her success. Every morning she would take care of her cavaliers, stream her favorite classical radio station through her laptop, scrub her counters, and go to work.

The months went by and Lyla expanded her basic bread menu. Fall was approaching and she wanted to introduce something new for the season. She thought about the things she made in the past and chose her reliable pumpkin bread recipe. It was an easy, dependable recipe that when baked in a bundt pan was impressive, smelled like cinnamon, warm spices, and reflected the season. She posted notices on the neighborhood internet group in early September. She was now marketing her products.

Lyla was overwhelmed with responses when she began taking orders for her pumpkin bread. The house was filled with the aroma of fresh bread, cinnamon, nutmeg, and clove. She added pizza dough to her available products and packaged it ready to roll, top, and bake. Mothers were delighted with the easy meals and had pizza birthday parties for their children. Everyone was rolling, topping, and baking. There were days when Lyla had so many pizza dough orders her refrigerator overflowed. When the dough rose inside the refrigerator it exploded every time the door was opened.

Everything was good.

Until late summer.

Until she began to get unsettling calls from Juliano.

"Hello, Lyla, yes, it's me, Juliano. Who else would it be? Do you know what I have to do to do my laundry? Well, I'm staying in a fifth-floor apartment and the laundry room is on the third floor. I have to drag the laundry basket, sometimes I even push it with my cane, into the elevator, go to the third floor and empty the basket into the washing machine and dryer. I have to do all this by myself and try to keep my balance at the same time. Sometimes I can't get into the elevator fast enough and the damn elevator door closes on me. It's a scene.

"And, I've been falling at work on my way to the copy machine. It's so embarrassing. Nobody says anything but everyone knows and I guess they feel sorry for me. I went to see a neurologist at the University of Miami Jackson Memorial Hospital and he thinks my diagnosis is similar to ALS but isn't sure. He just keeps telling me there's not much anyone can do."

"Well, Juliano, it just so happens that I got a call from your doctor's nurse at the University. She asked me to have a discussion with you about your drinking. She said the doctor has talked to you about stopping yet you persist.

"I was so embarrassed that this strange woman was asking me to talk to my husband to beg him to stop drinking. I had to tell her I didn't live with you there and had no control over what you did. You need to stop being so dramatic. Ask someone for help, there's nothing I can do for you from Texas."

It was not clear to Lyla what Juliano meant by these emotional displays. Had the disease progressed so much he was no longer able to be independent? Or was he tired of taking care of himself? He had a tendency toward the dramatic and was the consummate victim. What changed? What was he not willing to divulge? What was he planning?

He must have had ulterior motives and, of course, chose to share nothing with Lyla. He continued to complain how he didn't have the time to sit on the phone to discuss Social Security disability. He wanted

Lyla to take care of everything. Why was he on the phone with Social Security unless he was formulating some plan to quit working? Lyla tried to ignore his pleas and his pathetic cries for help.

He would call her and whine. "You're the only one who has ever been able to get anything done. I don't know how you do it but it's true. I just get hung up on after waiting for hours for someone to answer. Please help me; I can't do this anymore."

He manipulated whomever he could. Lyla grew tired of his whining and general complaints. To get relief, she agreed to take care of his latest problem. She was busy with her business and taking the time and responsibility to deal with his needs, whatever they were, became an imposition. She resented his intrusion into her life since he was the one who chose to leave.

In September, 2009, she helped him without realizing what she set in motion; she had provided the vehicle Juliano needed to make his move and complete his plan. She collected the disability information and re-layed it back to Juliano, hoping he would leave her alone.

In October, Juliano called Lyla to tell her he was leaving his job in November of that year and planned to live with her. He never gave her a reason. He insisted Lyla meet him in Sarasota, Florida. He thought he could likely manipulate her into leaving Texas by tempting her with a new home on the west coast of Florida.

What was he thinking? Why would she ever consider another major move and leave her business and children? Why would she trust him?

For the first time in her adult life, Lyla was feeling good about herself and productive. She was anxious her life would change if Juliano were to return to Texas and it wouldn't be for the better. Her business was booming. It was an incredibly busy time of the year, and she had obligations. But for some reason she eventually gave in and agreed to meet Juliano in Florida. Her customers would have to wait until she returned. It was as though her husband's imminent return melted all the independence she had gained.

Lyla's anxiety and fears began to increase at Juliano's impending return and she didn't know how or what to do to prepare. She knew the life she created without him would end. She wondered, *what made him stay away so long and why did he decide to return now?* The more she thought the more she reasoned he needed someone to rescue him, again. She was unable to find a way to protect herself.

Juliano leased a new vehicle before he left Miami and drove to Sarasota where he met Lyla. Part of his plan was to take her to an upscale 55+ community and discuss different models that could be built. When in Sarasota, he complained bitterly about his inability to walk without significant aid and insisted on a wheelchair. Lyla purchased a portable wheelchair not realizing how he would use this to control her even more. They left Florida with brochures of house plans and prices and Juliano hoped he had planted a seed that might come to fruition. After all, he still hated Texas.

The drive from Florida to Texas was barely tolerable for Lyla. Juliano insisted on doing all the driving. His driving skills had diminished and Lyla was afraid. The admissions she had made to Charlie, Dr. Horne's nurse practitioner, had increased her discomfort and distress being with Juliano, and she was afraid to be confined in a hotel room with him. More ugly rocks were piled onto her necklace and she was crumbling under the weight. Although Juliano drove, Lyla had to pump gas, get a room, drag the luggage, and push Juliano's dead weight around in a portable wheelchair.

"I can't walk by myself anymore because I lose my balance and fall. I'm still okay to drive but I can't get gas or do any of that other stuff. You have to take care of everything and don't forget to clean the windshield when you get gas. By the way, when you get a room make sure it's a decent room on the first floor and I want extra towels in the bathroom, lots of extra towels. Have you got that?"

She was exhausted and as she feared, she had to deal with his insatiable appetite for sex. When he approached her in the hotel room on their first night she said she was too tired. When they stopped on the second night she became frantic fearing he wouldn't accept her direct refusal. This caused her guts to be in turmoil.

"Hey, Lyla, how about we mess around?"

"No, Juliano, I'm tired and I'm not feeling well. I've been in and out of the bathroom all night."

"Well, I guess if you're not feeling well, we can wait until we get to Texas, we should arrive tomorrow."

Did Lyla stop to ponder who she had become in his absence and that there was a difference between rescuing someone and allowing someone to steal your life?

A familiar cycle returned. There was a fleeting honeymoon period followed by brief moments of Lyla's frustration turning to anger. She couldn't stand being bullied and bossed around as though she were incapable of generating a rational thought. The façade of the submissive wife began to deteriorate. Lyla was suddenly Juliano's caretaker and resented the role.

Lyla was too frightened of what Juliano might do if she openly confronted him and never forgot about the pills and handcuffs she found in his dresser drawer. She began asking herself. *Why do I have to take care of him, he never did it for me?*

He had returned. He had taken over.

Her bread business began to suffer from her lack of time and attention. Lyla was pulled in two directions, by her desire to continue her own work and passion, and by Juliano's need to dominate and accomplish his plan, whatever that was. Lyla worked diligently to make the necessary arrangements to secure his Social Security benefits. The process was time-consuming, and they had to appear in person for an interview. Juliano's mood was dark the day they drove to the Social Security office in Conroe, Texas. He hated being in the rain, and she hated dragging him around in the wheelchair. He was heavy and did little more than bark orders at her.

The temperature had begun to drop, the sky was overcast, gray, with intermittent rain when they left the house. When they arrived at the building, there was a light drizzle. Lyla pulled the car into a disabled spot several spaces from a ramp. She popped the trunk while Juliano sat in the car waiting. The temperature continued to drop and the wind began to blow harder.

Lyla struggled to drag the folded wheelchair out of the trunk, unfold it with difficulty, and wheel it to the side of the car. She made several trips back to the trunk for the separate parts and the bag on the back that contained Juliano's papers. When everything was in place, she opened the door for Juliano to grab the inside door handle. He adeptly pulled himself up and out of the car, plopping his entire heavy form into the chair. Lyla had to hold on to the back of the chair with all her strength to keep the chair upright and struggled to wheel him as fast as she could to the ramp, up the hill, and into the building. Once inside, she wheeled him to the front desk where they signed in and took a number.

The room was filled to capacity with people: young, old, disabled, many who spoke no English, sitting passively waiting like cattle for slaughter. The large room was darkened from the rainy overcast skies, cold, and smelled of wet clothing and shoes. She turned to Juliano and said.

"This is creepy."

Juliano's number was called and they were directed to a cubicle down one hallway and to the end of another hallway. Lyla parked the wheelchair at the desk facing the interviewer and found an empty chair for herself and sat next to Juliano. Lyla retrieved the folder of papers. The interviewer asked for a list of physicians. Lyla began to dictate the names and contact information, when Juliano interrupted her.

"No, don't give her that information first; give her the other name."

Lyla's face became blank, her neck arched in defiance, her jaw clenched, and she waited. She began again, "And this is Dr."

Again, Juliano interrupted her, his voice stern and bossy.

"No, give her the other information on the other doctor."

Lyla slowly turned her head to face Juliano. There was deadly silence and then she spoke to Juliano. "You need to stop interrupting me while I'm giving this information."

"And what will happen to me if I don't?"

Lyla leaned close to him and spoke in a hushed voice. "Well, I'll push the wheelchair out down the hall, let go, and let you get yourself back out to the parking lot. Is that clear? It's your choice."

The interviewer's eyes grew wide, her mouth dropped open, and Juliano laughed.

"My wife has such a sense of humor. Isn't she funny?"

Lyla wasn't kidding. A half hour later, the interview was complete and Lyla wheeled Juliano back to the car. She had to repeat the process of depositing Juliano into the car, dismantling his wheelchair, and placing the pieces back into the trunk while the rain and wind continued. Lyla was dripping wet from the cold and rain, exhausted, embarrassed by Juliano's abusive behavior and furious with him. Lyla drove back to the house without saying a word to Juliano. He either didn't notice her silence and anger or didn't care.

Lyla believed open confrontation with Juliano was risky. She had to bury her anger and resentment and find other ways to deal with her feelings. She retreated emotionally and mentally and continued to build her impenetrable wall of protection.

The social security experience was like an episode from the twilight zone. The person in charge of Juliano's case continued to request more information to verify his condition as a valid disease justifying disability.

"Yes, I understand Mrs. Masselli, said the case manager, "but we have to confirm that your husband indeed has a motor neuron disease by one of our independent physicians and is indeed disabled and qualifies for disability. Send me something that indicates his condition conclusively so I can move his file forward in the process."

Lyla was frustrated with a dysfunctional government system and at Juliano for dumping this on her at a crucial time in her business. She asked herself, "How much more evidence do these people require? What part of "he will not survive the disease" do these people not understand?" She was tired of fighting, tired of the entire nightmare, physically and emotionally exhausted. After five months of waiting, interviews, and submission of documents Juliano's case worker called Lyla to inform her Juliano's application for disability had been approved. Just like that.

Lyla had holiday orders as well as regular bread customers that kept her busy. The number of daily orders for baked goods increased to twenty loaves of bread and at least six pumpkin breads a day. Her kitchen was a constant hub of activity with flour flying, ovens pumping out proofed and baked goods, mixers whirling, and stacks of finished product ready for pick up. Juliano was behaving, for once, keeping himself busy with his television and computer. It appeared he accepted her work schedule. He had yet to complain about anything.

How long would that last?

Lyla woke up every morning feeling productive anxious to start her day and each new challenge. Every time another loaf of bread would come out of the oven 'perfect' or the pumpkin bread came out looking like it was a picture in a magazine, Lyla felt a rush, a tingling of excitement. She marveled at what she made. Lyla was obsessed with being organized and prepared with customer names, contact information, orders, costs, selling prices and pick-up times. She was a personal baker to every customer and insisted on having orders ready for pick up or delivery when they were fresh from the oven. Every moment of her day was occupied.

Lyla was convinced she made something wonderful from a bunch of dust, water, and shortening and what she accomplished was miraculous and delicious. And people liked it. Her little kitchen drawer was filled with money, and she was making people happy. One of her regular customers took the time to thank her.

"Lyla, I wanted to say a big thank you for making such a wonderful loaf of your Italian Cheese herb bread. I gave the loaf to a friend who is suffering from cancer and currently receiving chemotherapy. He's lost his appetite and lost weight as a result and is not doing well. But every time I bring him the bread his face brightens up with a smile and he slowly munches his way through the loaf, it makes him so happy. Thank you, your bread is a gift."

"I'm so glad to hear that he enjoys the bread. Let him know it is my distinct pleasure to bake for him, anytime."

If her 'flow,' as she called it, were interrupted by Juliano coming into the kitchen to talk or be served she would become angry. He was a distraction and it would ultimately result in her forgetting the number of cups of flour or spoons of salt, or sugar she was putting into her recipe. Making such mistakes wreaked havoc on her modified assembly line and drove her crazy.

Juliano would shuffle into the kitchen slowly pushing his walker sliding his unwashed hand along the island covered with baking ingredients. He would open the refrigerator door and lean back against the island to steady himself and just stand there staring into the refrigerator.

"Juliano," Lyla shouted, "what the heck do you think you're doing? I'm in the middle of making stuff and you're distracting me. I can't keep an accurate count of what I'm putting in and you're touching everything. I don't have time to take care of you now, you're going to have to wait. Find something fast and get out of here."

The dogs didn't help either. Lyla would be covered in flour in a world of her own when one of the dogs would sneak into the kitchen and begin to circle the island sniffing and licking flour off the floor. As soon as Lyla tripped over the small furry body or saw the criminal act she would begin to shout.

"Hey there, you, yes you with all the fur. Get out! Get out! Git... Git... Git... get your furry body out of here and don't come back." Just to make sure the dog retreated Lyla would use her foot to guide the dog out of the kitchen. Lyla's frustration and lack of patience with the dogs extended to Juliano when they both bothered her and got in her way.

People were in and out of the house every day. The front door was forever opening and closing like some great swinging portal. Customers walked in empty handed and walked out with their arms filled to overflowing. The adults were just as bad as the kids and weren't able to resist tearing into the bread before they reached Lyla's front door. Her customers, at times, came in hungry and tired but walked out with smiles happily eating. One customer arrived at Lyla's house after work hungry and tired. She picked up her loaf of bread and when she walked out said, "Ah, just what I needed after a long hard day at work. My day will end well with this loaf of bread, cheese, and a good bottle of wine."

Lyla never touched money while she worked and her front door was always unlocked during baking hours. Her customers knocked on the door and walked in smiling and salivating the closer they got to the aromas wafting in from the kitchen. Pleasantries and greetings were exchanged as long as Lyla wasn't too busy. The customers opened her money drawer and deposited their cash oftentimes giving her extra. Lyla's biggest customer complaint was that she didn't charge enough.

Because the business consumed most of Lyla's time and energy, Lyla hoped Juliano would participate in some way. Juliano was sitting on the couch in the living room when one of Lyla's customers knocked on the door and entered the house. The customer walked toward Juliano to say hello and Juliano immediately turned the volume up on the television. The customer tried shouting over the television to say hello. Juliano never responded, never looked in the person's direction. This scene was repeated often. Soon, people learned to ignore him and walk directly to the kitchen to find Lyla.

Juliano behaved like a pouting, rude child and believed he was being left out and rejected. He began to punish her. While Lyla was in the midst of her baking routine, Juliano purposely ambled into the kitchen and stood, without speaking, waiting for Lyla to acknowledge his presence. After several minutes he tried to get her attention. "Hey there, Lyla. Hey there. I want to talk to you, now."

Silence.... moments of silence.

Slowly, without looking up from her activity Lyla responded. "Well, Juliano, what is it this time? Is the game over, are you bored? You couldn't possibly be hungry I gave you a snack a little over an hour ago. So, what is it?"

Her indifference made him angry. He stood still for several more moments trying to block her way to the ovens. When she didn't respond he would make a snide remark, "Oh, yeah, sorry to be in the way, I know how busy you are. You haven't got time for me, your customers are more important." He turned and slowly shuffled out of the kitchen with his head down.

Right before the holiday, after a long day of baking, Juliano wandered into the kitchen and said, "Lyla I want you to give up the baking, give it up, for me. You are leaving me out, and I feel like I don't have a wife. You are constantly kicking me out of the kitchen just like you kick out the dogs and I'm not one of the dogs. That's all you do is spend time in the kitchen working. I want my wife to be my wife. What am I supposed to do here all day by myself?"

His speech began to feel like he was hammering nails into her coffin. A new year began, Lyla reduced her baking schedule and kept one or two regular customers, and was no longer the Lyla she had become. Juliano found other things to complain about like the weather, any thing he thought was inconvenient, and the distance he had to travel to go anywhere. Nothing about him had changed.

Several days after she reduced her baking schedule he tried to monopolize as much of her time as possible. He became totally dependent on Lyla to dress and undress him and respond to his every whim and desire. His litany of veiled demands would begin early in the day after his daily shower. He would sit in his bedroom chair and ask Lyla to dress him.

"Hey Lyla, can you come over here for a minute. I can't put my socks and pants on. I can't bend over. And by the way, can you get me that blue striped shirt in my middle dresser drawer, you know, the one I like?"

Lyla was in constant motion back and forth from his seat to the dresser to the closet to the dresser again. She started with his socks, unrolled them, stretched them, struggled to get them on his swollen feet, and pull them up. He was uncooperative and did things to make the task more annoying and difficult by spreading his toes when she tried to put the sock on and pull it up. During this process, Lyly would be forced to touch his skin and every time she did she shuddered, cringed, and became repulsed feeling like she was going to throw up. The trousers were even worse. He insisted on both legs being put on at the same time and then pulled up to his hips. He would stand with difficulty and purposely lean on her back to steady himself when she was bending over and force her to stand close to him as she pulled the pants higher. The only way she kept herself from screaming and vomiting was to separate herself from the tasks that placed her in close proximity to him that forced her to actually touch him. Each time she had to tuck those awful feelings away inside her, her guts would rumble and groan.

Juliano's demands made Lyla feel she was constantly racing around as if on roller skates.

"Honey, will you, honey, can you get me that, honey, can you put on a load of my laundry, honey, can you get my other shoes? Before I forget, when you vacuum my bathroom, don't forget to get the dog hair tumbleweeds in the corner, they just drive me crazy."

She would grimace at each command, grit her teeth, and remain silent to avoid confrontation at all costs. She pictured herself with a short-ruffled skirt well above her knees, a white off-the-shoulder blouse, tri-cornered cap, and roller skates whizzing and gliding from one room to the next like the carhops of the 1950's balancing trays of food and drinks.

Juliano had complete disregard for Lyla, his only concern was himself.

What happened to the busy, productive woman with the successful home bakery?

She retreated internally to the only place where she felt safe and able to survive.

Their life together, again, was strained as Lyla endured his endless demands by accommodating him without question. Lyla returned to a learned behavior pattern to deal with her emotional turmoil. In her desperation to escape Juliano's presence, she wandered away from the house without purpose. Her obvious intent was to accomplish simple errands, but she ended up wandering for hours. Lyla's unplanned excursions took her to places other than the grocery. She drifted through malls among crowds of people, taking refuge in her anonymity having contact with people who were not emotionally confrontational. She became just another woman out for an afternoon.

And then she adopted an idiosyncrasy she learned from watching her mother. She became obsessed with buying jewelry, handbags, shoes, she couldn't get enough shoes, and gifts for others that she didn't need and certainly couldn't afford. It was her drug of choice, a way to erase her melancholy. She had a closet stuffed with clothes, racks of shoes, cubby holes filled with handbags and shawls, and a jewelry box filled with gold and sparkling stones and no place to wear them.

And her guts were in turmoil.

CHANGE SOMETHING HAD TO CHANGE

The sun was shining on a beautiful Sunday morning and Juliano wanted to go to the car show at the convention center in Houston. He contacted the boys and convinced them it would be a great way to spend the day. Lyla hated the car show but had to attend, she had to drive. Juliano graduated from the portable wheelchair to a motorized scooter with accompanying lift on the rear of the car. The ordeal began. Lyla had to place a heavy portable ramp in the garage doorway for Juliano to ride the scooter outside the house. Once he was loaded into the car, the scooter had to be loaded onto the lift, strapped in, raised and locked in place. Lyla struggled with the heavy equipment and was exhausted before she began the hour-long drive to the convention center. She reached the convention center, turned off the street towards parking, and drove toward the parking booths to pay. Signs above the booths designated which booth to go to depending on the section. Lyla read the signs and drove the car to the booth on the left. Juliano interrupted her and tried to grab the steering wheel.

"No, don't go that way," as he pointed his finger to the booth at the end on his right.

Lyla automatically turned the car in the direction of the booth on the right when she read the signs again and changed the direction of the car left.

"No," he shouted at her, "no, don't do that. I told you go to the booth over there on the right. Do that."

Again, without thinking she responded by changing direction following his instructions. She zigzagged two more times as he continued pointing and shouting at her until she realized what she was doing.

Then she slammed on the brakes in the middle of the stream of cars and screamed at him, "STOP... STOP TALKING TO ME. SHUT UP... SHUT UP. If you don't shut up I'm going to dump you out of the car right here. I can't take this anymore. I know what I'm doing. I'm driving."

Juliano sat in stunned silence. Lyla found a disabled parking spot near the entrance to the building, repeated the process of removing the scooter and unloading Juliano from the car. Lyla was stoic, Juliano was unusually quiet. When they entered the building and found the boys, Lyla refused to walk around the exhibit with them and said nothing. She sat near the concession stand for hours while they collected brochures, kicked tires, sat in cars, and ogled the specialty cars. Lyla seriously considered leaving Juliano there with the boys to figure out how to get him back home but didn't want to burden her children, so she sat and waited. When Juliano and the boys were done, Lyla asked the boys for help to return the scooter onto the lift and Juliano into the car. She was furious and ignored Juliano, he didn't care.

Lyla thought, *I can't take this anymore, something has to change.* She confronted Juliano in the kitchen when they returned home.

"I am neither your servant nor your slave," Lyla said. Stop ordering me around and stop messing with the windshield wipers and other dashboard equipment while I'm driving. I don't want or need your help. If you want something you need to understand I will respond when I can."

He did not respond. Out of frustration she repeated herself thinking he didn't hear her.

"Juliano, you spend hours watching television. As soon as one sporting season has ended, there's another to take its place. You asked me to stop baking because you wanted to spend time with me. I gave it up but your behavior hasn't changed. Why is that? I have made numerous suggestions of activities for us as a couple, but you have refused to consider any of them."

Lyla stood there waiting for a response, there was none from Juliano. He merely looked away from her back to the television and acted as though she had not spoken. It took courage for Lyla to stand up for herself and just tell him, not scream at him. This time she voiced her rejection of him without the all-consuming fear of reprisal. Juliano made pseudo changes but they didn't last.

Lyla recognized who Juliano was and his inability or lack of desire to change. She had more clarity and understood her protestations were meaningless to him. He believed her rantings had nothing to do with him, she was the one who had problems and issues. He didn't need to change; there was nothing wrong with him.

Why did she bother to say anything? Did she begin to see her life from a different perspective? She realized she no longer wanted to give up her life for him and walked back to the kitchen to prepare a customer's order while she replayed the scene.

What a fool I am, she thought. *Why do I waste my time and energy telling him the same things over and over again? What am I hoping to accomplish? Am I venting my frustration with myself over the bad decisions I've made? Foolish woman, foolish...foolish woman. When will I learn that my life with that man will never change?*

And then the inevitable happened. With an empty house, no baking schedule, and an afternoon without any kind of significant sporting event, Lyla became a target.

"Uh, Lyla, how are you feeling? I see you're not busy right now, how about we meander to the bedroom and have a little afternoon delight? We can have a glass of wine first if you want. Come on, how about it? Just a quickie? Afterwards we can go to one of those famous Texas steak houses and then walk around the mall and shop? Aw, Lyla, you want to do this as much as I do, I know you do."

The moment Lyla feared might happen did, now what was she going to do? Juliano shuffled toward the bedroom confident she wouldn't deny him. He managed to get himself undressed and into the bed before Lyla had a chance to think up an excuse. She walked in the bedroom past the bed, said nothing, and locked herself in the bathroom. Just as she had done in the past, she looked at her reflection in the mirror searching for help. She thought, *well, Lyla, how are you going to get out of this mess? What will you do if he's taken one of those stupid little blue pills?*

She felt trapped, her feet were stuck to the floor. He was waiting for her, and he wouldn't wait long. What if she just walked out and told him no? What would he do? It would take him longer to get himself out of bed than it would take her to leave the room.

Don't do it Lyla, the voice inside her head said. *Don't do it, get out, get away while you have the chance. Don't give in; don't let him hurt you, this is against your will, say no.*

Why was Lyla being so compliant and submissive? Why wasn't she fighting back? What was she afraid of? Did she want him back? Was it impossible for her to establish a life without him? Why was she allowing herself to be trapped and used again?

Fear.

Lyla was afraid to move beyond the imaginary boundaries in place for so many years. She was comfortable knowing those boundaries. Sadly, whether her fears were founded in reality or not, they were real to Lyla. In order to grow, she would need to move beyond those boundaries. Was she able to do that?

Lyla did not examine or understand her fear. She felt its grasp on her and reluctantly opened the bathroom door believing she had nowhere to go. The six feet from the bathroom door to the bed felt like miles. As she made the guilt-ridden steps towards the bed she kept thinking, *I did this, I caused this to happen, I'm not worth saving.* She reached the bed and crawled under the covers and began to shiver. "Don't worry honey, Juliano whispered, I'll make you warm and toasty."

Juliano used all his strength and grabbed her body from behind so he could drag his body closer to hers. She didn't move. He nearly wore himself out trying to get closer to her so he could fulfill his sexual obsession. In the commission of that act, he crushed her, pulled on her, and grabbed her harder to steady himself. He became so lost and consumed in his efforts that he forgot she was there until he rapidly came to his conclusion in a convulsive series of movements.

Then he spoke in a hoarse voice, "That was great for me...you're so great. I've always been so turned on by you."

She was silent, still. "Hey, Lyla, are you going to answer me?"

"Juliano," she responded softly, "please get off me. I want to get in the shower."

He didn't move. The extraordinary efforts he expended exhausted him and she was ready to scream, NO MORE. He disgusted her. Lyla's revulsion of him prompted her to push him off her like he was a beached sperm whale. Her instincts told her to run. She left the bed and turned on the shower, her haven. Like so many times before, she felt the warm water run over her body hoping it would wash away his touch, his smell. And, like so many times before, she remained silent allowing her tears to fall and be washed away by the water falling from the shower head.

"Hey," Juliano called from the bedroom, "are you ever going to come out of there? I need a towel and I need some help getting out of bed. Hey, where's my walker?"

Juliano felt energized by his intimate encounter and his manliness. The abuse he performed put him in a good mood for the rest of the evening. His demands were couched in softer tones and he appeared to be more patient, satisfied as long as she submitted.

The next morning and every morning thereafter, Lyla was up and out of bed before he would wake and be aroused by her. Several days later Lyla was finishing her morning shower when Juliano pushed open the bathroom doors with his walker. He reached his sink and slowly went through his morning routine. Lyla stepped from the shower onto the bathmat, dried her feet, feeling uncomfortable with him staring at her. She covered herself with her towel, self-conscious of her nakedness.

"You're staring at me," she said, "I'm uncomfortable. Please don't do that."

Juliano laughed a wicked laugh and said, "I like seeing you naked."

"Come here," he said, as he leaned back against the counter and cabinet for balance. "Come on over here. I want to give you a hug."

She felt like there were bugs crawling all over her body. She began to shiver; her guts were churning in turmoil. She hesitated then slowly and dutifully walked toward him, clutching the towel draped around her. He pulled her to him, removing the towel to expose her body, pressing her against his nearly naked body. She tried to keep her arms folded across her chest but he shoved them aside as he squeezed and pressed her closer. He was rough, grabbing her flesh to satisfy his needs. Her body grew stiff and she tried to squirm out of his arms. "Stop, Juliano, stop. Your hands are cold and I don't want this to happen."

"Now, do you see that," he said looking down, "you see what has happened here? Look at that. How about we jump back into bed and finish what's started here?"

She struggled to free herself and he finally let her go. "Not now, Juliano. I've got to let the girls out, and I have a million things to do."

She left him in the bathroom wondering what happened, grabbed her clothes, and left.

Rejection.

Consequences.

THE ERUPTION

Lyla was spending long periods of time sitting on her blue bench under the crabapple tree, contemplating her past, present, and possible future. When she began her mental journeys in the gardens, she cried grieving for the life path she mistakenly chose and a lifetime of pain and suffering she no longer wanted to endure. Her grieving gave way to thoughts and desires of a better life.

Lyla was overwhelmed at the thought of moving on without her husband and children. This was the first time in her adult life, since her marriage to Juliano, that she seriously dared think about, let alone act on, moving towards something meaningful to her. She felt she had no other life before this struggle and at times was drowning in a pit of quicksand her entire existence. Moving out of the pit was a daunting thought. *Could she live on her own? How?*

How, was a difficult question to answer. Instead of being inspired to imagine happiness she fell back on what had been and resented the charade of living a lie. It took an incredible amount of energy pretending to be someone else. Her attempts to ignore her past with him were unsuccessful and that the past was not something haunting her like some skulking monster lying in wait, ready to devour her when she least expected it. As long as the children needed her protection, she had to live that way. Now that they were gone it was time for her to be free of that burden.

Living with him meant living with resentment and fear that remained just below Lyla's surface, simmering and bubbling over with the slightest provocation into anger and pain. Even small things she should have been able to ignore were irritating to her. The cumulative effect of living with him added more emotional rocks to her neck. Staying meant that Lyla would have to live with Juliano's daily monotonous routine and his demands. The tension grew between them with Juliano's refusal to leave the house because of the weather or his mood. This situation forced them to constantly share the same space. His pleas were wrapped in demanding tones of his victimization hoping she would feel sorry for him.

Daily contact with Juilano aroused painful, horrific triggers. Little by little bad dreams crept back interrupting her sleep. Her nights were spent thinking, replaying old tapes from the past in vivid detail and wondering how she could get out of the mess she was in before it was too late. *And what did too late mean anyway,* she thought to herself?

Unplanned ideas that come from a position of weakness and desperation often result in dramatic problems that can become dangerous. Lyla's fears and beliefs had become automatic and were no longer rooted in reality. It took little effort from Juliano for Lyla to remain afraid.

Juliano's touch and presence became agonizing discomfort and Lyla began to struggle with the inevitability of leaving him, finally, after all those years. Her guts were constantly screaming, she was in pain, anxious, and she couldn't get rid of the sensation of something crawling on her skin. She felt guilty leaving a man who was ill and unable to easily care for himself and afraid she would not be able to financially survive even though she had had success in her bakery. And despite the fact that her children were grown and out of the house, how would she explain the separation to them? Would they ever be able to understand? Would they believe her? Or were these excuses to talk herself out of leaving?

What on earth is the matter with me, she asked herself, *and why can't I forget the incidents, pain, and emotional horrors of my past with him? I don't want to worry about looking over my shoulder afraid and embarrassed by what my husband did in the past. I get stuck every Valentine's Day reliving the horrifying memories. I'm ashamed of my decisions, my life.* Lyla admonished herself in the lonely hours of the night when she couldn't sleep. *Just forget it,* she reminded herself. *It was a long time ago. Constantly thinking about it is making me miserable.*

The tension in their life continued. They were like two strange, cagey, softly snarling animals circling, just out of reach of each other. They shared, uneasily, the same space but little else. His behavior was becoming more erratic and unreasonable.

Lyla's morning routine was to usher the pack out the kitchen door to enjoy the sun and troll the yard. She was unable to be with them, take her pills, make her pot of tea and toast, and serve Juliano at the same time. She had to keep moving from kitchen, to pantry, and in and out of the garage responding to Juliano's veiled orders.

In the morning Juliano sat at the kitchen table next to the large bay window that overlooked the backyard and watched the dogs. He sat at the table hunched over, old bear-like, eating bits of dry cold cereal, drinking his orange juice with crushed ice. When he finished that he would devour fresh citrus leaning over the sink, slobbering, licking, and sucking the juice with sounds Lyla found disgusting. Lyla couldn't stand to be anywhere near him.

The final steps in his morning routine were to go to his favorite sites on the computer, spend time in the bathroom, and then return to the kitchen table for cereal. The morning began like every other morning. It had been two mornings after Lyla rejected Juliano in the bathroom after her shower. Juliano was sitting at the kitchen table while Lyla rushed to prepare the items he required for his morning meal. As usual, Lyla let the dogs out the kitchen back door to meander in the yard. She watched as they moved from place to place and saw one of them contentedly munching on something in the grass. Juliano locked his eyes on the one who was chewing on something and suddenly spewed forth bits of toast, cereal, and expletives, many of which Lyla had never heard before, cursing the dog and anything else that came to mind.

What ensued was a Krakatoa-like volcanic eruption from the bent form at the table. A flow of hateful profanity rained down, torching everything in its path, engulfing the room in noxious tension. Juliano's eyes were wide, his face was red, and his arms were flailing about as he pounded his fist on the table with each obscenity. The curse words and the insults grew louder and more objectionable and ended in a crescendo of anger. Juliano began choking, coughing and gagging on the toast bits and juice he inhaled during the explosion.

Juliano's outburst was his emotional response to Lyla's sexual rejection in the bathroom days earlier. He used the dogs' behavior as a vehicle to verbally assault Lyla and her beloved companion dogs.

Lyla stood still, remaining a safe distance in the kitchen by the island, as Juliano began his tirade, until there was silence. From her position, she spoke with a strong, steady voice. Looking at him she began, "If you have a problem with what happens when the dogs are outside, you have choices other than spewing out your venomous anger. Don't look out the window, close the blind, something, anything other than blasting everyone and everything within hearing distance with the ugliness that comes from inside you.

"I have been living with your volatile and destructive anger for too long and will not tolerate it anymore. It's putrid and fills the entire house with hate. You can take your hate someplace else; you will no longer spread it here. It is noxious and malicious and has had a destructive effect on me all these years making me physically ill."

Juliano sat in astonished silence and then spoke apologetically, lowering his eyes towards the table top. "Your point is well taken. I should know better, I shouldn't be doing this. You're right, this is not your problem, it's mine. I'm sorry, it was not my intention to..."

Lyla interrupted him before he could finish. "This has nothing to do with your intentions, or with you knowing or not knowing better. This is the way you are. Do not misunderstand; I am not asking you to change. I'm telling you, because of the way you are, you must stop these outbursts while you are with me. It's simple. All you feel is anger and hate. It's always there, bubbling and gurgling under the surface ready to blast its way out whenever you're unable to stop it, or choose to allow it to escape like geysers exploding when the pressure builds and must be released."

"You're right," he said softly averting his eyes and bowing his head. "I didn't mean to be so nasty."

"It's not nasty," Lyla said, "it's abusive, toxic, and hurtful. I have lived with its existence and the fear of what ultimately would happen when the eruption occurred. It was like living with a time bomb, waiting for the ticking to cease and the bomb to explode. The result is damaging to me and anyone else who is here. I have had to protect myself and my children for too long. If you do not or cannot check this explosive anger and vitriol, you will not be able to stay here. I will no longer live in fear of your words, actions, and the consequential fallout."

The echo of her words and then the silence that followed filled the stale air. She waited for a response, but Juliano said nothing. He sat at the table motionless. When there was no response from him, Lyla walked out of the room.

The kitchen scene was another one of their talks, a revealing moment when Lyla poured out her pent-up feelings as he sat at the kitchen table head bent, staring at her, then at the floor, ultimately shaking his head and apologizing. It was nothing new and nothing revealing, except this time Lyla meant every word.

His apology and contriteness were temporary. He may have meant the apology for the moment but never made much of an attempt to change. Changing would require him to make significant attempts at remaking himself and Lyla finally realized he would never be able to do that. His kind of love, dominating and possessive wasn't love, it was distorted obsession. Lyla hated to admit it, but her mother had been right about Juliano. Lyla spent a lifetime trying to change the quintessential makeup of Juliano and her attempts had made them both miserable.

He would wait for the opportune moment and he would find a way; she would be sorry she ever rejected him and treated him with disrespect.

THE BEGINNING OF THE END

Juliano was tired of being apologetic, drawing her to him fell on deaf ears, and chose to retaliate one morning when he thought Lyla would least expect it. He waited until she was not yet awake and then struck, viper-like. The strong smell of his cologne and deodorant sickened her and his heavy swollen body crushed her beneath him. He was awkward and unable to move himself without extraordinary effort. She saw him as a huge walrus attempting to mount her, dragging his body and legs over her to assume a position to satisfy his needs. There was no romantic banter or passion, just the lust of an ugly creature. When she realized what was happening, she let him labor, as she listened to him breathing heavily from the effort it took him to move his body.

It began. He was unable to place himself in a position that was comfortable matching the curves of her body. His clumsy attempts caused his head to press against the headboard, and with every forward movement of his body, he lurched and banged his head into the headboard. He ignored the discomfort just as he ignored who was lying beneath him. His only thought was of himself and his obsession to finish what he started.

Lyla remained silent and did not struggle. When he began, she closed her eyes, an unconscious habit, enabling her to mentally escape until the act was over. Her body was still as she tried to breathe under the crushing weight on top of her. Within the first moments she turned her head to her right side and kept her eyes closed knowing it would end swiftly. As his lust ascended, his body began to shudder and quake pressing her deeper into the bedding. He continued to be oblivious to who was beneath him. As he climbed to his peak, engrossed in his compulsion to reach his summit, he made strange utterances and primal sounds she had never heard before, garbled and mixed with saliva that poured into her ear.

When he was finished, Lyla slowly opened her eyes reorienting herself to the reality of where she was and what had just occurred. As a result of his movements, her head had been pressed against the headboard, compressing her vertebrae, and she felt a sharp pain in her neck. He managed to prop himself up on one arm to give her some relief to breathe. With a small, almost apologetic smile, he spoke in a breathless whisper.

"I guess that wasn't so great for you. I don't know what happened. What was all that shaking? My body was doing some weird stuff."

Lyla spoke without emotion. "You're right, it was horrible and..."

Before she could finish, he spoke. "Next time I'll find a different way, I'll do better. Although, honey, for me, it is always good with you."

The words stung her and propelled her to have the strength to use her free arm and leg to catapult him off her to the other side of the bed. She picked up the hand towel that had been siting on her nightstand and threw it on top of him and left the bed. She went into the bathroom, closing and locking the door behind her. Although he was no longer physically on her, she could still feel his touch and smell his cologne. Her nightgown had moved up to her neck during the encounter. She couldn't stand for it to touch her skin any longer and began ripping it off her body. She had to get into the shower to wash him off her and get rid of the humiliation and disgust feeling like she been raped, again.

There wasn't enough water or soap to remove and heal the trauma. She stood in the small space of her shower in the dark, letting the warm water wash over her body. She promised herself. *Never again, never again will I allow him to do that me. Never again. Ever.*

Lyla would be challenged by her utterances of never again near Valentine's Day. Juliano, spurred on by the romance of the holiday, was in the mood again for some of his kind of intimacy and invited Lyla to the bed. She was ready with her response and her resolve, knowing the moment would come. He conveniently forgot about the Valentine's Day when he was arrested, but it had been indelibly imprinted upon Lyla. "No," she said simply. "No, Juliano."

"Oh, OK, well, maybe later."

"No. Not today."

"Are you feeling OK? Is there something wrong?"

"No, there's nothing wrong, I'm not feeling ill. I am not in pain, not that it would have made any difference to you. It never did before."

He stood in her way to the bedroom door preventing her from leaving. She gently shoved past him and he asked again. "Then what's wrong; why not?"

"I'm not going to do that with you anymore."

She turned and faced him. "I'm not having sex with you again, not today, not tomorrow, and not any other day. I can no longer tolerate your brutality. It's terrible, and I'm not going to allow you to do that to me anymore."

She turned back around, faced the door, and left the room. She did not wait for him to respond. "Hey," he called after her, "what's going on here? Come back here. I want to know why. Why you are talking to me like that?"

She calmly turned around and slowly walked back into the bedroom and sat on the bed as he sat on his chair across from her.

"I'm not doing this anymore," she repeated. "I'm not going to allow you to bully me or emotionally blackmail me into having sex with you. And that's all it is: sex. It's not love making, it's not romantic, it's not even nice. You said so yourself the last time we had sex. I told you then it was awful, and I meant it. You make it an ugly criminal act and the only one who appears to be having a good time is you. I have nothing more to say."

Lyla walked out of the bedroom, ignored him, refused to make dinner, and no longer cared. For the remainder of the day, Juliano avoided her as much as possible and gave her the silent treatment. Lyla decided to move out of the bedroom and sleep upstairs, knowing he would not be able to follow her without considerable effort, if at all. Before she moved upstairs she asked Juliano if he wanted to say anything. He continued to ignore her and focused his attention on his 52-inch television.

"Juliano, you are behaving like an angry, pouting child who had his toy taken away from him. I will not change my mind."

She was acting emotionally, carelessly with no thought or consideration of the consequences of her speech and behavior. She had no guidance from anyone, and no one to warn her she was putting herself at risk. She had no one to advise her that women are vulnerable to harm when they refuse, say no, and when they try to leave. Unless she was in mortal danger, she needed to have a plan.

For the first time since Juliano's return, Lyla slept undisturbed in her old bed upstairs, surrounded by her canine companions. She believed she was safe. She was relieved the truth finally surfaced and she no longer lived in fear of him forcing her to have sex.

Did she have the strength to continue moving in this direction, or would she return to her old behavior out of fear? Did she stop to think about possible repercussions? Juliano didn't care who she thought he was. This speech, this revelation to him, only added fuel to the embers within him, giving him the justification, he needed to retaliate in some way that would hurt her.

It was mid-morning, the next day, when Juliano finally decided to lift the 'cone of silence' and approach Lyla. She was in the kitchen when he shuffled in and asked her to take a seat at the table so they could talk. She agreed but sat at the table as far away from him as she could.

"I don't understand why you said those things to me, about not being intimate with me. I am wondering if it's because of my physical condition, because of what has happened to me, because of this disease. If it is, I understand, but there's nothing I can do about that. I'll try to find some other way, some other position, or somehow try not to. ... Is that what it is? Or are you trying to get back at me for things I have done to you in the past?"

He rambled about the past, making excuses for his brutish, sexual performance, and his condition. He made no excuse for his needs and desires or his attempts to justify his conduct. He argued the importance of intimacy in a marriage and how imperative it was for a man to have a dutiful submissive wife, at all times. Lyla sat still without expression listening and waiting for him to finish and then she spoke in a calm, determined voice.

"What we do is have sex. It is not pleasurable for me, and it is most definitely against my will." She repeated, "It is against my will." There was a long pause in her speech where her eyes never wavered from his face. She continued, "It's degrading, humiliating, and painful, and I will not succumb to you anymore. It has little to do with what has happened to you because of the motor neuron disease. If we were a loving couple, we would find a way. But we're not, and I don't think we ever have been.

"I have tried to refrain from dwelling on the past to keep it from interfering with a relationship with you since your return. I'm saying no because I won't let you do that to me anymore. I refuse to be your receptacle any longer. I believe you are confusing intimacy and a loving relationship with the act of sex.

"Your selfishness does not surprise me. Did you hear yourself? Did you hear the words you used? You said, YOU had needs, YOU had desires, and I was the one who had to fulfill those needs and desires for you without any regard for me. Making love is supposed to be a loving and cooperative act, not some singular experience without consideration for the other person. Employing tactics to emotionally blackmail me, as you have done in the past when you didn't get your way, is not going to work anymore." Lyla sat back in her chair with her hands folded neatly in front of her on the table, waiting for him to respond.

He took a deep breath, "Will you reconsider? Will you please give me another chance? I'll do whatever it takes to change. I know I have done terrible things in the past, and I have hurt you and made you miserable. I want to change; I don't want to lose you. You're so important to me."

His pleadings fell on deaf ears. "No, Juliano. I will not change the way I feel, this is not a negotiation."

As he struggled to rise from the table, he spoke with a voice wrenched with emotion. "I can always hope. I promise you I am going to do whatever is necessary to change and make things right, however long it takes. If you loved me once you will love me again. I'll wait; I'll wait no matter how long it takes."

"Juliano, I don't think you heard me. I'm done, I'm finished. It's over."

Lyla took whatever she needed out of the bathroom and returned to their shared closet for her clean clothing when Juliano was not in there. For the next several days Juliano was quiet, almost submissive. One morning he cornered Lyla in the kitchen at the island, blocking her ability to get away from him. He left the walker behind him and moved toward her using the island to steady himself. She stepped back to remain out of his reach and warned him, "Juliano, don't do this," as he continued to approach her. "Juliano don't do this, stay away, don't touch me. Do not come any closer."

He looked at her and began to plead, his eyes red and swollen. "Please Lyla; I just want you to listen."

There was nothing on the counter for her to grab to protect herself. She was trapped. She backed up as far as she could go and immediately crossed her arms in front of her for protection.

"Listen, Lyla, listen to me. I've been up most of the night and I realize how horrible I have been to you. I know I did this; I caused this to happen. Please, listen to me. I love you; I have always loved you, and want to do anything …anything to…" His voice cracked and he began to cry. "Please, Lyla, what can I do? Please … tell me."

She felt nothing but loathing and disgust for him, "Nothing Juliano. There's nothing you can do."

"I don't believe that, Lyla. I don't believe that; there must be something I can do to make you change your mind."

"No, Juliano, there's nothing. This should have happened a long time ago."

Juliano retreated and spent his days wandering around the house from study to TV and back again, trying to convince Lyla to rehash their exchanges. His attitude and manner were contemplative, apologetic, and submissive. Nothing he said made any difference. Lyla knew this contrite phase would only last a short time and when his anger, frustration, and rejection took over he would be more cruel and nasty than he had been before. The next bout would be without gloves.

She was right. Juliano became more secretive, texting more rather than talking on the phone, and if necessary retreating behind closed doors to talk. Juliano commandeered her study and took possession of her intimate, beautiful things. He sat at her desk, in her room, at her computer.

He became devious and dangerous in everything he did. His act of stealing their community property and amassing cash by taking cash advances on all his credit cards led to the cataclysmic event that ended in open hostility. She realized he was systematically isolating her financially. His controlling behavior over money was the only power he had left over Lyla. He knew if he could succeed in keeping her dependent upon him financially, or continue to stoke her fears regarding finances, and convince her she was unable to take care of herself, he would maintain his grasp on her. A week after Lyla's final refusal to change her mind. Juliano was in the study and Lyla was in the kitchen.

"Hey," he called out to her. No longer did he call her honey or even her name. It was "Hey... hey, come in here for a minute, would ya?"

Reluctantly, Lyla left the kitchen and walked slowly into the study.

"Sit down. I want to tell you something," he said.

"No thank you, I think I'll just stand. What is it you want to tell me?"

"I want you to know that most of my friends would not be as generous as I have been if their wives refused to have sex with them. But, I'm not like my friends, so I wanted to let you know I sold most of the stock in the portfolio. I deposited the money into an individual account in my name only at a bank other than the one you use."

She said nothing. She had a feeling he wasn't done.

"I am going to be very gracious and generous and give you a small number of remaining shares of one stock. You can do with it whatever you like."

She remained silent attempting to brace herself for what was to come next. His announcement and admissions felt like he had punched her in the gut but she tried to maintain self-control. When Lyla could no longer contain her anger, she responded.

"And you think you're being generous? You think after all the sneaky, selfish, cruel things you have done I should be grateful that you threw me some crumbs? I want you to know there isn't enough money on earth that could compensate me for the torture you've put me through. I'm no longer the doormat who is naive and frightened. I can promise you if you're going to get ugly, I can be a formidable adversary, and I will not allow you to bully or scare me into submission. You have a moral and legal obligation to take care of me, and I am going to hold you to it."

"What's done is done and there's no way you can undo it," he said, thinking he was in a position of strength. "Go ahead take me to court and see how far you get when I present a pathetic picture to the judge of a disabled man sitting in the wheelchair and drooling. You will get nothing; you deserve nothing.

"Well, to be honest with you, Lyla, I don't want you to have access to anything of mine. After all, our status has changed. You're no longer my mate, my wife, and if you're no longer my mate then you don't have any right to anything of mine."

"Your ... mate? Do you want to explain that? Your Mate?"

Juliano paused and sat back in the desk chair folding his arms in front of his chest. "Well, you see, the day you said you would no longer have sex with me you stopped being my mate, my wife. And since you're no longer my wife, my business is not your business."

When the conversation began, Lyla was standing in the middle of the room, facing Juliano as he sat in the chair at her desk. As the dialogue escalated, she moved farther and farther away from him, retreating into the corner of the room beside the bookcase with her back to the wall. With folded arms and raised voice, she spoke the truth.

"This has nothing to do with whether I'm your mate or not, and not having sex doesn't automatically disqualify me from being your wife."

"Oh, yes it does. If you choose not to have sex with me you're not my wife. Dot period. I want a wife."

Lyla took a small step toward Juliano. "You don't want a wife. You want a female object you can boss around and brutalize with sex whenever you want. That's what this is all about, Juliano, what you want. It's always been what you want, and you've always had what you wanted one way or another until I finally said, NO.

Lyla took another small step toward Juliano. "This is about power, control, manipulation, and lies. You're a bully, and when you don't get your way, you get angry and punish me. I must have been very flawed to think an alcoholic, drug-addicted criminal would respond to the loving kindness I willingly offered and become a human being."

Then Juliano sat up straight in the chair, moved it closer, and put his hands on the desk. "You see," he interjected, trying to regain his superiority, "when you refused to be intimate with me you rejected me. I was hurt and because of that I got angry, and I did take it out on you, but."

She moved closer to him and interrupted, "INTIMATE? INTIMATE?

You don't know what intimacy is. You're confusing your obsession with the act of sex with intimacy which is something that never existed between us. It's really about subjugation, control, and power; it's not about some romantic, tender, loving act between two people who love each other.

"You're the consummate rapist. If you hadn't had me around to passively submit to you, you would have been raping other women. And God knows, maybe you did and I didn't know it. But I was convenient. Do you have any idea why I had my tubes tied after the last child? It's not because you refused to have a vasectomy. It's because I would not take the chance of getting pregnant again. I did not and would not have any more children with you ... ever. So, I had to decide to do something permanent.

"I have had enough. I suffered enough. I was determined not to succumb to any medical problems and refused to die, and God forbid, let you raise my children. Our issues are not about money. If we were trying to work together sex would not be the main topic of conversation. But's not, our issue is your desire to bully, control, and have power over me."

Her voice got louder. "You will never touch me again, NEVER. And because you will never touch me again, we need to end this charade of a marriage now, and let someone else decide who gets what. I'm paying for nothing because I have nothing. You will pay for everything, the lawyer, and whatever else has to be paid, and you will support me monthly as you are obligated to do. I will not live this way any longer."

Juliano tried to resume control. "I'll tell you what, why don't we get together tomorrow and take a look at the bills, what we have to pay and what we have left, and try to figure out what needs to be done?"

"What for? That changes nothing."

No, it'll be different this time, really, it'll be different."

"I don't think so. This is not just about money."

"OK," he said giving up. "Have it your way. I tried."

"You won't change and the issues won't either. I've been through this farce of a marriage too long and know better."

Lyla stood in the middle of the room waiting for him to respond, he said nothing. The silence between them became agonizing, she was finished. Her emotions were raw and bleeding but she didn't cry. She was determined to hide her emotional vulnerability from him. Lyla walked out of the room on shaky, wobbly legs, leaving him slumped in the chair at the desk in front of the computer. She put the dogs in their crates, said nothing to him, took her car keys, and left the house.

It was raining, the kind of summer rain that comes in waves. The pelting sounds of rain hitting the body of the car and the windshield, were comforting. Flashes of lightning and cracks of loud thunder accompanied the wind. She drove through the neighborhood to a small, deserted play area, parked the car, and cried hard heaving sobs. Moans came from her little frame, deep gut-wrenching primal sobs that come from one's core. And then she was quiet, listening to the rhythmic pulse of the windshield wipers wiping away the falling rain. She heard her mother's soft voice. "Cry until you can't cry anymore, dry your tears, and don't cry for him again. You're going to be all right."

It had been an hour from the time she left the house and left Juliano sitting in the study at her desk. How pathetic he was, hunched over the desk with his chin down, looking intently at the computer. He called out to her as she entered the house, "Are you OK?"

What an incredibly stupid question, she thought. She had no intention of revealing to him that she felt mortally wounded. "I'm just fine," she said.

Lyla's need to escape to the backyard was overpowering. She called to her companions and ignoring the light drizzle, stepped out the kitchen door. As she walked the perimeter of the fenced yard, she struggled to put past events into perspective and reached the conclusion that Juliano's apparent strength, power, and need to keep her in emotional bondage came from a position of weakness. She thought, *he needed to be in control. When he was not, he became angry, insolent, and acted out in antisocial but accepted ways by tailgating people on the highway, honking his horn at other drivers when they didn't leave a traffic signal fast enough, driving his motorcycle at dangerously high speeds, and dominating me for his sexual pleasures.*

Intuitively, she believed that she was the one who had strength of character and a strong sense of responsibility and determination. She was cognizant of how different he was from her in every aspect, and how unsuited he was for her. The mask had been removed, she was gaining insight about herself.

The beauty and freedom of the yard and the blue bench must have possessed magic. Every time she sat down to ponder her life, more things were revealed, bringing her life into focus, lifting the fog shrouding her. She concluded she spent her adult lifetime with Juliano keeping secrets, believing they had to be kept at all costs. They were Juliano's past, lies she told to protect herself and the children, and the lie of her marriage and the abuse she suffered. Keeping her secrets was what alienated her from her family and anyone who tried to get close to her.

As she watched her inquisitive dogs chasing bugs, her mind wandered and then focused on why she felt compelled to try so hard to repair their difficulties. Resolving the issues was her way to repair Juliano. She began to connect the dots, and thought she understood what had happened throughout their marriage.

A smile of understanding appeared on her face. *I understand,* she said to herself, *what it was and it was so simple. Why was I unable to see any of this before? Was it because I was so busy rescuing him? Was it because I was trying so hard to mold him into the person I thought he should be? Did my efforts make me incapable of seeing what was always right there in front of me? Or did this relationship have an addictive aspect I was powerless to perceive and overcome? We rarely had the same goals and aspirations as a couple. We were not compatible, not ever, and I didn't see it.*

My discomfort with him was so very basic. He was a taker and self-centered. I am a giver, willing and comfortable to sacrifice myself for someone else. I wonder if it was more difficult for me to discern if I was angrier with myself, for trying so hard to change Juliano, or with Juliano for being who he was.

The discomfort was more Lyla's, and she finally realized Juliano was in a situation perfect for him. He took everything and sucked the life out of her. The difference between them was that he knew he was a man who demanded much and gave little.

If she had been able to recognize these issues sooner, perhaps, she would have had a much different life, with or without him. Her constant struggle to force him to change and become someone he essentially was not, was a tug-of-war that caused conflict and remained impossible to resolve. It separated them, caused anger, pain, and a tension that was always there, no matter how they tried.

DEATH RATTLE

The last significant and tortuous summer conflict had faded and late summer was approaching. After a long hard day of baking, Lyla went out to the back porch with her cavaliers and relaxed on her porch swing. It was calm and clean in the back yard where Lyla felt free to think and breathe. The wind swept through the tall trees still clothed in the last of their summer wardrobe and the sound and movement made them look like they were in a corps de ballet, dancing in concert.

She was exhausted and focused on her beautiful yard and her playful companions. Juliano had been spending his days shuffling back and forth from his television to the computer. When he saw Lyla outside, he cautiously approached her without her realizing it, and maintained a safe distance before he spoke, "May I join you?"

"All right," she said, as she cautiously moved to the other end of the swing. It was difficult for her to be in close proximity to him and didn't want to give him the opportunity to be able to touch or grab her.

"It's beautiful out here," he began. "I never noticed before."

"Yes," she agreed. "I love it here, it's so peaceful and majestic. I often wonder how old these trees are and what they have seen and been through. I can just imagine the stories they could tell."

"Listen Lyla, I don't want to make you uncomfortable, but I wanted you to know I finally understand the difference between us." Immediately, Lyla could feel her body tense as she pressed against the end of the swing to sit farther away. "The difference is that I need to have sex first, before there can be intimacy, and you have to have intimacy before you can have sex. Can you just try and understand this difference? I also want to know if there's any chance you will reconsider and be my wife in a complete way."

She thought, *he's trying, again. This is another tactic to badger and manipulate me.* She could feel her body tense and stiffen more, and her guts began to churn.

He continued. "I know all this has been my fault, but I want you to know, again, I'll do anything to change, to make things better as long as you agree to be my wife again."

Lyla thought, *had it ever occurred to him I had always been his wife? I was dutiful, self-sacrificing, kind, and caring, always catering to him, his needs, wants, and desires. His stratagem had worked on me in the past; not now.*

Slowly she turned to face him, trying to mask her anger and frustration at yet another of his attempts to take away what dignity she had left, restrict her very existence, and bully her.

"I'm not quite sure I'm hearing you right, Juliano. You're saying if I agree to be your wife, whatever that means to you, you'll change your demeanor and the way you treat me, and if I don't you won't."

The expression on his face exposed his determination to try to explain who he is and why he feels the way he does and he became anxious to impart this to Lyla. His eyes grew wide with a pleading expression.

"I'm saying I want you; I've always wanted you. I can't think of my life without you. I've known you all my adult life and don't want to be with anyone else. I'm not asking you to give me an answer right now; you can tell me tomorrow."

"Listen to what you just said, Juliano. You're saying your manner and treatment towards me is predicated on me having sex with you. If you really wanted to change the way you behave, you would have changed already, and you would not have made it contingent upon whether I submit to you or not. I will not give you an answer tomorrow. You're being unreasonable and I won't consider it. The answer is no. You will never violate and subjugate me again for your own filthy, selfish pleasures."

Without forethought, she spoke unapologetically of issues that had haunted her for a lifetime like an old tape that kept replaying. She saw him now: an older version of his youth, but perhaps more set in his hateful ways. Lyla recalled how when he was much younger he privately made derogatory remarks about people who he thought were less than his equal and made fun of people who were disabled. Now that he's older he chooses not to hold back and speaks publicly unkind words and labels.

"I now know who you really are, Juliano. You're a self-centered, selfish bully who blames everyone else for his own bad mistakes and decisions. You see yourself as the victim, blaming everyone and everything else. You ultimately replace the blame with extraordinary anger and take most of the anger out on women, me in particular. Perhaps it was because I was convenient. Or, perhaps it was because I was the closest to you and you knew I was a vulnerable target and would not fight back.

"You destroy everything you touch; most of all, your wife. If you have any remorse, I'm not able to see it. Your apologies, which on the surface appear sincere, are not. You are who you are: a pathetic excuse for a man.

"It is very sad that in the last quarter of our lives your priority is demanding sexual submission from me. We're staying together out of financial necessity. Because of the circumstances, we need to find a way to co-exist without destroying each other. I have nothing more to say."

She was still sitting on the swing, placed her hands on the seat, looked at him one last time, and got up. She called in her pack and went into the house, leaving Juliano to digest the conversation. He was unable to maintain his emotional chokehold. Was he too weak to bully or manipulate her to get it back?

Lyla was busy in the kitchen, cleaning up what remained of the baking supplies, when Juliano shuffled in from the porch. He navigated his way to the island to steady himself and asked Lyla one more time to decide in his favor. She slowly turned to him with her arms full of flour containers and spoke softly.

"The children are out of the house now and I know now that my life is no longer closely intertwined with theirs. It's time I begin to have a life instead of sacrificing my own to live everyone else's. I'm not asking you to metamorphose into someone else. I know you are incapable and unwilling to move outside of your comfort zone. I made the decision to remain with you, at this stage of my life, because I believed it was the only option left to me financially.

"It would appear you merely think of me as some sort of servant. We have a limited time, and I would like to do what is most prudent. I will not leave you to lie in the gutter like some old dying, mangy hound, but

I will not allow you to hurt me anymore."

He acknowledged her words by nodding his head, letting her know he understood. He moved out of the kitchen slowly with his head bent, shuffling with an uneasy gait. She never spoke of those 'issues' again.

Why did she make this last attempt to reveal her thoughts and feelings when this had been a futile effort in the past? Was it because he was vulnerable and not able to fight back, her lack of fear, or both? Or was it that she was becoming stronger?

Lyla's awareness of herself was the important puzzle piece affecting her attitude change. She exercised more restraint of her anger and she treated Juliano without contempt. There was an uneasy truce with less tension and discomfort. Now, she could formulate a plan that would give her the permission to have a life with a productive purpose. She knew she could do this. She just wasn't sure how, not yet.

Lyla continued baking for her customer base and never missed an opportunity to take bread-making classes at the local market to become better at her craft. She maintained a balance between her classes, her customers, and making sure Juliano was cared for by professionals coming in to the house. Lyla was relieved the fighting and anxiety had subsided and there were other people in the house acting as a buffer. She and Juliano were barely polite but without the inevitable outbursts that colored their life together. It was different now. He was getting worse, requiring full-time professional care. It had been a long and difficult battle for too many years.

REALIZATIONS AND REALITIES

Lyla tackled uncomfortable issues with energy that had laid dormant since she was in college. She was paying bills with less anxiety and trying to work with Juliano in a nonconfrontational way. She chose to ask his opinion of how he would accomplish these tasks knowing she would ultimately do what she wanted. She discovered she was calmer, more grounded in her emotions in a healthy way, and better able to make sound decisions. She no longer spent hours on shopping sprees spending money she didn't have and began to volunteer in a local organization that serviced women who were victims of domestic violence. She liked stuffing envelopes, answering phones, and filing. It gave her a sense of purpose that she was helping other women and she was learning.

Little things no longer caused her such intense irritation and, magically enough, she began to sleep. Every morning from the comfort of her own bed, Lyla would sigh with an exhilarated feeling of relief and no longer spent the night replaying tapes of conversations resolving problems in her head. Her morning routine introduced a personal time of exercise on the Pilates reformer and an energetic walk on the grounds with her faithful companions. The Pilates conditioned her body and the walk in the fresh air conditioned her mind.

Lyla continued to experience a string of epiphanies about her marriage, her relationships, and what was so desperately missing in her life: her life. These realizations helped to guide her through her current ordeal and became the catalyst catapulting her on a new and exciting journey. If she noticed she was falling back into the same traps of impatience, resentment, and feeling a lack of self-worth, she chose not to respond in the same old way. She took time to examine her options and the reality of the situation making better decisions.

The early fall day was beautiful with temperatures near the mid-70s. The sun was shining and the skies were clear blue. After her morning routine, Lyla made a pot of morning tea and fresh toast. She decided to tackle the vacuuming while the aide attended to Juliano. The manual chore was something she found almost comforting. The sound of the vacuum acted as a sound barrier mentally and physically.

It helped to clear her mind and allowed her to focus on pleasant musings, but for some reason, that morning, ominous memories intruded upon her thoughts. As she worked hard to remove all the dust and fur from the rug in the study, she began to remember something her father said so many years ago when he fired Juliano. Harry's long held anger exploded onto Juliano the night before Juliano left Cincinnati for Tampa, Fl. Harry was heartbroken and spoke to Juliano with malice in his voice. "You're not right for my daughter and because of you, she will have to work for the rest of her life. She'll be miserable. You'll never be able to take care of her."

She remembered this like it was yesterday even though it was almost 30 years ago. Her father was right; she would work for the rest of her life, but it would be something she loved, something she had a passion for. The ideas were already forming and she ached to act upon them.

Lyla was left without a purpose and with no one to rescue her. She was in the process of discovery and planned to embark on a journey that would change and enrich her for the rest of her life.

Lyla's time away from the house were times of renewal. They provided the needed separation from the unspoken tension and discomfort living with Juliano and replenished her strength. After the last conflict, she ignored Juliano as much as possible and focused her energy on learning everything she could about her renewed passion, baking bread. When she had the opportunity, she drifted through the bookstore devouring everything she could find on baking bread. A book entitled, *Bread Alone*, captured her attention. It recounts the journey one man takes to become the baker he wants to be. She was fascinated reading about his journey to Paris to learn about the ovens, the ingredients, and the bread baked in them. The story enthralls her and she longs to be going on the same kind of journey and fantasizes someday she would.

Until then, she would continue to learn and hone her skills at home. Baking bread was her solace and a way to avoid feeling trapped and isolated. Lyla increased her baking from home again offering it to friends, neighbors, and members of her community.

Lyla had had a productive and rewarding week of baking classes and satisfied customers. As a treat to herself, she decided to stop by the mall and meander through the book store. She rediscovered the book, *Bread Alone*. She was flipping through the pages as she had done before and read a section that astounded her. The author mirrors how she felt about baking bread. It never occurred to her anyone else had the same feelings she had about the entire process. It was as though he was talking directly to her and knew what was in her head. It was this book that reignited her desires and solidified her plans for her immediate future. This time she really felt she had purpose to her life.

Lyla finally purchased the book. *This is what I need to do, this is where I need to go*, she thought. *I must go to Paris and I need to learn from the bread masters.* It made perfect sense to Lyla, although it might have sounded crazy to someone else. She couldn't pick up and leave at that moment, but it was clear to her that in time she would be on her way. Lyla became more determined than ever and felt a fortuitous tingle move through her body. This was right, she knew it. She just knew it.

The winter holidays passed and another new year began. Juliano's status changed significantly with the loss of his ability to swallow and soon he barely opened his eyes and refused to acknowledge anyone's presence. The decline began with a series of infections and aspiration pneumonia, leading to recurring hospitalizations. Finally, he went in the hospital and never left. One morning, Lyla received a call from the nurse caring for him.

"Mrs. Masselli, good morning. This is Hazel, the nurse attending your husband. I'm calling to tell you that Mr. Masselli passed away this morning at 10:39 a.m. Because he had a Do Not Resuscitate order, nothing was done to revive him when his heart stopped. I'm sorry, Mrs. Masselli, my condolences to you and your family. We have some of Mr. Masselli's personal effects. Would you like me to hold them here for you?"

Lyla was silent, sitting wide eyed on the stool next to the desk in the kitchen. She didn't know what to say.

"Mrs. Masselli," the nurse asked, "are you there? Are you OK?"

"Uh, yes, Hazel, I'm here ...I'm ... OK. Please call the number I left for the funeral home. They will take care of everything. I would appreciate you holding my husband's personal effects at the nurse's station. I'll be there to pick them up. Thank you for calling."

"Again, Mrs. Masselli, my condolences to you and your family."

"Yes, Hazel, thank you."

Lyla hung up the phone stunned, she was unable to move, as she kept repeating, "Juliano is dead, Juliano is dead." Somehow, she thought his death would cause her to feel relief, joy, not the strange empty nothingness she currently felt. She never understood how she knew she would never really be free until he was dead. Now that that happened, she didn't feel happy or sad. She sat there as if coming out of a reverie, raised her eyebrows, and heard her voice whisper, "It's over... it's finally over."

She closed her eyes and took a deep breath. Her lungs filled with the fresh air of freedom and she opened her eyes to something wonderful, the beginning of a new life.

THE JOURNEY

"Ahh," Lyla sighed as she stretched out her arms and legs to emerge from the night's cocoon of sleep. One by one, each little dog greeted her lovingly with kisses and tail wags as they snuggled next to her on her bed. Lyla smiled, comforted by the loving attention and affection from her cavalier spaniels. She whispered to them, "I can always count on you girls to wake me with soft kisses."

As she acknowledged each one with a stroke, a rub behind the ear, and a smile, she closed her eyes once again, just for a moment, contemplating what lie ahead. All five furry bodies made rustling sounds on the blanket that stirred Lyla from her thoughts.

"All right, ladies, I understand. It appears everyone is ready to bounce off the bed and start the day." Lyla pulled back the covers. "So, without further ado, let's be on our way," she said.

Her companions took turns jumping off the bed to the floor. They ran into the bathroom and patiently waited for Lyla to wash, shower, and change into her clothes. She then made the bed and walked to the kitchen back door surrounded by the din of jumping, barking canines who were pushing and nudging one another to go through the door first.

It was early spring 2010. The newness of the early Texas day felt cool with remnants of dew droplets on the grass reflecting the morning sun like glittering diamonds. The dogs scattered throughout the yard to find their favorite spots. They were happy to be outside and free, running with their long ears flapping and tails wagging. Lyla drew in a deep breath, as if to steady herself in preparation for the tasks of the day.

So much had happened here. So much pain ... so much change ... so much courage on her part.

She thought, it seems like it was a lifetime ago I was unpacking and trying to settle in. And now here I am packing my life's belongings of material things and memories, moving in the direction of a new and uncertain future. The doubts and uncertainties that came creeping back into her mind created disturbances in her gut. She instinctively knew being outside would help to calm her overwhelming fears and anxieties.

She looked into the yard at the tall trees swaying to the symphony of the wind. The landscape was alive with movement, refreshed after being nourished by the sun and morning moisture. She called to her four-footed friends. "All right ladies, time to come in and have breakfast. Hello, is anyone hungry out there?" She called once again having gotten no response. There was no glance in her direction; not one eyebrow was raised. "What, nobody's hungry this morning?"

As Lyla walked down the semi-circular, cascading concrete steps onto the lawn, she called once more.

"Yoo hoo … hey there, ladybugs."

She shaded her eyes with her hand, pursed her lips, and whistled the 'Rose' whistle her father had taught her. She finally got everyone's attention with the exception of the mischievous little Blenheim, who was busy hunting lizards by the front fence. Lyla walked over to Princess Penelope, the busy Blenheim cavalier, who was intent on her hunt and had not heard Lyla approach, let alone call. Lyla bent down and gently tapped Princess Penelope on the shoulder to get her attention and spoke.

"Now you listen here young lady, it's time to go in; we have a million things to do today."

Princess Penelope hesitated then turned and looked at Lyla once more as if to say, "Please, just one more minute," then scampered in the direction of the steps and joined the others waiting by the kitchen door.

"That Penelope," Lyla said. "I shall miss her."

Lyla walked slowly with cautious deliberation as she walked up the concrete steps to the porch and strolled across the patio to the kitchen door. Her movement was reflective of the monumental challenges she set for herself and the ever-present fears she was constantly quieting. Her pack of anxious and hungry companions crowded at the door barking. She opened the door and they flew into the house to their respective crates impatient for Lyla to appear with their bowls.

The cacophony of dog voices echoed and bounced off the walls, with a deafening sound. Magically, as speedily as the barking had begun, it subsided when the bowls were rapidly filled and distributed. The house grew quiet again except for the crunching and gobbling sounds as the girls ate their food and treats.

The granddaughter clock in the hallway began to chime the 8 o'clock hour, signaling the packers would arrive shortly. Lyla decided on an abbreviated breakfast of coffee, toast, and fresh fruit. She purposely kept only enough food for her and her pack for one more day. The kettle came to the boil and whistled as Lyla prepared her French press for fresh coffee. She poured in the water, affixed the press, and put on the timer. Six minutes: she needed lots of fresh strong coffee today.

The desktop by the kitchen phone was covered with small square pieces of paper neatly arranged in rows, some by themselves and some overlapping. These papers were Lyla's lists needing her immediate attention, such as the gardener, real estate agent, packers, and movers who played an integral part in this next phase of her life, as uncertain as that was.

She glanced hastily at the list for the day with times noted and checked off what she had already accomplished. A new note was made not to forget to have the car checked for engine oil levels, wiper fluid, gasoline, and tire pressure. It was critical she made sure there were no loose ends. She did not intend to return to this house … ever.

The dogs finished their food and immediately joined her in the kitchen, hoping for a morsel or more to drop from her hand. The bell of the timer rang and Lyla pushed down the plunger of her coffee press lingering long enough to take a deep breath, filling her lungs with the aroma. There was one disposable cup left and she filled it with the black steaming elixir.

"Ah," she spoke with a breathy voice, "if this doesn't keep me hopping today nothing will."

She barely had taken two long sips and two bites of toast when she heard the tapping of toenails on the floor running to the front door.

"I don't know how the girls know when someone is coming to the door. I don't know why I bother with a door bell," Lyla said to herself.

And as soon as she spoke, the barking began, climbed to a feverish pitch, and the doorbell rang. Lyla joined her pack at the front door.

"Packers," she said as she opened the door, "right on time. Good morning gentlemen; please come in and try not to let the girls out. They're cute and friendly, but once outside can't find their way back home."

"Yes ma'am, good morning ma'am, the one in front said. "Nice to meet you. We're here from the moving company to pack your large, fragile pieces like your pictures, lamps, and mirrors. That's right ma'am, isn't it?"

"Yes, that's correct. Please make certain all containers are clearly marked with contents and labeled. Do you gentlemen do the crating as well?"

"Uh, no ma'am, that's not us; that's a different bunch. If you just show us where you want us to start we'll get right at it, ma'am."

"Certainly, come this way. We'll begin over here in the study."

Lyla knew her pack well. Their friendly personalities showed an eagerness to help the packers, but they were underfoot, and in the way.

"Let's go girls and have a treat and relax in your crates."

Every eye immediately twinkled and tails were up and wagging, as the little dogs followed Lyla to the treat bag.

"I'm so glad bribing never fails," Lyla said to them with a smile.

Moments later, the doorbell rang again. Lyla opened the door and was face to face with two, tan, burly looking gentlemen.

"Let me guess," she said, "you're the bunch who will be doing the crating."

"Well, yes ma'am, that's who we are. If you'll just show us what needs to be done, we'll get right at it."

"Yes, no problem, please come this way. Everything has been assembled in the family room. You can take the pieces into the garage and make the crates on the driveway."

Lyla checked on each dog to make sure everyone was happily chewing on their treats and went back into the kitchen to finish her now cold, coffee and toast. She let out a soft groan. "This is just what I needed, cold coffee and rubbery toast; two of my least favorite things."

Later, when the craters and packers completed their tasks, papers were signed, and the house was once again quiet. Lyla released her dogs from their crates and took them outside for some fresh air and freedom. The day had disappeared fast, leaving just enough time to drive the car to the dealership for her scheduled checkup and gas, and be back in time to shower and meet the boys, her sons. The boys were coming to take her out to eat and say their final farewells. None of them was eager to see her embark on what they believed was an unreasonable, even crazy, thing to do.

Pandemonium reigned at the door once again. There were yips, barks, howls, and whines from the dogs as they jumped and popped up and down like grasshoppers.

"Great doorbells you got there, Mom," said her eldest as he bent down to give her a soft kiss on the cheek.

"Yeah, Mom, how about a little restraint here?" said the second-born as he greeted her warmly.

The third-born came in with arms outstretched and gave Lyla a big bear hug. "Hi Mom, are you sure about all this?"

The last to come through the door was the youngest. "I see you still have all those darn hairy critters," he said as he reached out to Lyla, tightly enveloping her in his arms for what seemed to her to be forever and whispered, "I love you."

Lyla's emotional world became complete when her boys were together with her, which was not often now that they were grown. Her face showed signs of fatigue and worry after a long day, but she tried to hide it. Even now, she was protecting them.

They left the house laughing and talking as everyone piled into the eldest son's car. He pulled out of the driveway and drove in the direction of Lyla's favorite restaurant for what they feared might be their last time together for some time. During dinner, no one brought up the subject of Lyla leaving. Instead they chirped and laughed about the past, video games, and what was currently happening in their lives. It was dark when they returned to the house and Lyla was feeling overwhelmed by the wine at dinner and the fatigue from her day. The cavalier pack was let out the kitchen back door by the boys and Lyla joined them on the patio by the swing.

The eldest spoke first. "Mom, I just don't understand. Why do you have to go so far? Why can't you do this here? You don't know anyone there. What if something happens to you or if you get sick or something? You'll be on your own. I'm not comfortable with this. Mother, how can you do this by yourself?"

She heard their voices speak almost in unison. Then the singular voices became clear, one after the other; everyone had the same message.

"What are you going to do there? Where are you going to live? What's the matter with you? You're too old. How can you possibly think you can do all that hard work? It's a lot of heavy lifting, long hours, hot ovens, and far from home."

"Yeah Mom," chimed in the next one. "Why can't you stay here? What's the big deal?"

Her third-born son turned to Lyla and spoke with a strong voice. "You know, Mom, I'm not real crazy about this decision, but I know how important it is to you. Do what you believe you need to do and if you need me you know how to reach me. I'll be there."

The youngest stood motionless, his eyes brimming with tears. When he finally spoke he whispered, "I know you can do this."

Lyla reached out and touched the hand of each one of her children, leaned in close to them as they sat crowded around her, and spoke.

"Boys, boys, take it easy. I've given this a great deal of thought and preparation, and I know what I'm doing. At least I think I know what I'm doing. Anyway, I've decided to live, temporarily, of course, in Paris and learn as much as I can about bread making. My life here, as I've known it, no longer exists and I must make changes and prepare for what is to be my future, whatever that is. When I think I'm ready, I'll return to Florida from France and open up my own bakery. Don't worry about me; I'll be careful. I've researched this and have located a nice furnished studio apartment I believe is safe and centrally located."

They spoke simultaneously with expressions of disapproval and exasperation, "Where is this place?"

Lyla responded with confidence, "It's on the Av Marceau in the 8th arrondissement and I am aware none of you have any idea where that is. It's a short walk from the Champs Elysees and it is not too terribly far from the bakery where I'll be working. It's safe, has security, and it's even got a concierge. It's a good area; I've done my research. I'll be just fine guys. I'm a big girl. It is 2010, and I have all the technology to prove it. I'll be in touch and will be available by phone and computer if you really want to reach me or I need to contact any of you."

The boys were silent, looking intensely at their mother, trying to figure out how things had gone wrong, wondering why she was running away. Instinctively, they knew they had to trust her and her decision to leave, knowing they would never be able to change her mind. Somehow, she seemed different.

"Listen fellas, I'll be leaving tomorrow to drive to Florida to put everything into storage and have made arrangements for someone to take care of my furry friends. I'll be staying one night in Miami then flying the next evening to Paris. My laptop will be my constant companion and I'll check in on a regular basis, really, I will, I promise. I know you think I've lost my mind, but I want ...no, I need to do this. It means a lot to me."

The cavaliers were brought into the house for the night and the boys left with loving embraces and concerns, spoken and unspoken. Lyla turned off the outside lights as her sons drove out of the driveway. She locked all the doors, set the alarm, and went to her bedroom to prepare for bed while her girls ran around the bedroom bouncing on and off the bed.

Lyla awoke early the next morning. The sky was dark and the air was still, waiting for the first signs of light. Lyla fed and walked the cavalier pack. Last-minute personal items for the trip were packed and placed in the car along with dog supplies. The movers were scheduled to arrive by 8:30 a.m. and the real estate agent by 9:00 a.m. Lyla paced the kitchen nervously waiting for everyone to arrive, checking and rechecking her lists and the contents of the car.

"Yes," she said to her dogs, "all gassed up, drinks, leashes, water and food for you, emergency kit, granola bars, fruit and nuts to nibble on, treats for all, check, check, check. OK."

The movers arrived as scheduled as did the real estate agent. Items were removed from the house efficiently without incident. The load took five hours and Lyla completed the paperwork with everything going to Florida into storage. The house keys were given to the agent with the Power of Attorney in the event of a sale while Lyla was away. The process was complete and it was finally time for Lyla and her pack to leave. She and her real estate agent embraced with a warm farewell, with Lyla trusting her agent to take care of the house and its eventual sale.

The crates and all five dogs were loaded into the car. Lyla made one more check around the house to make certain nothing was left behind, nothing that was tangible. She made calls to the boys to say goodbye, alerting them she was about to embark on her journey. Promises were made to keep in touch when she made her first stop.

One last check was done on the girls to make sure all crates were secure, and Lyla got in the driver's seat, and started her engine. She drove slowly down the long driveway to the street, pausing briefly at the end. It was then she turned around in her seat, took a long look back at the house, turned out of the driveway, and drove out of the development into the throng of afternoon traffic.

When she was out of the city on the open road, she placed her Lily Pons CD into the slot, turned up the volume, and sang along with Lily in a full vibrant voice, reflecting a freedom and anticipation of a life to come.

CONTINUING THE JOURNEY

The three-day journey from the Houston suburb to the north Miami area was long and exhausting. Lyla chose to kennel her pack with an old friend who had ample room for them to wander and play and plenty of other cavaliers to keep her girls company. The dogs were tired and anxious in their unfamiliar surroundings. The initial meeting of both groups of cavaliers was unsettling for the dogs, but Lyla's friend assured her all would change once her pack settled in and acclimated to the others; it would take time. Saying good bye to her companions was difficult. Neither Lyla nor her companions were convinced of anything except that they were being separated and they were scared. She promised each little girl she would return and they would be together again in their own home, safe and secure.

After Lyla said farewell to her pack, she continued to her hotel room near the airport. Her flight did not leave until the next evening, which allowed her to do last-minute shopping in the area. The activity was excellent therapy for anxiety; she always felt better when she was out mingling with people, looking at beautiful things. She was tired from the drive, hungry, and emotionally exhausted by the separation from her children and her only other companions, her dogs. Room service was available and she ordered an evening meal including a carafe of wine to be delivered to her room in a couple of hours.

Before room service arrived, she clicked on the icon of her favorite radio station on her laptop and prepared a bath with bath salts and bubbles for soaking. She dimmed the lights in the spacious bathroom, slipped into the large tub filled with warm bubbles, and submerged until the water was up to her chin. She closed her eyes and listened to the strains of one of her favorite chanteuses. Tension left her body and her thoughts drifted, as the warm water washed over her, and she breathed in the aroma of the perfumed salts.

Her dream-like state felt as if it had lasted for hours and daylight had become evening. Lyla stepped out of her womb-like vessel refreshed.

She dried her body with a large terry towel and then reached for the luxurious hotel robe that was hanging on the bathroom hook, wrapped it around her, and tied it securely around her waist. Her mirrored reflection prompted her to speak.

"Well, you look a lot better now than you did when you walked in here; the soak did you good."

She dried her short hair with a towel and ran her fingers through it, letting it fall softly around her face when a knock on the door interrupted her. She moved to open the door and usher in the waiter.

"Room service here with your evening meal," the waiter said and she suddenly remembered how hungry she was.

"Thank you, please wheel the table over to the large glass windows."

"It was a pleasure serving you, please ring if you require anything."

Lyla gave the waiter a generous tip as he exited the room and she turned to the window and looked at the panoramic sweep of lights in the night sky, an expanse of midnight blue canvas dotted with sparkling rhinestones.

Her meal was a small bowl of broth with stuffed tortellini, a plate of artfully prepared roast chicken with apricot sauce, jasmine rice, roasted asparagus, and a small carafe of white Moscato wine. She closed her eyes, breathing in the aroma and savored each bite and sip of wine.

Afterwards, she pushed the table aside and walked over to her laptop to change the music to a large file of Chopin Nocturnes. She leaned back against an abundance of pillows on the couch, closed her eyes, and let her thoughts drift deeper into a state of quiet reflection on the events that had brought her to this place at this time. The journey she was about to embark on was one she intuitively believed would change her life and provide her with new skills, enabling her to pursue her bread baking passion and give her financial independence. Everything was in order, her cavaliers were safely kenneled, and she was ready to go, spending the night before her departure in a deluxe room overlooking the city.

A compelling desire to record her thoughts overcame her as she listened to the soft strains of her favorite classical piano pieces, and sipped what remained of her wine. She clicked on the icon in Microsoft

Word and stared at the blank page when suddenly her fingers began to dance across the keys in rhythmic movements. The words tumbled out onto the page without effort. She was mesmerized and inspired by the music played by Vladimir Ashkenazi. Lyla was transported to a place that finally allowed her to open up and express what had been locked up for so long.

PARIS
HOW IT ALL BEGINS AGAIN

Lyla wrote, "Who I was as a woman was essentially defined by my role as a wife, a married woman, and a mother. When I lost those roles through my husband's death and the maturity of my children, I had to rediscover who I was. This was neither an easy task nor one I was certain I wanted to experience. My life had become set, familiar and comfortably uncomfortable. Moving away from this existence required a courage I hoped I had.

"The joy and excitement of a life that was fulfilling seemed remote and I wasn't sure I was willing to do what I had to do to find out, but there were moments when I welcomed the discovery of new people, skills and new experiences. These had yet to become satisfying considerations for me to follow through and act upon until now."

Lyla's ruminations turned to the woman she had become and unveiled who she had been and what she had done. She filled the pages of her laptop with the words that poured out of her.

"The consequences of my actions triggered my disgrace and embarrassment in helping him when he was arrested and marrying him to give him a life. Then I foolishly stayed, enduring misery and isolating myself from those I loved and could have trusted. This addictive cycle of abuse has a strange way of making the victim a seemingly willing participant.

"Sometimes the darkness and depression I felt from the constant anxiety washed over me like a thundering tsunami that engulfed and nearly drowned me. After Juliano's death I sold items that brought back memories of my life with him and I packed what remained. This was not the first time in my life that I had to pack, move, and start over. It wasn't easier because I've done it before. I am older and really on my own now. If I dared to dwell on this for more than a moment, I feared I would become stuck in a quagmire I believed I could not extricate myself from."

The more Lyla wrote the more she separated from the woman she was writing about. Lyla transferred her thoughts and emotions to the woman on the page revealing a woman who Lyla had not fully recognized before.

"I was filled with conflict that stopped me from moving on, even when the voice within urged me to go. There were occasions when my essence, strength, and fortitude would manifest and others would see what remained unrecognized by me. I was surprised, and at times shocked, when others commented on my strength and ability to persevere in the face of difficult issues and times. I was devoted to my children and spoke from the heart, drawing my words from the importance I placed on my essence as a Jewish woman, a life I had been unable to embrace.

"I recognize now that my strength to survive and my fortitude to overcome the adversities I faced was my greatest asset."

Lyla closed her laptop. She slept well that night and rose the next morning ready to take the path before her. The next day Lyla visited the outlet mall and found several irresistible treasures including a cashmere sweater on sale, an extra pair of walking shoes, and handbag perfect for the trip. When she returned to the hotel she had just enough time to pack her new things and organize the items she was taking on board. She called for the bellman and was escorted to her waiting taxi. Lyla gazed out the window of the fast-moving vehicle, silently saying goodbye to a place that felt like home.

"I'll be back," she said to herself. "I'll return and be so much more than who I am now. I will not be afraid, I can do this."

Lyla easily drifted through airport security as a first-class passenger and approached the boarding area for her flight. She was greeted by a gate agent.

"Good evening, may I see your boarding pass? Ah, yes, Miss Rose," said the agent. "Welcome, lovely to see you flying with us this evening. You're entitled to wait in our VIP lounge until the flight is called. We're experiencing a slight delay. May I offer you something to drink while you wait? I'm sure the delay will not be long."

The agent returned with a steaming cup of tea. Lyla sat sipping her tea as she recalled her life. She made several notes to remind herself about people she needed to contact when the agent announced that the flight was ready for boarding.

"Good evening ladies and gentlemen, Flight 0342 nonstop to Paris, Charles de Gaulle Airport is now ready for boarding. Please make your way down the ramp with your boarding passes ready."

Lyla boarded the plane and prepared her personal space, buckled up, and took out her Nintendo DS to pass time until the plane was ready to leave. Her window seat was in a row of two passenger seats and she was hopeful she would have someone nice to chat with. Lyla's seatmate entered the plane just prior to take-off. She was a small woman with short silver hair that fell softly around her face. She wore a pale blue knit pant suit with a sweater and jacket. Her jewelry was understated and her perfume faint and familiar.

Lyla was not a seasoned flyer and felt the need to close her eyes and say a silent prayer as the plane ascended into the sky up towards the clouds. Lyla's seatmate touched Lyla's arm as the plane climbed and acknowledged Lyla's silent prayer. She looked into Lyla's apprehensive face and spoke with a soft voice. "I always find it comforting to check in with God every time we take off."

Lyla turned to her seat companion and returned the woman's smile with a smile and a nod. When they attained cruising altitude, the attendants took orders for dinner and drinks giving Lyla and her seatmate an opportunity to get to know one another. Lyla's seatmate was Ethel Blum, a widow traveling to her home in Paris. Lyla was fascinated by the story of Ethel's life, a woman who traveled extensively, was accomplished in the legal field, and a woman who believed her husband was her predestined mate, her bashert (soul mate).

Mrs. Blum lived a full and exciting life with him and was now alone, using her time and energies for philanthropic endeavors. Her trip to Paris was to attend the dedication of a building and program for the foundation she headed. Lyla believed intuitively this encounter was providential and would have special significance in her life.

The building, Haussmann House, housed a unique Shalom Bayit program. Shalom Bayit, a Hebrew phrase meaning, "Peace in the Home," assists women, who have been victims of abusive relationships, to become whole. Lyla listened intently to Mrs. Blum explain how the program came into being, and what it hopes to accomplish for the victims and the women who give their time, energy, and hearts to the women they serve. Lyla thought, *this is why I had to go to Paris on this flight at this moment in time.* Lyla suddenly knew.

When their dinner trays and drinks had been removed, they made themselves comfortable for the night. Lyla wanted to confide in Mrs. Blum about her life but had misgivings speaking to this newly acquainted friend who she felt so drawn to. She was trying to find the words when Mrs. Blum reached over, took Lyla's hand in hers, held it tightly and whispered, "It's all right, you can talk to me."

Lyla shared her abbreviated story but excluded her most guarded secrets. Her story was revealed in the hushed whisper of the night, flying across the Atlantic. When Lyla recounted the story leading to Juliano's death, her plans, and her decision to go to Paris, Mrs. Blum smiled and acknowledged Lyla's incredible journey and courage in making the decision she had.

"We're not here by accident," Ethel Blum said. "There are lessons to be learned that will shape you and the rest of your life."

Lyla looked at Mrs. Blum, wondering what this woman knew? What did she mean? How could she possibly know? They got comfortable, reclining in their bed-like chairs and drifted to sleep: traveling companions, journeying together through the night.

The women awoke the next morning tired from an uncomfortable night, performed the basics of refreshing themselves, and were offered rolls and fruit or a full breakfast with fresh coffee or tea. By the time they finished their breakfast the plane was making its descent into Paris.

Mrs. Blum thanked Lyla for being a wonderful seat partner during the flight and invited her to the dedication of Haussmann House. Lyla was hesitant to accept and politely thanked Mrs. Blum, adding she would do her best to attend. They exchanged contact information and deplaned. As they walked and then rode the people mover, Lyla marveled at the beauty of the interior of the concourse that resembled the belly of a large transparent whale with dramatic rib-like structures overhead. The webbed dome ceilings fascinated Lyla and the large windows showered the interior with light. She delighted in the futuristic looking lounge chairs and the duty-free shops filled with treasures.

At the baggage claim, Mrs. Blum turned to face Lyla, kissed Lyla on each cheek, and they embraced, promising to stay in touch. Lyla returned the kiss. Mrs. Blum repeated her invitation to Lyla for the dedication. Lyla hesitated and politely acknowledged without acceptance. Mrs. Blum's chauffer, Philipe, collected her luggage and escorted her to a waiting vehicle. Lyla waited for her luggage, retrieved it, and placed it beside her. Lyla moved toward the waiting vehicles with her luggage hoping her message for a ride had been received. The airport was busy with people finding their way to their destinations. Lyla passed a crowd and noticed an older gentleman holding a small sign with her name on it. She walked up to the gentleman and did her best to speak in broken French.

"Pardonnez-mois Monsieur, je m'appelle Madame Rose." The gentleman's face lit up with a large grin, and he began to speak French rapidly.

"Je ne comprends pas," "I don't understand," she was able to say.

He grinned again and spoke slowly in English. "Welcome, Madame Rose. I am here to escort you to Mr. Albion, to your place of residence."

"Merci, merci," she said, as she followed him to his vehicle.

He opened the car door, ushered her inside, and attended to her luggage. Lyla tossed her carrying bag inside the vehicle and climbed into the back seat of the comfortable automobile. She was so excited she could barely settle down and did not want to miss anything. Although she was tired from the flight, she was anxious to see her new surroundings. For the most part, the ride along the highway was uneventful until they reached the city. Her driver, Georges, delighted in being her tour guide, pointing out landmarks and famous roads, adding a bit of drama and history to the ride.

As they traveled along the Boulevard Peripherique, known as the Paris ring road, Lyla's excitement continued to build. Georges exited the Peripherique to drive on the smaller thoroughfares through the city. He zigzagged his way through the streets, pointing out street names, buildings, and famous hotels he thought Lyla might recognize. When Georges looked in his rearview mirror to check on Lyla, he saw her wide-eyed astonishment, and was pleased with himself for the route he had chosen.

Lyla's life had changed entirely in six months. In Texas, her thoughts and dreams of baking in Paris were unfulfilled fantasies. Now, her wishes and dreams would become a reality. She was jolted out of her reverie by the vehicle's sudden stop and looked out the window to realize they had reached their destination.

Georges announced, "Nous sommes arrivés," we arrived. The 19th century building was several stories high and faced a tree-lined street off one of the other thoroughfares. It was a short walk from the Champs Elysees and was within walking distance or a bicycle ride to other amenities such as the supermarket, restaurants and the bakery where Lyla would apprentice.

She approached the front doors of her building, followed by Georges who carried her luggage, and was greeted by Monsieur Albion, the concierge doorman. He was an older gentleman of short stature dressed in a colorful uniform and hat. He wore white gloves and shiny black boots.

"Bonjour Madame Rose. I am Monsieur Albion, concierge, at your service. How was your trip? Comment allez-vous? You are well Madame? Très bien, it is a fine morning, bienvenue à Paris, welcome to Paris. Allow me to show you to your apartment; it is au deuxième étage."

Georges loaded her luggage into the elevator and the three of them rode to the second floor. Lyla followed Monsieur Albion to the apartment door and waited as he unlocked it and ushered her inside while Georges followed. The apartment was compact with a small terrace off the bedroom overlooking a private garden. It had everything she needed. It was tastefully decorated with bookcases, accessories, and tasteful artwork on the walls. It was clean, bright with lots of light, not at all disappointing.

"Is there anything you need Madame?"

"No, no, thank you, merci Messieurs Albion et Georges." Lyla was ready with a generous tip for both gentlemen.

"Au revoir Messieurs."

"Au revoir Madame."

Monsieur Albion handed Lyla the keys and turned toward the door. Lyla accompanied the gentlemen to the door and locked it behind them.

She turned to survey her cozy apartment, exhausted and excited at the same time. She couldn't believe she was finally there.

"Ah", she sighed, "alone, at last, in my own place a million miles, or so it seemed, from the life I left behind." She looked around once again and decided to unpack. Upon closer inspection, she discovered that the compact kitchen was equipped with a container to boil water for tea. Her plan was to set up her laptop and clicked on the icon for her favorite Italian language, Swiss, classical radio station while she sipped on fresh tea. She wrote a short email to the boys to tell them she had arrived safely as she listened to the familiar radio station. The small fridge had been filled with fresh fruit, cheeses, and small custard tarts. It was just enough to satisfy her hunger until she needed something more substantial. The day was beginning to warm up after an early, chilly spring morning. After sipping her tea and eating the custard tart, Lyla showered to refresh and remove the debris of travel.

The shower refreshed her, she was too excited to try to rest, and she decided to keep going until she dropped. Her first order of business was to pull up a map of her current location on her laptop and familiarize herself with the streets and businesses around her. Her next plan was to explore everything within walking distance, make a list of the places she wanted to visit, and draw a crude but functional map. The current temperature was still a bit cool so she took a light jacket and rode the elevator down to the street. Feeling confident, she stepped outside and started down her street. Her map helped her to stay on course, and she made a conscious effort to look for landmarks as she walked from street to street. She found a market, made a mental note of its location, and continued walking in the direction of the bakery.

On the way, she noticed the beautiful architecture of the buildings surrounding her on both sides of the street. Most of them were three or four stories with balconies made of decorative ironwork. Some had flowers on the railings, others had painted latticed shutters. One intersection she came to had a large island of trees separating the streets. Scooters, motorbikes, and bicycles lined the streets in stall-like parking places, standing like steeds waiting for their masters. Lyla remembered how much she disliked motorcycles but could perhaps make an effort to get used to those cute, moped looking things and eventually ride through the streets like so many other Parisians. In addition, she made a mental note of the clothing and accessory stores that caught her eye as she walked along the cobbled sidewalk.

The streets were busy, crowded with people as well as shops. The walk was longer than she anticipated but she found the bakery where she was to apprentice. Its large plate glass windows were splashed with 'Boulangerie' on the front. She recognized the delightful aroma of fresh bread emanating from inside from where she stood. People were patiently waiting in line for their respective loaves of rustic artisan breads and familiar baguettes. Small tables dotted the inside of the small establishment where customers were devouring their delicious purchases and sipping coffee, hot chocolate, or tea while engaged in animated conversation.

Lyla stepped inside and then to the side of the room and watched everyone. The bakers were busy in the rear of the shop, loading their pallets of unbaked bread into the huge brick ovens. There were stacks of bread coming out of the ovens and bread proofing in what looked like woven baskets. She was so immersed in the scene she didn't notice a tall gentleman walking toward her.

"Bonjour, puis-je vous aider? Hello, may I help you?"

Lyla looked up and was somewhat startled to see someone standing almost directly in front of her. "Pardon, uh ... Non, oh oui, pardon. Je suis cherche. Non non non." She had a look of exasperation on her face, shook her head, and gave out a small sigh. "Je suis à la recherche Monsieur Rinaldo, Monsieur Jacques Rinaldo."

"Ah, you are looking for Monsieur Jacques?"

"Yes, I mean, oui." Lyla apologized for her schoolgirl French, frustrated at her inability to speak the language with ease.

"Wait a moment please, I will tell him you are here, votre nom? Your name?"

"Lyla Rose. Lyla Rose is my name," as she stood on her toes and waved after him.

"I meant to say, Je m'appelle Lyla," she whispered softly. She was frustrated, exasperated with herself. Again, she didn't notice a gentleman who walked toward her, "Lyla? Lyla Rose?"

She turned and saw a middle-aged gentleman who stood about 5'10" tall. He had dark, almost black hair sprinkled with silver, soft dark eyes, a large trimmed mustache, and a warm smile. He was clothed in white shorts, a white t shirt and baker's apron with a white kerchief tied around his neck, and his hands were covered in flour.

"Bonjour, bienvenue à Paris, my name is Jacques, Jacques Rinaldo. I am the principal baker and owner of the boulangerie. We have spoken on the phone and emailed, and I am pleased to make your acquaintance."

Lyla was stunned into silence and her jaw dropped ever so slightly. She then recovered enough to acknowledge his greeting, she said. "Oui, oui, yes, yes. I am so pleased to meet you."

"Please, if you would come with me, I should like to show you the bakery, oui?"

"That would be lovely," she responded, trying hard to sound a bit more at ease.

They walked around and through the crowd of customers and emerged in the inner sanctum where the magic happened. It nearly took Lyla's breath away. The amount of heat that emanated from the open ovens was close to 500 degrees. Lyla felt the intensity that caused small beads of sweat to form on her face as she walked by them. The huge brick ovens along the entire wall had large openings that looked like wide gaping mouths ready to swallow the proofed bread to be baked. Bakers were loading the raised bread onto large wooden peels to be shoved into the oven, and others were removing the peels of baked loaves from the ovens to be cooled and passed to customers. The aroma of the freshly baked bread was intoxicating.

Monsieur Rinaldo introduced Lyla to the staff and gave her the complete tour of the establishment. He was particularly careful to explain the rules of the bakery in detail. She was told to be aware of the extreme heat of the ovens and surrounding area, how to remain safe, and some of the bread vocabulary she needed to know. The next few hours seemed to fly by.

There was a lot for her to learn. Lyla began to feel weak and faint. She was overwhelmed by the amount of information she was receiving and feeling the effects of jet lag. She placed her hand to her head feeling the beads of sweat and a sudden chill.

Jacques recognized her symptoms and remarked it was time for him to return to his work and for Lyla to have a light meal and return to her apartment. She would need the time to rest and prepare for the long days ahead.

"Baking bread is hard work and long hours; you must rest and be strong," he told her.

"Yes, thank you," she said weakly. "I think it's time I return to my apartment."

"You will return in a taxi, just wait here."

"Oh, no, monsieur, please, I can walk. I don't want to trouble you."

But before she could finish her sentence, he was out the door hailing a taxi and escorting her to the door. "Remember," he said kindly, "early in the morning, ready to work, get a good night's rest. Au revoir, jusqu'à demain, Lyla."

"Au revoir, Monsieur Rinaldo, until tomorrow."

"Please, Lyla, call me Jacques."

After they exchanged goodbyes, Jacques opened the door of the taxi, bid Lyla farewell, and closed the door with Lyla safely inside. She had not been willing to admit she was thankful to be riding and not walking back to the apartment. The day was beginning to wane and there was a slight chill in the air. Lyla asked the driver to stop at one of the many places that dotted the return route for her to purchase a takeaway meal.

It was late afternoon when Lyla arrived at her building. The short ride in the elevator seemed to take forever and the distance to the front door felt as though it was miles. She was exhausted, but proud of what she had accomplished. For someone who was afraid to step out of her uncomfortable comfort zone, she had come a very long way that day.

It was fortuitous that the apartment was small and compact. She unpacked her food and put the water on for a steamy cup of tea. The exhaustion and jet lag caused a slight tremor to come over her. She quickly removed her clothes, slipped into her flannel nightgown, and wrapped herself in a warm, snuggly chenille robe, fuzzy socks, and slippers. As she waited for the water to come to the boil, she turned on her laptop to find some of her favorite music and check her emails. Spam, spam, it even followed her to France. Emails were sent to the boys once again to let them know she was doing well with some pictures she snapped along the journey to describe her adventurous day.

The food she purchased was delicious, just what was needed, and it satisfied her hunger. She had just enough strength to wash her face, brush her teeth, and snuggle under the down comforter in bed. Her eyelids grew heavy and her thoughts revisited the highlights of her day, Mrs. Blum and the invitation to the dedication, and then she fell into a deep slumber. The early morning would arrive soon enough, and she would begin her first day as an apprentice.

LEARNING A NEW LIFE

"Thank you, Professor Blum," said the gate attendant. "You may now board your flight to Paris. Enjoy your journey."

As Alex walked down the long narrow walkway to the aircraft, he could hardly believe he was making this trip alone. The flight attendant greeted him as he entered the aircraft.

"Welcome aboard sir, enjoy your time traveling with us."

"Yes, thank you, I will," he said as he walked down the short aisle to his first-class seat. They had chosen to spend the extra money and go first class; that was Annie's idea. *Hmm*, he thought, *I wonder if this was the most appropriate thing to do considering the circumstances.* The empty seat next to him stared back in silence, making him question the decision even more.

Alex's flight was uneventful. The flight attendants served him with great care, as they did the other first-class passengers. He was appreciative of their efforts, but nothing could fill the void. Alex was well prepared, or so he thought. He and Annie had chosen several books to read during the flight, but he found it difficult to open any of them. Nothing seemed to interest him. Although he attempted to focus on his upcoming adventure, his thoughts always returned to what had happened to his Annie and how utterly alone he felt. He stared at the empty seat next to him, bewildered with how he could make this trip without her. After hours of trying to fill the lonely moments, he surrendered to the fatigue and sorrow and fell into a deep sleep. As he slept, he recalled his life with Annie and how he managed to be on this flight at this time, alone.

Alex and Annie were in their early thirties when they met and subsequently married. They lived a comfortable but not luxurious life. The thirty years they were married passed quickly. Although they never had children together, they filled their lives with the children they taught. Annie continued to teach full time while Alex achieved his doctorate and became head of the art department at a small local liberal arts college. It was Annie's idea to spend their 30th wedding anniversary in Paris, going to all the places Alex had described to her, and the ones she dreamed about seeing.

Alex and Annie Blum had planned a comprehensive, all-inclusive trip with much anticipation. They poured over guide books, looked on the internet, and talked to other friends about where to go and what to see. Although Alex had been familiar with Paris and France, he intended to make certain this trip was special for Annie. Alex's family was financially secure but Annie's was not and she insisted they not rely on any of Alex's family's money for anything, especially not for this trip; it was special. So, they saved a portion of his salary as a college instructor and then professor, and a portion of hers as a teacher, just for this kind of occasion.

Everything was in place. Tickets were purchased, itinerary was planned, and hotels booked with time left for some exploring and adventures. Annie reluctantly booked an appointment with her family physician for a general checkup as a precautionary measure prior to the trip. Bloodwork and other diagnostic test results were obtained, and she was shocked by the diagnosis and prognosis of advanced stage lymphoma. She left the doctor's office in disbelief, wondering how she would tell Alex. Perhaps it was all a mistake. She fantasized that the doctor's office would call and apologize for putting her through the pain and anguish of the diagnosis only to say files got mixed up or the lab gave them incorrect information. She hoped for anything to make this entire nightmare disappear.

She hadn't been feeling like herself and she thought those night sweats were just part of menopause. After all, she was in the right age range. She never thought it could be anything more serious. The cancer was everywhere in her body, and she had a very short time to live. As Annie drove home, lost in thought, the car seemed to drive by itself. "Should I tell Alex? What should I tell him? We've made so many plans. I have never kept anything from him before."

Their marriage had been based on their friendship and their mutual respect for each other. They were best friends and lovers, and their love grew from a trusting oneness to a comfortable and loving relationship.

She thought perhaps she could try to hide or mask her symptoms without causing Alex undue alarm and not tell him until they returned from their trip. It was a perfect way for them to spend what time she had left and not have to focus on what was to come. "Please God," she prayed, "let me have time to go to Paris, give me the strength to tell Alex when the time is right." Although this seemed reasonable to her, deceiving Alex weighed heavily upon her conscience.

Annie made a special dinner that night, deciding she would not reveal her secret until the time was appropriate. As usual, Alex entered the house whistling a familiar tune. He was eager to give Annie a kiss hello and nearly overlooked the beautifully set table. It was then he smelled delicious aromas emanating from the direction of the kitchen. He thought, *Uh, oh, I've forgotten something important, our anniversary? Annie's birthday? Why else would the dining room table be set and things look like there's a special occasion?*

As his mind searched for the answer, he decided to slip out, get flowers, return and act like he knew what was so darn special. If only he could remember what made today so special. Before he could get out the door, Annie came out of the kitchen looking beautiful. Her hair was brushed back off her face and she was wearing one of her colorful aprons. She was making one of his favorite meals.

He hesitated, and then said, "You remembered, so did I. What a coincidence!" She looked at him quizzically and wondered what had gotten into him?

"Uh, yes," she said, "special, yes. I remembered, but didn't think you would," searching his face for some kind of clue. "I'm so glad we're celebrating, aren't you?"

Then she remembered that today everything had been finalized for their anniversary trip to Paris.

"Yes, everything's done and now all we have to do is go. We must celebrate and you must help me practice my French and preview what we can expect on our trip."

She hoped she covered well for not knowing what was so important and Alex breathed a sigh of relief and laughed, "Yes, only three months to go, and we'll be on our way." He thought, *I have successfully dodged that bullet!* He kissed her gently on the neck smelling the aromas wafting from the kitchen.

The evening was a stunning success, the food was terrific, and the wine, perfect. They spent countless hours poring over maps of different areas they were planning to visit and places they hoped to see. It had been a long and difficult day for Annie and she was exhausted from the food, the wine, and the secret she was keeping.

That night, Annie and Alex fell asleep in each other's arms. She dreamt about her life with her best friend and lover and Alex dreamt of the trip he was anticipating with his wonderful wife. Finally, the trip they had gave up many years before and the city Alex wanted to share were becoming a reality. There was nothing more to do but wait until the school year ended. Annie had given notice to her principal that she would not be available to teach summer school. This would have been her first time not working through the summer. All that was left was for them to complete a smooth school year, pack, and be on their way.

The next several weeks passed speedily. Annie was losing her appetite and became easily exhausted. The night sweats grew worse, forcing her to change her nightgown several times a night. She became noticeably weak and had difficulty concealing her illness from the teachers at school. Her principal, Mrs. Gates, called Annie into her office after school one day, concerned that something was wrong.

Annie sat in Mrs. Gates' office trying hard to conceal her secret. But after several minutes of silence everything tumbled out of her mouth. Annie started to cry and then sob uncontrollably. She apologized to Principal Gates for not saying anything sooner. Together they planned for Annie to leave school without putting an emotional burden on her students and give Annie the time she needed with her family.

Alex would be home for dinner early that day as he had a short teaching schedule and no meetings. Although Annie felt nauseated and weak, she managed to prepare something simple for dinner and needed to lie down. She was chilled and relaxed on the chaise in the sun room with a soft coverlet. She promised herself she would only close her eyes briefly but within moments fell into a deep sleep.

Alex came bouncing into the house calling for Annie, carrying a large bouquet of colorful flowers. Annie loved fresh flowers. The house was unusually quiet, the table was set and Annie nowhere to be found. Alex called again and when he heard no response began to search the house. He found Annie lying asleep on the lounge in the sun room. Large maps and guidebooks were open, draped on her chest. Alex noticed her pale skin and gently bent over to kiss her. She slowly opened her eyes and reached out her hand to take his. He knew something was wrong. Her hand felt cold and frail, he became frightened. She looked at him and motioned for him to come sit beside her.

I've been waiting for you," she said weakly. We were walking in Paris, arm in arm, like all the other lovers. There's something I need to tell you."

She told him about her symptoms and her refusal to believe it was anything but menopausal silliness. And then she described her last visit to the doctor, the diagnosis, and the rapid progression of the disease ravaging her body. Alex stared at her in shock and disbelief. He blinked his eyes and tried to wake up thinking he was in the middle of a nightmare.

"Wait a minute, wait a minute," he said. "When did you find this out? Why didn't you tell me? I could have done something. I should have done something. I have to do something," his voice trailed off to a whisper. "I don't understand."

"I thought we had more time," Annie said. "I thought we would be able to take our trip. But I don't think I'll be leaving for Paris with you."

Alex said nothing more. He lifted her into his arms cuddling her, holding her, stroking her hair, and wanting the moment to last forever. She felt comforted in his arms. He buried his head in her neck and closed his eyes as the tears rolled down his cheeks.

PARIS MOVING ON

The sound of muffled voices and the clattering of metal containers woke Alex from his distressing sleep. The conversations of nearby passengers, the aroma from freshly brewed coffee, and trays laden with steaming breakfast brought him back from his haunting and painful remembrances. Somehow, he had survived the night. He left his seat, walked down the aisle to the first-class lavatory, and splashed some water on his face. After returning to his seat, he was served a full breakfast tray, but merely picked at his food. He no longer had an appetite for food or for life. The attendant removed the used breakfast trays and last-minute drinks as the plane flew closer to its destination. Alex began to prepare for the landing as the pilot announced their final descent and approach into the Paris airport.

After Alex deplaned and retrieved his luggage, he boarded one of the shuttles into the city. As he traveled from the airport to the city, he once again thought of Annie. Her absence created a significant void in his life that left him with a definite ache. Perhaps his decision to take the trip and the year-long sabbatical was a mistake.

He was deep in thought when he spoke out loud, "Alex this is a mistake...a big mistake, taking the sabbatical and position at the Sorbonne. What did I think I was doing?" he questioned as he shook his head in disbelief.

He believed making decisions, at least major life decisions, was not advisable during times of distress. Perhaps he acted without thinking, perhaps he acted out of grief, perhaps...perhaps. He focused on the images speeding by outside his window as he continued his journey, uttering the words echoing in his head, "What am I doing here...alone?"

Alex breathed a deep sigh and settled back into his seat. The van had been on the road for nearly 20 minutes when Alex's discomfort began to ease and a tender smile showed on his face with the thought of Annie, their life together, and the trip they had lovingly planned. "Look at this Annie," he said, "I'm here." The van was in the city dropping off passengers. The sights and sounds of a busy city interrupted his reverie, bringing him back to reality.

There was quiet chatter from the other passengers in the van as the vehicle continued along the streets of Paris snaking its way down avenues and boulevards.

"Vous-êtes un Américain? Are you an American?"

The voice came from beside him: soft, gentle, and definitely French. He looked at her with surprise, realizing he had been totally absorbed in his musings.

"Uh, Yes, I mean oui." Alex responded almost apologetically. She was young and very beautiful, with long auburn hair that fell in long luxurious curls around her face. He was caught and drawn in by her amazing emerald green eyes.

"D'accord monsieur, I speak English. Are you in Paris to visit?"

"Yes, I mean no, well, actually I'm here to do both. I'm a visiting professor at the Sorbonne and hope to travel during my free time."

"Mais oui, mon Dieu, it is fortunate for me. I'm currently a student at the Sorbonne."

Alex couldn't help but feel immediate discomfort at this initial encounter with a beautiful woman as an unmarried man but became more relaxed as he moved into his professorial role. The conversation focused on familiar subject matter and ended when the student, Jacqueline, reached her destination. As she gathered her bags and bundles, she gave Alex a familiar, French departing brush on the cheek, said, "Au revoir," and exited the vehicle. Before going on her way, she turned back to face the van as though she had forgotten something. "Monsieur, votre nom ? Your name ?"

Alex opened the window of the van and responded, "Professor Blum, Alex Blum, enchanter."

"Àbientôt, Professor Blum. Perhaps we will see one another at the Sorbonne, perhaps in class, yes?"

"Perhaps," he responded as the van moved on to its next destination.

The van moved through the city continuing on its journey to other passengers' respective destinations. The next stop was the Hotel Design

Sorbonne, directly across the street from the Sorbonne itself, and near the Luxembourg Garden, Pantheon, and other places of interest. Alex was anxious to check in. He left the van driver a tip and thanked him for the ride. The streets were already busy, crowded with students and tourists. He entered the hotel lobby where he was struck by the artistic use of color and design.

The reality was as alluring, even more so, as the pictures he had seen online. The lobby was a visual feast of colors that were used in exciting and unusual combinations. He noticed one couch sitting in an alcove that was black with turquoise stripes surrounded by chartreuse accents and turquoise and black wallpaper. His room arrangements were made for him by his staff and he was anxious to see his accommodations. On his approach to the front desk, his senses were bombarded by the color, movement, and texture of the walls, floor, and furniture. Alex approached the desk clerk and asked for assistance.

The clerk greeted Alex, "Bonjour, Monsieur."

"Yes, Bonjour, my name is Alex Blum. I believe arrangements were made for my accommodations. I would like to check in and go to my room."

"Ah oui, Professor Blum, with pleasure. Did you have a good journey? Bon, Oui, oui, ah we have your room ready for you as was requested. If you would sign in, please, I will have someone assist with your luggage."

The clerk reached for the keys as Alex signed the register.

"Monsieur Blum, le professeur, I almost forget, you have several messages for your attention. Someone from La Sorbonne has been here inquiring about your arrival. They left a note and there have been other calls for you. You may return the calls here in the lobby or wait until you reach your room."

"Thank you, I'll return the calls from my room."

"Very well Monsieur, someone will take you there. Enjoy your stay with us."

The bellman appeared at Alex's side with his luggage and Alex followed him across the open area of the lobby into the elevator. When they disembarked from the elevator, Alex's senses were again struck by a barrage of color and design from the furnishings of the hotel that seemed to engulf him. The hallway was carpeted in a dark red rug dotted with a colorful yellow design. The walls of the hallway were covered in dark red mahogany fabric dappled with an eclectic collection of artistic works.

The bellman and Alex walked to the end of the hallway where they faced the doorway to Alex's room. The bellman opened the door on a suite bathed in light and decorated in shades of taupe and gray accented with pale green. It was a distinct difference from the large bold color he experienced elsewhere in the hotel. It was a welcome solace and an excellent place for him to unwind and relax. He tipped the bellman and thanked him.

"If le professeur needs anything at all, please call. I am at your service." The bellman acknowledged Alex's tip and exited the room.

Alex surveyed the space, unpacked, and organized his clothing and accessories. Jet lag had not set in. He could feel the stubble on his face and hadn't bathed since the day before. He turned on the shower, steamed up the bathroom, and let the hot water wash off the dirt and grime of travel then dressed in his favorite jeans and soft flannel shirt. His next priority was to respond to the messages. Alex made his first call to his mother, Ethel Blum.

MRS. BLUM

Mrs. Blum's chauffeur maneuvered his way through traffic to her gracious home in the 16th arrondissement of Neuilly Sur Seine. She lived in an area known for its well-appointed homes and inhabitants. The homes stood behind clean, quiet, tree-lined streets and were architecturally handsome and reflective of the architecture of the early 1920s. Philipe opened the iron gates with the remote and drove up the short drive to the front entrance. As Mrs. Blum passed through the gates she smiled wistfully recalling the loving memories of her life there with her husband.

Her smile turned bittersweet, happy to be back in Paris, but not alone. She picked up her handbag and other personal items on the seat next to her as Philipe opened her car door and then carried her luggage inside the house to her room. Mrs. Blum was greeted at the front door by Hildi, her housekeeper. The drapes over the large windows by the hallway had been pulled back to wash each room with the glow of the morning sun. The vases were filled to overflowing with colorful fresh flowers.

Hildi accompanied Mrs. Blum upstairs to help her unpack and lay out her clothes for the day. As they walked up the staircase, Mrs. Blum spoke to Hildi. "Hildi, I am so pleased to see the house looking so warm and inviting. Thank you to all of you."

"Thank you, Mrs. Blum," Hildi remarked. "The staff has worked hard to reopen your home. We were anxious for your return, especially on this momentous occasion."

Mrs. Blum's room was graceful and refined, tastefully decorated in a country French style reminiscent of Louis XV and Louis XVI that captured her sophistication and warmth. The walls were painted café au lait and cream. The draperies were muted blue silk covered with a small print of cream and brown flowers and vines that pooled onto the floor. Her bed was footed in pale cream carved wood with a floral and scrolled headboard.

Mrs. Blum showered and changed from her traveling clothes to something suitable for her appearance at Haussmann House. She worked in her study, sorting documents and other papers and was ready to depart the house. Philipe had already been summoned and was waiting with the car door open as she walked through the doorway. He greeted her with a pleasant, engaging smile and gathered her into the waiting vehicle. He sped her away into the morning traffic and advised her they were near their destination. He opened her door, assisted her with her departure from the vehicle, and she walked into the building.

Mrs. Ethel Blum entered the building through the tall wooden double doors eager to conclude the final preparations for the dedication.

"Good morning, Mrs. Blum, how are you?" the young receptionist inquired.

"I'm well, thank you, Vivienne, and you?"

"Oh, exceptional Mrs. Blum, exceptional."

"Très bon, très bon, Vivienne. Please find Genevieve and ask her to meet me in my office in about 45 minutes, merci."

Mrs. Blum walked through the building and was pleased to see the women wholly engaged and focused, preparing for the dedication and daily activities. The building had been renovated to bring back the beauty of its former life and designed to accommodate space essential to its function. The first floor contained the administrative offices. The second floor housed the classrooms, dance/workout rooms, art/music, counseling, and training suites. The third-floor housed small apartments designated for women and their children who had to escape their homes and were unable to seek refuge in a local shelter.

Mrs. Ethel Blum was a remarkable woman. She knew everyone by name and personally acknowledged those she passed on the way to her small, tastefully appointed office. The room was an accurate reflection of her containing pictures of her husband, children and grandchildren, small sculptures, and art glass she collected during her life. She had a great appreciation for all forms of art but was particularly fond of her grandchildren's drawings and art projects, which were framed and mounted. When Ethel entered the office, she walked over to her antique mahogany desk and adjusted the needlepoint pillow on her chair. The leather-bound notebook on her desk contained the plans for and details of the dedication. She heard a faint knock on the door as she opened the book and put on her glasses.

"Ah, Genevieve. Bon matin. Good morning. Please come in. There are a multitude of issues I want to review with you."

Mrs. Blum was interrupted when Alex made his first phone call to Haussmann House.

"Bonjour, bon matin. C'est Martine à la Fondation de Haussmann House."

"Yes, I'd like to speak to Mrs. Blum, s'il vous plaît," Alex inquired.

"Of course, sir, may I ask who is calling?"

"Yes, you may, this is Alex Blum."

"Just a moment, if you please. I will connect you." The main operator connected Alex to his mother's secretary.

"Bonjour Professor Blum, just a moment. Mrs. Blum has been awaiting your call."

"Alex, is that you?"

"Yes, mother, I've arrived." Mrs. Blum motioned for Genevieve to give her a few moments of privacy and turned her attention to her son. When her conversation ended, she asked Genevieve to return. "I would like to start with the guest list." The guest list for the dedication was personally compiled by Mrs. Blum. It included political figures, members of the Jewish Community, and other influential people of Europe. Genevieve reported there had been an enthusiastic response. The guests were anxious to learn about the comprehensive program Mrs. Blum had been able to create and were eager to learn and absorb every aspect and return to their respective cities and initiate similar programs.

"Are there any invitations not yet posted?"

"No, Mrs. Blum, with the exception of the last name you gave me upon your arrival."

"Do you have that invitation with you now?"

"Yes, I do."

"Thank you, I want to include a personal note and want it hand-delivered today."

"Of course, it will not be a problem."

"Good. Thank you. Now, let's go over the schedule of events and the protocol necessary for the dignitaries."

Mrs. Blum knew it was essential to have concrete follow-up to her verbal invitation to Lyla. She believed it would require a great deal of mental courage and emotional fortitude on Lyla's part, not only to accept, but to actually appear. In a way, this was a test. Mrs. Blum instinctively recognized Lyla's shyness and hesitancy to accept the invitation and attend the dedication. This was not the first time someone with similar circumstances as Lyla who had crossed her path. Mrs. Blum intuitively recognized this particular group of women who had been submissive and victimized over a long period of time. Throughout her life time Mrs. Blum learned there was usually a cataclysmic emotional event the women had to share/confront that would catapult them into revelations and insights, enabling them to access their essence and the strength that could be drawn from it.

She wondered what Lyla's event was. Ethel didn't recall hearing anything specific or alluded to that would produce a cataclysmic emotional event hearing Lyla recount her story on the plane. Why did she stay with her abuser when she had clear opportunity to leave? What was it that kept Lyla there? It had to have been something emotionally extreme for Lyla to linger until her husband's death. Ethel wondered if Lyla would ever be able to reveal this.

Ethel Blum knew their meeting was not coincidental and wondered if this was the woman she had envisioned taking the program back to the United States. Only time would tell, and of course, Lyla's willingness to participate.

LYLA THE BAKER

Lyla's shrill alarm woke her from a deep sleep. The residual effects of her travel the day before from Florida left her feeling achy and sore. The excitement and anticipation of her apprenticeship clouded her perception of how demanding and taxing it was to be a baker. The hours would be long and unforgiving and involve active physical exertion.

When Lyla was fully awake, she climbed out of her warm bed to shower, then stood, staring at her clothes, wondering what would be appropriate to wear on her first day. She decided on a clean, long-sleeve T-shirt and comfortable jeans. Her breakfast consisted of some fresh apple and yogurt from the refrigerator, and a piece of bread from the day before. She brewed a mug of strong tea and crisped the bread.

The invitation that had been hand delivered the day before caught her eye. Monsieur Albion had placed it in her mailbox the day Lyla arrived, while she was exploring, and called it to her attention when she returned from her outing. When Lyla retrieved it, she placed it on the corner of the table by the door. This morning, she picked it up and read it as she nibbled on her breakfast. "You are cordially invited to the ceremonies for the dedication of Haussmann House on Sunday..." Lyla had been procrastinating. She knew she had to decide but chose to ignore the invitation for the time being. She placed the card on the table and left for the bakery.

Lyla's first weeks at the bakery were like a blur of early mornings and long days spent learning the language of bread. Lyla's skill in French was still elementary but hearing the language daily and using the words and phrases helped to train her ear and grow her vocabulary. Every evening she returned to her cozy apartment, thankful to shed her working clothes covered with flour dust and soak in a hot tub filled with lavender oil.

Lyla lounged on the small settee relaxing after her soak, cuddled in her chenille robe and fluffy socks. She clicked on the icon for classical music and poured a glass of wine, a perfect way to finish her day. Not once since her arrival in Paris, had she thought about Juliano and her life with him. How strange, she mused. He was not in her head and not in her life. She wondered what happened to the anger and resentment. Where did it go? Did it just disappear?

Lyla got up to refresh her wine, not wanting to dwell on those thoughts for too long, when the card sitting on the table by the door caught her eye. So far, she had been successful in ignoring its presence. Was it that she was busy and tired, or was it something else? Was she purposely avoiding the invitation, not wanting to deal with having to make the decision? She picked up the envelope, walked back to the couch and sat comfortably, drawing her legs close to her body, and covered herself with her throw to stay warm. Slowly and carefully she opened the invitation and read the hand-written note from Mrs. Blum.

"Dear Lyla, I wanted to express again how lovely it was to travel with you. I enjoyed our time together. It would mean a great deal to me if you would join me and attend the dedication of Haussmann House. I realize how difficult it might be to come, not knowing anyone, but I want to assure you, you will not feel alone once you arrive. It would be my pleasure to introduce you to some splendid people who I'm certain you will enjoy meeting and getting to know. If you have any questions or concerns, please do not hesitate to contact me. I look forward to seeing you. Fondly, Ethel Blum."

The dignified invitation was pale cream linen paper imprinted in dark eggplant-colored ink. Lyla rubbed her fingers over the raised letters, unable to decide. It was nice of Mrs. Blum to invite her in the first place, let alone send a personal note. But Lyla continued to hesitate.

"I'm not so sure about this," she said, speaking to the invitation. "I really don't know this woman. She was just a nice lady I sat next to on the plane. Well, that's not quite true, there was something special about her and something special about the time we spent together."

As Lyla put the card down, she waved off the thoughts with her hand.

"How can I go there all by myself? I don't know anyone. This is not for me. She's a nice old lady but I don't think so. Besides, I don't have anything to wear and what the heck do you wear to a dedication?"

She got up from her cozy spot, having convinced herself the decision was made. She turned off the music and looked at the invitation one more time, noticing the bottom which read, "The favor of a reply is most appreciated." She thought. *It's late, I'll reply with a decline tomorrow.* The entire issue was dismissed. She dropped the card onto the table and retired to bed.

Lyla got up the next morning anxious to see what the day would bring. Jacques had given her the day off, and she was grateful to have some time to herself. As she walked to the kitchen, she noticed the invitation on the table. It appeared to be glaring at her. She tried to ignore the uncomfortable feeling she had and entered the kitchen to make her morning tea.

The fridge contained a fruit custard tart and a brioche she brought home the day before. Lyla popped the brioche into the microwave, thinking, *what cruel injustice to microwave the luscious and delectable bread,* and waited while her water came to the boil. Suddenly, she felt uncomfortable as though someone was staring at her. Lyla turned to look behind her to see if someone was there. No one, but she glanced in the direction of the table and became fixed on the card.

"OK, OK, OK," she said out loud, "OK, I can see this is going to be a problem until I make the phone call. A girl can't even have a morning cup of tea without being harassed by a silly piece of paper."

She walked to the table as her water came to the boil, picked up the invitation, and returned to the kitchen. *This is ridiculous,* she thought. *I'll make the phone call and be done with it as soon as I have my tea."*

She sat and stared at the menacing invitation and slowly sipped her tea. It wasn't the card that was so very intimidating. It was the act of moving outside of the comfort zone she had already made for herself. Here she was in Paris, a vibrant and exciting city. She had journeyed a great distance to leave her past behind emotionally and physically and begin a new life. The transplant required a distance of more than 4,500 miles and still she was alone and isolated; comfortably uncomfortable.

There was no Juliano, children, or dogs to blame who relied upon her for all their needs. It was only her and her self-imposed isolation. Her almost monotonous daily routine, working at the bakery left her little to no time to herself. But why was that? Was Jacques such a taskmaster that she was never given time off? On the contrary, he had, from the very beginning, encouraged Lyla to move beyond the confines of her world and experience the beauty and wonders of living in Paris.

She made no attempts to engage with anyone and was always alone. It was as though she once again created a safe, comfortable world without being totally engaged with the world. Each day she ventured out, walking the streets to the bakery, barely acknowledging the crowds of people walking past her. Her eyes were downcast as she walked, intent on her path to her destination. The journey to Paris required her to take a great risk and a giant step into the unknown. Now she needed to find whatever it was that got her there and use it to move her forward out of the little box she had put herself into.

All right, Lyla, here you are half way around the world and you're frightened to leave the safe place you've made. It's time to venture forth, open the door, and experience life. Now I know I'm in trouble, she thought. *I'm talking to a piece of paper and myself.*

She picked up her cell phone, called the number to RSVP to the dedication, and waited as the ring-ring, ring-ring, echoed in her ear.

"Hmm," she said to herself, "guess it's too early to call; no one is responding. She was relieved, secretly hoping no one would pick up."

The longer the phone rang unanswered, the more fear Lyla felt. She stared at the words on the invitation that were beginning to smear from the moisture on her fingers. Her anxiety rose as she admonished herself, "it's only a voice, take a deep breath." Just as she was ready to end the call, a young woman's cheery voice answered. Breathless as though she had been running, the young woman on the other end said, "Bonjour, bon matin. C'est Martine à la Fondation de La Maison de Haussmann, bonjour ... bonjour. Est-ce qu'ilya quelqu'un? Is someone there?"

Lyla brought the phone back to her ear and responded.

"Ah yes, I mean to say, je m'excuse, oui, bonjour. Je m'appelle, Lyla Rose."

"Ah oui, Madame, it is with pleasure to hear from you."

"Oh, you speak English," Lyla responded, with a hint of relief. "Thank you, yes, this is Lyla Rose and I'm calling to accept Mrs. Blum's invitation to the dedication on Sunday."

"Merveilleux, marvelous. Mrs. Blum will be pleased to know you will attend. Do you have any questions of me?"

"Well, as a matter of fact I do. I'm not quite sure what one is to wear to this type of event and was wondering if you would be kind enough to assist me."

"Bien sur, of course," she responded in her cheery voice. "The event is black tie, optional, but formal. A lovely evening gown would be appropriate."

Lyla's eyebrows arched and her eyes grew wide as she repeated the words, "Evening gown?" Lyla did not want to appear foolish, and acknowledged, "Oh yes, well, of course, yes, naturally," and then there was silence.

Martine noticed Lyla's anxious voice and responded. "Mrs. Blum anticipated your possible need for some assistance in finding an appropriate garment. She has taken the liberty of offering to send her assistant to take you shopping if you have the time."

"Oh, yes that would be wonderful," Lyla said, and then began to babble uncontrollably. "You see, when I decided to come to Paris I never anticipated needing anything more than casual, well, actually, jeans and ... something very comfortable ... and I thought, well, actually I never thought I would need or have to wear...anything...that required... I'm rambling, I'm so sorry. Yes, yes, I would appreciate having someone to help."

"Bon, good. How about today, perhaps, later this morning? Oui?"

Lyla looked at her clock to establish a time frame for herself and responded. "I think 10:30 would be fine for me. Is that agreeable?"

"Yes, perfect. Genevieve will pick you up at your apartment at 10:30. Please, may I have your exact location?"

Lyla confidently rattled off her address in an acceptable accent and was pleased she had taken the time and effort to learn to recite her address with ease. The call ended with Lyla realizing what she had done and she stood holding the phone tightly in her hand against her chest. She stood perfectly still, took a deep breath, and said softly, "I can do this."

Lyla stood for several moments, trying to organize her thoughts.

She finally put the phone down and once again checked the time. Sipping the last drops of her morning tea, she calculated she had about an hour before she was to meet Mrs. Blum's assistant downstairs. It was barely enough time to shower, dress, and assess the deficiencies in her wardrobe. She struggled to remember the name of the assistant but was so nervous and excited when she spoke to Martine that she remembered only vital pieces of information: shopping, downstairs, 10:30.

Before going downstairs, Lyla made a personal inventory. She checked her keys, cell phone, and credit cards, where would she be without those plastic beauties, and walked out the apartment door to ride down the elevator to the ground floor. As she stepped out the door of her building, she met a well-dressed woman looking definitely Parisienne and self-assured. The woman approached her saying, "Bonjour, my name is Genevieve, Mrs. Blum's assistant, and you are Lyla, Lyla Rose?"

"Oui, yes, it is a pleasure to meet you," Lyla responded.

"Mais oui, but yes, it is lovely to make your acquaintance, Lyla. I have made the presumption of bringing my own vehicle to make rapid maneuvers in and out of tight spaces if necessary. Have you any particular place in mind you would like to go?"

Lyla had no idea where to start or where to go. "I'm sorry, Genevieve. I have done little shopping since my arrival in Paris and will defer to your experience and better judgment."

"Mais non, you have no need to apologize, Lyla, and by the way, everybody calls me Genni, Genevieve is too formal. Anyway, do not apologize, you are fortunate. I have great familiarity with the shops in Paris. I love to buy clothes, but especially shoes and handbags. I shall take you to some of my favorite spots. I know we will find something exceptional.

"Our first and only stop will be to the Galeries Lafayette on Boulevard Haussmann, a sumptuous feast for the eyes! It is a shopper's paradise you will never want to leave. The galerie's atmosphere reminds me of a mid-eastern bazaar where you can find everything from gourmet food to scrumptious clothes and accessories. I am most certain we will find what you need there."

The two women stepped into her compact Citroen as Genni adroitly drove the car and joined the rest of the swiftly moving traffic. Lyla and

Genni chatted with ease, getting to know each other as they darted and wove their way through the morning traffic. If Lyla had any reservations about her shopping companion before they met, they were now rapidly dissolving. Genni rattled on about her favorite fashion haunts in the Galeries Lafayette so much that Lyla could barely stand the anticipation.

When Lyla and Genni arrived at the Galeries Lafayette, Lyla was struck by the sheer enormity of the buildings. "How big is this place?" Lyla asked in wide eyed wonderment. "Well," Genni began, "technically, the galeries is made of three buildings, five floors or about 750,000 square feet, an entire block on Boulevard Haussmann. It contains a very diverse assortment of merchandise for shopping and restaurants."

They walked into the main hall and Lyla became speechless. The glass domed ceiling in the main hall was breathtaking. It was made of glass panels reminiscent of neo Byzantine art. The multiple floors of balconies showcased merchandise that sparkled from the spotlights perched above them. Every pore in Lyla's body was tingling with excitement.

Genni looked at Lyla and smiled, "You can take a breath now, Lyla, just relax and breathe. We have a lot to accomplish."

As they walked, Genni pointed out specific sections, giving detailed information on what each contained like a docent moving through a museum. Genni suggested, "If you would like, there's a free fashion show on the 7th floor of the Coupole Building at 3 pm. I like to attend when I can and will make a call for reservations if you want me to. We must make certain to be there early to get front row seats."

"Yes, oh yes, I would love that." Lyla couldn't take much more.

Genni continued, "I can't think of a better way to spend a day. It is like being a child in a candy shop. One wants to take a taste of everything. Now that we've taken a small tour, let's sample some of the beautiful evening gowns."

The women walked toward a department with racks and stands of beautiful gowns. They began to search the racks, moving from one gown to the next, too light, too dark, too bare, not the right style. The gowns they chose were hung together on a separate rack and put into a dressing area.

"Well," Genni said with a smile, "I think we have something to start with. Let's try them on."

Lyla easily slid them on, one by one, looking lovely, especially in one beautiful gown that became the favorite. It was a stunning long gown in draped petal chiffon with small spaghetti straps in a luscious muted eggplant color with a matching long-sleeve, lace bolero jacket. It was understated, simple in its lines showing the shape of her body but was not too tight, and the modified scooped neckline accentuated her neck and shoulders. It was a refined beautiful reflection of Lyla.

Lyla was surprised by her mirror image, reminiscent of the simple classic beauty of her youth. The innocence and youth were gone and, in their place, stood an older and hopefully, much wiser woman. There was no question this was the dress she was to wear. Lyla studied her entire image in the mirror, stunned, and then spoke softly.

"Lyla Rose, where have you been?"

Lyla was hoping to find an equally simple, classic shoe with a hint of sparkle that would not overshadow the dress. They found an irresistible number of shoes capable of tempting any seasoned shopper. Lyla settled on a pair of black silk 3-inch heels with lovely shape and curve. The shoe was finished with a simple rhinestone design that looked like someone had sprinkled tiny diamonds on the tip of the toe.

Lyla's gown was covered for protection and was left with the department sales lady to be picked up when they completed their shopping. Genni turned to Lyla. "Well, Lyla, what do you have as an outer garment? It will be chilly in the evening and you will need something to keep you warm. Just follow me to another department I know very well; too well, I'm afraid to say. I know we will find something appropriate there."

As Genni led Lyla to their next stop, Lyla was so busy looking at the merchandise she nearly ran into another woman who was shopping. "Pardon, pardon, please excuse me, I'm so sorry," Lyla said. "I...I just couldn't stop looking." The woman smiled and nodded and knew exactly what Lyla meant.

Genni wasn't wrong. They walked through several other departments and walked up steps to one floor above and were surrounded by racks of fashionable outer garments. Lyla found a full-length cape of fine spun wool in a dark eggplant color with a short stand-up collar that hugged her neck.

"Genni," Lyla said with a voice like that of an excited child. "I can't believe we found so much. Where do we go for gloves and a small bag?"

"Not to worry Lyla, it's not far from here."

Lyla had forgotten how exciting it was to shop for a beautiful dress with a special occasion in mind. She had a twinkle in her eye and couldn't stop smiling, at everything and everyone. "I feel like Cinderella preparing for the ball," Lyla said. "All I need now is a pumpkin, four mice, and a horse."

Lyla's life had already begun to change. She was feeling positive and productive and didn't have to save anyone to feel that way. She was learning new skills, language, and interacting with people who treated her with respect and dignity.

"Ah, Lyla," Genni said, "before I forget, I must tell you, Mrs. Blum has made arrangements with her driver, Philipe, to pick you up and return you to your apartment on the night of the dedication."

Lyla smiled and said, "My pumpkin and driver."

At 3 pm their temptation preempted their hunger and the women arrived for the fashion show. The had front row seats and Lyla was enthralled by the models who moved so wonderfully to the music. When the show ended and the crowd dispersed, Genni reminded Lyla they had to go back to each department to pick up the packages.

On the way to the car, Genni took Lyla to a store to purchase a memento of her visit to the Galeries Lafayette. The women chatted with animation and were ready to end their triumphant day with a good meal.

Genni said, "Mon Dieu, I'm famished, how about you?"

Lyla had forgotten all about being hungry until just then. "Me, too," she answered.

"Bon, I know just where to go."

The ladies enjoyed their meal and afterward Lyla returned to her apartment. Now all she had to do was wait the final two weeks for the evening of the dedication.

THE DEDICATION OF HAUSMANN HOUSE

"Good evening ladies and gentlemen, Mesdames et Messieurs. My name is Simone de St Etienne. I have been given the honor and privilege of being chosen Director of the Program Mrs. Blum has created, embodied in this lovely building, Haussmann House. Mrs. Blum is a remarkable woman who has risked much in helping women and girls from the horrors of World War II to the present. Without her tireless efforts and generosity, Haussmann House would not have become a reality."

The waiters moved respectfully around the room serving the guests as Mrs. Blum was acknowledged and the sound of plates, cutlery, and hushed voices mingled with the initial introductions.

"It is my distinct pleasure to present Mrs. Ethel Blum, the lifeblood and inspiration for this most unique and comprehensive concept. I give you, Mrs. Ethel Blum."

Mrs. Blum rose from her seat at the head table and walked to the podium with confidence and grace as polite but generous applause erupted. She looked to the guests who were there to honor her, her work, and her Foundation and was pleased, humbled by the number of people who were in attendance. The attendees were acknowledged with her nod and gracious smile as she waited for the applause to subside.

"Thank you, thank you so much for this lovely welcome. I am overwhelmed and extremely pleased you chose to join us in this celebration and dedication. This is a very meaningful evening for me."

She looked slowly around the room and silently acknowledged individuals with a slight nod of her head and a brief smile. "I want to begin by thanking my wonderful staff, headed by Simone de St Etienne, for organizing and bringing this entire evening to fruition.

"I would like to take this opportunity to speak briefly about how all this began for those who do not know me well. My career began many years ago in the United States, in Miami, Florida, as a secretary in a large law firm. I met and worked for a young attorney who subsequently became my husband. His initial interest was in family law and later international law which enabled me to become involved in aspects of the law that would later become my life's work.

"My husband and I became partners in our own firm, when I became an attorney, and we began to work nationally and internationally as representatives of families, specifically women and children. I endeavored to assist in the rescue and emigration of women and children at the end of World War II, helping women and orphans resettle and rebuild their lives. I chose Paris as a central location, to develop the Program and the Foundation, to continue our work.

"Haussmann House has a special significance. Although it was once a fine home filled with a loving, caring family, it was brutally commandeered by the Nazis and used to interrogate and torture Jews. There were many who entered and never returned to their families and the lives they had once known. Haussmann House will no longer be associated with the horrific atrocities committed here, but will become an oasis to help women rebuild their lives. The building has been meticulously renovated with one solitary reminder remaining out of sight, but not out of mind.

"The purpose of this structure and the program it houses is to provide an environment that is nurturing and safe, nonjudgmental and supportive reminding us we are not alone. That, in spite of our frailties, mistakes, and misjudgments, we can survive, we can change, and we can become more than we could have ever imagined. Each woman's life is a symphony composed of her choices, missteps, foibles, and successes, moving from movement to movement, each with a distinct beat and tenor.

This oasis has been created to help women rebuild their lives enabling them to blossom and become the extraordinary people they were meant to be. The program is comprehensive and brings together many disciplines for a holistic approach to healing and transformation."

Mrs. Blum continued to talk about the concept of Haussmann House, the overall blueprint, and how they were going to accomplish their goals. She spoke of the dedicated women, members of the team, who from the moment they crossed the building's portal, were carefully chosen for their related tasks. "Every woman involved is dedicated and committed to serving this population," she said. "They possess a strong desire to guide others along this journey, to share their experiences, talents, and expertise, and to be an integral part of a life-changing program." As she continued to speak, the room became still. The waiters stopped in their places or retreated behind the scene, respectful and mesmerized by Mrs. Blum's voice and her words. Mrs. Blum's voice echoed throughout the room. As her speech began to crescendo, her voice grew louder and stronger, building to an emotional climax.

Lyla had been lost in her own thoughts when her attention was redirected to Mrs. Blum's words and she felt a small burst of electricity move through her body. When Mrs. Blum spoke about the effect the program would have on the women who would cross its threshold, Lyla heard her say, "We think every one of the women who comes to our sanctuary needs a multidimensional approach to enable them to heal. I firmly believe we all have an innate ability to draw upon a part of us I call our 'essence' to overcome immeasurable odds and move beyond our current circumstances. It is a trait found in all women regardless of ethnicity, physical location, or spiritual belief and often remains unrecognized and underutilized. If we, and that is a collective we, are able to tap into our reservoir, I believe our lives would be very different and exciting, to say the least.

"There are those of us who are unaware of this source in us, as it is deeply buried, or we do not know how to access it in order to be liberated from our current circumstances and become the women we were meant to be. There are some, perhaps many of us, who become redirected through our choices and missteps, and are unable to access this 'inner source' without the kind of environment Haussmann House offers.

"Some call this process empowerment, but we, at the foundation, refer to this change as transformation. We come to recognize our essence, embrace it, and allow ourselves to blossom and emerge as a multifaceted woman filled with the ability to leap tall buildings in a single bound. Of course, I'm not saying we become a 'superwoman.'

"We become a woman who grows and transcends from an isolated, frightened victim of ourselves and others to a woman who overcomes... a woman who goes beyond...a woman who emerges without baggage of anger and resentment...a woman who is richly textured, comfortable, and confident in herself, wanting to share her discovery with others.

"Many years ago, I watched a skilled florist work with a single gladiola flower stalk. She chose individual petals from each complete flower, removed each petal, and wired each one individually and then to other petals carefully forming a new blossom more exquisite than the original flower. This new, fully formed, unique flower blossom is called a glamelia. I realized this was how we could help women metamorphose into the persons they could become. As a result of this transformation, we learn to see not only with our eyes but with our souls.

"We become guides along the journey who partner with the women to facilitate their transformation from being the gladiola to the glamelia. The process can be challenging requiring determination on the part of the women and patience and support from another who cares and understands.

"The woman takes the individual petals, the singular parts of themselves, and changes those aspects or petals into a more complete and fully blossomed flower. We are not enablers but facilitators. We are not crutches. We are support rungs on a long ladder of steps to a woman's freedom and development. We are not here to change a hair style, or educate and teach new skills, or administer a hand for these women to hold.

"We are here to lead and mentor. We are here to provide a safe, nurturing environment. We are here to help every woman break the shackles and release the pain of the past. We are here to take the broken pieces and help them create the women they have always had the potential to become. This requires commitment on their part and ours.

"This is who we are. This is what we do for other women and ourselves, creating a ripple effect of epic proportions not only here in France and other European countries, but around the world.

"I want to thank each and every one of you for your support this evening and in the future. We make a formidable team. Now that you know who we are and what we are trying to accomplish and provide, I would like you to take a look at the centerpiece arrangement on each table. The center flower is a glamelia surrounded by gladiola stalks of the same color. We hope this helps everyone visualize this transformation.

"We have planned a lovely evening with a sumptuous meal and an opportunity to meet our faculty. We encourage you to ask questions and tour what we have accomplished here at Haussmann House.

"Thank you again for joining us. Mesdames et Messieurs, bonne soirée. "

Lyla sat silent, transfixed in her seat, oblivious to her surroundings. Her eyes were brimming with tears. While Mrs. Blum spoke, Lyla was overcome with emotion, recalling Mrs. Blum's calm and reassuring voice on the plane the night they met. Mrs. Blum's words had a gentle strength that pierced Lyla to her marrow. They continued to echo in Lyla's mind: powerful source, embrace it, victim of myself and others, overcome, transformation. For the first time, Lyla noticed the floral centerpiece arrangement at each table.

Every table had cloths and napkins in pale smoky lavender with a centerpiece created in a different gladiola color, displaying a spectrum of colors throughout the room. The focal point of the arrangement was an unusual blossom. Lyla stared at the blossom wondering why it triggered a feeling of familiarity and then remembered using the pink glamelia as her wedding bouquet. She thought, *Was this a coincidence?* There was a small card at each table setting, explaining the process of transformation from the gladiola to the glamelia.

At the end of the speech, the guests stood and shouted their praise, "Brava, Magnifique, Superbe, Well done," in support of Mrs. Blum and her program with thunderous applause. Mrs. Blum, humbled by the response, walked back to her seat. Haussmann House was her last major effort and her proudest moment and she wistfully thought about her husband, wishing he had been there to experience it with her. The thought didn't last long when her attention was redirected to those who approached, congratulated her, and offered their support.

Moments later, waiters streamed in from the kitchen, carrying trays of the remaining courses of the evening. Guests returned to their tables tempted by the aromas that came wafting through the room. Lyla was forced out of her shyness by a guest at her table inquiring who she was and where she was from. Conversations began to flow across and around the table and soon everyone was chatting and enjoying the meal.

The table conversation was about Mrs. Blum, the Foundation, and her past achievements. Then Lyla's seat companion asked her what she was doing in Paris at this time of year so far from home in America. When Lyla talked about her apprenticeship at the bakery, her eyes sparkled. She timidly stepped into the spotlight and then moved to address the questions and comments from her table companions. As the evening progressed, Lyla's demeanor began to change. By dessert, Lyla was engaging with everyone at the table. When Lyla finished her desert, she excused herself from the table, bid her companions adieu, and navigated through the throng of guests to find Mrs. Blum.

Ethel Blum was surrounded by friends, dignitaries, and well-wishers. Lyla hesitated, not wanting to intrude. Mrs. Blum noticed Lyla standing there, acknowledged her presence, and motioned for Lyla to come closer. Mrs. Blum excused herself from her conversation and asked Lyla to sit beside her in a vacant seat. She took Lyla's hand, smiled at Lyla, and Lyla began to melt.

"I want to thank you for sending the personal note and Genni to be my fashion guru," Lyla said. There were times during your speech when I felt as though you were talking directly to me. Thank you for your dedication, wisdom, and Haussmann House. This is where I need to be. I know that now."

Mrs. Blum sat quietly, holding Lyla's hand tightly, letting her know that no matter what, Lyla would not be alone any more.

"Lyla, I'm delighted you chose to come, and I look forward to spending time with you." Mrs. Blum turned to acknowledge her son sitting adjacent to her. "By the way, I would like to introduce you to my son, Alex. Alex, excuse me Alex, I'd like you to meet a new friend of mine, Lyla Rose." Lyla was already looking at the gentleman seated near Ethel. "Lyla, this is my son, Alex. He is a visiting professor on sabbatical for a year at the Sorbonne."

"Hello, Alex, it is a pleasure to meet you," Lyla said. Alex interrupted his conversation with another gentleman to say, "Yes, enchanté, Lyla."

"Thank you again, Mrs. Blum, for a superb evening, I must leave."

"Thank you for coming Lyla, I'll have Philipe take you home, "Bon Soir."

"Thank you, Mrs. Blum, I look forward to seeing you again. Bon Soir."

They brushed light kisses on each cheek of the other. Lyla retrieved her cape and exited the building to the waiting car. Neither Alex or Lyla recognized each other from their brief introduction years earlier in Florida. Tonight, was another brief encounter neither chose to expand. Lyla was still closed off from much of the outside world, wary and untrusting, and Alex was still grieving over the loss of his wife. They were polite but distant, each lost in their own world.

Lyla's evening at the dedication of Haussmann House felt as unreal to her as Cinderella's night at the ball. Everything about the evening was like a fairy tale. There was much for Lyla to digest: Mrs. Blum's moving speech, the people she met, the food and music. She had come to Paris not just to learn how to be an authentic bread maker. This is where she was meant to be. She was emotionally and physically exhausted and was appreciative of the warm ride to her apartment. Lyla was deep in thought on her way home to her apartment in the City of Lights trying to put the evening's experiences in perspective.

A faint smile appeared on her lips. *I'm not going to ask how all this happened or why I was chosen to receive this rare and miraculous gift. I am just going to drink it all in.*

Lyla was startled when the driver, Philipe, told her they had arrived. She collected her personal items just as the driver opened the door for her. He held out his hand to her as she exited the vehicle and thanked him for the comfortable ride. The elevator ride was short and fast. She was in her apartment in moments. Lyla hung up her beautiful dress in the armoire, tucked away her shoes and bag and put on her warm nightgown. She quickly brushed her teeth, splashed water and moisturizer on her face, and climbed into bed under her comforter. She fell to sleep to the sound of raindrops gently falling on her window pane and succumbed to the night, to her dreams.

Bread was merely the vehicle that got Lyla to Paris.

TRANSFORMATION

Early morning arrived quickly and Lyla was reluctant to emerge from the warmth of her comforter. She shook the sleep from her eyes, showered, dressed, and was filled with warm pastry and a steaming cup of tea. From the time she reached the bakery, her focus was on her work. Dough needed to be prepared, ovens readied; and baskets and sheets had to be filled with baguettes, brioche, croissants, and other breakfast breads that were an essential element of people's lives. Lyla became totally immersed in her bread world and momentarily forgot about the night before.

Jacques' bakery was scheduled to participate in the "The Paris Chocolate and Pastry Food Tour," the walking tour to pastry, chocolate shops, and bakeries, led by an expert food connoisseur. Tourists and locals gathered as part of the tour. Lyla was responsible for all necessary supplies, and enough products for sampling and sale. There was neither room nor time for anything else. She was growing in her profession and becoming more confident.

That day, Lyla left the bakery exhausted but satisfied and was looking forward to a hot shower and a relaxing cup of tea. Lyla prepared for a restful evening and nestled into a cozy, spot on her couch with her tea. Her thoughts returned to the night of the dedication and the effect it had had upon her. She felt the need to write and opened her laptop to add to her continuing journal. Her last submission recalled emotions she carried throughout her married life.

"The aloneness engulfed my entire being. It covered and suffocated me, my voice, like a dark shroud. There were moments when I was able to peek out from underneath the darkness of isolation only to retreat again, comfortably uncomfortable and unable to move beyond it. Feeling this way, justified or not, created an environment of stagnation. The inability to overcome the aloneness and isolation was limiting, destructive, and painful."

She continued writing. "The night of the dedication provided the support and reinforcement I needed." The words continued to pour out onto the laptop screen with breathtaking speed.

"All my feelings seem to be stuck in the past, and I'm wallowing in a quagmire of my isolation, fears, and my inability to move beyond this. I realize in order to move on I must leave the past behind, and I don't quite know how to do that. I've been this way for so long I don't know what it's like to be any other way. I've merely transplanted myself to a different physical location; the rest remained the same. I'm still locked up; I'm still afraid, just in a different place.

"Haussmann House can breathe life into me to ignite the spark within me. The flame of my essence was smothered and grew cold from the continual suffocation of abuse. This is where I belong along with my desire to have my own bakery as a way to have financial independence allowing me to create something I love.

"I know in my innermost being I am a bud not yet ready to blossom. There's a key to unlock all this, and I know it must be with the Foundation's program. I need to find the key. I will find the key. I can do this."

Haussmann House will introduce her to other women who journeyed down a similar path and were involved in a toxic relationship. For some, the consequences affected them physically; but healing the emotional wounds and scars will be difficult for them all. The meetings with the therapist will prove to be an invaluable place for Lyla to allow herself to share with others without the fear and shame associated with revealing her story, her feelings about herself, and the man she chose to marry.

Lyla welcomed the next morning with the determination of one who had been starved and thirsty. Without hesitation, she called the Foundation, asked how to participate, and was sent the necessary information via email. She was excited and scared and tried to convince herself not to dwell on the negative and unknown. Her first encounter would be that evening after work. The required activity was group therapy under the leadership of the therapist, Dr. Merkavah.

Lyla was completely immersed in her work at the bakery and lost all track of time. Her focus was on learning, building her skills, and becoming more comfortable with language. She rarely took time to eat during the day and was often given brioches, bread, and or custard tarts to take home. Jacques had to remind her to go home. Today was no different and she hurriedly bade farewell to her fellow bakers. She had just enough time to return home shower, change, and eat.

Lyla arrived at Haussmann House, walked through the tall wooden main doors, and down the hallway to the elevator past suites of rooms already occupied. The elevator rose to the second floor and she walked what felt like miles with trepidation to the designated room at the end of the hallway. "Just my luck it would be the last room," she muttered to herself. The door was open, revealing a softly lit room resembling a lounge. Lyla walked into the room and no one acknowledged her in any way. It was the way she liked it; she was almost invisible.

There were nine other women of various ages sitting comfortably in a small group; she was the 10th woman. The other women engaged in quiet conversation in anticipation of the moderator's arrival. Lyla sat in a small lounge chair separate from the others and tried to hide her fear and apprehension

The longer Lyla waited for the group moderator to appear, the more her anxiety climbed. Lyla was ready to leave at the precise moment, Dr. Merkavah, the moderator, walked in. Dr. Merkavah introduced herself, her credentials, and explained how the group would work. *Oh, no, here it comes,* Lyla thought. *Here comes the 'touchy feely' stuff. I knew it; perhaps now would be a good time to leave.* Just as Lyla finished her thought, she allowed Dr. Merkavah's words to enter her consciousness.

"Now, if any of you ladies think or expect that these sessions will be filled with a lot of touchy feely nonsense, you need to either get over it or get up, leave, and join us when you have a better understanding of our purpose here."

Dr. Merkavah's seriousness caused Lyla to lean forward in her chair, still anxious but interested to hear more. She was embarrassed by her behavior and body language and settled back in her seat to listen intently. Dr. Merkavah continued, "This is a place where we find comfort, we find support, we share, and we learn about ourselves. The dynamic of the group will evolve and grow, and I will serve as the moderator giving you direction and feedback. As individuals and as a group, we will explore major issues: We will recognize who we were. We will develop a sense of who we are. We will begin to build on those aspects of ourselves, becoming who we can be.

"Now ladies, let's begin with an introductory exercise that is more often than not, difficult for everyone. I've given mine, so now, let's hear yours one by one. Do I have any volunteers?"

Dr. Merkavah looked at each woman seated in the room and was not surprised by their reluctance to volunteer. "No volunteers this evening? Ah, that leaves me the task of getting this group moving by choosing someone to break the ice. Lyla, how about we begin with you?"

Lyla was not expecting to be singled out to begin. As soon as Dr. Merkavah started talking about introductions, Lyla tried to sink as far as she could into her chair and appear inconspicuous. Lyla thought, *No ... no ... not me ... not me first. Oh, my God she's noticed me.* Then a soft, small voice inside Lyla's head encouraged her to speak. *Just say your name and where you're from. You can do this.*

"Hello everyone, my name is Lyla Rose, and I am an American. I traveled to Paris to become an apprentice to Monsieur Jacques Rinaldo at his bakery. It is my desire to become a bread baker extraordinaire. I was married for over 30 years and have four wonderful sons who are now grown and on their own."

"Thank you, Lyla, and who's next? How about you over there, your name? Renee, yes, you. Would you like to tell us something about yourself?"

The introductions continued by each woman. The meeting lasted for two hours with all the women interacting except Lyla. Lyla returned to her apartment as soon as the group ended tired and emotionally drained but felt compelled to make an entry in her journal.

"I am overwhelmed and confused. How do I find my place? What is the matter with me that I cannot forget, and why is it I'm so afraid to take a chance at a new life? I have never been able to reconcile issues of the past that have haunted me my entire existence with him. I don't know what drew me to him in the first place and what flaws resided within me that caused me to do what I did. Am I able to forgive myself? Is it my inability to forget that gnaws away at me, making me feel unworthy to be loved, by anyone, even him?

"Did I place more value on his life and neglect my own as a result of the anger and disappointment I harbored for myself? I have spent nearly a lifetime saving others and never recognized before that I was the one who desperately needed saving. How do I go about saving myself?

"I am emotionally falling apart, like Humpty Dumpty, afraid I will never be put back together again. I feel like I'm drowning in emptiness. I feel so very lost; will I ever find my way out of the forest of fear and confusion? I don't want to be this way anymore. I must develop a positive sense of who I am now. Can I do that?"

Lyla was insightful, intelligent, shy, and unsure of herself, certainly not the personae of a courageous, confident, goal-oriented person she showed to the world. She was an enigma with a terrier-like tenacity, was loyal to a fault, and preferred to have a one-on-one relationship with one woman at a time instead of belonging to a group. It required extraordinary effort for her to be outgoing and social, much like the lone little girl sitting in the background, like some wilting wallflower. Ultimately, she expended a great deal of energy pretending to be someone she was not as a way to hide.

The weekly sessions forced Lyla to face aspects of herself and the consequences of her choices. Her predominant emotions were anger and fear, and although she had opportunities to share with the group, she remained untrusting of others, unwilling to expose her intimacies. When she felt like that she revealed uncomfortable, long hidden feelings to her journal where she felt safe.

"I felt unbearable pain and anguish when his hatred and anger tormented me. I wondered how I survived the onslaught of his words meant to destroy my emotional equilibrium and cause fear. My internal moral compass told me to do 'what was right.' When he used this against me, I doubted myself. I trusted no one, had no one to confide in, or ask for advice. If I did and Juliano found out he would yell at me, berate me, insult me. He told so many lies I never knew what the truth was anymore.

"I had to use all my strength to survive and protect my children, no matter the cost. I became paralyzed with fear, afraid to confront him."

Each time Lyla attended the meetings with Dr. Merkavah, she came away with as many questions as answers. The meetings were forcing her to think about things she had successfully tucked away for a long time. Dr. Merkavah entered the room one evening with her usual greetings and got immediately to work.

"Good evening ladies," she said, making visual contact with each woman before she took a seat. "I trust you have had a good week and are prepared to embark on an important journey this evening. This evening we're going to explore the power of 'touch.' Most of the time when one speaks of this 'power,' it is in reference to the physical sensations we have as we touch things around us and the sensation of how we feel when we are literally, physically touched by someone.

"The sense of touch is a powerful conveyor of emotion, capable of taking us to the heights of pleasure and joy or to the depths of despair and fear. This is an important physical aspect of our beings, yet many of us tend to shy away from this. We put up walls and hesitate to allow others to come anywhere close to our space, let alone touch us. Why is that, do you think? What has occurred to cause some of us to withdraw from something so essential to our well-being? Because of its importance in our process of transformation, we are going to spend the next five sessions discussing one of the following questions. Please give the first question thought this week. This is where we will begin.

"I have provided pens and paper for everyone to write down the following: 1. What was 'touch' in your family with your parents and siblings, if you had siblings? 2. What is the kind of 'touch' you know and understand? 3. What role did 'touch' play in your relationships? 4. What was the 'touch' you received from your intimate partner and how did it affect you? 5. Who do you 'touch' and in what way do you allow others to 'touch' you?"

Lyla's anxiety began to climb as she watched and listened Dr. Merkavah continue to speak and to lightly, touch the shoulder or arm of each woman as she moved about the room. Instinctively, Lyla began to recoil just as Dr. Merkavah reached her chair. She grew stiff anticipating what was about to happen. Lyla's body language did not escape Dr. Merkavah's attention. Instead of touching Lyla as she stood beside her, as she did the others, the doctor rested her hand just beside Lyla's on the arm of the chair. Lyla drew in a deep breath, slowly exhaling a soft sigh of relief. Dr. Merkavah hesitated for a moment, then continued to speak and moved on to someone else.

The session and the assignment caused Lyla considerable discomfort. Lyla said her goodbyes to the group that evening and did not stop to chat as she had done on some previous occasions. She felt driven to return to her apartment where she knew she was safe. Lyla looked at the questions once again. One voice inside her head kept repeating, "Stay away, don't do this, it's dangerous," and the other voice said, "Yes, I believe I can."

Each week was devoted to one question from the original list. Dr. Merkavah would open the discussion by presenting the question and its significance relative to the women. The participants had an opportunity to respond to the question and then to one another.

At first, Lyla began to share with the group in a timid voice. "I don't think my family knew much about a loving touch. My father was physical, rough, and struck me over seemingly insignificant transgressions I never understood. When he hit me, his large square ruby ring left red marks on my skin. I longed for my mother to protect and hold me but she didn't. I loved her, why didn't she love me back? Why didn't she protect me, stop him?"

Lyla continued. "I think the touch I know and understand is not one of nurturing kindness except for the times I was taken care of by a nanny. I can remember her holding my hand, cuddling with me, and brushing my hair. She would lie down with me when I took my nap until I fell to sleep and I felt comforted."

During the next session Lyla contributed by sharing, "I confused the act of sex for intimacy and emotional attachment. My mother never had the requisite talk about sex and intimacy with me. My mother could barely explain what would happen to me when I came of age. And when it did happen, she acted like it was something terrible and left me to find out on my own. Most of the time, the touch I knew from men was lust and pain, not love and tenderness. They were always so anxious to touch me and use me for their pleasure."

Lyla's familiarity with intimacy and touch with her partner, her husband, was reflective of her perception of how relationships were supposed to be and this was based on what she thought she knew about her parents.

"My husband's intimate behavior was different in the initial stages of our relationship. But, after I was married to him, he began to change the way he treated me when he wanted to have sex. He became selfish, self-absorbed, and was interested more in his own pleasure. I began to feel uncomfortable and fearful of his touch. But I accepted his aggressive, romantic engagements and submitted. That was when the walls went up. I didn't consciously decide one day that in order to survive I would retreat to safety behind an emotionally blank wall. I built the wall brick by brick, piece by piece, over the years, each time something happened; each time it was against my will. It was the only way he couldn't touch me. Now, I realize breaking down the wall will be a difficult task."

It will be necessary for Lyla to begin to trust others, allow herself to reach out to others, and allow them to physically and emotionally touch her.

"Now that I think about it, I was a very physically loving mother. I held and cuddled my children when they were very young. I would always take their hand to hold when we walked even though it wasn't necessary for their safety. But I was not like this with anyone else. I kept my distance and felt uncomfortable if anyone got too close to me physically. I don't like to be touched by anyone, particularly my husband. And I find it difficult to be in a large crowd jostled by others. I need my personal space. My skin crawled every time my husband touched me. I don't know what it's like to have a loving touch."

During the many sessions, the women revealed, most for the first time, their most intimate feelings and experiences. This continued until the entire list of original questions was discussed. The women were beginning to understand an essential component of who they were then and now. It was time for them to participate in a final exercise centered on how they could begin to build on what they learned. The final exercise consisted of receiving a massage, the epitome of touch.

When Dr. Merkavah made this announcement, Lyla was uncomfortable with some stranger touching her in such an intimate way. Dr. Merkavah exited the room to return moments later followed by a beautiful young woman whose golden locks were braided and wrapped around her head, revealing a flawless complexion and bright blue eyes.

"Ladies," Dr. Merkavah said, "I would like to introduce you to Bruni, the licensed masseuse at the foundation. Please feel free to ask questions."

Bruni's soft, non-threatening voice helped to ease some of the tension in the room. "Each session will, of course, be private for 30 minutes,"

Bruni said. "We will discuss, together, how I will proceed and nothing will occur without your express permission. I am well aware of your apprehension and want to assure you that your massage will not be painful or embarrassing."

Lyla was the last to sign up for her session, but was determined to have this experience; at least she hoped she was. The sessions were scheduled in place of the next week's meeting time. Lyla's day at the bakery had been busy when the day and time for the massage arrived. She barely had enough time to shower off the dust and sweat of the day before going to Haussmann House.

When Lyla arrived, she was directed to a small suite behind heavy glass doors. She stepped inside the softly lit room and heard the faint sound of trickling water and the soothing rhythms and melodies of instruments. She sat down on a long soft bench that ran the length of the room. Several small tables were scattered in front of the bench and were covered with magazines and journals about meditation, health, and nutrition. A young woman casually dressed in a printed midi dress came into the room to greet Lyla.

"Bienvenue, welcome, my name is Honoré may I get you something to drink?"

Lyla noticed a large pitcher of water with fresh lemons sitting on a tray on the opposite counter.

"No merci, not right now."

Lyla tried to relax, listening to the sounds of the water and music. Lyla asked about the music and Honoré explained. "We believe it's essential to create an environment conducive to balance, harmony, and healing. For centuries sound has played an integral part as a healing tool. Bruni will be with you shortly. Until then, please relax and enjoy your time here."

The sounds were intoxicating as Lyla sat still with her eyes closed, taking deep breaths in through her nose and exhaling through her mouth, relaxing from the top of her head down through her body to her toes. Her eyelids grew heavy as she filled her lungs with slow, deep, even breaths. As she continued to breathe deeply, she encouraged her mind and her senses to become permeated with her surroundings.

Her ears gathered in the sounds of the water and music. Her body responded to the ambient temperature helping her to release tension. Each sense, one by one and then collectively, drank in the sensations. The last and most subtle was the faint fragrance of a mixture of scents that were delicate, delicious, and disarming filling the air with beautiful notes of exotic spices and soothing flavors of almond. She had no idea how long she was sitting there when a light touch on her shoulder forced her to open her eyes.

"Looks like you have already started to relax," Bruni whispered. "Shall we go into the room and get started?"

Lyla picked up her handbag and followed Bruni into a small, dimly lit room. There was a high narrow table in the middle of the room covered with a clean white sheet. Across from the table stood upper and lower cabinets with a granite counter top covered with containers of aromatic oils.

"Lyla, we can begin by focusing on one specific area and then move on."

Lyla thought for a moment. "I feel I carry a lot of stress in my neck and shoulders. I often feel my shoulders hovering around my ears."

Bruni smiled and nodded. "Yes, that's very common with many of us. I would like for you to take off as much as you're able to without distress but particularly everything from the waist up and get comfortable on the table, face down under the sheet. I will give you some privacy and will return in a few moments."

Lyla did as she was instructed and had to remind herself she was not in some doctor's office about to undergo a painful procedure or get poked and prodded like some piece of meat. Her hands trembled as she removed her shirt and bra and then got under the sheet face down placing her face in the towel-covered head rest. The muscles in Lyla's body began to tense. To compensate, Lyla concentrated on the sounds and the aromas in the room but still felt anxious and distressed no matter how much she told herself to calm down and relax.

Bruni entered the room, speaking softly as she passed the table on her way to the counter to choose the oils she was going to use. Bruni lightly touched Lyla's shoulder area and said, "Now, Lyla, I want you to let me know if you feel uneasy. Since you have never had a massage before, I will start with a very light touch, and if that's acceptable we'll move on to something deeper. How does that sound to you? I'll stay within the area you mentioned and not move on unless you ask me to."

Lyla could barely say okay. In the past, Lyla had difficulty asserting herself, saying no, or setting limits. She had acquiesced and said 'yes' out of fear, when she really wanted to say 'no.' Her lack of verbal protection significantly impacted her sense of self-worth.

"Now relax Lyla, let me take care of you. I won't do anything you don't want me to do. I want you to tell me if you become panicky, have discomfort, or if there is something you do not like. You have the ability to say no here."

Bruni gently slowly removed the sheet from Lyla's torso, folding it down to her waist exposing Lyla's soft white skin. Bruni put a combination of warm oils on her hands, rubbed them together creating more warmth and friction, gently placed her hands onto Lyla's shoulders, and began to massage her muscles. Lyla flinched when she was first touched. She was not used to the touch of a stranger, but as time went on Lyla began to relax and accept the soothing, healing, rhythmic movements of Bruni's strong fingers.

Bruni interrupted the massage at short intervals to ask Lyla if she was comfortable. When Lyla felt the tense and knotted muscles, she asked Bruni to concentrate on the troublesome spot. All of Lyla's senses were infused and awakened by the healing music, the aroma of scents and incense, the oils applied to her body, and the warmth created by Bruni's touch.

Bruni moved to Lyla's middle and lower back, manipulating the muscles there, working out the years of tightness. Over and over Bruni rubbed and massaged the stiffness out of Lyla's muscles. For Lyla, the sensation of Bruni's touch was remarkable, gentle yet strong, like nothing Lyla had ever experienced. At the end of the session, Lyla had completely succumbed to Bruni's healing touch.

When the massage ended, Lyla slowly opened her eyes. Bruni explained to Lyla the necessity of drinking plenty of water to stay hydrated after the manipulation of her muscles and recommended a good long soak in the tub.

"Thank you, Bruni, for this extraordinary experience. I never thought

I would welcome anyone's touch," Lyla said. "But, now, I would do this again. Would it be possible for me to schedule another session with you?"

"Of course, Lyla, it would be my distinct pleasure to take care of you. I'll make the arrangements."

Bruni warned Lyla she might be sore in the morning, the way she would feel after a hard workout, even though she may be feeling fine now. So, the soak and the hydration were important. Lyla assured her she would do both and a soak sounded like a wonderful way to end the evening. Bruni exited the room to give Lyla privacy to dress and met Lyla again in the reception room.

"Thank you again, Bruni for taking care of me."

They reached for one another to brush cheeks. Lyla left Haussmann House feeling centered aware that her body was no longer drawn in to make herself small with her shoulders rounded like she was carrying the burdens of the world. Instead, her shoulders were pulled back, her posture was erect, and she held her head high, like a dancer. When she returned home and looked in the mirror, she saw the reflection of the woman she was becoming.

The glamelia was beginning to emerge and take shape.

CONTINUED EMERGENCE

Lyla's attendance in the group had spanned several months and another new year arrived. Her days were spent working at the bakery and her evenings and weekends were spent at Haussmann House socializing and participating in activities with the members of her group and others. She had moved beyond her self-imposed isolation. Lyla's feelings of fear and anxiety began to fade as the process of transformation progressed.

When Lyla arrived in the suite for the next therapy session, the women were talking amongst themselves, anxiously anticipating how the evening would enfold. They asked about Lyla's massage and began to share their experiences. Dr. Merkavah walked in with her usual greeting making eye contact with each woman.

"Good evening ladies. I hope you are well and ready to explore another important pathway to transformation. If you recall from our last session, I hinted this session's topic would be related to the issue of touch, but not as obvious. But, before we begin our new topic, I would like to extend an invitation to our members to share what you have learned since we began our time together and how your perceptions of yourselves have changed. I am asking each one to participate and share."

Lyla did not hesitate to volunteer first. "My self-talk became positive. I saw that as I moved farther along the path of freedom I was inching my way closer to the personality characteristics that reminded me of me as a young girl. The quick rise and uncensored eruption of anger of the woman I became dissolved into fragments and were replaced by a more settled, almost reserved attitude. I had fewer conflicts and problems were resolved in a more mature and effective manner. Working my way through issues this way helped me learn how to interact with people and not be confrontational and demanding.

"I dared to look back on 'why' I stayed in the marriage, but didn't dwell there too long," said Lyla. "I realized I had become convinced there was always something that denied me the opportunity to leave, or so it seemed."

Another group member responded. "I know exactly how you mean. I felt trapped every time I would even think about leaving. I was so afraid I thought he could read my thoughts. But most of the time, I didn't know what I was afraid of most."

Again, Lyla spoke. "I was becoming a better listener allowing others to speak and finish their thoughts. I began to understand that demanding perfection, spoken or unspoken, was as destructive as it was a goal to be attained. It became less and less important to hold onto the rigid demands made of myself and others; perfection was exhausting."

For the next several sessions, Dr. Merkavah asked the women to share their observations about what they learned and each week Lyla was the first to volunteer.

"I was becoming less anxious. I began to overcome obstacles in a more positive way rather than allowing the issue to recklessly consume me and in turn consume someone else. I remember one time when I was feeding the dogs and I accidentally spilled a whole bowl of food on the floor. Before I could scoop it up, the dogs had me surrounded and were gobbling up every morsel. I was so mad at myself and mad at the dogs that I said the same horrible things about myself that my husband did punishing myself and took it out on the dogs."

Renee, one of the group members began to share. "I understand. Now that my attitude has changed, it's okay for me to make a mistake."

As the next weekly session began, Lyla shared an insight relevant to all the women. "The characteristics of the Lyla I had become were falling away and were replaced by a stronger, more mature, less fearful woman," said Lyla. It was acceptable to think of myself and take care of me and not be self-sacrificing and submissive. I don't even feel guilty when I do something just for me like the massage. I no longer have the need to rescue someone else."

"I now understand that my thoughts and responsive behavior were not built on reality. In the past, my husband didn't have to be present for me to be overcome with paralyzing fear and anxiety. He no longer has the overwhelming power and control I automatically attributed to him. My misunderstood beliefs were no longer a determining factor in my reactions. The immediate heart palpitations, the profuse sweating, the shortness of breath and panic have disappeared."

Talula, another group member shared with the group. "It's amazing but all my partner had to do was say a word or make a gesture and I would immediately feel the tense pressure, anxiety, and fear associated with it. It got to the point where he didn't even have to be there, all I had to do was think about something or hear something for me to become paralyzed in fear."

Some of the other group members nodded their heads. Cleo, another member said, "It sounds like all these men have similar behavior like they went to the same school and learned the same things. They all sound alike."

Lyla contributed, "I can remember if I wrote a check for $20.00 over the amount of the groceries and got the cash back I would momentarily freeze in fear that he would find out and find a way to punish me. I never thought, how would he ever know? It was like he was all knowing with ears and eyes everywhere, but that wasn't reality."

"I am learning to stop the self-condemnation for not having left what was a long-standing, painful, and toxic relationship," said Lyla.

Dr. Merkavah believed she needed to participate in the group to reassure the women. "It's never easy for anyone to understand the 'why' women stay. Perhaps it's equally difficult for the woman who is the one caught and entangled in the relationship."

Lyla concluded with, "My relationship with my father and his relationship with my mother, and others did portend my choices in partners, something that was telling but remained elusive to me for most of my life. I was more comfortable choosing someone who was similar to my father, it was familiar and was what I knew and understood. I stopped asking myself 'why,' and have chosen to move forward standing on the shoulders of the weak crumbling structure of the past and am using it to build a positive today and future."

Dr. Merkavah took control of the group and began the lessons for the next topic. "Thank you, ladies, for sharing your insights and revelations for the past several weeks. You see we share many of the same issues and understandings. Let's begin.

"One of the things holding us apart from the rest of the animal kingdom, or so we like to think it does, is our ability to speak. Several languages are represented in our small group and our topic this evening is not limited to any one language; it occurs in all. It's not the language; it's the one who speaks it. Verbal and/or psychological, emotional abuse is the secret form of abuse causing as much or more long-term, trauma than the physical.

As Dr. Merkavah spoke, Lyla immediately flashed back to a time when she had her annual gynecological exam. The doctor asked several routine questions and it was Lyla's answers that alerted the doctor to the possibility that Lyla was being abused. Lyla denied ever being hit by her husband. That was the first time Lyla ever heard about verbal and psychological abuse.

Dr. Merkavah's voice interrupted Lyla's thoughts. "Often, women are in denial, believing if they are not physically harmed, the action of the perpetrator is not recognized as abusive. The physical abuse leaves evidence, scars that can be seen; verbal leaves scars of a different kind.

"I have drawn up a list of verbal assaults I would like to discuss this evening. I want you to keep in mind the perpetrator's motivation and intention is to control and establish dominance, manipulate, and create shame and humiliation that is traumatizing and crippling to the receiver causing lingering mental and emotional paralysis. It is powerful enough to convince us we have no value.

"This type of destructive atmosphere, language, and the resultant trauma often manifests in us physically in the form of stress-related diseases. We cannot change the people who speak the words, but we can survive, change the way the words affect us, and if possible, leave the one who is causing the carnage. We are at great risk if we do not."

Lyla thought about her churning guts and the many years she suffered. It was all making sense. The room became painfully quiet as Dr. Merkavah was speaking. As she began to read and discuss each type of verbal abuse, Lyla could feel her heart beat faster and her guts begin to churn. She could identify with many of the examples, evoking memory of specific incidents.

The recall brought back the disgrace and humiliation again, something she thought she had overcome. She thought of the time when she had made the children's wing of the Texas house downstairs into a modified apartment. The wing was located on the opposite side of the house beyond the laundry room, a safe distance from Juliano, or so she thought. Her vivid memories came rushing back.

There was a door that led to the bedroom she occupied that formerly belonged to one of her children, another door that was adjacent and down the hall with its door and a bathroom in the middle that connected both rooms. She moved her clothing into the bedroom she slept in, put her toiletries in the bathroom, and set up the other bedroom with another small computer, television, and Pilates exercise equipment

She established what she thought was a safe place. After all, there had been no other incidents or attempts to force her to have sex, no confrontations of any kind. Although the tension remained, there were no outward signs of aggression or danger from Juliano.

She awakened that morning, just before sunrise, to walk and feed the dogs, spend time on her exercise equipment, shower, and change into her baking clothes to work in her kitchen. She had a large special order that day for several different varieties of breads and pumpkin breads that would take all day to prepare and deliver outside the neighborhood. It was late in the afternoon by the time she completed and delivered the order and she had gotten caught in heavy Houston rush hour traffic on her way back to the house.

It had been a long but successful day. The woman who ordered the bakery goods couldn't stop complimenting Lyla on how beautiful everything looked and how delicious it smelled. When Lyla arrived home, the dogs greeted her enthusiastically and needed to be walked, fed, and walked again before she could think about taking care of herself. She was too exhausted to prepare an evening meal and chose some leftovers to nibble on. She presumed Juliano found something to eat on his own.

The evening sky had changed from sunset streaks to an inky black and Lyla was overcome with exhaustion. She put the girls in their crates for the night and used her last ounces of strength to shower, put on a lightweight nightgown, and prepare for bed. She closed the door to her bedroom and the adjacent bedroom and crawled into bed. The sheets were cool and clean and smelled of fresh air. Crickets chirped outside the bedroom window and she could hear the howls of the coyote pack in the distance. She closed her eyes replaying her day feeling proud of her accomplishments. In moments, she was deeply asleep.

She never heard him shuffle down the long hallway or open the bedroom door. *Dazed and in a state of twilight sleep, she could feel her nightgown being pulled away from her body. As she awakened, she felt a heavy object pressing on top of her back crushing her small frame. And then she heard a voice, a gruff, gravelly, unfamiliar voice that kept repeating, "I want sex, I want sex," over and over again. She had been sleeping on her right side and was suddenly flipped like a pancake to her back fully exposed with one of Juliano's heavy legs pinning her to the bed.*

She never screamed but when she realized what was happening she began to fight back trying to shove him from her with her hands. She began slapping and punching him wherever she could to get him to release his grasp. It didn't work.

His hands were groping her body and at the same time fending off her frantic efforts to free herself. She could hear him breathing heavily from the exertion required for him to move his body and legs. The smell of his cologne sickened her, throwing up was not an option. She had to concentrate on getting away. The adrenaline was coursing through her body and she was breathing rapidly. She wasn't thinking, she was fighting for her life. In the midst of the chaos of flailing arms and hands, he must have resisted her attacks and wounded her because there was blood on the sheet and pillow.

He repositioned his body and tried to get his other leg over her body to mount her. When he moved slightly she was able to free one of her legs long enough to begin kicking him. She kicked him as hard as she could over and over again. He tried pinning her legs, she kicked harder trying to twist her body free. She must have found a vulnerable soft spot on his body while kicking because he momentarily withdrew his attack long enough for her to scramble away from him and get off the bed.

She began to run, in the dark, in the night, through the house toward the stairs leading to the second floor. By the time he got off the bed and, on his feet, she was up the stairs hiding in her old bed under the covers. She sat rigid, paralyzed in fear, listening to her frantic breathing and placed her hand over her mouth trying not to scream, hoping he wouldn't follow her.

She could hear him shuffle and stop when he reached the foot of the steps. Her breathing had slowed and she became quieter as she listened acutely for any clue as to where he was. She waited, nothing, and didn't hear him struggle to climb the steps.

Silence, dark silence.

Then she heard his voice, no longer the gruff, raspy voice that woke her.

"Lyla, Lyla, are you up there?"

She didn't move, she didn't speak.

"Lyla, Lyla, are you up there?" His voice became louder. "Hey, listen, I know you're up there. Listen, listen to me. I'm...I'm sorry, hey I'm sorry, I didn't mean to jump your bones like that."

Dark silence.

"Lyla, did you hear me? I said I'm sorry. Come down, we can talk."

Then a voice from upstairs echoed her warning. "If you ever touch me or try to rape me again I will call the police and have you arrested. You will be sent to prison and there will be no one to rescue you. If you don't believe me, try it and see what I do."

It was then she began to feel the horror of what had happened. Cold droplets of sweat began to form on her brow and above her top lip. Her body began to quake and the inside of her right wrist was throbbing. She began to cry, deep quiet moans and sobs that came from the core of her being.

Suddenly she had remembered the dogs. They had been in their crates safely tucked away. Or were they? Was he crazy or angry enough to do something awful to her girls? She put her hand back over her mouth to muffle her agony. She was paralyzed in fear and couldn't go down the steps to check. Softly she repeated, "Please God, please God, don't let him hurt my girls."

The horrifying thoughts and memories faded as Lyla heard Dr. Merkavah's voice. "Women find it arduous to have an intimate relationship with the partner who is verbally abusive. A woman naturally withdraws as a way to protect herself, and when she ignores her instinct, she puts herself at risk," Dr. Merkavah continued, capturing the women's rapt attention.

"Real intimacy requires trust. I would suspect some of you have learned that trying to change and/or placate your partner did not work and caused more friction, frustration, and pain." Lyla tentatively raised her hand to speak. Dr. Merkavah recognized her and nodded her head for Lyla to speak.

"I find it distressing that I am able to identify with many of the ways words can destroy. For most of my life with that man, I said nothing in my own defense and internalized the attacks. The regret and indignity associated with the act of staying in the marriage was overwhelming.

Even though I made many attempts to leave I never followed through, and I endured the pain and suffering. I withdrew each time, afraid, and I never really identified exactly what I was afraid of. Perhaps I was afraid of reprisal and believed I was totally unprepared to function successfully on my own.

"I hated it when he made fun of me in front of other people, but especially in front of my children. I hated it when he made me feel like I was stupid. I hated it when he ignored me and treated me as though my input was unimportant, worthless, a waste of his time. I hated it when he punished me for things he thought I did wrong or badly. I hated it when he was gracious and charming to other women and treated me badly. I hated the way I felt every time I had to have sex with him. I hated it when I didn't say no when that was really the way I felt. I hated it when I had to pretend all the time. I hated myself for not being able to protect my children and leave him.

"I hated his anger, I hated his hate …I hated it when …I hated it when he … even now, after his death, the memories and the old feelings rise in me as though they were current. I need for this to be over. I need for this ugliness to be part of the past I can leave behind. I need to leave the anger behind too, and I don't want to hate him anymore."

She couldn't finish. There were no words left. Huge tears began to roll down her cheeks as she spoke in a whisper, "I have felt so damaged, so broken, and afraid I would never be able to recover. I was once a beautiful young woman with so much potential and now, and now."

She covered her face with her hands and sobbed, shaken with emotion. Dr. Merkavah walked over to Lyla, sat close to her, and whispered, "You have been badly bruised but not irreparably broken. You're safe and you're not alone. You have recognized what happened in the past, you have permission to leave it behind, and allow yourself to heal. It does not mean that the one who did those things is absolved of the words and acts. It means you are no longer the victim or the survivor, but have the ability to be a thriver."

When Lyla looked up, she saw the faces of the other women who were in tears as well. Dr. Merkavah continued as she spoke to the women.

"It will take time, and you will heal. It will take time, and you will trust. It will take time, and you will rebuild your lives, becoming the women, you were meant to be. The relationship you entered into was not one of mutual respect or peace with security or harmony. It was not a relationship you alone could make, fix, or complete on your own, no matter how long or how hard you tried. While you were unable to recognize this before, you have the ability to do so now, and that is what is important. It is time to shed the ugliness of the past, rebuild, and look to a future filled with purpose and fulfillment.

"Part of the healing process is learning to trust yourselves and others, enabling you to express thoughts and feelings previously kept hidden. The meetings are an invaluable place for each woman to allow herself to share with others and let go of the fear associated with revealing her story, her feelings and anger about herself, and the partner she chose. Ultimately, was the partner someone you chose or one who saw particular aspects in you that he knew he could use to control and dominate?"

Haussmann House, while at first intimidating and uncomfortable, became a powerful place of refuge and discovery. Lyla's experiences there introduced her to other women who journeyed down similar paths. Women who were strangers when they first met, learned to trust one another and form a strong bond of friendship. They were no longer alone and frightened, struggling with the pain and heartache of their pasts. For some there were physical consequences that disappeared, but for the entire population there were emotional wounds and scars that were difficult to heal.

DINNER WITH MRS. BLUM

Lyla's days were filled with learning her craft both as a baker and as a businesswoman and she soon became accomplished in her trade. She had a knack, an intuitive, intimate relationship with bread and was astute, learning quickly about the business aspects of running a successful bakery. Jacques would often tease her, marveling at her skill and how quickly she had developed. He was astounded at her ability to 'know' just when the dough was ready and how she almost lovingly caressed the dough as she kneaded and shaped the loaves and other products. Jacques said it was as though she had been born with flour on her hands.

For the next several months, Lyla's life was completely immersed in her baking. The only times she relaxed or socialized outside of Haussmann House were the times she spent with Mrs. Blum dining out, going to the theatre, or just sitting and talking. Their relationship became one of love, trust, and friendship. Mrs. Blum was the mother figure Lyla had longed for and Lyla was another daughter who Mrs. Blum wanted to love, nurture, and help heal.

In late spring, Mrs. Blum invited Lyla to dine at her home as she had done so many times before. Although Lyla had made significant progress in her transformation, there was something carefully hidden, something too painful for Lyla to confront and/or reveal. Mrs. Blum wondered if Lyla would ever find the courage to move beyond her emotional obstacle.

That day Lyla was up before dawn and arrived to the quiet solitude of the baking sanctuary to begin preparing the first loaves of bread and croissants for early morning customers. When she was alone with her thoughts and bread ingredients, she pondered issues she had discovered that helped her to shed fears and doubts about herself that led to and existed during her relationship with Juliano.

As Lyla fired up the large brick ovens and kneaded the first of the morning loaves, she began to dwell on the one aspect of her relationship with Juliano she was never able to deal with and had never revealed to anyone. It made her uncomfortable just to think about it, and she noticed the more she allowed it to surface, the more anxious she became. Her heart began to beat rapidly and her breathing became faster, shallower. She was lost in thought when Jacques interrupted her by asking why she was squeezing the life out of her dough.

"Oh, uh, bon matin Jacques, ah yes, well, you see, I wasn't thinking. Actually, I was lost in thought and wasn't paying attention to what I was doing."

"Yes, I noticed that. Those were some very interesting thoughts, bien sûr. Perhaps you need to show mercy on that dough, put it out of its misery by shaping it, and allow it to recover in its proofing basket."

"Forgive me. Yes, of course, right away."

Lyla was embarrassed by her emotional distress but quickly regained her composure. Neither she nor Jacques spoke of the incident again. Her day at the bakery was complete in late afternoon, in time to catch some sunlight before the temperatures began to fall. Late spring in Paris was cool during the day. The occasional night time showers nourished and gently nudged the cherry, apple blossoms, and other spring flowers to show their colors.

Lyla stopped at a small boutique that was along her route home. She often passed the shop, but never succumbed to the temptations inside until that afternoon. To her delight and surprise, she made a wonderful discovery of vintage Courreges clothing and accessories. She found a pair of lightweight wool trousers, a sweater and a short leather Courreges battle jacket in sky blue. When she tried everything on she had to have them all, they were meant just for her. The purchases were extravagant, but Lyla thought she deserved the treat after her many months of hard work and the purchase reminded Lyla of the Courreges sweater and accessories her mother brought home from one of her trips to Paris. This was the perfect outfit to wear to Mrs. Blum's that evening.

By the time Lyla arrived at her apartment, the outside temperature had dropped. Her newly found treasures were left in her bedroom and she went to the kitchen to put water on to boil. A sudden chill coursed through her body from the long weary day, and Lyla thought a flavorful cup of hot tea would chase away the fatigue and discomfort.

She opened up her laptop, found music, and browsed through her unread emails until her tea was ready. She sent emails to the boys and responded to others that couldn't wait. There was just enough time to shower and dress and meet Mrs. Blum's driver downstairs.

This evening would no doubt end late; she was not working over the weekend. "I might even sleep in," she whispered as she took the elevator to the street floor. Philipe was waiting with the large black town car.

He greeted Lyla as he opened the car door for her. "Bon soir, Madame."

"Bon soir, Philipe. Lovely to see you this evening."

The car was comfortably warm. It was hard for her to believe how much had happened since the dedication. The transformative process was reflected in her countenance and attitude. Philipe turned into the driveway through the iron gates and drove up to the front door of Mrs. Blum's residence. He then quickly moved to assist Lyla.

"Thank you, Philipe," Lyla said as she stepped out of the vehicle, turned her coat collar up, then gathered the heavy wool and fur scarf around her neck hurriedly walking to the front door. As she reached to ring the bell, the door opened, bathing the opening with the light and fragrance of the house's interior.

Lyla was greeted by Hildi. "Bon soir Madame, Rose. It is a pleasure to see you this evening."

"Bon soir, Hildi. Thank you; it is a pleasure to see you as well."

"Mrs. Blum is waiting for you in the library. May I take your garments?"

"Yes, thank you, Hildi I will join her."

Lyla entered the library where Mrs. Blum, seated by the fire, looked up from her book as Lyla entered the room.

"Bon soir, Madame Blum."

"Bon soir, Lyla. Why is it you have such difficulty calling me Ethel? Surely, by now we can dispense with the formalities. Non? Oui?"

"Oui, Madame Blum, I mean, Ethel."

Lyla reached down to Mrs. Blum to brush each cheek with a light kiss as Mrs. Blum returned the greeting.

"Lyla, you look lovely. Are you wearing something new?"

"Yes, thank you for the compliment. It's wonderful to see you, Ethel. On the way back from the bakery I couldn't resist stopping at a boutique where I found vintage Courreges. I pass the shop every day on my way to the bakery and have resisted going in until today. Believe me, it's not a weakness I shall succumb to on a regular basis. I suppose I conveniently forgot how beautiful but also how expensive Courreges is; I splurged. The clothing reminded me of when my mother returned from one of her Paris trips and gave me several Courreges items. When I tried them on, mother commented on how lovely I looked. I was so pleased she had remembered me. It's been years since I thought of those things. With everything packed and in storage, I have no idea if I still have them. It felt good to have a connection with mother, she has been gone for several years now and I am missing her."

Lyla sat down beside Ethel to chat about the rest of her day at the bakery and Ethel's plans for her latest excursion. Hildi entered the library to announce dinner.

"Thank you, Hildi. I don't know about you, Lyla, but I'm starved. The menu this evening is roast lamb with a lovely mustard and herb crust."

Lyla responded, "Sounds luscious, I'm famished."

They walked slowly, arm in arm, from the library to the dining room. The table sparkled with fine china, crystal, and the glow from the candle-lit candelabra. The table was covered with a fine linen tablecloth and napkins.

"Dinner was absolutely superb, Ethel. You're going to spoil me, and I fear I've had much too much wine."

Mrs. Blum sat quietly watching Lyla, who seemed to be struggling with something. "Lyla, Lyla?" she said softly. "Is there something wrong? Is there something on your mind? You have suddenly become quiet, contemplative."

Lyla toyed with her wine glass and then began tracing a nonexistent image on the tablecloth. With her eyes downcast she hesitated and then spoke. "No, it's probably the long day, the delicious meal, and the wine."

"Lyla, I have a suggestion. It's late, you're tired, feeling the effects of dinner, how about you stay the night? Philipe can take you back in the morning after a good night's rest. You could probably use it."

Lyla was not accustomed to anyone looking after her and didn't know how to respond. "I don't want to impose upon you Mrs. ...Ethel."

"Don't be silly, Lyla, it wouldn't be an imposition; the guest room is always ready. Besides, it would do you good to allow someone to take care of you. I suspect that hasn't happened in a very long time."

Lyla was silent with her eyes focused on the tablecloth. Slowly she looked up at Ethel. "You're right; it has been a long time, an agonizingly long time. Thank you, I will stay."

"Good, come with me we'll get you settled."

Lyla and Ethel climbed the staircase and walked down the hall to the guest room. It was a generous sized room bathed in the warm light of the fireplace and fixtures.

"You'll be comfortable here. I'll get Hildi to bring you some night clothes and anything else you might need. I'll return to say goodnight once you're ready to climb into bed."

In a matter of moments Hildi appeared at the bedroom door and knocked lightly. Her arms overflowed with everything Lyla might desire. "Madame Blum said you might require these things. I'll place them here on the bed."

"Merci, Hildi, these things are perfect."

Lyla felt like she had been tapped on the shoulder by a fairy god-mother's wand. It took only moments for her to change into a flannel gown, wash her face, and brush her teeth. She heard a light tap on her door, and recognized Ethel's voice.

"Lyla, Lyla? May I come in?"

"Of course, of course, please come in."

Lyla greeted Ethel who was carrying a carved silver tray with two small pots of tea and delicate china tea cups.

"I thought we would both enjoy a hot cup of chamomile tea. Would you like some?"

"Yes, that would be wonderful, thank you."

Lyla climbed into bed, propped up the pillows, and got comfortable. Ethel asked, "May I sit at the bedside with you for a few moments?"

"Oh, yes, please stay."

Ethel sat on the edge of the bed facing Lyla. They sipped their tea quietly when Ethel spoke. "I noticed how quiet you became after we finished eating. May I ask again if there is anything causing you distress? Is there something on your mind?"

Lyla's thoughts raced back to the incident at the bakery earlier in the day. What a question to ask. The circumstances were similar to the question posed to her by Charlie, the nurse practitioner. And just as it happened with Charlie, so it happened with Ethel.

"Well, you see," Lyla said, with her eyes fixed on her tea cup, "something did happen at the bakery this morning. I was lost in thought as I was kneading a batch of dough by hand. Memories of past events, and my feelings about my behavior back then became intense and I was temporarily overcome by the old paralysis and pain."

Ethel sat still, knowing Lyla was about to expose something painful. Lyla began her story, haltingly at first, uncertain what Ethel's reaction would be. She continued with her eyes fixed on her tea cup as the words, the emotions, and the anger at herself, her husband, and her family came tumbling out.

"Even though I've worked hard and have gained so much understanding, I have yet to reveal how I felt about myself for what I did and the foolish, incomprehensible decisions I made. I rescued him, gave him a life he never would have had, and in return sacrificed my own and compromised the lives of my children. How was I to reconcile that? I have had such monumental regrets and now understand why my mother thought I had lost my mind when I married him."

"Anger at myself matured into self-loathing when I realized I knowingly rescued a sexual predator, a monster, and contributed to his eventual release from incarceration. I defended him to my family and continued to support him when he obviously took advantage of me and my family. I tolerated his cruel behavior and buried how I really felt and continued to hope he would change. I could barely admit this to myself let alone to anyone else. I began to feel I was the one who was guilty of the reprehensible act or somehow caused his behavior, not him. I would ask myself, "How could I help him? How is it that I initially was able to recognize the magnitude of what he had done but after time somehow bury and ignore the reality of his true nature and horror of his actions? What kind of person was I who could do such things? Why was it that everyone else could see how wrong my decisions were and not me? Lyla recounted the specific events of her past that led her to rescue, support, and provide a life for him ignoring all the signs and pleadings of her family.

"I chose to accept the stigma, the shame, the humiliation, and the burden of his criminal act. I believe I became addicted to the life I made and the man I felt compelled to save. I carried an extraordinary amount of guilt, concealing my real repulsion for what he had done, keeping him from the fate he was most likely destined to have.

"I defied the laws of the universe; I made my Frankenstein."

Again, and again, she repeated her self-disgust and inability to absolve herself of her past decisions.

"Letting go of the critical, damning self-judgment, and the horror of my decisions was a monumental task. I have told no one until now. I needed to find a way to understand, forgive myself, and allow myself to be human and make mistakes without condemnation. I couldn't face what I thought you and everyone else thought of me, my past behavior, and beat myself up harder than anyone else would have. Revealing myself to you makes it possible for me to be released from my self-imposed prison and forgive myself."

Words were tumbling out quickly and tears were running down her cheeks, splashing onto her cup. As her sobs grew in intensity, Ethel took Lyla's teacup and placed it on the table beside the bed along with her own. She then sat on the bed next to Lyla and gently placed her arm around Lyla's shoulder, cradling Lyla in her arms. Ethel could feel Lyla's intense pain coupled with her anguished cries.

"I'm here, Lyla, I'm here," Ethel whispered, "You're safe. I'm here with you. You have a kind and loving heart. You never recognized that the one you were trying to save was wrong for you, for anyone. The anger and pain can no longer dwell within you. The decisions and choices came from a culmination of your experiences and emotional state at the time. You must also remember you were never responsible for his actions. While we may be shaped by the past, it does not have to dominate our present and certainly not our future. You are now beyond that. Cry until you can't cry anymore. Dry your tears and don't cry for him again or for what happened in the past. You're healed and whole now."

As Lyla's cries began to subside, Ethel gently rocked Lyla to give her comfort and security. Lyla's body began to relax as she nestled against Ethel's breast until she could hear Lyla whisper. "Mother, Mother. I know you tried to rescue me and I didn't, I wouldn't, let you, I was such a foolish child."

Ethel's voice was soft and comforting. "I'm here, you are safe, shah, shah; I'm here, you are safe."

Minutes later, Ethel could feel Lyla taking deep even breaths. Lyla had fallen sound asleep. Ethel never suspected the gravity of what she now knew, after hearing what Lyla had bravely revealed. It was painful to hear what happened to this once beautiful, innocent young woman. As Ethel held and rocked Lyla, she recalled Lyla's words, and she too began to cry.

"Never again," she whispered, "never again."

Ethel gently laid Lyla's head on the pillows and covered her with the comforter. She left Lyla sleeping with the peace of a comforted child.

Lyla was emotionally distraught and the repetition was reflective of her shame and guilt, which was central to her view of herself. She had to continually repeat her confession in order to get it out, in an attempt to make sense of something she could not. She perceived herself as much a monster as he was; until now.

TRANSFORMATION COMPLETE HEALING

Although Lyla woke up the next morning with a slight headache and puffy eyes, she felt better, different. She stood in front of the sink, brushing her teeth, and noticed the heavy necklace of rocks she had worn for so long was nearly gone. Then the realization of what she had revealed to Ethel the night before, gradually made its way into her consciousness. The churning feeling in her guts began and the sickening feeling changed from discomfort to nausea and dizziness. Was it simply too much strong wine from the night before? She looked in the mirror and spoke to her reflection.

"Yes, that's what it must be, too much wine, of course. What's the matter with me? How silly."

She finished brushing her teeth, undressed, and stepped into the warm shower, feeling relief, convinced she was merely being foolish. And then it happened again. The thoughts came rushing back just like the water raining down upon her. The churning guts, the nausea, and the feelings of anxiety crashed in on her. She held her face in her hands, as she leaned over in obvious distress, as the water fell about her.

She whispered, "What have I done? I've revealed a closely guarded secret. They were painful, horrendous pronouncements that I was embarrassed to utter even to myself let alone to someone else. My God, what I have done?"

When she stood up the anger rose in her. "Stupid, foolish woman. How could you do something so stupid? You never should have trusted anyone, even Ethel. You had everyone convinced. You covered up everything so well, until now. What will Ethel think of you? How can you face her?"

Her churning guts were ready to explode and the nausea was overwhelming. As she stepped out of the shower and began to dry herself off, she closed her eyes and took a deep breath. "Deep breath in through the nose and out through the mouth," she repeated over and over again until her heartbeat began to slow down and the nausea and gut pain began to subside. She spoke aloud again.

"Wait a minute. Let me consider what's happened here. I've said some very intimate, painful truths about myself to someone I have grown to love, trust, and admire. Ethel would never expose and betray me. Still ... the shame ... the embarrassment."

Lyla, in her anxiety and fear, was unable to forgive herself, and unsuccessful in convincing herself that what she admitted the night before was not harmful. She decided to make her excuses to Ethel, skip the morning meal, and return to her apartment to sort this out. Perhaps she would be lucky and Ethel would sleep in this morning, and Lyla wouldn't have to see her at all.

She dressed hurriedly gathering her personal items when she heard a soft knock at her door. Lyla called out, "I'll be down in a moment," thinking the knock signaled Hildi's presence. Again, there was a soft knock at the door. She presumed Hildi had not heard her and called out again, "Yes, yes, Hildi, I'm dressed, I'll be down in a moment."

Lyla was frantically stuffing whatever she had into her handbag when the door opened slowly, revealing the figure of Ethel. Lyla turned to face the door and became transfixed, Medusa-like, casting her eyes towards Mrs. Blum's feet in submission. Lyla looked up with a sheepish grin as though caught in a transgression.

She said, "Oh, good morning, good morning. I was just gathering my things and taking care of things, and *My God,* Lyla thought to herself, *I'm babbling.*"

Ethel walked toward her and spoke softly. "Good morning, Lyla, I trust you slept well?"

Lyla was obviously uncomfortable and anxious. "Yes, yes, very well, yes I did. And you, Ethel?"

"Well, Lyla, to tell you the truth, I did not. I thought about the things you told me last night and was concerned."

Lyla could feel the heat rising up from her toes to her gut and up towards her throat. The thoughts were racing through her mind. *My God what is she going to say? My God what have I done?*

"Please, Lyla, come over here where we can be more comfortable."

They walked to the two boudoir chairs in front of the large bay windows. "I have taken the liberty of asking Hildi to bring up some morning tea and warm croissants. I hope you don't mind."

"No, of course not. Thank you."

Lyla could barely speak. She hoped her anxiety didn't show and wasn't sure if she was going to be able to drink anything let alone get a rich croissant down.

"I want to begin by thanking you, Lyla, for trusting me to lay bare your innermost thoughts and feelings. I listened carefully to everything and believe it must have taken great courage to speak of those things that have caused you so much pain. I want to make sure I convey to you I will in no way, ever divulge anything that passed between us last night. This is a solemn promise I make to you. In addition, unless you choose to speak of those issues again, I will never allude to them nor mention them. I am a woman of my word."

Lyla sat still, stiff with her hands folded in her lap and her legs crossed tightly at the ankles, hanging on every word. The more Ethel spoke the less Lyla's guts rumbled and the nausea began to fade. Ethel spoke again, reassuring Lyla.

"As we grow older we attain wisdom. It is from the experiences of life that we become wise. We build upon this wisdom for a lifetime and pass this on to our children and they pass it on to their children.

"You have had a life experience that will stay with you for some time to come. These and others, hopefully less painful, are part of the foundation upon which your insight and your wisdom is built. It will take time to heal. Part of the process is trying to make sense of something one cannot and perhaps never will. Wisdom does not come just in knowing. Wisdom comes from the choices you make when you do know. Does this mean you never should have done or felt the things you revealed to me? Well, perhaps, perhaps not. But these were the choices made at the time. I strongly suspect you believed if you disclosed your innermost feelings about yourself others would hate you as much as you hated yourself. Don't be afraid to trust again. This takes time.

"I would gladly take your pain upon myself if I could, if it would alleviate yours, but I cannot. Because I cannot, I can only attempt to ease yours with the love, wisdom, and insight of my years. I am proud of you and your efforts, your strength, your courage, and this journey you have embarked upon."

A small lump grew in Lyla's throat as her eyes filled with tears. She spoke softly, unable to lift her eyes from her teacup. "I feel a tremendous weight has been lifted from me. I was uncertain how you would respond and I was afraid I was wrong to have spoken. I was afraid I would lose you. There were many times when I wanted to confide in my parents, especially in my mother, and could not. I knew she was angry, hurt, and worried about me. At the same time, I believed she suspected I was suffering and could do little to help me and the children. I missed my chances to communicate with her and rely upon her, and when I was able to do so, it was too late; she was dead.

"There have been times when I needed to cry to her, ask for her help and wisdom, receive her comfort, and I could not. I have many regrets and have lamented she never knew I was finally free and moving in a positive direction. I could not tell her then and cannot do that now. This is a significant loss I have not been able to deal with.

"I can recall times as a young girl when I became frightened and upset and my mother was not there to console me or protect me. I would run to her bedroom and crawl onto her bed resting my head on her pillow, curling up on top of her covers. I closed my eyes, burying my face in her pillow, taking deep breaths to take in the scent that was hers alone.

"As I lay there, infused with her aromatic presence, I began to feel safe and the fear would subside. Being on her bed and on her pillow, had magical properties that brought her to me when I needed her. Being with you and telling you last night felt like I was with my mother on her bed, and it helped to heal and soothe my aching heart and finally better understand, acknowledge, and forgive myself.

"I used to think if I could just be strong enough to survive until he died I would be free. Now with the help from everyone at Haussmann House and you, Ethel, I know I was wrong. My internal freedom came when I eventually let go of the hatred and pain, when I stopped judging myself, and I focused on me. I never expressed this to anyone before and the weight of this was agonizing, until now."

The women sat sipping their tea as the filtered morning sun covered them with the warmth of a new day. Lyla finished her cup of tea and croissant, feeling, knowing, the last of the stones had finally fallen from her neck.

"Ethel, thank you. I am fortunate to have your friendship and love. It was a difficult night, and I've got the red puffy eyes to prove it. There are many things I need to consider in the next several months, in particular, when I will return to the States, and the direction I want my life to take. I can focus on those things now and feel the glamelia getting larger and more beautiful each day."

Lyla and Ethel stood up from their chairs and embraced, each holding the other for a tender moment. Ethel stepped back to look at Lyla and once more made her promise known and offered her ever-present support.

"I'll have Philipe take you home as soon as you're ready. We'll see each other soon."

They parted and Ethel left Lyla's room to make arrangements for Lyla to be taken back to her apartment. As she descended the stairs the telephone rang. "Mrs. Blum," Hildi called, "it is Monsieur Alex."

"Thank you Hildi, please tell him I'll be there in a moment."

Lyla picked up her handbag, took one more look in the mirror, and saw a red, puffy-eyed woman, who for the first time in many years truly felt free. She left the room walking a little bit taller, with the confidence and well-being of a woman who was about to embark on another incredible journey.

Mrs. Blum took the phone call in the library. "Good Morning, Alex. How are you this morning?"

"Fine, Mother. How was your evening? I wanted to come by and see you today; would you like some company?"

"Of course, Alex, it's always good to see you. Would you like to have some breakfast? I'll have Hildi prepare something for you."

"I don't think so, Mother, just some pastry and coffee, thanks. I'll be over in about an hour. How's that sound?"

"I'll be here."

Lyla spent the ride back to the apartment reflecting on the previous night feeling like the chains of emotional bondage had been broken. The feeling of real freedom was intoxicating. She began to make mental notes and lists of her priorities. For the first time, Lyla was directing the course of her life with renewed energy, positive purpose, and without fear. The first part of her plan was simple. She would continue to learn about bread, the ovens, and the other pieces of equipment it would take to run a bakery of her own and perhaps she could convince Genni to take some time to celebrate with a bit of a shopping spree; her time in Paris was coming to an end.

Lyla began to construct an outline of her plan as soon as she returned to her apartment. She was making lists and organizing her ideas into a workable document laying out what she would need to start her bakery business. She chose to name her bakery, Sweet Aromas, recalling her home bakery in Texas. The proposal would have to be done properly to convince the bank she was a good risk for the loan. It would be necessary to talk to Ethel and ask her advice on that and on one other matter.

Alex arrived at his mother's house and greeted her with a soft kiss on the cheek and an embrace.

"Alex, you look a bit tired. How are you doing?"

"I guess I'm all right Mother. I can't seem to find my way, and I'm missing Annie. I thought if I came here for an extended stay and kept myself busy with classes it would help me move on, but I don't seem to be able to do that. Here I am in this vibrant City of Lights, and I feel very much alone. I have a hard time being social, and it's not because I haven't been asked. I feel it's time I move on, and I'm not quite certain how to do that."

Ethel studied her son's face, wishing she could take his pain; but she knew too well how it felt to miss someone you loved.

"I have an idea, Alex. Have you ever heard of "The Paris Chocolate and Pastry Food Tour? It's well-known, and I think you would really enjoy it. How about we go together next week? I would love to have you as my escort. I have some free time; what is your schedule like?"

"Well, let me think. I do have some time next week on Tuesday. How could I refuse to escort such a beautiful woman? Of course, I'll go with you."

SYMPHONY OF HER HEART

"Good, then it's settled. We'll go on the tour next Tuesday and indulge in life's sweet confections: bread, pastry, and chocolate, a most decadent trio."

Mrs. Blum took her son's arm, "Come, let's have a little something to eat and visit more. I know there must be something in this house that will tempt you. I'll tell you all about my upcoming trip to the cottage, and perhaps you'll come with me."

"The cottage? You haven't been there since ...."

"Yes, I know since your father died. It's time I went back." Alex's concern for his mother's well-being was evident in the tone of his voice. "Are you sure you want to do this?"

"Yes, Alex, it's something I must do."

A RELATIONSHIP THAT IS NOT BREAD

Early Monday morning, Lyla called the foundation to meet with Ethel later that same afternoon. The phone call was the easy part, talking about business to Ethel was another matter. Lyla hoped she was not being presumptuous in asking Ethel for help.

Lyla arrived at Haussmann House anxious but hopeful. Her frequent visits to Haussmann House had given her the time and opportunity to become familiar with everyone at the foundation, and she acknowledged them by name as she walked down the hallway to Mrs. Blum's office. Lyla greeted Genni at her desk with a warm smile and an air of confidence.

Genni looked up to see Lyla coming toward her. "Good afternoon, Lyla, how are you? You are looking exceptional this afternoon. What happened? Did you change your hair, your make-up? What's different?"

"All the rocks are gone," Lyla said, "every single one of them. It feels great."

"Rocks? What rocks, Lyla?"

Before Lyla reached Mrs. Blum's office she turned back to Genni and said, "Why, the ones that were around my neck."

Lyla walked into Mrs. Blum's office. Ethel stepped from behind her desk and the women embraced.

"Hello, Ethel, thank you for seeing me on such short notice."

"Don't be silly, Lyla; you're always welcome, any time."

"I wanted to thank you again for giving me my life back. I have been desired, lusted after, used and abused, but this is the first time I have been the recipient of a loving, unselfish relationship."

"Come, Lyla," Ethel said, let us sit down and talk."

"Ethel, there's much I want to do and I have dozens of ideas swirling around in my head. I've made some important decisions."

"Well, Lyla, let's take them one at a time."

"I've given this a lot of thought," said Lyla. My time here in Paris is coming to its end and I believe it is time for me to move on. It is essential that I spend my remaining time here making contacts and solidify my working knowledge of what will be necessary for me to begin my bakery." Ethel's eyes grew wide, she was about to speak, when Lyla continued, "I want to go back home, Ethel, to south Florida."

"My work here is done. I want to build a bakery with a small shop area with seating, and offer an assortment of cheeses and jams. My plan is to bake the kinds of breads I have learned to bake here and others. It is my hope, with what I have gained here, I will be successful. Please forgive me, Ethel, I am asking for your help with a business plan.

"It's strange," Lyla continued, "but when I think about it, it is not. I came to Paris to learn to be a baker. It was a way for me to run away from the horrible memories and events of my adult life. At the time, I believed it was the only way I could shed the past and not be haunted by it. I didn't realize that I was carrying my past around with me the whole time.

"It took you, your program, and the wonderful women here to help me understand I needed to shed the issues of the past to reshape myself and rebuild my life. It was a difficult and painful journey, but one I do not regret. For the first time, since I was a young woman, I believe my life has purpose. I am in the third quarter of my life, and I am choosing not to waste a moment."

Mrs. Blum sat listening intently, amazed at Lyla's convictions, her strength of purpose, and desire. Lyla was there for several hours during which time phone calls were made to Mrs. Blum's attorney for documents and legal advice. Lyla made a call to her friend and real estate agent in south Florida, requesting that she begin the search for a bakery location and Lyla's new home. Things were coming together without effort; it all felt right.

"Ethel, I want to thank you again for your loving kindness, friendship, and support. It's getting late and I must go." Ethel invited Lyla to dine with her that evening.

"No, thank you, I'm meeting the ladies from my group this evening. It's going to be a French pot luck. Of course, I'm bringing the bread!!

Au revoir, à plus tard, Ethel."

"Au revoir à plus tard, Lyla." The women embraced and parted.

Mrs. Blum and Genni watched as Lyla left Ethel's office. Heads turned as Lyla walked from Mrs. Blum's office toward the front door to exit the building. Mrs. Blum and Genni looked at each other and smiled at Lyla's obvious changes. The sadness in Lyla's eyes was gone and she walked like a woman unburdened and self-confident. The flower Lyla was when she arrived in Paris had transformed into a multi-layered, richly hued blossom, petal by petal, and the change was heart-warming to witness. Mrs. Blum marveled at the changes and remarked, "Genni, I believe she's the one."

Lyla woke to the stillness of the early morning and nearly jumped out of bed in her eagerness to get to the bakery. She rushed through her morning routine, nearly forgetting her tea, swept up her bags, and was out the door. She hurried past the doorman, nearly running him over, and grabbed a taxi to the bakery. She worked briskly and efficiently to make sure she had enough bread and croissants for the early morning customers and for those who were coming through the bakery on the food tour.

Jacques was pleased with her idea to fill baskets with samples for the people on the tour. Lyla's ideas were fresh and well-received by customers, and the bakery became a favorite place on the tour. Business increased and the bakery was making more product now than ever before. Lyla was in the back of the bakery, putting together more samples when Ethel and Alex arrived with their tour group. The bakery was an explosion of activity with everyone rushing to fill morning orders and special items for the tour.

Lyla stepped from the back of the bakery, her arms laden with baskets brimming with bread and croissants. She was navigating through the crowd to deposit her baskets when she noticed Ethel standing among the guests and customers. She stood on her toes to get Ethel's attention and called to her.

"Ethel, Ethel Blum, over here; it's Lyla." They moved toward each other embracing with great affection.

"Bonjour, Ethel. You should have told me you were going to be here. I would have made something special for you."

Mrs. Blum turned to her son and remarked to Lyla, "I'm here with my son, Alex. I believe you met him at the dedication. Lyla, my son, Alex; Alex, this is Lyla Rose." Before either of them could exchange greetings, Lyla was called away for several moments. She excused herself and said she would return momentarily.

Alex turned to his mother and said, "I don't remember meeting her at the dedication. When did I meet her? Are you certain I met her? Are you sure it was at the dedication?" Mrs. Blum smiled and reminded him of their brief introduction.

"You would think I would have remembered meeting her, she's beautiful; so vibrant."

"Yes," Ethel acknowledged, "she is."

Alex was right. Lyla looked radiant that morning. Even though she was wearing a large baking apron and was covered with a dusting of flour, her beauty was unmistakable. Her silvery hair was away from her face and was covered by a brightly colored kerchief revealing her velvety brown eyes. It was difficult to take one's eyes from her as she moved through the crowd, smiling and helping customers. She eventually maneuvered her way back to Ethel and Alex and apologized to them both.

"I'm sorry it is hectic here now. How do you like our bread?" They were both so enchanted with Lyla they had forgotten to taste the samples.

"Here," she said, "if you please, take some. I made them myself just this morning." Lyla gave a small piece to Ethel and then handed a sample to Alex. Lyla looked into Alex's face and smiled as their hands touched for a moment.

"Well, how do you like it?" asked Lyla. Ethel noticed Alex had somehow lost his ability to speak, so she responded for them both.

"Excellent, marvelous, wonderful flavor and texture, you can bake for me anytime."

"Thank you, Ethel, it would be my distinct pleasure."

The tour guide began to round up his participants for the next stop. As Alex walked toward the door he called out to Lyla, "Lyla, do you do anything?"

She smiled, "Yes. I do. I bake bread."

Alex partially covered his face with his hand still holding the unfinished croissant and asked again. "No, how silly of me, I mean do you do anything aside from bake bread? I mean would you like to do something? How exasperating. I sound like a teenager. I mean there's a wonderful exhibition at the Louvre this weekend. Would you like to accompany me?"

Accompany me? Alex couldn't believe the word came out of his mouth. *Accompany me?* he thought. *What kind of way is that to ask out a beautiful woman?* Alex followed the rest of the tour group toward the door feeling slightly perturbed by his verbal clumsiness. Lyla turned away as her attention was taken by some passing customer.

As Alex reached the door, he turned back to see Lyla as she waved goodbye to them, saying, "Yes, I would like that."

Ethel turned to Alex and noticed his entire countenance had changed. She knew something happened back there, she could feel it.

"Alex, what happened back there?"

"I don't know, Mother; it was the strangest thing."

"Yes, I know Alex. I felt it, too."

"Must have had something to do with the magnetic gravitational pull of the earth at that exact moment in time," Alex said with a wry smile.

"Sure, sure that's what it must have been, whatever gravitational thing you said," Mrs. Blum acknowledged, wondering how long it would take the two of them to realize what happened.

When the tour ended with the last shop, Philipe was at the appointed meeting place, ready to take Mrs. Blum and Alex back to the house.

"If you don't mind, Mother, I think I'll find my own way back. I'd like to take some time to meander."

"No, I don't mind at all, Alex. Thank you for escorting me today. I have enjoyed spending this time together. I believe I've had enough chocolate and pastry to last a long time or at least until tomorrow morning." They embraced, holding each other for a long moment, then Mrs. Blum got in her vehicle and Alex took a taxi back to Lyla at the bakery.

Lyla was busy in the back of the bakery when Alex returned. He stood inside the door watching her as she removed pallets of finished loaves from the hot ovens. Lyla was covered with flour dust working in a pair of white trousers cut off above the knee and a loose-fitting T-shirt twisted and tied at the waist. She worked efficiently depositing her freshly baked loaves and went immediately to her table to razor the tops of the loaves that were finished proofing.

Lyla felt uncomfortable, as though she were being watched. She thought, *How foolish, Lyla, there's no one there. You've got all these loaves to get into the ovens, stop being so paranoid.*

She returned to her work and tried to focus, but could not. This time she couldn't shake the uncomfortable feeling. Then she slowly turned and looked over her shoulder to see Alex standing there, watching her. He met her gaze and approached her.

"Uh, hello there, Lyla, you're not going to believe this but I suddenly had an overwhelming urge to have some bread and thought perhaps. Well, I thought maybe you would have some extra I could buy, or something. Sorry, I seem to be stumbling around here looking for the right words to say. I'm not very good at this. I've sort of been out of practice. Perhaps I should stop talking."

"No, I think it's quite charming, I like it, I mean the stumbling. I found myself doing the same thing when I first came to Paris." Her brown eyes twinkled and her brows lifted as she leaned in to hear his voice. "Are you really still hungry or was that just an excuse to come back?"

"Well, honestly, I'm not really hungry. In fact, I don't think I could swallow another chocolate or pastry. I just wanted to come back to see you and ask if you'd like to spend the evening with me. I mean, would you like to have dinner later or something to drink?"

Lyla's smile was coquettish as she walked over to Alex wiping her hands on her apron, brushing short wisps of hair from her face.

"It would be my pleasure to do 'something' with you this evening, Alex Blum."

Lyla liked his soft-spoken voice and his easy-going manner.

"It will be awhile before I'm finished here. How does 7:30 sound?"

"Fine, just fine, how about I meet you at..."

Lyla interrupted him and said, "How about you meet me at my apartment?"

"Sounds good, excellent. Great, sounds good, yes, good." As Alex turned to go he pivoted back to face her and asked, "Where is that? Your apartment I mean."

Lyla laughed sweetly at his schoolboy awkwardness and took a piece of paper from her pocket and wrote her address and phone number.

"Now, if you don't mind Alex, I must return to my bread. I have much to accomplish before I leave today."

"Yes, I see that," Alex said. "I'll see you later."

"Yes, Alex, 7:30 it is," she confirmed as she turned and walked back to her work. Before Alex could move, she turned around to face him.

"Thank you, Alex, for coming back. Thank you for your invitation. I look forward to seeing you later."

Lyla disappeared into the back of the bakery and Alex continued out the front door. She had no time to think about what happened in the bakery with Alex until she was finished for the day. When she arrived at her apartment, she opened her laptop, navigated to the site for some soft mellow jazz to stream, and made a cup of tea. She filled the tub with hot water and bath salts and submerged. As she listened to the music and relaxed, her thoughts turned to what had happened at the bakery earlier that day.

Strange, she thought. *Something did happen in the bakery today that I just can't put into words.* Lyla closed her eyes and remembered his smile and his voice. She wondered if she would have been attracted to this man in the past and what it was that drew her to him now. He was handsome and refined, tall and somewhat lanky with a full head of beautiful black hair that was generously sprinkled with silver. His expressive eyes were warm brown surrounded with long black lashes and his voice was gentle seamlessly moving from English to French and Italian. Perhaps it was because he was Ethel's son.

The alarm that she set before her soak signaled it was time to get out and dress before she shriveled into a prune confection. It was amazing how her mirrored image reflected the transformation from a dusty flour maiden to an attractive woman. She put on a comfortable pair of trousers and sweater, ran her fingers through her hair, and put on her lipstick.

Lyla heard a knock on her door. "Just a moment, I'll be there in a moment." She sprayed some of her favorite perfume on her sweater, walked to the door, and looked through the peep hole to see Alex, holding flowers. She smiled as she opened the door.

"Hello, Alex, please come in. Are those for me? They're lovely."

"Yes, I hope you like them."

There were a few awkward moments as he stood inside the door and she stood with the flowers. Alex was immediately drawn to her beauty. There was something about her that rendered him speechless. He interrupted his intense stare to follow her as she placed the flowers in a container of water in the kitchen.

"Lovely," Alex said with Lyla's back to him. Without turning she responded, "Yes, they are, thank you."

"No, Lyla, I didn't mean the flowers I was speaking about you. How lovely you look; you almost take my breath away."

Lyla did not know how to respond to the sincerity of his words. She desperately tried to find a way to relate to him and his expression of feelings for her. Lyla was a woman, who, for most of her life, trusted no one, and was unaccustomed to being treated this way.

Alex made no move to take Lyla's hand or touch her in any way, but waited for her to turn and face him. They stood staring at each other, unable to speak or move, searching each other's face, eyes, trying to identify the intangible energy that brought them together. Finally, Alex spoke. "Hungry?"

"Famished," she whispered. "I'm sorry," she continued, "I find it difficult to move. I feel like I must drink in every moment as though I had an unquenchable thirst. I don't understand what's happening."

Their fingertips touched, sending a wave of warmth and electricity through them. Alex barely touched Lyla's waist and led her to the door, trying to be free of his inebriated feeling.

Finally, Alex spoke. "We're going out to dinner, aren't we? Where would you like to go?"

They decided to have a late dinner at a small café near the apartment. It was a place frequented by locals with delicious home-cooked French fare. The café was quiet and conducive to intimate conversation and the food and wine were satisfying and filling. After dinner, they decided to take a leisurely stroll talking for hours, engrossed in the Paris night and each other. Lyla interrupted the comfortable silence that descended on them as they came closer to her apartment.

"Thank you, Alex, for a lovely evening. I never realized how much we have in common. Well, this is where we began, it's time for me to go."

They walked in the building, to the elevator, to her apartment. Alex followed Lyla and they stepped just inside her apartment to linger there for a moment.

"I never imagined I could feel comfortable and easy with anyone, especially since Annie's death," Alex said in a voice choked with emotion. "But, here I am with you feeling like I've always known you. I am having a hard time leaving you. May I?"

Alex bent down towards Lyla, brushed her cheeks with a light kiss, and said, "Good night."

Lyla closed her eyes and felt the warmth of his skin. She drew in a deep breath smelling his subtle cologne and was dizzy, overcome with emotion. She could barely open her eyes, and stood there not wanting the moment to end. Finally, she spoke, "Good night Alex; à plus tard."

Alex left the apartment and walked to the elevator in a daze. Lyla stood motionless just inside her door. She reached up her hand to feel each side of her face where Alex had kissed her so tenderly. His touch felt like soft cashmere stroking her skin. When she regained her composure, she entered her bedroom remembering the evening, as a soft tingle moved through her body. She drifted to sleep with Alex's image and his touch.

Lyla no longer recalled what it was like to be on a 'date.' Her memories were predominated by those early days of seemingly carefree abandon with Juliano where life was lived in and for self-indulgent moments. What was so different about this man?

Lyla woke early the next morning filled with energy. It was her day off. Her plan was to see the beautiful sights of Paris and she wanted to make each day an adventure. Her apprenticeship was ending and her schedule had been reduced to two days a week. She made her morning tea and consulted her laptop for a map of well-known sites of Paris. Her short list consisted of another visit to the Louvre, the Eiffel Tower, the Palace of Versailles, and a cruise on the Seine before returning to the States. As she made her last notation, her phone rang; it was Alex.

"Good morning, bon matin, Lyla, how are you? It's a beautiful day today. How would you like to tour the city of Paris on the back of my motor bike?"

"Good morning, Alex, I'm delightful, how are you? Let me think. A tour of the city on the back of your motorbike. Will you be driving?" It was impossible for her to conceal the laughter in her voice.

"Very amusing, my little macaron," he responded. "Of course, I'll be driving. How about it? I haven't had anything to eat this morning. We can stop for some café and croissants and ride, eat, drink, and amuse ourselves through the day. Would you like to take a chance on my driving in the city? I would like to show you the enchantment of Paris."

"Do I dare? Yes, I'm going to throw caution to the wind. I would love to go with you as my tour guide."

"Bon, good, how about I pick you up in an hour ready to ride?"

"I'll be ready."

Alex arrived at Lyla's apartment and greeted her with another kiss to each cheek that lingered longer than the night before.

"Alex, I hope you aren't cross with me. I've packed some bread, cheese, and wine, of course, and a little something else special I brought home from the bakery last night."

"What a grand idea. I know just the perfect spot where we can stop later for a picnic. Let's get going. Ready?"

"Oh, yes, just let me get my scarf for my hair."

They stepped out of the front door of Lyla's building to the street where the scooter was parked. Alex strapped the basket onto the scooter, climbed on, and Lyla climbed on behind him. He started the engine and Lyla lightly grasped his waist with her right arm. Alex smiled at her touch, started slowly so as not to startle her, and then swiftly joined moving traffic.

Alex remembered everything Lyla had mentioned the night before about wanting to see the memorable sights of Paris. He carefully chose his route to the Champs Elysees, stopping briefly for a café, and continued to their first destination; the Arc de Triomphe for a 1.5-hour guided group tour. The tour included an ongoing history and art lesson that concluded at the top of the monument where visitors had a panoramic view of the city.

Lyla was impressed by the beauty and majesty of the structure, and the magnificent sculptures that encrusted the building. The history of the city came to life before her eyes and she was stunned.

Alex and Lyla walked up the steps to the roof of the building to view the exhibition at the top and the city laid out before them like a huge intricate quilt. Alex, as an art historian, as well as an accomplished artist and sculptor, told Lyla interesting and obtuse facts.

Lyla and Alex stood, on their cloud-like perch, absorbed in the vast images below. Lyla broke the silence and said, "I wish I could imprint these images on my memory. I don't ever want to forget what I've seen here."

"Lyla, are you, all right? You are so quiet. I hope my bringing you here has not made you upset."

"No, Alex, please don't think that at all. I'm pleased you took the time and effort to do this. You chose to do something important to me that we could enjoy together. I'm grateful I was able to experience this and feel privileged to experience this with you. You've made this come to life for me."

Lyla sensed the serious tone the conversation was taking and to lighten the mood asked, "Well, Alex, does this mean I should be looking out for a pop quiz? Should I have taken notes?"

Alex thought for a moment and took both her hands in his and raised them to his lips.

"No, my lovely bakery lady, not today. How about we return to the Champs Élysées and continue to our next destination? Next stop, les Jardin des Tuileries, the Tuileries Gardens."

Alex and Lyla climbed onto the scooter and rode down the tree-lined thoroughfare of the Champs Élysées, crowded with people and vehicles. The juxtaposition of modern and historic buildings was a mixture of old and new. Alex spoke to Lyla over his shoulder when they came to a stop and asked Lyla if she would like to window shop along the way. For the first time in a long time, she was content to be right where she was.

They arrived at one of the Tuileries' many entrances from the Place de la Concorde. Lyla was mesmerized by the sights and sounds of the grounds that were filled with people. Many singles and couples were strolling, chatting, reading, and absorbing the beauty around them. Couples young and old dotted the canvas, admiring the sculptures, the scenery and each other, some in affectionate embraces. Lyla and Alex stopped to watch children sailing their boats on the glassy surface of the large basin.

"This is beautiful it looks like a Monet painting," said Lyla

"Yes, artists have found this site inspirational."

Alex and Lyla strolled down a wide walkway flanked by rows of majestic trees, lush well-manicured lawns, and beds of flowers bursting with color and bloom. They found a place with two unoccupied chairs under canopied trees with shade, comfort, and seclusion.

Lyla emptied the basket's contents and Alex poured the wine. They shared their bread and cheese in silence. Lyla was unable to find words to describe the tranquility of their surroundings and her feelings of vulnerability. She turned to Alex, reached out, and touched his hand while searching his face for clues.

"Hello there, my handsome guide and professor, my Renaissance Man. I have been overwhelmed and stunned. I've been thinking about us and the time we've spent together these last two days. I keep thinking I've met you before. There is something I can't identify about you, me, us being together; it is like we fit. I know it sounds crazy."

Alex gently took her hand in his. He looked in her eyes and spoke tenderly. "You did; that is, we have met before."

"Where, when, what lifetime was that?"

"My mother introduced us the night of the Haussmann House dedication. Perhaps you forgot; it was a very short encounter. My wife had

recently passed away and you were, I understand, a very recent transplant from the U.S."

"Ah, yes," she said, "the dedication. I seem to recall meeting you and
then running out like Cinderella. I'm afraid I have been known to
make quick exits."

Alex continued, "And once I thought about it, you made another of
your quick exits when we were introduced many years ago at a party
in Miami Beach, an anniversary party or something for your aunt and
uncle. I believe your mother introduced us and before I realized it you
were gone. I was with my wife, Annie, that afternoon."

"Alex, I apologize for my sudden, ill-mannered hasty retreats in the
past. I have no desire to run off this time."

In the mottled shade of the overhanging emerald canopy, Alex
touched Lyla's face under her chin, gently, as though she was made of
fine porcelain. "May I?" he asked.

Alex leaned toward Lyla, nearly touching his lips to hers. Lyla drew
in a breath and moved to meet his in a tender kiss, but hesitated. Lyla
withdrew at the precise moment their lips were to touch and retreated
to her place of safety, placing physical and emotional distance between
them. They parted from one another with Lyla wanting more and not
understanding why, how, what it was that caused her to feel this way.

*Lyla was deeply touched by Alex's tenderness but didn't understand it or know
what to do, with him. What was so natural for Alex was not so for Lyla. She was
feeling consumed by a loving gentleness unfamiliar, yet so comforting and safe.*

"Alex, I need to share something with you. I need for you to know
things about me that are not easy for me to talk about. I know we have
not mentioned our pasts, and I have been grateful you have not probed
or intruded with questions."

Lyla sat back in her chair just out of his reach. Her hands were
folded neatly in her lap with her legs crossed loosely at her ankles.
Slowly, carefully, she began her story of struggle and transformation.
At first, she was timid, but as she continued, she noticed his steady,
tender eyes focused upon her face. He was listening to every word she
spoke, watching her body language, hearing the soft tremors in her
voice.

"I have felt so broken, so damaged, so unwanted, and frightened. It has been a lifetime since I have trusted anyone."

As Lyla continued her story, she could feel her emotions building and tears filled her eyes. Alex gave her a moment to collect herself and reached inside his pocket handing her his handkerchief. She smiled, thanked Alex for coming to her rescue, and apologized for being so emotional.

"I am so sorry this has happened to you," Alex said softly. I believe you are a brave and courageous woman, and I admire you for what you have accomplished against insurmountable odds. You raised four children, suffered and survived many health obstacles, beyond my comprehension, and also began a successful business."

Lyla's eyes grew wide with surprise at his response. Alex continued, "I cannot imagine what you have been through. I come from a loving family and have been blessed with my life. Although I never had any children, I was married to a wonderful woman who was my best friend. I was fortunate. I would like to continue seeing you, if you will allow me, and hope you will trust me."

"I don't understand all of this, but I want the same," answered Lyla.

Alex leaned toward Lyla and reached out to cradle her hands in his. She let him hold her hands. She could scarcely breathe from the quickening she felt and searched his face once again. It was a touch she had never before experienced from a man. Should she trust this? Was this real? She took a deep breath, raised her hand to touch his lips and then became enveloped in his embrace. The aroma of his faint cologne mixed with his perspiration of the day filled her senses as his smooth skin brushed against hers. Her eyes became filled with tears that dropped gently onto his skin. She met his embrace and never wanted to leave his arms.

Lyla was flooded with buried and forgotten emotions. This was not the way it had always been for her but was what she instinctively knew it should have been. For someone who was so conflicted about trust, vulnerability, and the physical and emotional aspects of 'touch,' this experience was huge. It was only a simple touch but it was so much more.

Lyla opened her eyes. They let go and sat back in their chairs facing one another in silence. Alex picked up his glass of wine and gave Lyla her glass. He filled both with the last of the wine, lifted his glass to hers, tapped her glass, and spoke.

"A toast to my beautiful baker extraordinaire. The last two days have been remarkable; may we have many more."

They tapped their glasses and drank their wine. The picnic was a prelude, enough to quench their thirst and calm their appetites until dinner.

"Alex, I am impressed by what we have seen today and the incredibly brilliant history lesson. You've made everything come alive for me. The gardens are amazing and stretch forever. I can understand why it would take a long time to see everything. If you don't mind, I would like to take a long walk in the gardens before we think about dinner. I am hoping to see as much as I can. My schedule has been full at the bakery and I have missed the beauty and excitement of Paris. It feels life affirming to be able to experience Paris. And it is a pleasure to see it with you."

Alex had impeccable manners. Lyla had to force herself to allow him to treat her like a lady. His manner and behavior made her feel special, like taking her arm as they walked along the street and insisting on carrying packages for her. He remembered everything about her, the foods she liked and the kind of wine she preferred. This attention to her detail delighted her.

They packed up their basket and left the seclusion of their brief hideaway to join the rest of their fellow wayfarers. Lyla snapped pictures of everything: sculptures, flowers, trees, and people. She needed to capture every detail.

The fresh air and breeze brushed across Lyla's face, wiping away traces of her impenetrable wall. As they strolled, their shoulders touched for a brief moment when Alex stepped closer to allow someone beside them to pass. Lyla could feel the warmth of his skin as her muscles tensed for a moment but then relaxed again as they continued to walk and talk.

Lyla became animated as she spoke. Alex saw her taking deep breaths and briefly closing her eyes to savor the sensations. Lyla's well-guarded speech and actions gave way to spontaneous laughter while she relayed anecdotes about her experiences at the bakery. Her eyes were bright, her voice clear, almost bubbly. She no longer carefully censored her every word and movement and was merely acting and reacting to her surroundings and her companion.

Their final destination was a small restaurant, Café Louise, between the Tuileries and the Louvre, where they enjoyed an intimate meal. It was a family-owned establishment, with hearty portions artfully plated that tasted delicious, a gathering place for good food, company, and conversation. The restaurant was neatly tucked into the corner of the building on the Rue Crois des Petits Champs. This restaurant became one of their favorite places.

During dinner, Alex mentioned that he had several classes to teach until the term ended. He asked Lyla if she wanted to visit his class and take a tour of the Sorbonne.

"Of course, Alex," Lyla said. "I would love to sit in on your class. I wonder if you mesmerize the students as much as you do me!"

It was late when they arrived at Lyla's apartment and Lyla was exhausted. They said good night in her apartment with a gentle, loving embrace and the whisper of a kiss on each cheek. Alex left Lyla to complete her evening with memories of her day.

Lyla walked into her bedroom, undressed, put on her night gown, and carefully put her clothes away. She crawled into bed bathed in a flood of emotions filling her to completion. She didn't want anything to intrude on the feelings, and memories, of the day they had shared. Her eyelids became heavy and she closed her eyes, wanting to remember every detail of his face, longing to recapture his scent from her hair and skin. All she could think about was Alex: his touch, his face, his voice, his embrace.

Lyla thought, *how amazing to feel these emotions and feel so connected to someone.* If this is all she would have, she wanted it to last as long as possible. She filled her lungs with an untroubled breath and fell into a deep, restful sleep.

The question now: Will Lyla trust herself, this man, and her reawakened feelings? Will she have the courage to let herself be the loving, passionate, woman she always was and has become again?

FEAR TEMPTATION RESOLVE JOY

Lyla's days were different now that she didn't have to wake early and go to the bakery every day. She bathed and dressed comfortably and began her day with a steaming cup of tea and a simple breakfast.

Lyla thought about Alex and their budding relationship as she sipped her tea. The more she thought the more uncomfortable and unsure of herself she became. The fears and uncertainties from the past caused her to doubt many of the things she learned at Haussmann House. The old familiar voice reared its ugly head, trying to convince her she didn't deserve to be happy, she was unworthy. She knew what it felt like to feel badly, this new feeling was so unfamiliar.

How could she trust herself and this man she barely knew? She tried to compare how her husband had been in the beginning of their relationship to her experiences now with Alex. She thought, *her husband had brought her flowers, Alex brought her flowers. Her husband had taken her out to dinner, Alex had taken her out to dinner. So, where were the red flags?* They were not obvious to her. *Was this the same?* She wondered if she would notice them if they were there with Alex? The trust that took so long for her to rebuild in herself had begun to erode.

The conflict growing within Lyla caused the familiar and uncomfortable feeling in her gut. Alex was her first real encounter with a man after completing the program at Haussmann House. She was having a crisis in confidence and knew she needed to have reassurance about herself, her decisions, and the relationship she wanted so badly to develop. Her instinct was to call Dr. Merkavah at Haussmann House and ask to join one of the follow-up groups that night.

Lyla arrived at Haussmann House, just as she had so long ago, seeking answers. Only this time, without realizing it, she was not the same. Her strength and confidence grew with each step that brought her closer to the front door. Once inside, the familiar sights and sounds helped to bring her thoughts and feelings into perspective. She reached the group therapy room with more clarity and resolve and immediately chose a seat near the other women.

"Hello ladies, I'm so very glad to see you. It feels like home."

The ladies nodded in agreement. Dr. Merkavah entered the room, acknowledged everyone, and presented the topic for the evening: discernment and crisis in confidence. Lyla smiled and thought Dr. Merkavah must have been a mind reader.

"I think we need to review what we learned and discussed regarding discernment of our actions and feelings, and the behavior of others we interact with. The red flags in us and in others were always there but were overlooked. I am asking you to recall now your recent interactions with people, men in particular.

Lyla immediately flashed back to her dates with Alex.

"Even when drawn up in the moment and feeling like we've forgotten everything we've learned, we have not. It is there ready for us to access when we need to. We must remember everyone is on their best behavior in the beginning of a relationship. Time is critical, especially if we're considering continuing a relationship that may someday lead to permanency.

"I believe it is equally important to revisit the issue of 'feeling' again. We must recognize that women who are in toxic situations, especially long-term environments of abuse, utilize a natural way to protect themselves, which is to suspend or isolate their feelings. Not feeling is an important tool to survival.

"We learn, over time, to build walls which serve to protect us from the onslaught of words, actions, and physical experiences. This becomes automatic. But what happens when it is no longer needed? How do these impenetrable walls come down allowing us to become trusting and vulnerable to others?

"We have been working diligently in our group sessions to bring down the walls piece by piece. We have gained confidence in the integrity of our group members. We know what is said here will never be used to hurt us. We have invested in building an enduring trust that happens with time and the commitment of a meaningful relationship of give and take.

"When you become involved in potential relationships outside of this group, please keep these things in mind. You may experience feelings long buried that may surprise, even frighten you. Acknowledge them, accept them, talk about them, and allow them to become part of who you are. Trust takes time and the feelings you have are part of establishing and maintaining a good relationship. They are a part of who you are."

Dr. Merkavah's words encouraged Lyla to reflect and focus on Alex's characteristics. His tender voice and gentle mannerisms were not so unlike the young men she spurned in her distant past. Lyla's distorted perception of a man's strength was framed by her knowledge and encounters with her father and the men in her life. She believed a man's strength was shown by his fierce attitude and his complete dominance and control over others. Her knowledge and wisdom gained at Haussmann House changed all that.

Lyla raised her hand and was acknowledged by Dr. Merkavah. When I think about Alex, I realized his strength was in the gentleness of his soft voice. He was refined and did not pretend to be someone he was not. He was informative, fun, and easygoing. His light-hearted and engaging sense of humor and his boyish manner were enchanting and refreshing. He even asked permission to embrace me which astounded me. Alex's strength was in his self-assurance, his willingness, and desire to share. He asked; he didn't demand. He delighted in the beauty and skill of the artists he loved and admired. His language was genteel and not boorish and he enjoyed and appreciated life."

Renee, one of the group members, asked, "He's sounds so wonderful. Does he have a brother?"

Lyla and the other ladies laughed and Lyla continued.

"I realized Alex's manner and behavior were not weaknesses, but the traits of an intelligent man comfortable and confident in who he was," Lyla said. He was not afraid to demonstrate his loving kindness and treated people with dignity and respect. He was free of the demons of hatred and anger and the insecurity of the need to control. Alex was the antithesis of my knowledge and perception of the men of my past."

Dr. Merkavah thanked the women for participating and encouraged them to continue sharing, returning to the group on an occasional basis for reinforcement and support. "Remember, ladies, we are here for support, you will always have someone to talk to. Bon soir, until we meet again."

Lyla ended her limited work schedule to concentrate on her relationship with Alex. She attended the remaining two weeks of Alex's art history class and met many of his colleagues. The campus and students were invigorating and refreshing. The vibrancy, thirst for knowledge, and openness was contagious and it reminded her of when she was in college. Each time Lyla and Alex were scheduled to meet, Alex would confirm their time and meeting place. If anything happened he would call Lyla to let her know; his consideration captured her attention.

Lyla observed how Alex interacted with his students and peers. He was confident and well respected with a commanding knowledge of his field. She saw that he could be demanding of himself and his students but was not overbearing or controlling. Alex rarely raised his voice in anger, preferring to resolve issues in an understanding, thoughtful, and compromising manner. He was not a fighter, and he admired and encouraged others to have their own thoughts and independence.

Alex eagerly introduced Lyla to everyone he knew. He had established friendships with other faculty members and was frequently invited out for the evening. Lyla became his constant companion and he proudly shared her with his new friends and colleagues. Towards the end of the semester Alex and Lyla were invited, as a couple, by Alex's colleagues to the award-winning restaurant and wine bar, Ô Chateau on the Jean-Jacques Rousseau for a wine tasting adventure.

The adventure began as soon as they walked in the bar. The room was decorated with painted walls of pale wine and the floors, bar base, tables and chairs were polished wood. Tall bar stools with seats covered in green and cream leather surrounded the magnificent bar of green granite with swirls of cream. The bar area sparkled from the polished wine glasses, colorful bottles, and overhead lights.

The couples were greeted warmly and shown downstairs to the spectacular wine cellar to participate in a lesson in all things wine. The floors looked like green slate and the walls were covered with large stones that arched over the long wooden table. Book cases of wine bottles filled the shelves on either side and the back of the room. Each place at the table had several wine glasses in preparation for the tasting.

The lesson was informative, the accompanying cheeses and meats were delicious, and the company was exceptional. Before long, everyone was laughing, singing, and toasting with each new glass of wine. "Ah, formidable," said one of Alex's colleagues who raised his glass to toast everyone there. Then another toast and another and he broke into a rendition of the Marseillaise, the French National Anthem, joined by everyone in the group. Neither Alex nor Lyla drank much prior to living in France, but when in Paris they joined in assimilating into the Parisian culture. Lyla had never laughed and drank so much in her life, and she loved every moment of it.

Alex completed the school year, summer began, and Alex and Lyla were constant companions. Knowing Lyla's time in France was coming to an end, they were together every day visiting the famous sites of Paris. Lyla never kept her plans to return to America a secret, and Alex never pressed her to change her mind. They accepted their situation and the separate paths they had to follow at this juncture in their lives. Mrs. Blum and everyone who met them saw their ease with each other and their love.

To their delight, they discovered they both liked dancing to the old rock and roll tunes of their youth. A club frequented by the Sorbonne students became one of their favorite spots. When there, Alex would lead Lyla onto the small dance floor with ease. They would jitterbug like they had always been a couple and made a promise to jitterbug into the sunset, together, forever. When the music's tempo slowed, they remained in each other's arms on the dance floor lost in their embrace and in time. Lyla became lost in the moment and acknowledged her burgeoning feelings for Alex.

"Thank you, my Renaissance Man, my bashert," Lyla whispered.

Several weeks later, Alex and Lyla were having dinner with Ethel at her home. During dinner, Ethel said she was seriously thinking of selling the mill cottage, now that she and her husband no longer took holiday there.

"The cottage holds many loving memories, but it's emotionally challenging for me to go there without your father, Alex," Ethel said. "I have not been there for some time and don't plan on returning before putting it on the market for sale. Alex, would you consider going to the cottage and doing that for me?"

"That's not a problem, Mother. I have time and will take care of it. It's been awhile since I've been there, and I would like to take one last look myself. The weather is warm now, it should be beautiful." Alex turned to Lyla and asked if she would accompany him to the cottage.

"Yes, oh yes. It sounds like an exciting adventure. I would love to see the French countryside."

"Good, that's settled then, Ethel said. "Thank you, Alex, Lyla, for taking care of that for me. Would you two like to have a cup of tea before you go?"

"No, Mother, we must be on our way. I have a three-day workshop starting tomorrow and Lyla must be up early, she and Genni are spending the day together. Who knows what treasures they will unearth."

Ethel smiled at Lyla and Alex and gave them a loving embrace before she retired to her room.

"Good night, children."

Alex and Lyla planned to visit the mill cottage the very next weekend. The cottage was about a two-hour drive from Paris. Lyla planned to bake some goodies and pack a good bottle of wine and some cheese. Alex had rented a small vehicle for their trip. He picked Lyla up by 8:00 am that Saturday morning, and they were on the road early to take advantage of the day. The roads were clear and the weather was warm and sunny. They meandered along winding roadways through quaint villages and towns that dotted the hillsides and valleys, arriving at the mill cottage.

The mill cottage was a secluded estate situated on 10 acres of pasture land and woodlands. Alex described the history of the area and the mill cottage. It had been originally built hundreds of years before by English soldiers to grind grain. He made the history and art of the time and place come alive. The cottage had been painstakingly renovated with modern amenities, but Mrs. Blum was careful to retain the original character.

Lyla and Alex walked through the lush gardens and woodlands before going into the cottage. Once inside, Alex took Lyla on a tour and recounted some of the many times they had been there as a family. Lyla was impressed by the beauty, solitude, and peace that enveloped them.

"I've never been anywhere or seen anything like this, nor have I felt so wonderful. It is an amazing reflection of your mother and the love that was here."

Alex looked at her as she spoke and walked toward her and took her hand.

"You're right," he said. "This place is the mirror image of the love my parents had for each another. I realize you're committed to return to Florida soon, and I had no intention of trying to stop you but..."

Lyla put her hand to his lips to keep him from speaking, but he continued.

"I don't know how it happened, but when I met you at the bakery there was a force that drew me to you that I couldn't resist; it was almost magnetic. Ever since then, I have felt completeness; no, wholeness, something indescribable that I have difficulty putting into words. I was with Annie and loved her for a long time but never experienced anything like this before. I don't understand how this happened and..." Alex's voice was a whisper as he repeated, "Mi mancheria se te ne vai, Mi mancheria se te ne vai, I will miss you if you leave, I will miss you if you leave."

Lyla was bathed in the warmth of Alex's tenderness. They touched lovingly, Alex gently kissing her as they embraced. She took a step back, giving her enough space to look in his kind eyes and was mesmerized by his touch and his voice that nearly took her breath away.

"I must go," she whispered. "I must return."

Alex could not find the words to explain that he could not let her go, and he knew he must. He whispered, "I know, I know."

He reached out to her and gently touched her face, wiping away a wisp of hair. His gentleness and strength were communicated in the way he lovingly, delicately drew her to him, and folded her into his arms. He waited for Lyla to respond, not wanting to overwhelm her. She was drawn to him with a desire to fulfill a preordained bond, feeling, knowing she was where she belonged. They found each other becoming one in the cottage on that summer day.

For the next several weeks, Alex and Lyla visited the cottage often and used it as a jumping off place to explore the country, the people, and each other. Each time they returned to the cottage, it sealed the loving relationship that had developed between them. Lyla had to remind Alex once again she was resolute to return to Florida to continue her journey.

They planned their last romantic weekend at the cottage before Lyla's intended departure. Alex approached Lyla and again asked her to stay with him in France. They sat together on the couch in front of the stone fireplace, sipping wine. Alex said nothing, searching Lyla's face, trying to imprint her upon his consciousness. He took a deep breath and spoke lovingly to her.

"Your presence and love have ignited a creative spark in me I cannot let go. I have decided to stay abroad in France, at the cottage, and work fulltime on my sculpting and painting. The pieces are inside me, yearning for me to bring them to life. I must stay. I no longer want to teach but desire to create, to embody my love for you and make tangible, visible, what our union has created. Will you stay with me? Will you consider delaying your return?"

"Alex," she began, "it is profoundly difficult for me to find the words to explain why I must continue my journey now, without you. You are an extraordinary man, Alex Blum, who has showered me, embraced me, and enveloped me with love. You have nurtured me to return the same and have given me a life I didn't think possible. It is because of who you are and who I have become that I am able to fulfill my raison d'être. But I must return. It does not diminish my love for you, and I believe that what has begun here will not end; but I must go... I must go."

Alex realized Lyla was determined to return. He spoke to her with as much honesty and clarity as he could. "I know you must return and I understand; at least, I think I understand. Your absence will not minimize my feelings for you, and I, too, believe we will not end here. This is just the beginning."

The day came for Lyla to return to Florida. Alex picked her up at her apartment and loaded everything into the car. He brought her to the bakery and then Haussmann House to say her final tear-filled farewells to Jacques and everyone at the bakery, the women of Haussmann House, and the friends she had made. Everyone exchanged email addresses and phone numbers, promising to keep in touch. Lyla's departure from Haussmann House and her goodbye, to Ethel Blum was heart-wrenching.

"Lyla, please remember to stay in touch once you get settled in Florida, and send me the remaining documents," Ethel said.

Mrs. Blum's voice began to break, exposing the emotional intensity of the moment as tears glistened in her eyes. "I shall miss you. I feel when you leave you take a small part of my heart with you, but that is the way it should be. It's a part of me I want you to have with you always."

Ethel looked at Lyla and Alex, who were standing next to her.

"I want you to know I love you both. Seeing you together and the love you share has reminded me of my husband and me. May you both be blessed for many years to come and may I be fortunate enough to see this."

Lyla and Ethel embraced and exchanged another teary goodbye. Alex then embraced his mother and led Lyla out to the car. The ride to the airport was filled with moments of laughter and quiet reflection.

The airport was filled with people arriving and departing for destinations unknown. Alex and Lyla walked to the counter to check her bags and check in for her flight. It was on time and boarding in the next half hour, just enough time to get through security and to the gate for boarding. Alex handed Lyla a manila envelope before they reached the security area.

"Lyla, this is a little something to remind you of Paris and the life that you found here.

Lyla took the envelope and carefully placed it into her bag.

"I'll look at it on the plane, thank you," she said as she reached up to kiss him on the lips and then on each cheek. Alex had to leave her at the security checkpoint and watch from a distance as she went through the line, the body scan, and then collect her belongings. She turned to him and waved, smiling as she put her hand to her lips, blew him a kiss and said, "A plus tard mon amour, à plus tard."

Alex raised his hand to catch the kiss and held it tightly as he watched her disappear into the depths of the terminal. The gate was not far, she arrived just in time to board, and went directly down the gateway into the plane. Her seat was near the front of the aircraft. She sat in her seat organizing her things for the long flight looking forward to a seat companion who would be someone nice to chat with. She put her essentials away, just as she had on the flight she took to Paris so long ago. Lyla opened the envelope and took out the canvas inside as other passengers were seated and settled.

The envelope contained a painting on canvas. There was a Monet like image artfully reflecting the transformation Lyla had undergone. In the center there was a multi-dimensional heart in shades of pink like quartz. Radiating from the base of the heart, on either side, were stalks of gladiola in various shades of light to dark pink. In the center of the heart where the stalks met, there was a glamelia in shades of the pink gladiola. The initials AB in black script were inscribed on the lower right.

The preflight instructions were given to the passengers, the plane taxied down the runway and became airborne. Lyla said a prayer for a safe flight and arrival as she had done on the journey that brought her to Paris. When she finished, she opened her eyes and noticed her seat companion still had her eyes closed. Lyla reached over and touched her hand.

Lyla spoke and smiled, "I always find it comforting to check in with God every time we take off."

The young woman turned to Lyla and smiled.

HOW IT ALL BEGAN AGAIN

Late spring was ushered into south Florida with great fanfare. The sun was shining and big, puffy, cotton candy clouds floated in a sea of bright blue sky. The air was warm and the breeze light as Lyla opened her eyes. Today was special. Lyla planned introducing another new group of women to the center. She looked forward to these 'first days' with anticipation when she welcomed the women whose lives she hoped to help change. Although today's group was diverse in age, culture, and socioeconomic status, they all had experienced similar issues; domestic violence, abuse, was nondiscriminatory.

Lyla looked at the clock on her nightstand and listened to it chime the 8:00 a.m. hour. It was time to shake off sleep and dreams and begin her day. She ran her fingers through her short-tousled hair heavily sprinkled with bright silver and put on a comfortable robe over her gown.

Her first task was to take care of her faithful furry companions. She portioned out the morning meal for her 'girls' and when they were finished, let them outside for their morning constitutional. When everyone completed their morning ritual they returned to Lyla's bedroom.

Her master bedroom was unpretentious, painted in muted colors of aqua and cream, with a spacious, bright bathroom in coordinated colors. Her creams, lotions, powders, and perfumes filled the bathroom with their pleasing aromas and were displayed on the granite counters and glass shelves.

She slipped out of her robe and nightgown and stepped into her round-shaped glass shower. The bathroom was custom designed to have a view of a tropical garden on the other side of a large glass wall that bathed her in bright natural light. She didn't need to hide in the shower. It wasn't a sanctuary of tears anymore.

After her shower, she walked into her well-organized closet trying to decide what to wear. She stood in her spacious room, waiting to be inspired, when she saw a pair of sunny yellow, lightweight, cotton capri pants, and chose a coordinated t-shirt. "Perfect," she thought. "It's the exact color to reflect a bright new day." Her red sandals added a touch of spice to further brighten her outfit. She looked at herself in the full-length mirror.

"Well, Lyla, you look like a little bit of sunshine!"

Lyla's home reflected her qualities of love and joy. It was airy and bathed in bright, natural light that streamed in through the panoramic full-length windows. It was filled with her favorite objects scattered throughout on table tops, and baker's racks with some peeking out from unusual places. Plants were everywhere in all shapes, sizes, and colors, especially her beloved orchids and African violets. She waved goodbye to the 'girls' and her housekeeper, Nelba, and drove off in her little convertible with her short hair blowing in the wind.

The Center, as she liked to refer to her foundation, was an outgrowth of her struggles to become whole and create a life that was worthwhile and free from the pain of the past. It was the initial extension of Hauss-mann House in the U.S. and Lyla was proud of her accomplishments. The Center, ever ongoing, changing, and growing, had become her main endeavor. The bakery would always be her first love, but the Center was a way for her to give to others what had been so hard for her to find, and a place where others would not have to do it on their own, alone.

Lyla had created a welcoming oasis filled with the promise of life. Here, women and girls were provided a place of safety, emotional nourishment, and support. Lyla wanted the design and appearance of the building to reflect the purpose of the center. She achieved this with the help of a talented landscape architect who was able to take what she envisioned and make it appear.

Lyla drove into the parking lot of the one-story building nestled in the arms of tall palms, hibiscus, and other lush tropical foliage. On her way to the steps, she tiptoed and dodged the spray from the early morning sprinklers emitting that wonderful hissing click, click sound. She walked up the steps, through the front, glass double doors into the lobby. When the building was designed, the one aspect she insisted on was lots of natural light, with the ability to support the plant life she loved.

"Good morning, Miss Lyla," said Abby, the young receptionist. Abby's job was to greet everyone who entered the building. She sat behind a glass-topped, kidney-shaped desk. "You look like a reflection of the sun this morning," said Abby.

"Good Morning to you Abby, thank you so much. It was just the look I wanted today, and, how are you?"

"It's a beautiful day and I'm feeling terrific. I finish my finals this week and graduate from Barry University. The ceremony is after that, and I'm so very excited."

"Abby, that's an amazing accomplishment, I wish you all the best."

"There's only one thing, Miss Lyla. I will miss being here; seeing you and all the other ladies who walk through our doors. This has been the best experience of my life, and I'm so thankful. I don't know what I would have done or what would have happened to me if I had not met you and come to the Center. I am now a college graduate, on my way to law school, and I could not have done it without you and the women at the Center."

Abby bowed her head, unable to hide her emotions, as tiny pearl teardrops fell from her eyes. Lyla walked behind the desk and took Abby in her arms embracing her with strong, yet tender warmth, similar to those embraces Lucille had given Lyla long ago.

Lyla whispered in Abby's ear, "Congratulations, I'm so proud of you. I knew you could do it."

Lyla released Abby from her embrace and held her at arm's length to get a good look at the confident, young woman Abby had become. "Beautiful," Lyla said to her, "beautiful and strong with the world at your feet and prepared to meet it."

Abby called to Lyla as Lyla walked toward the hallway, "You'll be there, won't you?"

"Oh, yes, I wouldn't dare miss seeing you walk down that aisle dressed in your cap and gown carrying your lit candle."

Lyla, turned and looked back toward Abby and spoke. "Abby, please make a general announcement for drum circle early at 3:30 p.m. this afternoon. I will need to leave soon thereafter, thanks."

Lyla walked down the passageway past open doors filled with women busy at their respective jobs on the phone, on computers, and in conferences. As one of the reporters so deftly put it when they had their grand opening, "... women were everywhere, all ages, sizes, shapes, and colors, and the place looked like a beehive bustling with activity." The article continued.

"As one walked down the hallways showered with light, doors led to offices and meeting rooms filled with women attending to their responsibilities and in the middle of it all was Miss Lyla, the Queen Bee."

Lyla knew everyone by name and greeted them as she passed. It was a long walk to Lyla's office. The building's unique design reminded everyone of a multiple winged butterfly. There were outstretched wing like halls on either side of the building, each meeting in the middle, that opened onto a lush garden. Lyla's office was at the end that looked onto the gardens. There was light everywhere and lush plant life could be seen from every window. The building was an oasis of light and life.

"Good morning, Miss Lyla," said Gabby, Lyla's secretary and personal assistant. "It is a beautiful day today. You look like a ray of sunshine."

"Why, thanks, Gabby, another beginning today for many of us, and I'm looking forward to it. How about you?"

"Oh, yes, Miss Lyla. The women are in the baking room getting acquainted and receiving instructions about our rules and conditions. They are waiting for you. I have assembled their folders for you to look through before you go in, if you choose to do so."

"No, I don't think so, not this morning, Gabby. I don't want to be influenced by any prior reports, it just feels like the right thing to do."

Gabby left the women's folders on her own desk, and asked Lyla, "Are you ready for your morning tea?"

"Ah, yes, I believe so. I have several calls to make and would appreciate a fresh cup. Thanks so much, Gabby. Just leave it on my desk when it's ready."

Lyla's office reflected her life and her passions. Artwork covered the walls, tasteful small sculptures dotted the room on shelves along with her extensive cookbook collection, and fresh flowers filled several small vases. The pictures of her children and grandchildren were on her desk and scattered across a long credenza behind her. The wall opposite her desk was a large frameless window that framed the gardens, which filled her with awe and delight no matter the weather or time of year.

Lyla often stood at her window gazing at the large koi pond in the garden area, reflecting upon her life, and the path she had taken that led her to this place, at this time. *What a journey I have taken,* she thought. *It was at times long and painful and seemingly never ending.* She had accomplished so much for herself and was now doing it for others. Lyla finished her phone calls, Gabby tapped on her door, and walked in to let her know everyone was ready.

"Thank you, Gabby. Please make sure all arrangements are complete for Abby's graduation celebration. I want to make sure it's special. You can let the ladies know I'm on my way."

Lyla left her office and walked down one of the fingered hallways of the building to the baking room, which was the place where beautiful things began. Francis, her administrator and head instructor, greeted Lyla as she walked in.

"Good Morning, Miss Lyla. I'd like to introduce you to the newest group of ladies to enter our program. Ladies, this is Miss Lyla: founder and life-force behind our Center. Please welcome her."

Lyla received good morning greetings from the women as some stood still, some applauded, and others looked apprehensive about what to expect. Lyla was aware of their discomfort and acknowledged them throughout her greeting.

"Good morning. Thank you for the kind greeting. Please, everyone be seated and get comfortable. And for those of you who are anxious, it is my hope, you will come to feel less apprehensive as you move through our program. Others have had similar feelings, you're not alone. Let me repeat that: you are not alone; no one who comes here is alone.

"Today we're going to make bread. We're going to produce something delicious from some dust and water; it's pretty remarkable when you think about it. I imagine you are wondering, after your introduction to the Center, why the first activity you would be involved in was to learn how to make a loaf of bread. It's simple, making bread is similar to how we live our lives. Breaking it down into its simplest terms, it teaches us how to prepare and measure, the techniques to prepare the dough, how to incorporate all the ingredients, the patience to wait for the dough to proof, and recognizing when the bread is ready to be removed from the oven.

"We are all here to leave behind a trail of failed attempts at making bread, so to speak. For one reason or another we have not been able to assemble the ingredients with the patience and skills necessary to produce good decisions and to live a life worthy of who we are.

"We learn here by making bread first, thereby modeling how we make bread successfully, to how we live our lives. Now, I realize some of you are here because you have been ordered by the court and are opposed to being here. It is a place of last resort, a last chance for you and the children who have been taken from you.

"I hope that when you have completed our program, you will have learned how valuable your life is, and in knowing this, be able to give those skills and knowledge you have acquired to your children and others. You have come to a veritable oasis, filled with women who are here to teach and guide you, take care of your needs both physical and emotional, and who will send you back into the world with knowledge and confidence to be able to say, 'I can do this.'

"Welcome, everyone, to our wellspring, to a place where you are safe, to a place of comfort and care, to a place where you learn to acquire life skills, and to a place where you are not alone. Feeling alone, in emotional pain, in confusion, and unable to move through our lives in a meaningful way is not an exclusive club. Women are consumed by lives that are out of control. When our life is complicated by destructive relationships, we lose sight of ourselves and survive from one crisis to the next, with energy poured into trying to limit the damage. When this occurs, we neglect and forget to nurture and develop the nurturer. Here, we become aware; we learn, nurture, and develop the best parts of ourselves, together.

"Ultimately, we are all sisters of the heart. I would like to personally welcome you to Glamelia House or the Center for short."

When Lyla finished speaking, some of the women wept and rose to thank Lyla for the opportunity to be there while others held back, skeptical of this strange woman who wanted them to bake bread. Lyla broke away from the women and walked toward the kitchen to pick up an apron hanging on a colorful hook. At that moment, Gabby walked in with a note and handed it to Lyla. As Lyla unfolded and read the note, a smile crossed her face.

She motioned to Gabby saying, "Please tell Mr. Alex yes, yes, 7:30 is fine, I'll see him then."

Lyla turned back to the group of women and directed them to take an apron from one of the hooks and meet her in the bakery.

"Today, ladies, we're making oatmeal bread. It is a light, nutritious dough, with a delicate crumb and flavor with a bit of crunch to the crust."

Lyla turned and walked into the bakery with her chicks behind like a mother hen, calling out to each participant to take a place at the table.

She stood at the head of the table and said, "It's time to begin."

Lyla spent the greater part of the day working with the newest members of the Center who had opportunities to get to know one another. Lyla chose this exercise to give the women a chance to begin a project that looked impossible and bring it to completion. Everyone was able to make bread, a task some women believed they could not achieve, and were pleasantly surprised when they did.

The participants learned they could achieve something when they worked together cooperatively, persevered learning new tasks, and developed patience. The task helped them to know they could make mistakes without harsh judgment. This activity helped everyone relax and let go of the anxiety that was present when they had begun.

Once the loaves were cooled, some of the women couldn't resist and took generous slices. Others took tastes and saved some to be shared with new friends and family. The women were then divided into groups and given tours of the Center. Each woman was assigned and introduced to her respective counselor who would be her guide and mentor throughout the entire process.

The program was comprehensive and required the cooperation of the women who entered the program and the women who served them. Everyone worked together to accomplish the transformation and everyone shared the women's difficulties and triumphs.

Lyla returned to her office, beaming from the successful bread-baking experience. During the lesson, she carefully observed all the women, and made mental notes to check against the information in their folders. She hoped each woman would be successful in completing the program, and move on to a better life. Before she became distracted with other matters, she opened each folder, read the contents, and added her comments. In addition, she answered phone calls, emails, and questions from staff members.

Her thoughts were interrupted by Gabby knocking on her office door.

"Hello, Miss Lyla, I'm here to remind you about the early drum circle."

"Oh, thank you so much, Gabby; I didn't realize the time."

Lyla carefully read through all the messages on her desk and prioritized them from urgent to, "Oh, no, not again and this can wait." The urgent phone calls were returned and matters disposed of with precision and confidence. Non-urgent messages were addressed in the same way, leaving those that could wait until the following week. Next, she turned to other documents strewn across the desktop, prioritized those, and placed them in her receptacle for work 'to be addressed.'

Other papers were designated for Gabby to file and complete and Lyla's writing instruments were placed in their respective vessels and drawers. She scooped up the china teacup with its last few drops of cold, herbal tea that sat on the side of her desk, and took it to her bathroom to rinse. She returned with a moistened paper towel, wiped her desk, and stood back to survey her surroundings.

The week had been particularly stressful and Lyla needed the time to let go of the issues, people, and problems she had been required to confront. She walked over to the sitting area in her office and picked up the drum in its place of rest. Her instrument was larger than the other ones at the Center and was embellished with carvings and a fabric band from which hung long, ornate rainbow-hued tassels that danced with its movement. The drum was gently cradled in her arms as she walked to the office door and she turned slightly to survey her personal domain. She hesitated for a moment and then walked out the door smiling. This activity was her favorite time of the week.

The use of this specific type of percussion was a concept Lyla had adopted after meeting a woman whose business and life passion was conducting drum circles. Lyla strongly believed that she and the other women at the Center worked in an emotionally charged environment.

The issues and people they encountered, the crises, and the pain impacted them all.

The group activity was an important event that occurred every late Friday afternoon. The women who worked at the Center chose to be there, to follow this career path, and work with this particular population. It was a way for them to release stress and shed internal and external issues from the successes, failures, and frustrations they faced daily and those which had built up over time.

Activity levels throughout the Center began to slow down. Projects, reports, and files were closed and/or organized and placed in their respective cabinets and folders for their weekend respite. The buzz became a soft hum as the women attended to their end-of-the-week tasks.

Lyla's secretary, Gabby, checked her calendar to make sure nothing was overlooked then closed her book and nestled it beside her phone. She carefully placed her tools in their respective drawers and compartments and dusted the top of her desk. When she was satisfied her office and 'command center' reflected the coming calm, she smiled and began her weekly journey.

A cylindrical drum embellished with the art and symbols of the African village where it was made was tucked away in the corner of her office. Small, multicolored fabric tassels hung from the rim of the stretched goat skin surface that moved, mirroring the movement of the instrument. When Gabby picked it up and cradled it in her arms, the tassels swayed and jumped with life. This was her favorite time of the week.

Gabby walked down the hall with a bounce in her step, eager to fulfill her mission. She tapped lightly on Lyla's door once more, checking to see if Lyla was ready. Lyla's office was empty, with everything neatly stacked in its place; calm had already begun to descend.

The route Gabby chose led her down the hallway to her right that curved around the central atrium. As she approached each room, she could hear the faint sounds of women's voices chatting. She gently tapped on the door and poked her head inside, filling the room with her radiant smile.

"Hello ladies, just came by to remind everyone, but I see you girls have already begun to wind down your day. Drum circle is at 3:30 p.m., see you there."

This congenial activity was repeated throughout the complex. Gabby had timed the process and knew exactly how long it took, leaving her enough time for last-minute conversations and preparations, to arrive at the circle, ready to begin at the appointed hour. This was the best part of everyone's week.

Lyla arrived at the rear patio and garden area behind the Center and was emotionally prepared to let go. She carried the object of her affection slung over her left shoulder. As she entered the patio, she walked over to the storage closet and picked up a folding chair with her free hand. The chair was placed on the patio beyond the screen in the open space of the garden.

By 3:30 p.m. all staff members were seated with their prized, percussive possessions loosely cradled between their knees. Lyla's eye searched her flock to see if everyone had arrived. She closed her eyes, trying to focus and clear her mind, and began to tap softly. It was her habit to begin with a single rhythmic tap on the top of her faithful companion. The single soft tap was soon followed by another accompanying tap that was somewhat louder.

One by one the ladies joined as they felt inspired to do. The air became filled with the rhythmic taps, each with its distinct beat and tenor. The rhythm moved in irregular impulses and patterns from simple to complex with differing intensities and duration. The sounds changed as people stopped playing momentarily to dance in the center of the circle and others were moved to tapping.

The mesmerizing sound reached a crescendo only to slow down, undulating like a great sea serpent. This symphony continued for about 35 minutes, when the final cycle of diminuendo began, first with the entire group. As it continued, the individual drummers would end their participation until only Lyla remained, softly tapping with a single tap as she had originally begun; the cycle and exhalation of stress was complete. Everyone remained quiet with eyes closed for a moment to feel the power of the energy the group had created.

Then one by one they each took a deep cleansing breath to drink in the final moments, opened their eyes, and dispersed with parting embraces, ready to step outside the doors to their lives outside the Center.

ONE DOOR CLOSED ANOTHER OPENED

Another new year had come and gone and the weekend was rapidly approaching. Lyla no longer had time to frequent the bakery because of her long hours at the Center. When the stress and responsibilities of the world were too much or she needed grounding, Lyla chose to spend the day baking her favorite breads, embracing her passion, and mentally meandering through the past. Lyla knew baking bread was her way to feel centered. It gave her the opportunity to be alone with her thoughts in an emotionally safe and comfortable place. She needed to bake today; it was the anniversary of Ethel's death, her yahrzeit. Her death left Lyla struggling with a gaping emotional wound that had yet to heal.

The house remained dark and still before dawn. Lyla slowly opened her eyes, awakened by the soft tick of her mother's Dresden china clock poised on the desk. She rolled over toward her nightstand looking at her small digital alarm clock when she heard the soft tinkle of her mother's clock chime 5 a.m. She was drifting into a light slumber when she felt her companions stirring on her bed. Her cavaliers had taken up residence some time during the night on the top of her bed. They were stretching, yawning, and signaling their intent to awaken her. Each furry little dog crawled their way up to Lyla's face and showered her with their pink-tongued kisses, shaking the bed with their wagging tails.

"All right ladies, I can see you're awake and ready to start the day. How about one group hug here and we're up and on our way? I'm going to the bakery today."

Lyla completed her morning routine while the cavaliers patiently waited their turn to go for their morning walk outside and get fed. Once complete, Lyla secured the house, waved good bye to her faithful companions, and stepped outside embraced by the fading night sky.

Lyla drove her little car through the empty streets to her bakery and parked in a space close to the door. She unlocked the glass door, turned, and pulled down the shade to be left undisturbed. A dozen small tables covered with green and white checkered cloths dotted the floor, waiting for their morning customers to arrive.

Lyla walked past the empty glass display cases to the rear of the bakery, turning on lights and surveying her sanctuary. She put on her apron, tied her brightly colored kerchief over her hair, and fired up her ovens to begin the morning ritual of mixing and preparing her dough. Lyla worked methodically, carefully kneading and shaping her bread while lost in thought. As she worked the dough and readied it for proofing, she recalled the night she met Mrs. Ethel Blum on that fateful flight to Paris.

Lyla stood alone, bathed in the warmth of her womb-like kitchen, and brushed away a wisp of hair that had fallen into her face. Her thoughts were of Ethel Blum, Paris, Haussmann House, and Alex, and how it had all come together almost magically; well, perhaps it was never really magic. Her thoughts were interrupted by the pinging sound on her phone, signaling an incoming text. She wiped her hands on her towel and reached into her pocket for her phone.

The message read, "Good Morning Bakery Lady; see you at home. I love you, Alex."

Everyone Has Their Paris

ACKNOWLEDGMENTS

I would like to recognize and publicly acknowledge my extraordinary friendship with Jaqueline Berger. We were brought together eight years ago during a dark and tumultuous time in my life. She became a close confidant, friend, and soul sister whose unwavering kindness and support kept me together when I was continually falling to pieces.

Special thanks must be paid to my friend from high school, Joanne Sudman, who I reconnected with after 50 years. Her ongoing support and friendship have been paramount in my recovery and healing.

Many thanks and appreciation to Debi Edge and the remarkable women who are the life-blood of the Montgomery County Women's Center in The Woodlands, Texas, and were instrumental in germinating the seeds of transformation. I believe our association was fortuitously planned and orchestrated by a force greater than us all. They created a safe, non -judgmental and nurturing environment of compassion and strength providing the rungs of the ladder I had to climb.

Thanks, and kudos go to Elizabeth Ball the talented graphic designer whose creativity and sensitivity enabled her to transfer the essence of the story so well reflected in the original cover design. It was an illuminating and satisfying experience working with her.

This book would not have been the final product it is without the guidance of my final editor, Joan Alden. Joan became my task master, teacher, mentor, and friend. During the process, I learned about language, structure, technique, my bad habits, and often times would become frustrated at the tasks she required of me. I persevered and as a result of her time and efforts it helped me to produce a story that had to be told. Thank you, Joan.

With great fondness,

Sheri

CPSIA information can be obtained
at www.ICGtesting.com
Printed in the USA
FFHW020028040419
51442055-56884FF